# RIDE,
# BOLDLY
# RIDE

# RIDE, BOLDLY RIDE

## AN AMERICAN NOVEL

*Over the mountains of the moon*
*Down the valley of the shadow*
*Ride, boldly ride...*
    – Edgar Allen Poe, 1849

THE CONCLUDING NOVEL IN THE MARCHION-HARRIS TRILOGY
*Over the Mountains of the Moon, 1846-1849*
*Down the Valley of the Shadow, 1849-1857*
*Ride, Boldly Ride, 1857-1869*

## MARY RAMSTETTER

C Lazy Three
PRESS
Golden, Colorado

RIDE, BOLDLY RIDE
An American Novel

Ramstetter, Mary
ISBN 0-9643283-4-8
Library of Congress Control Number: 2005903538
SAN 255-5271

Copyright © 2006 by Mary Ramstetter

Copy reading and copy editing by Julia A. Ripley
Cover and interior design by Troy Scott Parker, Cimarron Design,
www.cimarrondesign.com

⊘ PRINTED ON RECYCLED PAPER
Printed in the United States of America

First printed 2006
5  4  3  2  1


Published by
C Lazy Three Press
5957 Crawford Gulch
Golden, CO 80403

---

*Dedicated to my grandchildren*

Gina, Mary, Matt, Mike

# THE UNITED STATES
## 1 8 6 9

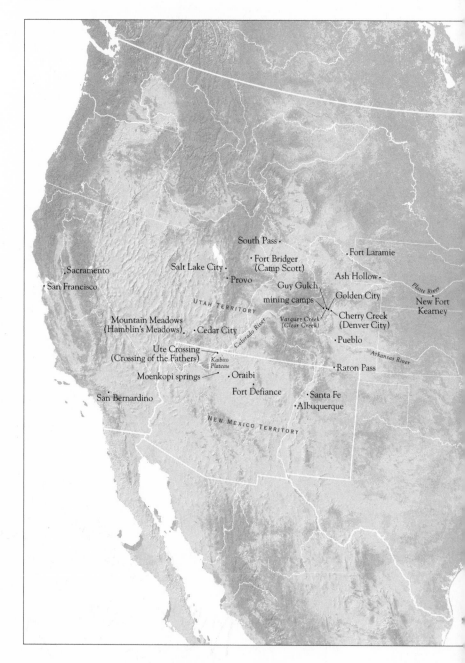

South Pass

Fort Laramie

Sacramento · · Salt Lake City · · Fort Bridger
(Camp Scott)

San Francisco · · Provo · Ash Hollow ·

Guy Gulch

Platte River

mining camps · Golden City · New Fort Kearney

UTAH TERRITORY

Mountain Meadows
(Hamblin's Meadows) · · Cedar City

Vasquez Creek
(Clear Creek)

Cherry Creek
(Denver City)

Colorado River

· Pueblo

Ute Crossing
(Crossing of the Fathers) · Kaibito
Plateau

Arkansas River

· Raton Pass

Moenkopi springs · · Oraibi

San Bernardino · Fort Defiance · Santa Fe
· Albuquerque

NEW MEXICO TERRITORY

For background on the characters,
refer to THE CAST OF FICTIONAL CHARACTERS
page 519

# PROLOGUE

UTAH TERRITORY, 1857. President James Buchanan names new officials for Utah and sends a military escort, the Utah Expedition, to support their authority. By September advance companies of the Expedition reach Ham's Fork near the Green River. The civilian contractors hired to equip and supply the escort are already there, along with 2,000 head of beef cattle.

Holed up in his mountain fortress, Brigham Young thumbs his nose at Washington. Captain Stewart Van Vliet, in Utah to arrange for the receiving and provisioning of the army, is sent packing. Martial law is declared and the Territory closed, the supply wagons burned and the cattle run off.

It is the Lord's will. The Gentile cattle will better serve the Lord's purpose in the settlements. More important is what those cattle represent. The ongoing Reformation, launched by the church to hide economic blunders, has now been joined by persecution from the outside world.

The ensuing uproar will snuff out interest in the botched massacre of the Fancher emigrants, and the trail back to South Temple Street will grow cold.

# PART
# ONE

# O N E

*What were you thinking, John Lee, as you drove into the city?
Sitting there straight as a ramrod on the buggy seat, the high-
topped black silk hat at your side? Did you really expect to find
the acceptance in your Prophet's eyes that you can't find in your
own? You were only following orders. It wasn't your fault the
Indians betrayed you, none of this was your fault.*

GREAT SALT LAKE CITY, Wednesday night, the last day of
September. Bishop George Harris is making his weekly
visit to the house on Second North. Not, however, to
see this wife who, after tending to the door, discreetly withdraws
to the upstairs sitting room.

The parlor lamp has been turned low, the drapes drawn. Tom
Stenhouse waits in the shadows.

"John Lee's in the city…Iron District boys got an emigrant
train in Hamblin's meadows."

"An emigrant train?" The bishop sounded a cynical note.
"What's our excuse this time?"

"Territory's closed, they're *persona non grata.*"

Somewhere in the house a rat was gnawing. *It's good we
can't see what happens to the nice things we build,* the bishop
reflected, *otherwise we'd never start.* "That would give us the
right to attack them, I suppose."

"It's this damn Reformation!" The Scotsman gave the plank

floor a smart tap with his cane. "We're becoming unbalanced as a people. Bound to…to all sorts of secrets, all sorts of dreadful oaths…good Lord! I'm too old to play hide and seek." He took a deep breath, winded by his brisk walk through streets where men after dark kept to the center and carried their pistol at their side, fearful of the deadly influences now ruling Zion.

"Well, it seems to be doing the trick. No one's talking about being hungry anymore."

A shaming silence filled the room. What cowards they'd become, staying quiet as cobwebs in a corner while Brigham's men ran amuck.

The house smelled of duck fat from the evening meal. Out in the darkness a horse clipped-clopped by on the hard dirt road.

George worked a knotted willow root into the little potbellied stove, and resumed his seat. "We've strayed too far off the civilized path. How many of us invited Justice Stiles into our homes? or any of the other federal officers sent here to enforce the laws of the United States? or stood up for those officers when Brigham encouraged the riff-raff to pelt their carriages with garbage? Buchanan's only doing what we lack the courage to do."

"Is that any way to talk, George, as fond as the good churchman is of you."

"Fond of separating the poor from their pennies." The bishop made a sound of disgust. "We're a country of fools, watching each other instead of Brigham. He's stealing us blind."

"People don't think of it as *stealing*. No. In fact, they take great pains *not* to think of it that way. Making a living in this desert isn't easy. Anything extra to worry about is just one more stick on the camel's back. And look what's waiting for us beyond the grave—a beautiful Kingdom along with the promise of Kingdoms to come. Not that tired old Christian philosophy with its European ghosts. Ours is genuine New World, we can each be gods in our own right. Exciting stuff, George.

"In the meantime, jobbing along, we can all pray and sing and be God's spies."

The Scotsman's low voice had an iron ring to it. In the old days he'd performed in numerous plays in the Council House, but with the introduction of the Reformation there was no longer any theater in the Valley.

An upstart of wind banged a loose shutter. Both men jerked.

"Brigham's insisting I take another wife and live my religion."

"That's bad news, bad for both you and Fanny."

"She's quite sick about it, we discuss it very little. I think she thought since we've been married for eight years that we'd escaped Brigham's notice. Mmmmm…oh well. She'd like me to scotch the idea, but I can't do that. Not and keep my newspaper going. I've mentioned several names, but she refuses to choose. It will probably be Apostle Parley Pratt's daughter, Belinda."

"Belinda…" George hesitated, sorting through Parley's children. "What is she? twelve?"

"Thirteen, but there's no hurry. We'll have a suitable courtship."

"I courted Sister Phoebe when she was thirteen. Some courtship that was. I hauled her out on the prairies and put her to work for Constance."

"You've given her a good living."

"Yes, if that's all there is to living."

"Girls marry young here. They have to, their families can't feed them. She'll be happy enough with us."

"Rubbish! What she'll be is lonely. I don't spend any time with my wives, with the exception of the two I live with. This whole city's full of lonely women married to men just like me."

Remembering Appella, George laughed depreciatingly. "Except for the one who lives in this house. Sister Appella left her husband when he wanted sex, she took a vow of celibacy and asked me to marry her." He laughed again. "Apparently I don't cut quite the figure I thought I did. Anyway, she's very good-natured, probably well-read, probably has all sorts of interesting opinions on all sorts of things, I wouldn't know.

"You want my advice, Tom? Be kind. Let Brigham's little trifle for being a good soldier go find a boy her own age."

A sudden backdraft wreathed the little stove in grey streamers.

"President Buchanan's an old batch," George mused. "That must be peaceful."

"My dear friend..." Tom tapped the bishop's boot lightly with his cane "...are you nae wanting to hear about tha emigrant train?" Having determined years ago to be an actor, he had weaned himself from the dialect of his native land, and now used it only for his own enjoyment, liking the sound.

"No, no I don't. I hate it, *just hate it!* God is not on our side when it comes to stealing." George rubbed his eyes and reminded himself to stop. The wood smoke bothered his eyes. It didn't use to, but now it did. He sighed deeply. "So what'd our painted Indians get away with this time?"

"Lee, McMurdy, Knight, killed the wounded in the wagons..."

"...*killed the wounded in the wagons?!!*" George straightened in disbelief. "What are you talking about?!"

"John Lee went in with a white flag and told the emigrants we'd protect them if they gave up their guns. They sent their guns out..."

"...and?..."

"...we wiped them out." The words sounded of incredulity.

"Good Lord! What are you saying?!"

"The whole train's been used up. Lee confessed everything. Brother Woodruff was in the room, he wrote it all down. The

President says it's the most unfortunate affair that ever befell the church. It's a sacred secret, he says, don't even tell Heber. Go home, he says to Lee, write your report laying everything to the Indians. I need it to keep off troublesome inquiries, that's what he says.

"Lee asks what to tell the people in the south who are bothered by what happened. The President hems and haws around, says he wouldn't have cared about the men, but killing the woman and children is a sin. Well, Lee, he gets a little hot under the collar and reminds his holiness where those orders came from. They were written orders, he says, right out of Great Salt Lake and carried south by George A.

"So then the President tells Lee to leave and come back today. Today, he tells Lee he prayed on it. Says the brethren acted from pure motives, trouble was they acted a little prematurely, that they were a little ahead of time. I sustain you and all the brethren for what they did, he says."

"...prematurely?" George puzzled. "...a little ahead of time?" The bishop's head buzzed. "What does that mean?"

"Damned if I know. At any rate, it seems that while Brigham was praying on it, he asked God to take the horrid vision of that massacre out of his sight if what the Saints did at the meadows was a righteous act. And, wouldn't you know? Poof! away it went. Cheered our little tin Jesus right up."

"When in God's name did we start killing off whole wagon trains?!"

"Brigham couldn't resist, that's my guess. His power's corrupted him. This was a rich train. He wanted the money *and* the goods, and he thought he could depend on the Indians to do the dirty work. Apparently it was too dirty even for them. When they wouldn't, Lee thought he had to. Once started, our boys couldn't stop, there couldn't be any witnesses."

"This will cost the King his throne," George said, trying not to picture the sickening betrayal.

"Ah! never. His footmen will compensate and the blame will stick to them. The ultimate purpose of manipulators, George, is to be manipulated themselves. John Lee will do whatever it takes to keep the church blameless, even to putting his own neck on the block."

"God will not accept this."

"Who knows what God accepts and what he doesn't?"

"*I* know. Children know. Have you ever watched the little children when the President walks through a crowd? They're afraid of him, he's like a Pied Piper in reverse."

"When did it ever matter what children think? We build them no schools, we have no hospitals, no parks, no libraries, no reading rooms."

"Certainly when Brigham's replaced…"

"…maybe not even then."

"You don't think Buchanan will back down?!"

"No, of course not." Delighting in his perversity, Tom laughed heartily. "Brigham will, and what a glorious retreat it will be. Mark my words, someday somewhere there will be a magnificent public edifice erected in his lordship's honor—a library, a school, a hospital—something he himself will never build because he's too busy building stables for his wives and buggies."

"And killing poor apostates and unsuspecting emigrants," George sneered. "When the army does get in here, we need to report what we know about the massacre."

"That will take awhile. Yesterday afternoon Wells marched over a thousand men off to close the Narrows."

"There's nothing to fear in the American Army."

"That fey talk will put you on Brigham's enemy list in this world *and* the next."

George winced, reminded for some ungodly reason of

Constance. He wished her well *somewhere*, of course, but not too near in that other world, certainly not struggling for his attention.

"By the way, John Bernhisel is assuring Brigham that the South will bolt the Union," Tom said. "If our esteemed delegate is right, the American soldiers won't stay around long enough to investigate the massacre. Oh, and that reminds me of something else."

The stentorian tones thickened wickedly. "Auld Brother Lee poured a high-topped black silk hat full of rings and gold and silver chains and watches and tongs out over Brigham's desk. Tha President threw a handful back and yelled and stomped around in a high dudgeon. What does that tell ye?"

"Well...nothing."

"Nothing is right. Because guess what? Brigham's billing tha government for tha goods gie tha Indians." Leaning forward, the Scotsman gripped his friend's shoulder affectionately. "Now's ye chance tae stand and be counted, my guild mon."

"The Indians?" George puzzled. "He's never spent a dollar on Indians. We send Washington signed vouchers, and they reimburse us, but we don't really furnish Indians anything, never have. You know that."

"These goods came from tha emigrants, tha Fancher train."

# T W O

NEWS OF THE DREADFUL Indian massacre of over one hundred emigrants en route to California reached San Bernardino on Thursday, the first day of October, with Matthews and Tanner, Mormon freighters. The freighters told of being guided past the site after dark by Mormon soldiers and ordered to stay with their wagons and keep moving until well clear of the meadows. They also told of the gruesome discovery of what looked to be human remains, dragged into camp by the dogs.

That same Thursday George received a voucher from Levi Stewart in the Iron District for work pants, shirts and other clothing, pipes, powder, lead, and firing caps, "furnished to sundry bands of Indians, near Mountain Meadows...on Superintendent orders." Stewart's claim totaled $3,527.43 and was supported by two trustworthy witnesses. Also swearing to the claim's validity were Indian interpreter Dimick B. Huntington and Brigham Young.

"I certify on honor that the above accounts are correct and just," Brigham had written above his signature, "and that I have actually paid the amount thereof."

Fixing his attention on the figures, the Director of the Tithing Offices dutifully recorded them one by one.

At supper that evening the bishop's first wife told of hearing the Territory was to be closed. "Brigham's just plain squirrelly. But surely he'll let the trains out that are already here, wouldn't you think?"

Pushing the conversation back behind his other worries, the bishop didn't reply. The times were so damnably unsettling, what with the large Gentile merchants being forced out, leaving idle buildings up and down Main Street. And now the President wanting guns to fight the American invaders and wagons to relocate the church in the south. Such a farce.

"George?"

"What? Oh yes, dear, I'll check."

Ellen did a double take. The only place he called her "dear" was in the bedroom.

Later in the parlor, hunched over the usual fistful of papers, George made himself concentrate on office work. Ellen was working at the sewing machine. They didn't have to be talking to enjoy each other's company, but tonight, for George, the absence of conversation was horrible, accusing him of cowardice and worse, complicity. The leather-covered chair, usually so comfortable, wouldn't give. The room was stuffy, making it hard to breath.

*I have until tomorrow night,* he told the damning silence. *Maybe by then she'll hear it somewhere else. Such an awful thing.*

Jeremy came in. The bishop swept the paperwork aside and pulled the boy into his lap as if to buffer himself. Plainly uncomfortable, Jeremy suffered his father's hug.

"I just love you so much," George said, releasing the boy, and broke into tears.

"Leave the room!" Ellen told Jeremy sharply, and stiff with anxiety turned on George. "What's wrong, what's Brigham done?"

"I can't..." George stopped and began again. "...I just can't bear it."

"What? You can't bear what?"

"Such pretty little girls, such a nice little boy." He was weeping, the words coming out in pieces.

"Dinky?!" Ellen cried. "Are you talking about Dinky?"

George didn't answer. His chest was heaving, and he was having trouble breathing.

Frightened, Ellen loosened his tie and worked his coat off, feeling the judder in the shoulders under the white shirt. "What happened?"

"They got her train."

Ellen felt her scalp crawl. "Who got her train? what are you talking about? where?"

"Down toward the desert."

"Toward the desert beyond Cedar City?"

"Hamblin's place, in his meadows."

"George! listen! I told Dinky to leave the train in Cedar City. Is that before Hamblin's place?"

"Yes." George ran his hands through his hair and down the back of his neck. "I think so. Yes it is. Tom told me last night, I didn't realize at first..." the wild sobbing resumed "...who he was talking about...not until he called it...the Fancher train."

*"Listen to me! Dinky's with Emil in Cedar City!"*

"Good, good." Struggling to regain his control, the bishop pressed a handkerchief to his face. "Good people. Oh, this is good."

"Dinky is fine," Ellen said firmly, making it so in her heart. "I told her to leave the train before it reached the desert if she had any suspicion of trouble. I gave her Emil's note and marked it 'paid' to pay for her keep. Were many killed?"

"Everyone, every single one!" Undone anew, George howled against his hands.

"Stop it!" Ellen cried shrilly. "You're scaring me! What are you saying?" She pulled his hands free to hear the answer.

"The Indians wouldn't do it, we did it."

Ellen shook her head. "No, there must be some mistake, that can't be what you heard."

"And do you want to know what else?" The bishop was pounding the arm of his chair with his fist. *"What else is we charged the American government over $3,000 for goods we allowed the Indians to take from the train...we have made a commercial business out of killing emigrants!"*

George slept late the next morning, and Ellen sent a note to the office saying he wouldn't be in. By supper he felt better. A touch of a cold, he thought. Phoebe and his children filled the supper table with their chatter. Nancy told a funny story about a top getting away from a little boy in Reece's Mercantile and rolling down the aisle, and her father laughed uproariously, desperately drawing strength from his dear family, who eyed each other uneasily.

The next day was Sunday, and for the first time ever George did not go to church. Instead, the family bundled itself into a buggy and left the city. A noxious pall of dust and putrid smoke from burning horse manure shrouded the streets, but in the mountains, yellowing with aspen, the day was beautiful. George, his thin, wind-tousled hair resembling a drift of cottonwood seed, played catch with Jeremy and Nancy and laughed at his clumsy attempts to throw the ball.

The next morning he stayed abed with chills and fever, and Ellen sent a second note to the office. The bishop had influenza and would be at home the rest of the week. Tuesday, the fever increased, his muscles ached, his throat felt sore. Phoebe blamed the dirty air. Friends dropped by and visited quietly. George was asleep when a delegation of clerks paid a call.

"Your bishop has worked from sunrise to sunset since coming here," Ellen told the high priest in charge of the clerks. "He is sixty-five years old and due a rest. The books are up to date, all that's necessary is to accept the tithes and record them. As for distributing the P.E. funds, Bishop Harris will take care of that on his return."

Thursday night gale-force winds cleaned out the city, and the next day Phoebe was sure Mr. G. looked better.

In the meantime Brigham was becoming a nuisance—talking about war and making plans to evacuate the city, with airy disregard for all the disconnecting such a move would require.

"If George isn't better, we won't be leaving," Ellen confided to William Godbe, editor of the *Utah Magazine* and a close friend.

Godbe warned strongly against staying. "Brigham is determined to show unanimity. If you don't leave, you may very well suffer a house fire."

George returned to work Saturday. Ellen wrote Verity to ask about Dinky, but a warning like a sliver in her finger stopped her from backing the letter.

George slowly got better. Several fine carriages belonging to the Fancher party were brought into the city and parked in Brigham's yard. The Prophet's wives buzzed with details of the wagons' contents. Appella, with close friends inside the Beehive, described bundles of fine dresses and all manner of shoes, paired and tied together with strings. She also told of those wives who, picking up the valuables scattered about after Brigham's meeting with Indian farmer Lee, were each given a jeweled ring.

None of this gossip was shared with George, who, for his part, carried home no rumors from the Tithing House.

# THREE

ARLY SUNDAY MORNING, October 3, inside the California boundary. Henry and Malinda Scott and their four children have reached the end of their long journey from Clarksville, Arkansas. There's plenty of work in the mining camp of Volcano for a good wheelwright, and land to be had for the taking.

Lying in the bed of the wagon, the new babe at her breast, Malinda counted her blessings. Four-hundred-fifty miles back down the road in Great Salt Lake City things had looked pretty bad. Henry's deciding to abandon the Fancher party and keep to the main California road worried her to death. But they'd made it, praise God, they'd made it.

Then she heard the dogs howl.

"Henry, those dogs crying like that before dawn? it sure ain't a good sign."

"We ain't going no further," Henry mumbled. "We gotta quit sometime."

The next day, fishing in her bag for the letter carried all the way from Utah, Malinda stuck herself with a pin. The letter, when she found it, had three bright red spots in the corner. The postmaster wanted postage.

The anguished woman stared wildly about.

*It wasn't us the dogs cried for! something's gone terribly wrong with the wagon train!*

"You gotta give me ten cents, ma'am, or I can't mail it."

Malinda emptied the bag on the counter and found the coin Dinky had given her.

Clunk went the liberty dime in the change box.

"Next," said the postmaster.

*Aug. 5, '57. My dearest Mun, our party is being sent south by the church because of poor food supplies on the north trail. I'll write at every settlement and meet you in San Bernardino. Come on your fastest horse, I love you my dear. Dinky*

Mun asked if there were more letters. The clerk looked through the unsorted mail and shook his head. At the newly rented house on Harbor Street in Sacramento the disappointed man repacked the gifts laid out for his children and told the landlady he'd be picking up his family a little further south.

Fifteen days and five hundred miles later, in the wagon yard outside San Bernardino, Mun inquired if the Fancher train were in yet. Learning of the massacre, he traded his worn horses for two fresh mounts, replenished his supplies, and bought an extra pistol. The last person to report seeing him was a freighter at the Mojave crossing who warned the worried rider it was noonday madness to enter Utah Territory.

Houlton, Maine.

A burlap-wrapped package arrived at the old Clare residence out the Calais Road. Inside was a painting done on an old cabinet door, so signaled by the worn hinge markings on the back. An accompanying note read,

*For Jed and his family from your favorite sister. This was done by Phoebe, love Dinky*

The board measured roughly 12 by 18 inches. The scene was that of a waterfront—a blurry-edged, ragged row of black silhouettes vaguely resembling buildings overlooking white boats sitting cork-like atop violet-hued water. Yellow sails appeared to flutter above the boats. The sky was the color of fresh butter dotted with pink clouds and reddish splotches. In the lower right-hand corner of the picture, scratched through the thick paint while it was still wet, were the initials PT.

"Stand back," Dr. Clare ordered rather too loudly, determining the reddish splotches to be birds. "You can see wings."

Julia gamely hung the roily extravagance in the front room and pointed it out to guests as having been done by an acquaintance of the family. Making clear—out of earshot of her husband—that the artist was a charity case.

Two weeks later (after confessing to Bettina, "I simply can *not* leave it up another day, or I *shall* throw it in the fireplace!") she announced her intention to redecorate for the holidays and deep-sixed the oil-on-oak monstrosity in the cellar.

The coal man came with the first load of coal for the winter. Jed went down to open the chute, and the early sun, flowing straight through the chute, caught the painting hanging in the adjacent tool room. And Phoebe looking around the edge of a sail.

Jed could see the light glint on her thick glasses. He could see her short, curly hair. Charmed, he stepped closer, and the chubby, near-sighted little girl met on the Oregon Trail disappeared in a smear of white-edged wave.

Coal was rattling down the chute and the black dust boiling up. Jed closed the coal-room door and carried the painting upstairs, and that afternoon took it to the mill, where it hung

on the wall across from his office window. Here, whenever
he happened to think about it and catch her just right in the
even winter light, Phoebe looked over at him, touching off an
undercurrent of something a little bit lonesome.

*God, that was a long time ago, that Oregon Trail business.*

# FOUR

Sergeant Charles Reeves left Captain Van Vliet's escort at Fort Kearny on the Platte River, October 15, 1857, to be placed under the command of 1st Lt. Elisha G. Marshall, 6th Infantry. In the weeks that followed, the sergeant took patrols down the Little Blue and upriver through the sand hills. And except for witnessing a minor skirmish between the Pawnee and the Sioux, found the buffalo pastures quiet. This despite a briefing that warned the Cheyenne might want revenge for the ill-got gains of the past summer's Cheyenne Expedition.

The Cheyenne had jumped their ancient enemy, the Pawnee, for old-time sake, and the Pawnee whipped hell out of them. Custom called for revenge, but before the Cheyenne could get their act together, the army declared the Cheyenne in violation of the Fort Laramie Treaty and moved Bull Sumner up from New Mexico.

Why the brass thought a colonel who'd failed to chase the Navajo out of New Mexico, who couldn't even locate their cornfields to burn, would do any better up north against the Cheyenne was a mystery to the sergeant. Out on the High Plains, true to form, Colonel Sumner fizzled again, spending all summer mindlessly marching his 1st Cav boys to and fro. Settling, in the end, for a peaceful camp of Cheyenne on the

Solomon fork of the Kaw and wasting twelve men, women, and children, including two chiefs.

Poor bastards.

On his fourth reconnaissance in as many weeks, pushing through one lonely draw after another, the sergeant reached the summit of a hill overlooking the Platte. Glowing orange and gold, the lowering apron of trees lent the flat water an odd bluish tinge. Except for a small herd of buffalo bedded down, the wide Oregon turnpike was empty. Across to the north the endless pastures quivered in an autumn mist of drifting seeds.

Adrift in his own thoughts, he studied the countryside. The white man never kept a treaty, the Indians never broke one. How many Bull Sumners would it take to change that? and what difference did it make? Every day in New York City someone got off a boat and headed west. It was like watching a Mexican woman throw clay on the wheel. Slow but sure there'd be a bowl come. Slow but sure the whites would own all the land, and all the Indians would be dodging for dimes on the street corners.

A cold rain pelted the prairie. The rider who appeared in the gloom outside Fort Kearny led an extra horse and looked beat to the bone. A soldier led the spent horses away to the stables, the courier reported to the fort's commander.

> Col. S. Cooper
> Adjutant General, U.S.A.
>
> ...On the morning of the 5th of October, the Mormons burnt two trains of government stores on Green River, and one on the Big Sandy, and a few wagons belonging to Mr. Perry, sutler of the 10th infantry, which were a few miles behind the latter train....
>
> Colonel Alexander
> Camp Winfield, Utah Territory

The exhausted courier reported the countryside's being burned ahead of and along the flanks of the advancing army— 52 heavy freight wagons full of provisions burned, over a thousand head of oxen and beef stolen.

Lieutenant Elisha Marshall dismissed the courier and returned the dispatch to its leather pouch. The rain was turning to snow, the heavy flakes sliding down the window, reminding the lieutenant of what, as a child, he'd called "Christmas" snow. God help the regiments in that cold, wind-whipped South Pass country, that was going to be one hell of a Christmas.

*I wish Indians was all we had to worry about,* he reflected, recalling another piece of news relayed by the courier, that of a large number of emigrants having been lost to Indians near lower California.

Colonel Alexander's dispatch was forwarded with a fresh courier the next morning. Later that same day the Leavenworth courier brought news that was easier to chew. The contractor detained at Fort Kearny since the middle of August due to late arrival from Springfield, was to proceed to Albuquerque.

The newly planked floor sounded hollow under the sergeant's boots. The fort's commander had taken dinner at his desk, and the office smelled strongly of corned beef and cabbage.

"Our civilian contractor is being routed to Albuquerque. As the only sergeant left on the post familiar with desert freighting, you've been reassigned to the 3rd Infantry. You'll take five men with you.

"Pick up your orders from Chief Clerk Card in the morning. Captain Steele will brief you as to the distances and latest reports on the southern road. See what the Springfield boys have left in the way of rations and grain, make sure they got enough to get as far as Fort Union. Any questions?"

"No, sir." Hot damn! *QueQue!* Sunshine, hard roads,

beautiful senoritas, fine wines, fandangos. He could already smell
the *punche*.

The contractor, a man by the name of Potter, and his four
wagonloads of hardware originally earmarked for the Utah
Expedition, left Fort Kearny the next day. Six mules in the
hitch, a cavayard of four extra mules, and a military escort. The
prairies were adazzle with two feet of new snow under a hard,
blue sky. The wind was calm.

More than happy with having drawn the short straw, the
sergeant led out. The teamsters, too, were pleased to be headed
for a southern depot. But the barely literate Irish boys assigned
to the detail were long-faced.

"Look at it this way," the sergeant told them. "You're trading
a winter where the cold wind blows for a land of milk and
honey."

But they'd signed up to kill Indians, not nursemaid freight
wagons.

That night, two soldiers rode to the highest points near the
camp, dismounted and let their horses graze while keeping a
lookout until sunset. Wagons were parked so as to form three
sides of a square open side to the river. Mules were grazed outside
the square until an hour before sunset, when they were brought
inside and picketed on half-lariat. Army mounts and pack horses
were fed a full ration of corn, working mules half, idle mules
none. Supper was salt pork, hard bread, a gill of beans, and
coffee. A man could, if he wished, add his allotment of vinegar
and salt to the beans and dunk his bread in the broth. Two soldiers handled the night sentry shifts, Potter also put out two
sentries.

At the forks of the Platte the train swung south away from
the main trail to follow the fork that followed the mountains—
the fork the Indians called the fat-meat river. The recent snow

was all but gone, the as-yet-warm earth having absorbed it like a sponge, and the little-used trace, although slippery in places, was mostly dry.

A day down this lesser-traveled road the whiskery grey stubble of a vast prickly pear flat seeped over the horizon. Sharp plants made up of round, flat disks about three inches across and covered with long spikes that pierced the flesh. The infestation ran as far east as the eye could see and was home to owls, prairie dogs, and rattlesnakes. Occasionally an antelope or deer, following a dry arroyo, appeared in the bleak distance as if marooned. For the most part the wagons were able to skirt the inhospitable fields, but not always, making it necessary to check the animals' fetlocks nightly for spikes and infected sores.

Some two hundred miles upriver of the forks of the Platte the old St. Vrain trading post was reached, the first in a line of posts—St. Vrain, Jackson, Lupton, Vasquez—all empty now. The heaps of brown tumble-down walls, coming one after another like they did, reminded the sergeant of a broken string of clay beads left out on the prairie by giants.

He thought about the woman he led south from Fort Laramie ten years earlier in a crazy stunt that could have wasted both their lives. Right about here was where they hit the river. Ellen was her name, ran away from a Mormon train. And that Marchion kid hot on her trail.

*I wonder whatever happened to them.*

Mr. Indian was nowhere to be seen, tepee rings abandoned, rickety game poles empty. But ho! what was this? In the cottonwoods above Fort Vasquez a handful of dolls sat side by side on a limb low to the ground, their round, blank leather faces turned eastward toward the prairies. The sergeant dismounted for a better look. The dolls, about a foot tall, were dressed in trade-blanket scraps and tied so as not to be easily dislodged by wind or animals.

"I hope you make it back," the sergeant told whoever it was said good-bye and went away. "Cause this little family's watchin' for you, it sure is."

At the mouth of Cherry Creek the old trappers' corral was gone—washed out along with the shelter dug into the bank. The sergeant crossed the creek and halted for the night.

"I stayed here a spell in '46 when I broke my leg," he observed, helping a teamster who earlier had snapped off his peg leg.

"Trapper name of Dork lived here. Got killed a year later by Indians, Blackfeet, so I heard. That's a mistake men make living off all by their lonesome in Indian country. They get to thinking they keep their scalps 'cause they're smart, 'stead of laying it to good luck that could peter out any time."

"Yeah," the teamster agreed nervously, studying the desolate lay of land. "That's right."

"This here's where we leave the Platte," Charlie told him.

"How so?"

"'Less you wanna get right cozy with those mountains."

The teamster eyed the dark saw of fangs in the west. "Yeah, I see what you mean."

Nightfall in the loneliest camp at the end of the loneliest road in the world. Skies overcast, cooking fires hesitating circles of light in a sea of darkness. Tucking an ear against the monotonous whine of wind in the high cherry bushes, the peg-leg teamster hard at work on a new stick, the men cheered themselves with stories of other places.

"Sooner or later some nester's gonna show up here with ever'thing he owns," the sergeant said, hanging his washed-out socks on a willow sprig. "Plow, goats, kids, chickens."

But no one else thought so.

Up on the high plains south of Cherry Creek the game wasn't so plentiful as along the river bottoms. The weather held cold and dry, a hard wind out of the west whistling in the riggings, whipping the wagon sheets. Men and animals hunkered against it, closing their eyes against the gritty dust.

At the mouth of Fountain Creek the Spanish pueblo waited like a blood-stained ghost in the gloom of early evening. A Christmas-day massacre three years earlier had emptied the pueblo and put the quietus to nearby settlements. In the months following the massacre, American soldiers pushed the Ute and Apache marauders so hard through the valleys and mountains of the Southwest that the Indians had no time to stop and hunt. In June 1855 the Utes began making peace offers, by September a treaty had been signed with the Muache and Jicarilla Apache. But still, settlers avoided the region.

A hitch railing, broken in the middle, leaned into itself. Little pens with untended gates stood deep in brown, curled-over grasses. The party set up camp in a square once worn to dirt by the passage of animals and men, and went to sleep seeing ghosts in the hollow-eyed walls.

The sergeant's biggest worries were the cholera and Raton Pass. Every mile out of the river drainages lessened the threat of cholera. That and the sergeant's insistence that the men lay their blankets on boughs instead of the damp ground and go to bed with dry clothing. Now he set his sights on the 8,000-foot pass. Seen from the distance under tall, grey skies, the mountains in the vicinity of the pass showed no snow, but what had blown off the trees could still be on the ground.

He'd crossed the pass in the summer of '47 and remembered the twelve-mile grade up the north side as not bad. But these wagons were heavy. Each carried a mountain howitzer in addition to breech-loading carbines and metallic cartridges, making for 3,500-pound loads. It wouldn't take much snow and they'd be double teaming, splitting the detail and setting themselves up for trouble if renegades showed up.

*The Micks'd probably like a little excitement,* Charlie reflected wryly.

The Irish boys had done alright, followed orders and learned a thing or two, particularly from Potter's teamsters, older fellows from Vermont. But the sergeant doubted they knew anything about the grunt work of moving heavy loads.

In the plus column, the Green Mountain teamsters were used to deep snow. And the Fort Kearny briefing had listed no troubles reported since the pueblo massacre.

Crossing the Purgatory River near the mouth of Raton Creek, a wagon dropped a front wheel in a hole, snapping an axle and costing the better of the day to repair. The wind picked up. Snow showers separated by fits of pale sunshine charged down the long valley that headed on the Culebra Range. Late afternoon the party moved a mile up Raton Creek and stopped for the night, with winter in the moon. At this elevation the bushes were sliding into reds and yellows.

By ten o'clock the next morning the wagons had reached the twisted Indian trail that led over the pass, with patches of bare ground showing clear to the top. But the rocky, north-slope road, in places holding the snow and ice of earlier storms, was wearing down the teams. Every hour they were halted for fifteen minutes and their feet checked.

Nightfall and a good six miles to go.

The next morning was hazy with cold. Early afternoon a sudden, deep fog engulfed the mountain. Moving from one dry patch to another, the sergeant kept the trail lined up. Most worrisome were those stretches where the narrow, badly

washed ruts, crossing a rocky shoring, swayed out over white
nothingness. Snowflakes began drifting through the fog as if
lost, and the sergeant sent word back along the line that there'd
be no more rests and to work the teams accordingly. Shortly
afterward, the fog lifted and a steady slant of snow began.

In the heavy wheeling the big mules made shorter and shorter
gains, the line jerking forward, stopping of its own accord, and
jerking forward again. Shoulders to the wheels the men shouted
obscenities at the mules, at the mountain, at each other. Piñons
began to straggle by, wispy shadows in the storm. Gritting his
teeth, Charlie kept going, holding out for a place wide enough
to give the animals good standing between the wagons and the
mountainside. And wishing to hell he'd called a halt when the
fog first rolled in.

The slant eased off. He could stop now. From all the yelling
he could tell the mules were going to their knees. His hands and
feet were numb, it was time, it was past time. Where the hell
was the goddamn top?!

As a boy he'd paced off the distance from his home to the
oaks across the field at a hundred yards. More than once over
the years, he'd flogged himself with the memory—*100 yards, I
can do 100 yards.*

Doggedly counting, he realized they'd made it.

That night the wagons were chocked on level ground. The
weary mules lay in a rope corral in the stubby pines, and fires
popped and cracked through the dry kindling hauled from below.
Celebrating, the teamsters toasted the sergeant and his men
with their last cask of rum.

Morning dawned clear and cold. The party walked through
several feet of new snow to where they could see the black rim
of the southern prairies under the far, orange edge of sunrise. A
day of rest and the wagons were rolling, axles locked, down the

long, south slope—rocks steaming in the sun, snow melting on
the burning bushes.

Down to the junction of the Mora and Sapello Rivers
where the huge, useless trading post built by the Englishman
Alexander Barclay and his friends stood empty—a victim not of
Indian depredations, but of business agreements gone sour.

At Fort Union, Colonel Loring took one load of hardware
and ordered a second wagon off-loaded at Fort Marcy in Santa
Fe. The colonel had lost an arm at the Belen Gate outside the
City of Mexico. *That's what it means to be an officer,* Charlie
thought, watching the erect, soldierly figure going over the
lading bills with Potter. *You still got a job.*

At supper that evening one of the teamsters allowed as how
whatever else civilization was, it began with the act of sitting on
a chair and eating from a table.

Snow fell the next day, slowing the wagons, but causing the
sergeant no worries. Groceries restocked and the high ground
behind them, he took his time. The following morning the
forest of pine and piñon was white and silent under a clear blue
sky. A heavy rime covered every trunk, every branch, every
needle.

The splendid fairyland was in sharp contrast to the mean
huddle of adobe and stick houses that waited down the road.

"This don't exactly make me hilarious," one of the Irish boys
complained, eyeing the dirty, dog-haunted lanes and blanketed
inhabitants of Las Vegas. "What happened to the land of milk
and honey?"

"Wintertime," his sergeant told him. "Come spring they get
rid of them blankets, cows freshen, bees buzz around like crazy."

That afternoon the party stopped for an hour at the ranch
of Dr. Boise, an American. Always happy to see American
soldiers—especially when they were serving as an escort for

war wagons—and to learn the news of the northern trails, the jocular doctor fed the men bowls of red chile followed by dried currant pie and hot coffee in his large front room, and repeated his own gossip.

"There are over twenty thousand savages out here." The doctor waved his arm about. "In addition to our own friendly Navajo." He laughed and ran a finger across his throat. "It's impossible to appreciate the immensity of this land, or the danger. Only the Indian can fully appreciate it, and that's because it's in his veins, its breath is his breath.

"We have the Gila Apaches to the southwest, not the friendliest people you ever met, and off to the southeast the Mescaleros. Any feast they serve you will include you. Then along the edges of the territory are the Kiowas, Comanches, plains Apaches, and the Utes. The poor Mexican, unable to field an army with teeth, has no choice but to huddle in his little villages and pray. So you see, señors, how much you are appreciated! Have some more pie!"

At San José, Señor Don Antonia José Sena, his fortunes since the Mexican War now firmly hitched to the American cart, was also deeply appreciative of any commerce that promised to do what over three hundred years of Spanish rule had failed to do. The stately courtesy with which the señor greeted the American sergeant was followed by a feast of barbecued goat carried in large platters to the campfires of the little caravan, along with melons and bowls of piñon nuts.

Twenty miles out of Santa Fe, in the valley of the Pecos River, the trader Jim Pidgeon, a funny, stray little Frenchman, when asked about the ruined pueblo passed earlier in the day, replied, "It's called the Pecos Church. Montezuma, the brother of God, brought the first fire to the pueblo and gave strict orders it wasn't to go out until someone came for it. Don't ask me why, you can't second-guess God or his brother.

"So the Indians keep it going, day and night, night and day. Then along come the Spaniards, and *voila!* the priests haul it off to another pueblo. That's the way it is with life, you never know whose fires you're tending."

Christmas Eve, Fort Marcy depot, Santa Fe.

The plaza pulses with light and music. Invited to eat in the Governor's Palace, the civilian contractor and his sergeant join a crowd of military officers and local inhabitants milling around the long tables on the main floor. The feast includes a bonanza of colorful Mexican dishes in addition to mouth-watering reminders of home—platters of oysters, fresh shad, delicate little frosted cookies, cinnamon rolls accompanied by cherry preserves.

At the far end of the tables an old soldier pours drinks from bottles of fine champagne, El Paso wines, and brandy. And tells stories. He came in with the Army of the West in 1847. In those days men went to bed without their supper, the supply wagons miles behind and the Mexicans having no extra food. Stayed on half-rations for a good month —nine ounces of ground wheat per day, no sugar, no coffee—before marching south down the Camino Real. Those were hard times, hard times, nothing like now. The young bucks now don't know how easy they've got it.

After supper Charlie strolled about the city, enjoying the narrow streets with their hodge-podge of low houses and tiny yards. Encountering dusky men wrapped in coarse blankets and smoking *cigarillos,* he murmured low greetings in Spanish and went on. He liked the Southwest, liked everything about it—the empty spaces outside the settlements, the settlements them-selves, forever awash in Indian summer laziness.

Coming at length to the Church of St. Francis, the sergeant paused, thinking he'd like to see the Christmas decorations.

In the dim vestibule behind the heavy church doors, on

a table covered with a dark cloth, a nest of candles in little colored bowls shown like stars. Nearby, a clay jar held straw sticks. He touched a straw to one of the stars and set a fresh candle ablaze, the brief flare of light catching his smile.

*Ain't you surprised to see me in here, Sarah? Merry Christmas.*

Inside the sanctuary tall candles held aloft by wrought-iron holders filled the church with a soft, yellow gauze of light. At the back of the alter a row of round, squat pots breathed a sage-smelling incense. Cedar boughs lined the alter. Standing in rows in front of the boughs small children dressed in long, white dresses and sporting lopsided wings practiced Christmas hymns. The angels themselves couldn't sound any better.

Charlie sat for a while before wandering back outside, easing through the people entering the church. A group of singers in holiday finery and carrying lighted candles was collecting on the steps that led up to the little yard in front of the church. They opened an aisle for the *americano soldado,* and a lovely Spanish woman wearing a brilliant shawl favored him with a warm Christmas smile.

Made him feel *so* good!

General Garland, a tall old hero of the Mexican War and the fort's commander, was entertaining the populace with a concert by the 3rd Infantry band in the Plaza. The sergeant paused briefly and headed for the house of Carmelita, a well known *arpista.* There he spent the rest of the night drinking *mestela* and dancing to the music of harps and violins and guitars, the hard dirt floor flaking under his boots.

At one point he ran into a couple of the Micks, who were sloppy, puking drunk, and realized he was getting old. Either that, or he was already beginning to think like an officer.

The next day one of the Irish boys decided to desert in favor of a pretty little thing whose father ran a string of mule wagons to Chihuahua. As luck would have it, the love-struck soldier told his sergeant, who put the boy in irons until he sobered up. By then the wagons were a day south of Santa Fe.

"You wanna run, go ahead," Charlie said, unlocking the small wagon-box chain and paddock that served for cuffs. "I won't come looking for you. Leave your gun and your horse."

But the shamefaced Irishman got on his horse same as usual and made a beeline for Albuquerque.

# F I V E

WINTER CAME AND FILLED the valleys of the Utah mountains with snow. And the Army of Israel came marching home through the streets singing their boisterous camp songs, and the snow fell like white roses on their coarse woolen uniforms and on their laughing faces.

> Old Sam has sent, I understand,
> Doo-dah! Doo-dah!
> A Missouri ass to rule our land,
> Doo-dah! Doo-dah day!
> But if he comes, we'll have some fun,
> Doo-dah! Doo-dah!
> To see him and his juries run,
> Doo-dah! Doo-dah day!
> Then let us be on hand,
> By Brigham Young to stand,
> And if our enemies do appear,
> We'll sweep them from the land.

*Doo-dah! Doo-dah!!* sang the soldiers. *Doo-dah! Doo-dah!* sang the people.

Songs of victory were published and handed out on street corners. And if the titles were clunky and overlong, such as "Welcome to the returned warriors of Zion, dedicated to Lieutenant General Wells and his co-champions in arms," the music itself was joyously sweet.

> Strong in the power of Brigham's God,
> our name's a terror to our foes.
> Ye were a barrier strong and broad
> As our high mountains crowned with snows.
> Fear filled the myrmidons of war,
> Their courage fell in wordy boast.
> The faith and prayers of Israel's host
> Repelled the tyrant's gory car.
> Then welcome! sons of light and truth,
> Heroes alike in age and youth.

Forgotten were the hand-cart calamities, the failure of the lead mission, the grasshopper plague, the closure of the iron works. Blotted out by the wonderful news of the dreadful suffering and privation being endured by the wicked army encamped on the far side of Emigration Canyon.

The winter trees were decorated with lighted candles, and the homes hung with evergreens. Dancing and theatre were everywhere encouraged. Possessed of a terrible joy after the long, dark months of the Reformation, the Lord's chosen embraced the invigorating themes of death and revenge. And danced and danced and danced, so hungry were they to witness their Lord's power. And when the sweet singers of Israel sang

> Here our voices we'll raise and we'll sing to thy praise.
> Sacred home of the prophets of God,
> Thy deliverance is nigh, thy oppressors shall die,
> And the Gentiles shall bow 'neath thy rod.
> O Zion! dear Zion! home of the free,
> In thy temples we'll bend, all thy rights we'll defend,
> And our home shall be ever with thee.

to the sweet air of "Lily Dale," even strong men wept.

In Sunday worship the sparkling promises of fire and brimstone fell in an electrifying rain.

The Government of the United States will be broken to pieces. The Kingdom is the stone which will grind into powder all upon whom it falls. The whole United States, the whole world, can not prevail against the Saints. This is what Brigham said, and the howling congregation lifted their arms in supplication.

And Heber said, "Brigham is to become President of the United States. I am to be Vice President. Brother Wells is to be the Secretary of the Interior. In the meantime, the Saints are just as sure to go to hell as they live, and I know it, if they consent to dispossess Brother Brigham as our Governor!"

And people said "Amen" with the sound of a river falling.

And Heber said he hoped the army would not come, so his wives would not have to hurt them.

And the people laughed to hear him, erupting in hand-and-heel applause that filled the ears with the thumping of a demented drummer.

And those who knew better, who know sure as the sun rose in the east and set in the west that the American soldiers *would* come, tried not to hear. Tried instead to live inside their heads. As did George, letting a gurry of remembered tithing script and emigrant registrations, contractor receipts, stage-ticket stubs, purchasing and reimbursement orders, close up his sore ears.

And when the singing began,

> Up, awake, ye defenders of Zion!
>     The foe's at the door of your homes;
> Let each heart be the heart of a lion,
>     Unyielding and proud as he roams.
> Remember the wrongs of Missouri,
>     Remember the fate of Nauvoo:
> When the God-hating foe is before ye,
>     Stand firm, and be faithful and true.

those most damned of souls who could not believe, sang in their black hearts where no one could hear them the words that belonged to another time and place,

> O Columbia, the gem of the ocean,
>     the home of the brave and the free…

And always after service, women whose hearts would be moved at the violent death of a spider and men who would not suffer an animal to go hungry, these most pious of people, having sung themselves hoarse, walked home at peace through the snow-white world, scarves bunched carefully around their necks, the happiest of mortals.

And no one dared argue with Brigham. Nor tell the believers that they could not possibly win.

For the army huddled against the stone walls of the burned outpost of Fort Bridger the season was not so gay.

> 2,720 pounds ham, burned
> 167,900 pounds flour, burned
> 8,580 pounds Rio coffee, burned
> 68,832 rations desiccated vegetables, burned
> 134 bushels dried peaches, burned
> the groves along the river, burned
> the winter corn for the animals, burned
> over 1,000 head of oxen and beef, stolen

Brigham sent 800 pounds of salt with Brothers Henry Woodard and Jesse Earl to Colonel Albert Sidney Johnston, along with a letter attacking the American President. Colonel Johnston threw the Mormon messengers out of his camp and their salt with them. And the Indians, hearing the army had no salt, packed their own salt into the American camp and sold it for five dollars a pound.

And harsh storms raged, and the thermometer fell to minus sixteen degrees, and soldiers pulled grass by hand and fed it to their horses, along with tumblers of whiskey to revive the poor brutes' spirits. And horses and mules and the remaining cattle grew too weak to search under the snow for the grass and tried to eat sagebrush and died by the hundreds of starvation and the critical cold. And Colonel Johnston ordered Captain Randolph Marcy, 5th U.S. Infantry, together with a command of forty enlisted men, to cross the mountains by the most direct route into New Mexico to procure replacement supplies.

And all through the long winter American soldiers, worn down by the cold and scant rations, hitched themselves to wagons and walked five and six miles to the mountains to get fuel.

And all through the long winter Mormons scouts watched from the high points overlooking the wind-swept prairie where the army who would wage war on Zion huddled, and messengers rode back and forth between Great Salt Lake City as fast as the deepening snows would allow.

Thrilled by the penalties being extracted of the ungodly by the Almighty, the faithful in Utah sent news with Mormon freighters using the southern route to California that the times that would favor Zion had come at last. Hosanna to God in the highest! Victory for Israel and defeat and disgrace for the Gentile Nation!

A lady in GSL City wrote to her children in Providence, Rhode Island.

> I expect you have heard the loud talk of Uncle Sam's great big army coming to kill the Saints. Now, if you did but know how the Saints rejoice at the folly of the poor Gentiles. There are about four thousand on the border of our territory, and six hundred wagons—one naked mule to draw them—all the rest having died. The men are sitting in the snow, about a hundred and fifteen miles from us, living on three crackers a day, and three quarters of a pound of beef a week. Thus you see the old Prophet's words are fulfilled—whoever shall fight against Zion shall perish. The time is very near when one man shall chase

*a thousand, and ten shall put ten thousand to flight! Zion is
free; she is hid in one of the chambers of the Lord. We are a
free people. We do not fear "Uncle Sam's" soldiers. We only
fear our Father in heaven. We are learning His commandments
every day from His prophet, and I am determined to keep them.
If you were here, and could hear the Prophet's voice as I do,
and could hear the Lion of the Lord roar from the mountains,
as I do, and know how near the scourge of the Lord is upon the
Gentiles, you would flee to the mountains with haste. The time
has come when the Lord has called all the elders home, and
commanded them to bind up the law and seal the testimony.
They are now coming home as fast as possible. What comes
next? The judgment, hail-storm, thunder, lightning, pestilence,
war; and they that will not take up the sword against their
neighbor must flee to Zion for safety. Will you come, oh! my
dear children?*

Oh, yes, indeed! the gayest winter ever known in Utah.

> Old Squaw-killer Harney is on the way,
>     Doo-dah! Doo-dah!
> The Mormon people for to slay
>     Doo-dah! Doo-dah day!
> Now if he comes, the truth I'll tell,
>     Doo-dah! Doo-dah!
> Our boys will drive him down to hell,
>     Doo-dah! Doo-dah day!
>
> Then let us be on hand,
> By Brigham Young to stand,
> And if our enemies do appear,
> We'll sweep them from the land.

# SIX

HAVING NO CHOICE but to postpone their visit to Utah Territory, Nathan and Daphne settled for the winter in San Francisco in a modest third-floor walkup overlooking the hustle and bustle of Sacramento Street. Nathan hired on as a bookkeeper with the *Evening Bulletin*, where he gathered information on the local swells. Daphne took employment with the assistant decorator to Mary Bell Gwin, wife of United States Senator William McKendree Gwin. The Gwins lived in that new neighborhood christened "South Park."

As the daughter of a Virginia tavern keeper, Mary Bell's social skills were honed to a fine edge. She knew whom to visit and whom to shun, leaving Daphne with no choice, after spotting Mme. de** in Mary Bell's parlor one foggy afternoon, but to plead a family emergency and quit on the spot. Were Mme. de** to remark, even in the most idle fashion, on the resemblance between Mary Bell's decorator and the thief who lightened the de** bank account by a considerable amount—ahhg! Daphne shuddered to think.

She next went to work as assistant to the assistant secretary to Abby Eastman Meagher Parrott. Abby wore diamonds big as strawberries. John Parrott boasted the largest fortune in the city. The Parrotts occupied a new home on Rincon Hill *overlooking* South Park.

On her first day in her new position, after being given a tour of the house, Daphne was put to work reviewing dusty stacks of framed prints with an eye to suggesting where they might hang, an assignment she soon circumvented by selecting a pencil drawing of Beethoven and carrying it to an unfinished room nearby the recital stage.

Intent on where to hang Beethoven, she happened to mention her intimacy with romantic locales in France, Italy and the Caribbean. The assistant secretary told the secretary, who, after conferring with her employer, gave Daphne free rein to decorate the room.

A month later, invited to view the "Beethoven Room," Nathan was ready. The unfathomable jumble of exquisite bric-a-brac cluttering every inch of wall wrung from him only the most effuse of compliments.

Several times, first in the Gwin home and later in the Parrott home, Daphne had the good fortune to encounter that wickedly handsome Mr. Uergin, who never failed to make gracious mention of his interest in procuring additional paintings. But Daphne knew, from the warmth in the saloon keeper's dark eyes, what Conrad Uergin was really interested in procuring.

In dusty little Albuquerque, change came slowly. That flagpole there in the plaza, posts spliced together and reaching upwards of 150 feet—that was new. So was the regimental band, along with several new mercantile businesses and a ferry boat on the Rio Grande.

Everything else was the way Charlie remembered it from ten years earlier during the Mexican campaign. Old mud houses with clay floors and little yards. Big-hatted ranchers sporting fancy silver buttons and red sashes. Laborers in *sabanilla* trousers and shirts. Shaggy little, big-eared burros tottering under their loads. The tinkle of wind bells in the patios, the cries of Pueblo Indians selling their wares on the *plaza de armas*. Mouthnumbing tamales and those flat little cornhusk cigarettes. Pretty women with their limp skirts and limpsy gait and inviting smiles.

In February the famous camel supply train of U.S. Road Superintendent Edward Fitzgerald Beale sauntered through the streets of Albuquerque. Seventy-six gigantic white camels all the way from the Gobi Desert in Asia. People clapped as the queer looking brutes passed by. A Mexican drummer took his place at the head of the column and was soon joined by others who knocked sticks together and shook gourds.

The amazing beasts of burden had crossed the ocean in sailing ships and landed at Indianola, walking inland from the gulf to Albuquerque. From Albuquerque they hiked through the desert lands to Fort Tejon, ninety miles north of Los Angeles, turned around and hiked right back in the dead of winter. Over four thousand miles without an accident, carrying up to seven hundred pounds per animal.

Watching the parade of camel jockeys, the sergeant decided he'd like to go for a camel ride. So he followed the strange procession to the army corrals, and soon found himself inspecting the countryside from the top of a real live, twohumped Bactrian called Sir Speedy.

Swaying back and forth in the high saddle, he encountered a donkey grazing peacefully along. Mr. Donkey took one look at Sir Speedy and scratched air getting out of the way. Sir Speedy belched and spit and broke wind and took off after the donkey in slow motion. The sergeant whooped and hollered. It was the best fun!

Fortunately for the American soldier on patrol in the Middle Valley, life stayed downright monotonous. An occasional Navajo foray, the usual fruitless chase, the usual escort duty for travelers and freight up and down the *Camino Real de Tierra Adentro*.

This held true for most of the Southwest. A dust-up in the Ladrone Mountains when the Fort Craig boys under Lieutenant Overell killed five Kiowa and took one prisoner. Three 2nd Cavalry boys wounded on the south branch of the Llano River in Texas in a brush with an unidentified band of savages. An officer and twenty enlisted men wounded in the Huachuca Mountains in a fight with Apaches. That was about the extent of the troubles.

Which sure beat Kansas, where Freebooters were tangling it up with companies from the 1st Cavalry. Likewise the Spokane Lake country of the far Northwest, where companies from the 1st Dragoons and a 9th Infantry detachment got into a real fire-fight with more than a thousand redskins.

And Utah Territory? The Southwest very definitely beat Utah Territory all to hell! Those poor bastards nailed down east of the Wasatch Mountains since last fall still hadn't made it into the Basin.

Yessireebob! For a man waking up every morning to the sounds of reveille, QueQue—with its great dome of cottonwoods bare, its flies and mosquitoes gone, and its nightly riot of entertainment—could not be beat.

There was only one small wrinkle.

The winds of war were blowing west. Most *mexicanos* seemed determined to ignore the fierce storm building in the East, unwilling to compare their own large numbers of peons and captive Navajo children with the black servants owned by the Southern army officers.

But the big landowners at Bernalillo and Ranchos de Albuquerque were coming down hard on the side of succession.

The noisiest of these, the *Tejanos,* who called themselves the Texas Mounted Volunteers, regularly staged parades in the plaza.

Within the Post itself, the right and wrong of a man's owning slaves triggered serious arguments up and down the ranks. If the South abandoned the Union, officers with southern sympathies could resign their commissions. But for the enlisted man to be similarly cavalier with his allegiance made him a deserter.

No one thought the war would last long. Six months, a year at the most, to dissolve the Union or slap the South down, depending on who was doing the talking.

Promised a commission as a second lieutenant if the South bolted the Union, the sergeant convinced himself the war would be short and the Southern countryside beautiful to see.

# S E V E N

LIKE A SEISMIC WAVE sweeping inland from far out in the ocean, news of the Utah disaster moved inexorably eastward in cataclysmic explosions, reaching upstate New York the tenth of December 1857 with headlines that screamed

### Horrible Massacre of Emigrants
### Over 100 persons murdered!!

December 31 the news reached the Ozarks. A month later to the day, Houlton, Maine. Locked in the grip of winter, the Marchion brothers waited for spring and prayed.

Maine, March 1858.

There is a whistling in the woods and the sound of teams hauling buckets and taps. The sugar maples are being spigoted and the fresh sap pulled down from the back fields. Barrel stoves billow smoke night and day. Bulges in the frost heaves break the roads, and in the center of the frozen pond below the potato house a ghost breath of water is making space for itself.

It was time.

Jed drew up a letter asking Shep Cary for a six-month leave of absence and showed it to Julia, who went to pieces.

*"What in blue blazes are you thinking of?!* You belong here!"

"We've talked this thing to death. I don't have any choice."

"Oh, for heaven's sake, Jed! *It's March everywhere!* Mud season! The roads are full of mud and snow. You just want to go out there."

"Believe me, there's no 'there' there. Except for my sister and her children."

"She's got a husband!"

"Yes, if the Indians haven't killed him, she's got a husband."

"And I have a husband and a one-year-old son who needs his father, and I don't want the Indians to kill him!" Julia broke into wild weeping and would not be comforted, stomping down the cellar stairs to sit in the winter-dark tool room.

But later, in bed, their nightshirts pulled down like armor...

"I read in the newspaper that Utah Territory's closed."

Jed didn't answer.

"What about Walker, he's her brother too."

"I don't know what Walker's doing."

"Well, find out! What about Yam, those are his people."

"Those are not his people, they're wild savages. Besides, Yam's up in that Allagash country."

"You can wait and meet him in Bangor. I'll feel better if you don't go alone. If he really is your half-brother, I think he'd be glad to help out, after all you've done for him."

Jed punched his pillow into a comfortable lump and tried to relax.

"Are you asleep?" Julia curled against him.

He rolled over and drew her close.

"It won't help you or your sister to go running around like a chicken with its head cut off," Julia whispered with tears in her voice. "Promise me you'll wait for Yam, please, dear, and I won't harp another word."

Later, likening the western desert to a kind of Indian

promised land, Julia's cousin and dearest confidant Bettina remarked, "Yam will never come back."

"Oh my goodness!" Julia threw up her arms in mock horror. "Why didn't I think of that!"

In the Great Basin Brigham's plans for vacating the northern settlements were reaching a crescendo.

> We have an abundant supply of grain and cattle, and if necessity compels us to flee to the mountains, bread and beef will appease our hunger. Every preparation is being made to preserve ourselves in case the administration does not relent…We can but lose our improvements, and 'twere better to lose the little that we have of this world's goods, than our liberty in this life, and our hope of salvation in the world to come. Rather than see my wives and daughters ravished and polluted, and the seeds of corruption sown in the hearts of my sons by a brutal soldiery, I would leave my home in ashes, my gardens and orchards a waste, and subsist upon roots and herbs, a wanderer through these mountains for the remainder of my natural life.
>                     President Young
>                     Deseret News

The peach trees were in full bloom. A midwife brought an armful of peach-tree branches to the Tithing Office, and George scolded her for breaking the tree in such a fashion. Even so, the delicately scented blossoms, propped in a cream can filled with water, added to the bishop's day in ways he could not have imagined.

Phoebe set up her easel at the side of State Road, returning several hours later to prop her masterpiece on the sofa to dry. Asked his opinion, George pronounced it beautiful and suggested it be hung in the entryway.

"What are you going to call it?" he asked, angling for a hint as to what it was.

"Plum Saplings," Phoebe replied, surprised he had to ask.

Plum saplings? The globs of red, blue, and orange overhanging what looked to be a goat track were the spindly plum saplings bordering State road?! *She might be blind,* George mused, *but no one can ever accuse of her lacking imagination.*

Ellen was in the kitchen churning butter and reading the *Deseret News.*

"We're like Abraham," she told George and handed him the paper. "Putting our children on the chopping block for Brigham."

George glanced at the article. "He's crazy."

He walked out the back door to the barns. He loved being outside, catching the last of the sun on his gardens. Passing between the barns, thinking about them being burned, he recalled Brigham's letter with loathing. Such a tyrant. Always threatening this, threatening that, never any talk of peace or conciliation or common sense.

He treated himself to a carrot and seated himself on the bench so as to have the sun in his face. His mother had always hated to see the sun go down, waiting until almost dark to light the lamps. He used to think it was to save on coal oil, but now he knew better. In a way it was a death, the going of the light.

On March 18 the First Presidency officially abandoned the idea of armed resistance to federal forces. It was the Lord's will. All spring work was stopped, and plans drawn up to destroy the city. That Sunday the Saints were told to go south as soon as possible, that United States troops were determined to kill them all.

Soldiers were advised to quit using tobacco and be valiant for the kingdom of God. John Pulsipher, Mormon soldier, wrote in his diary,

> The prophet Brigham is as calm as if there was no danger—says *move South & see the Salvation of God*. And almost the entire people say Amen to it & are as happy as were the children of Israel led by Moses, anciently when they passed thru the red Sea.

Speaking in the Tabernacle, Brigham said,

> It is all I can do to hold back from killing those Infernal scoundrels out yonder at Bridger, sent by Government to destroy this people. Pres. Buchanan has violated his oath of office in sending that army against us, as peaceable citizens as are in the union.
> They are determined not to pay us one dime of what they owe us—But are paying thousand & hundred of thousands of dollars to hire the indians to kill us.
> I need a breeching as strong as that of Dutch harness to enable me to hold back from killing every Devil of that army—But is best to hold back & let them whip themselves. It is the will of the Lord that we leave this city & the north country—Move south—& if our enemies come upon us, when we are doing all we can to get away we will send them to hell across lots—& if they hire the indians to help them, we are good for all of them. Amen.

Monday Jeremy brought home a writing exercise entitled "How to leave your house." Copied from the school blackboard, the instructions called for shavings, kindling, and dried grasses to be left in the doorways. Personal possessions could be taken out, but no furniture. If the Sevastopol treatment were ordered, the Lord's soldiers would burn the buildings and chop down the trees.

"We shall not be given to the halter!" Jeremy exclaimed, bug-eyed. "They shall not set one foot in this house!"

Face frozen, Ellen stared at the uneven march of stick letters back and forth across the ruled sheets. "And where will we live?"

"In rocks and deserts, hidden deep in dens and caves." Jeremy pulled a second page from his school sack, this page asking that he be allowed to remain behind to guard the house and garden.

Ellen scarcely knew what to say. "You're going to protect our house, or you're going to destroy it?"

"Protect it until the evil Union troops get here, then fly at a moment's warning and leave nothing behind!"

"You would set your own house afire?"

"We'll build another one."

"And chop down the trees you yourself planted and cared for all these years, trees budded with fruit?!"

"Of course." Jeremy lifted his chin. "God will give us more."

How tall he was getting. What a wonderfully fierce face he made. Ellen wanted to cup that face in her hands, to tell her son he looked like his father, that all he needed was some paint and he could be a mad Indian chief. Instead she said, "You're blaming all this…all these bizarre plans on God?"

"Mother," the tone sounded a warning note, "just because you don't believe in God."

"Don't change the subject. You're ten years old, you don't know squat about what Brigham's up to."

"Eleven…almost. And I know that, unless you leave, you are going to be exterminated."

"Exterminated? Well, that's a big word. If that's the case, I certainly will go, but I'm not leaving you behind, and you can not pile fire starter in the doorways. That's silly. No one's going to set fire to our house."

Wanting to tamp down the anger she saw building, she added lightly, "You know how, when you're playing with your friends?

how you talk about keeping low in the saddle? keeping low in
the grass, so your enemies don't see you? That's kind of fun, isn't
it? That's what Brigham's doing, he's playing a game, he's trying
to outsmart his enemies, only they aren't really…"

"…he is *NOT* playing a game! We are in grave danger!"

"Just hear me out, I heard you out. The American Army is
bringing us a new governor and…Jeremy? Jeremiah George! you
get back here *right now!!*"

The boy was walking out of the house and out of earshot,
unless Ellen wanted to scream. Unless she wanted the neighbors
to spring to their windows and afterward to report the argument
to Church Authority. As he walked, Jeremy snatched up
handfuls of dried grass defiantly.

Rejoicing to exchange the comforts of home for the trials of
the wilderness, a strange army began to crowd the road down
from the northern settlements. Many without shoes or hats,
driving here a little bunch of cows, there a little flock of sheep—
women and children walking merrily along as if going to a corn
husking.

On April 12 the American official sent by President
Buchanan to replace President Young as Governor of the
Territory arrived in Great Salt Lake City. Determined to
overlook the insult visited on him, and in larger measure on the
sovereignty of the Federation, by keeping the American Army at
bay throughout the winter, Alfred Cumming arrived in the city
eager to reassure the faithful that the government wished them
only goodwill.

The first thing to catch his eye was the parade passing
through the main street. Drawing close, he saw wagons and carts
piled high with what looked to be personal belongings. Some
drawn by livestock, others pulled by people. Inquiring as to their

purpose for being on the road, he was told they were fleeing the American Army.

At first he thought his leg was being pulled by a prankster. Nevertheless, with heartfelt entreaties, he implored them to return to their homes. To no avail. Aflame with salvation and sacrifice, moving under the hand of God, the poor beings kept walking, reminding the new governor for all the world of lemmings marching themselves determinedly into the sea.

Having no time to waste on religious zealots, Cumming hurried on about his business—that of meeting the legendary Brigham Young.

On April 25 the newly appointed governor attended Sunday service in an overflowing Tabernacle, where he had the following announcement read.

> NOTICE
>
> It has been reported to me that there are persons residing in this, and in other parts of the territory, who are illegally restrained of their liberty. It is therefore proper that I should announce that I assume the protection of all such persons, if any there be, and request that they will communicate to me their names and places of residence, under seal, through Mr. Fay Worthing, or to me in person during my stay in the City.
>
> A. Cumming, Govr. Utah Ty.
> April 25, 1858

After the reading, performed rather poorly by a church clerk, the new governor stood to acknowledge that the purpose of his presence in the territory was to vindicate the national sovereignty.

Wreathing his words in smiles, the medium-sized, well-dressed Gentile called on those embittered by remembrance of real and imaginary wrongs to look to the future. He was not there to judge the Saints' social and religious views, they had the right to serve God in any way they pleased, but Utah must move toward statehood.

Ellen was sitting with Phoebe and the children toward the front of the Tabernacle—a location they avoided except when George was being honored with the opportunity to speak. Today it was the corpulent, good-natured Georgian they wanted to see. A man in his fifties, round face made rounder by black sideburns. The speech was going over well. George had warned of fireworks, but the people were listening calmly. Ellen smiled with relief.

*The children will learn their Constitution in school, there will be regular policemen on the streets instead of Danites.*

Governor Cumming spoke for thirty-five minutes, humbly conceding, "I do not expect mine will be a path of roses…if you see me go a little astray, do not treat me harshly but counsel with me as a friend." He concluded his remarks with, "I will be glad to hear from any who might be inclined to address me upon topics of interest to the community."

The topics of interest broached by the speakers who took turns ascending the platform were the assassination of Joseph Smith and his brother, the services rendered to an ungrateful country by the Mormon Battalion, the persecution endured by the Saints in the States, the suffering encountered in fleeing the States, the unlawful introduction of national troops into the territory.

Each accusation was followed by a wave of cries and murmurs, each wave higher than the last. The Four Horsemen of the Apocalypse charged down from the rafters wearing U.S. Army uniforms. The congregation howled back like snapping dogs. Overlooking the frenzy, the President and his apostles could scarcely contain their glee.

Hearing her son's voice in the madding chorus, Ellen leaned around Phoebe to shush the boy, noticing behind him a sea of faces singed with hate and fear. Nancy poked Jeremy in the ribs and told him to be quiet, and Jeremy hit his sister hard with his shoulder.

Brigham rose slowly to his feet, and the crazed congregation burst into a wild roar. Governor Cumming, ashen faced, continued to stand. Brigham lifted his arms.

Silence. Instant. A blow in itself. Nancy covered her ears.

"There is no good reason to have the army thrust upon the Saints of Salt Lake Valley," Brigham said sweetly, soothingly.

"It is my judgment it will bring evil, crime, and perhaps open warfare and bloodshed. Because we are not prepared to meet such a blow, we will lay the territory waste and go into the desert. This move will redound to God's honor and glory. Be patient. Go to your homes, purify yourselves and let the Lord work."

As the President spoke, a humiliated Governor Cumming, unable to answer a single charge leveled against the Federation, was ignobly hustled out a side door.

That night after dinner, George asked his family if they wanted to leave the church. "I understand the army will provide safe escort."

Phoebe voted for far-away places, Jeremy declared himself a soldier of the Lord to the death.

"All my friends are here." Nancy began to cry.

"Be quiet, you baby," Jeremy ordered.

"The time is drawing close for responsible men to step forward," George explained. "Otherwise Brigham will continue to paralyze the transfer of power as he did today. I want you to leave while you have the opportunity. You may be able to come back later, either that or I'll join you."

Drawing a short, quick breath Jeremy straightened in his chair. "I don't understand why we'd go anywhere. It isn't our

President's fault people are so stupid. He isn't even going
to fight, he's going to retreat. I wish he would fight, but he's
thinking of us, he doesn't want us to get hurt."

"He isn't going to fight because he can't win," George said
gently.

"He can too! He can do anything with God on his side. How
can you say he can't win? It's like you're arguing with God,
you're not supposed to do that."

"I love the church very much, Jeremy. It's a beautiful church,
full of beautiful promises. But I can no longer follow Brigham,
and neither can many others. Just because people say they're
talking for God doesn't mean..."

The boy was getting red in the face, unwilled tears stung his
eyes. "...he *is* talking for God! God talks to him all the time. We
should trust him, we've got lots of really nice things all because
of him."

"But he wants to burn them." George bowed his neck to
scratch the top of his head. And gave his son a sideways grin.
"You know, there's only one church in the Valley."

"That's alright, it's our Valley."

"But if someone came along, some fellow your age, and he
was, say, a Methodist. Would you care if he had a Methodist
church to go to here?"

"Well, I wouldn't, but I don't see what difference that makes."

"And if you had a job for him, or if he wanted to live in one
of your houses, would that be alright?"

"Well, sure. He'd have to pay me." Jeremy giggled. "No
charity."

"So you don't really care if not everyone believes in
Brigham?"

"Well...no."

"Good," George said happily, and before Jeremy could muster

further argument, added, "That's all. Your mother and I will let you know what we decide."

"Just so you know, I'm not going anywhere."

"What about me?" Nancy asked. "I get my say."

"By all means. And it is?"

"And it is…" the little girl made a whooshing sound "…I don't wanna leave my friends, that's for sure, so I'm not going either. But this question is for mama and Sister Phoebe. If we do go, who gets to be the wife? because in America men only get one wife."

Ellen swallowed a smile and looked at George who, pursing his lips, studied the silverware on his plate.

"I think," he spoke slowly, "the thing to do is to allow your mother and Sister Phoebe to draw straws, to see who will be the lucky one."

Everybody howled in protest. He was cheating.

Ellen and the children began clearing the table. George covered Phoebe's hand with his own, wanting to talk with her a minute longer. "You understand, don't you, what I'm telling you? There will be sacrifices. You'll be able to take very few of your belongings, no paintings, there won't be room."

"I always wanted to go to California."

"That would be my choice too. I…" (he might as well get it over with) "…you could be my daughter by my first marriage. Ellen would be my wife, and there wouldn't be any mention of other wives. Are you comfortable with that?"

"Oh, I don't care, now Constance might." Phoebe broke into a sudden laughter.

"So I'll only have to pull a third of the peas," Nancy said.

"Nancy Jane!" George said sternly, "this is hard enough without your two cents worth, just keep clearing."

"Start the dishes, Nancy," Ellen said, returning from the kitchen to resume her seat at the table.

"It's Jeremy's turn."

"Then Jeremy should start the dishes. Go tell him." Ellen looked at George. "I don't think it's necessary for any of us to leave, not with the American Army here."

"The American Army isn't here yet, Sister Ellen. Brigham still sits on the throne."

Hearing the irritation in George's words, Phoebe beat a hasty retreat with the last of the dirty dishes.

"I'm not going anywhere without you," Ellen shot back. "And if anything happens to you, I'm going straight to the authorities. In the meantime, I'm going to bed."

"What authorities? Whatever happens here happens *because* of Brigham."

"If you want to leave, put the houses on the market. We paid the church for them, we'll take our things and leave together. This is America, and I'm done pretending it's not."

"You confuse yourself with your expectations, Sister Ellen."

"Oh, stop with the smoke and mirrors, talk English!"

"Alright, you're being stupid. This is not America, this is Utah. There is no market."

"I'm saying there *will* be a market! that we *will* be part of the Union. The American Army did not come all this way to lick Brigham's boots, and I'm saying goodnight!"

Upstairs in her darkening room Ellen moved aimlessly about, loath to light the lamp and blot out the lingering sunset. Without his family, George would have no protection. There'd be no quiet Sundays, no picnics. The church would be at his door every minute—adding meetings onto meetings, never giving him a minute's rest. They'd kill him with work, he'd never get out in time. And what did he mean about stepping forward? He wasn't young anymore, his friends weren't either.

Oh, dear God, what to do?

In seven days, keeping his office open all hours of the day and night, Governor Cumming registered 56 men, 33 women, and 71 children as desirous of protection and assistance in proceeding to the States. The church promised to furnish the go-backs with flour and to assist them in leaving. For their part, the apostates signed papers abandoning all claim to their improvements. None of the Harris family asked for protection.

Having done all he could do, the Governor returned to Camp Scott, where he had spent the previous winter. What, on entering the city, had looked to be an aberration was in reality a much larger movement. For reasons that were not clear to him, the Saints seemed determined to flee the advancing army.

Shortly thereafter Brigham signaled the evacuation of the city itself by joining the exodus from the northern settlements. George's entourage consisted of a buggy, which he drove, and two small covered wagons—one driven by Jeremy and the other by the hired man.

"Can anyone hear me?" George asked softly, his eyes unnaturally bright. His fever had returned. He lay on a pile of quilts in the wagon bed, the sunlight through the yellowed canvas lending his face a waxy cast.

Ellen shook her head. She was holding his hand, idly smoothing his fingers.

"If anything happens to me, you must be on your guard and not expose yourself to punishment…"

"…nothing's going…"

"…be quiet and listen. There's a very important piece of business you must remember. When the house contents are inventoried, save something aside for when you meet with Brigham alone—some little gift, some very valuable little gift."

Fifty miles below the salt lake, at the outskirts of Provot, gambling the First Presidency wouldn't miss the bishop, Ellen ordered the wagons pulled aside. This was as far south as she was going, they had friends in Provot. The precaution proved unnecessary. Brigham set up headquarters on the block east of the meeting house in Provot—moving his belongings from the Lion House and the Bee House, together with his wives and children, into the large number of newly-erected lumber shanties.

George knew the court would stay in Provot, but had forgotten to tell anyone.

# E I G H T

The government at Washington, by its shameful misman-
agement of this whole expedition, has placed Colonel
Johnston and his whole army in a dangerous position. What
does that government intend to do by way of getting them
out?

    Horace Greeley
    New York Tribune
    January 14, 1858

Yam and his wife Mouse worked the winter in a timber
camp in northeastern Maine. The principal was a quiet
man who knew his business, the crew included the farmers
from around Cold Stream Pond. This did not make life easy, but
easier than it might have been otherwise.

Reaching Bangor that spring with the harvest, Yam collected
their $570 in wages and gave Mouse $200 to buy horses and
supplies for the long trek home.

"Look me up in three days, and stay out of fights."

Free at last to enjoy himself, he plunked down two dollars for
two tubs of warm water at a bathhouse on Washington Street.
One tub held a soupy wash of shaving soap, ammonia, and
saltpeter to get rid of the vermin. The second tub came with a
soap bar scented with attar of roses.

A trip to the barber followed these pleasant ablutions. Next it was a shopping spree in Wheelwright and Clark on West Market Square. New boots and britches, a fancy red-checkered shirt, a snappy low-crowned, wide-brimmed hat, and he was ready for business.

But no sooner had he rendezvoused with the drivers in a tavern on Broad Street, then a most unexpected event occurred. Who should walk in the door with tickets on the *Maine Central Railroad*, leaving Bangor 8 a.m. sharp the next morning for Portland, but Jed Marchion, looking like warmed-over death.

Poor Yam. The cruel winter and the dangerous ride down the · churning waters of the Penobscot behind him. The glass raised to his lips. And now this.

There was still a party—of sorts. But not much of one. To make sure there were no hitches, Jed followed the Indian everywhere but upstairs with the lively ladies.

Yam left a message with the barkeep for Mouse, telling her to buy only one horse and go home. Shortly after daylight he followed his charge through the crowds of loggers and sailors and rats from the harbors that roamed the streets of Devil's Half Acre. Hotfooted it across the railroad bridge over the Kenduskeag, and eased between the drays and delivery buggies on Railroad Street. And parked himself in Central station to wait for a train

So much for three days in Bangor.


For Jed, routinely checking his pocket watch to see what Julia and J.C. were up to, the excitement of that first train ride soon wore thin. But Yam was mesmerized. The clang-bang stops and starts, the constant rattle-rattle, click-click-click when the wheels rolled, the countryside gliding effortlessly by.

From Portland the brothers caught a succession of cars down to Baltimore, and at the head of Chesapeake Bay climbed

onboard an iron horse with the words *Marietta & Cincinnati*
printed in dark green on the sides of the yellow cars.

Every chance he got, Jed visited with railroaders about freight
charges, with timber men about what was being cut and at what
prices. Run-of-the-mill stuff that gave him something to do
and kept him from going insane. The trains were rife with talk
of succession, much of it loud and argumentative. The eastern
region of Minnesota Territory was entering the Union as a Free
State. Kansas Territory wanted in Free too, but the abolitionists
had their hands full with Southern senators and Pro-slavery men
from Missouri.

"And just how do you feel about the black question, sir?" a
well-dressed man with a layering of chins and a fried-ham-and-
grits accent looked up from his supper to ask.

"I don't have a dog in that fight."

The businessman wanted to argue economics, Jed shook
off the words with a smile and concentrated on his plate. The
dining car smelled of stale food. It rocked comfortably back and
forth, lime-green linen tablecloths swaying gently. Outside the
windows, dusk was in the trees. The large clock at the end of the
car said seven-thirty.

If he were home, he'd be lying on the floor by the baby's bed
trying to stay awake. Julia would be singing nursery rhymes so
soft he could hardly hear her. Pretty soon she'd whisper that
J.C. was asleep, and they'd go out in the kitchen and talk about
what all went on during the day. Good Lord, it was hell to be
homesick.

Not that he had much time to wallow in self-pity, Yam's
buying habits being what they were.

"You just give that kid a quarter for a penny gumball! You
gotta watch how much you pay for stuff."

And later. "You're attracting vendors like flies, you won't
have any money left! We gotta buy horses in St. Joe."

"I will walk."

"Not by a damn sight!" In the end, he gave up and paid for everything, which meant there was always someone approaching with a hand out, but at least he kept them from jacking the price.

Equally troublesome was Yam's inclination to wander off. The Indian had to be watched like a hawk at the stops. In Parkersburg, Virginia, he disappeared completely. Jed searched the station and adjacent sheds, stuck his head in doorways up and down the street bordering the track and, time running out, found Yam back in the waiting room.

"Where in the hell have you been?!" Jed plopped on the wooden bench and jumped up. The train for Athens, Ohio, and points west was being announced. "Let's go."

At a stop on the Hocking River to load hogs he saw something he'd never seen before—wood hogs crossed with Bedfords. The resultant light-colored crosses were smaller than the Bedfords, but heavy hammed and square as a kitchen table, with big square-like black spots rounded on the corners. The heavy jowls sagged to the ground. The poll over the head was huge, covering the eyes. Ears the size of squash leaves lopped forward over the savage faces.

"Now them's real money makers," he said to Yam, or would have, had Yam been within hearing distance. He walked amongst the sheepfolds and hog pens and yelled, and returning to the train, stood on the steps to look over the yards. The cars eased slowly forward, the steam popped, and the little stock pens slipped from view with no Yam running wildly to catch up.

Taking his seat, he rested his forehead against the sooty, grit-pitted window glass. *I ain't coming after you, I gotta get Dinky. I'll meet you back in Houlton.*

At the next stop, here was Yam.

"Where'd you come from?" Jed asked curtly, hiding his relief.

Yam put a finger in the air reprovingly. At a passenger stop outside Athens, he hustled Jed off the train and down the line of cars to a baggage car. There in a corner, kept upright with a rope, stood a wooden Indian. A slender, brightly painted fellow who looked to have been carved from a discarded ship's mast. His mouth was frozen in a howl, in one hand he clutched a sheaf of tobacco, in the other an upraised tomahawk.

"Jesus H. Christ!"

"He was not happy."

"He still ain't. What'd you pay for him?"

By way of answer Yam produced a crumpled baggage-claim ticket from Parkersburg on which a wit had written "injuns ride free long as they ride west."

Exactly how Yam came by his wooden friend, Jed never did learn. Be that as it may, the carving solved the problem of Yam's wandering off. When he wasn't where he was supposed to be, he was in the baggage car with Frank—Jed's name for want of a better. In Cincinnati the brothers switched to the *Ohio & Mississippi*, Frank with them, and rode those tracks west all the way to the city named for King Louis XV of France—and the end of the line for all train travel west.

In the cavernous St. Louis train station a plump, bare-chested maiden carved from a tree trunk proffered a fistful of cigars. Her bright headdress fell the length of her skirt, her bare ankles were modestly crossed. Yam wrapped his arms around Frank and muttered something against the poor old wooden head. And left his friend with the voluptuous maiden.

"I'm curious," Jed said. "What made you decide to park Frank here?"

Yam's face was a wall. "I can not take both."

The journey from Maine to Missouri—a journey that before the railroads would have taken a good month—on the cars took less than seven days and cost $32 apiece. From St. Louis

the brothers rode the *Tobacco Plant* up the wide Mississippi
to the mouth of the muddy Missouri, and up that yellow,
snag-filled current to St. Joe. A not unpleasant journey of 556
miles—shortened as it was by the colorful assemblage that trod
the steamer's planks. Negroes in purple and fine linen, slaves
in chains, hornswogglers, men of the cloth, soldiers and sailors,
drunkards, peddlers, barristers, nuns, conjurers, respectable
families, merchants, courtesans, wanderers, cotton speculators,
land speculators.

The *Tobacco Plant* was twice as big as the *John Golong,* the
steamer Jed had ridden downriver to Independence twelve years
earlier with Spoon's mules. The banks of the Missouri were twice
as civilized. Brave little patches of open ground, hard wrested
from the trees, boasting buildings and plowed fields.

At Robidoux's old fur-trapping station, now given over to
grain elevators and foundry smokestacks, the brothers caught
the ferry *Ebenezer* to the Territory side of the river, purchased
supplies and four horses, and lit a shuck for the prairies.

It had gotten wearisome, watching spring unfold whilst
sitting idle inside the bellies of crowded stages and trains and
jostling for space on the crowded steamer decks. How much
better to smell the lush greenery and swampy dampness, to fall
asleep to the night sounds of the river bottoms and wake to
grasses and trees silvery with dew. To ride young, strong horses
through silky soft, early-morning mists and be serenaded with
birds' cries.

The crooked wagon route along the high ground between the
Missouri and Kansas River bottomlands swarmed with sad little
clutches of the Kansa Nation. The wretched populations, having
developed a taste for the white man's provisions, howled and
begged, but were easily outflanked by the horsemen—Yam riding
as his white brother rode, turning not only his horse aside, but
also his face.

West of Wolf Creek on Mission Creek a half-dozen Iowas galloped out of the trees to challenge the passersby to a race. Failing in that endeavor, they peddled groceries—leading the way to a large storehouse on their government mission grounds. Jed bought jerked meat and a dozen fresh eggs broke in a lard bucket. And some bad whiskey for fifteen cents a dose. Yam didn't find the whiskey that bad, but then it didn't make Yam sick.

That the thrifty-looking farms surrounding the mission belonged to the Iowas cheered Yam considerably. The white man was never going away—the large number of wagons and droves of stock on the road attested to that—but he could be lived with.

Jed wasn't so sure. That nothing stopped the western migration—not ignorance of the countryside, not cholera, not the threat of Indian attack, not the Utah War—meant there wouldn't be much sharing when push came to shove.

Slow but sure the trees began to falter. Yam hated the increasing desolation. He kept looking for a place to hide, the way deer, coming into the open, keep the forest in mind. One day he found himself staring at an Indian sitting in the shadow of a small clump of sage. Bam! right there! not a stone's throw away. The Indian, grey as dirt, had let himself be seen, his eyes locking on the rider's. Otherwise, Yam would have passed by unknowing.

But the naked earth did offer one gift. To see the moon get up and go to bed, to roll over in his blankets and see how the stars stood—these things made the journeying good.

The further west they rode, the longer the view across the never-ending prairies. Recalling Uergin, catching himself reacting as Uergin would to the bob-ups in the trail, Jed wished the guide well wherever he was.

"We might get lucky," he told Yam, sharing another of Uergin's stories. "He could be somewhere on the road." At the same time, he hoped not. Uergin had wanted to own a saloon, a fancy one where he could put on the dog.

Late one late afternoon, cresting a high ridge overlooking the upper fork of the Platte, the riders came out above a long train of white-topped wagons bumping its way downhill through the ruts worn into the sandstone. To the south along the ridge line a village of Indians was on the move, travois piled high, children and dogs scooting about. Yam wanted to follow the village, he'd catch up with Jed the next day.

The only sign of the Indians' passage was the disturbed dirt. Unlike the white man's road, littered with the things the white man could not live without until his teams gave out.

After supper Yam offered his tobacco. The warm pipe bowl passed slowly from hand to hand. The chief, a tall, stately man called Bull Bear, invited the visitor to speak.

"I come from a land of trees and water and many white men," Yam said, relishing being in the quiet camp of the Dakotah. He took off the cross. "A holy man told me this wood is on a journey. Perhaps here to this place."

The warriors studied the trinket carefully, passing it around the circle in the same direction earlier traveled by the pipe. There was no priest in this camp, but there was a very old woman who possessed mysterious powers. She was brought into the circle to sit at the left hand of Bull Bear. Her name was Bird That Whistles. Hunched in her thin robe she dangled the trinket against the firelight.

The cross began to turn, slowly at first then faster, wrapping the string as it turned. That it turned in the opposite direction the pipe had traveled, troubled Bird that Whistles. Gently she stopped the circling. Now she held the cross in both hands against her mouth and blew softly, as if to comfort it.

"The wood comes from a great distance, it doesn't belong here." She held the cross, folded from sight, a minute longer, head bowed, before returning it to Yam.

"It is a gift. Don't be so careless with showing it around, a dishonest person will take it from you and interrupt the journey."

## N I N E

In Washington John Bernhisel, Utah's Delegate to Congress, suggested a pardon for President Young. President Buchanan balked. For all the wrong reasons, he knew. With the South beating the drums ever louder for succession, America could ill afford to keep two-thirds of its standing army in the bog hole that was Utah. But Buchanan didn't trust Bernhisel and he despised Brigham.

In Provot Brigham spoke ominously of moving the church into the Muddy River country of the southern desert. And waited patiently for Washington to bow down.

Fort Kearny, May 1858.

> *The road between Missouri and California is closed for all commercial, postal or social intercourse throughout Utah Territory.*
>> Handwritten notice posted on wall
>> behind emigrant registry

Jed gave his name and listed his business as woodman. In response to his question about the road, a clerk explained that the Utah cut-off was being patrolled by Brigham's so-called destroying angels.

"The devils are even hurrahing the trails above Bridger's.
Oughta hang every last one of 'em."

The brothers made camp across the Platte in the trees and
the next morning returned to the fort for supplies. The air had
a crisp, clean smell to it. In a few hours the dogged heat would
clamp down, holding in the smells of the fort and giving it the
breath of civilization. Jed was walking across the yard leading a
horse for the farrier when he heard the monotonous whine of
cursing, and then his name.

He glanced in that direction and kept walking, thinking he'd
misunderstood.

"You don't know me? Or maybe just don't want to."

Jed tilted his head, looking out from beneath the brim of his
hat at the man standing off against the sun. "Walker?"

"That's right. Walker. You knew I'd be here somewhere."

"Well, I guess I could of figured. Dinky's our sister."

"She's my sister, Jedrich. She ain't yours."

"What's your problem, Walker?"

"If it wasn't for you, she'd still be alive."

"She is alive, I can feel it."

"You're the one told her all the stories about going out West,
what a great place the West was. The last time I saw her, she was
talking about you."

*The last time I saw her, she was leaning out of the carriage
blowing kisses,* Jed thought grimly, feeling oddly vulnerable.

"Mun's out there, Walker, that's why she went." He moved
toward the voice. "I got someone with me I want you to meet.
We're leaving in the morning, you can ride with us."

"That's far enough, stop right there. You never was no good
for nothing."

"You been drinking."

The cursing started up again.

"Brother, we can ride out together or not, it's your call. But we ain't arguing." Jed turned away. A gun fired, and a bullet plowed a furrow in the dirt beside his boot. He jumped as far as he could and rolled, but the shooting was over. Behind him, Walker writhed in the dirt. Stunned, Jed watched Yam pull a knife from Walker's arm and walk away, wiping the knife on his trousers.

A soldier hurried up and together he and Jed hauled the wounded man off to the post hospital. Then Jed went hunting for Yam, finding him on the previous night's campground.

"Ain't no one looking for you, but it don't hurt to make yourself scarce just the same."

"Why did he shoot at you?"

"It's an old fight, he's our brother."

Yam didn't answer. The stranger was not *his* brother, this was not his family, these white people.

"It's always been that way," Jed said, seeing the disbelief in Yam's face. "You just gotta keep an eye on him. You saved my life, for that you might have to save your own someday."

Yam didn't argue. Setting his mind against the Marchions was as useless as setting his mind against the wind. It went right on whirling around him, blowing him along like a painted-wing.

Giving themselves two days to rest up, Yam headed for the Sioux lodges upriver and Jed returned to the fort. Walker was lying on a cot in the small, one-story adobe hospital, his right arm in a sling.

"You're in no shape to ride, Walker."

"Yeah." Walker gritted his teeth, wishing he'd been given more opium. "Your red pal saw to that, the bastard, he'll be seeing through bars by the time I get done with him."

"No, he won't. The law's different out here."

"I guess that's why you're here."

"Go home, Walker. You got a wife and kids and mama to look after."

"Yeah, that's the way it goes. You got a wife and a kid, but you don't got no responsibilities. That's my little brother."

Jed was to the screen door when Walker stopped him with, "I wasn't aiming to kill you, I just wanted to get your attention."

Jed didn't turn around. "Doc says that's a clean cut, hit the bone but didn't tear up anything. You need money to get home?"

"Go to hell."

Drinking alone in a corner of the sutler's store, Jed toyed with the notion of finding an Indian to take them into Utah Territory. There were surely Indian camps to be found in the vicinity of Bridger's. If that didn't work, hell, he'd sign on with the army. Kind of dumb thinking. He laughed softly. Talk about dumb! what in hell did Walker think *he* was going to do, messing around in that godforsaken wilderness? Walker couldn't find Dinky, he couldn't find a fish in a rain barrel with both hands. He always did do things the hard way.

The clerk in charge of the emigrant registry took a nearby table. He thought something might break pretty quick on the road. "A peace commission went through here a week ago headed for Utah."

Asked about a rumor heard earlier, that it was Mormons, not Indians, that wiped out the wagon-train on the Lower California road, the clerk agreed. "It was Mormons alright, and I'll tell you how I know. The book listing the names of last summer's emigrants is missing, which means we gotta depend on the families to let us know who all's in that train. Which means anybody without a family ain't gonna be counted, much less looked for. Now you tell me, what Indian's gonna give a damn about that."

The next morning Jed paid three dollars to have his saddle horse and the pack horses grained and penned with a manger full of hay. And visited the hospital. Walker was gone, a soldier mopping the floor reported the injured man's having caught a ride home with a freight train.

That afternoon, standing in front of a stack of canned oysters in the sutler's store trying to justify the price and the extra weight, Jed spotted a slight man in a threadbare coat timidly keeping off to himself. That's what gave the fellow away, that uneasy awareness of who was around him.

Leaving off with the grocery buying, Jed retrieved his saddle horse and settled down in the shade near the front gate. It wasn't long before the fellow rode by, a lumpy sack thrown over his shoulder. That he left alone didn't bode well. Mormons didn't favor visiting the forts alone, particularly now, with feelings running so deep against them. But it was still worth a shot.

On the ferry across the Platte Jed made small talk with the ferry's operator. Reaching the north shore, he meandered off in a different direction from that of his quarry. Eventually the fellow disappeared up a draw to the west. A narrow, crooked draw choked with willows. Rounding a rock outcropping, Jed heard a man say, "That's far enough."

*I ain't a fast learner,* Jed reflected wryly, recalling Emil James at the camp outside Independence. He reined in his horse. "I don't mean no harm, I need some help is all."

No answer.

"I'm looking for a job."

Still no answer. Jed turned his horse around.

The man standing behind him held a pistol in both hands. "Why are you following me?"

"Like I say, I need help."

"You running from the law?"

"No, I need to get into Utah Territory, me and my brother. Scratch back. We work for you, you pass us off as Mormons."

"I ain't going there."

Jed shrugged. "It don't hurt to ask."

"What made you think I was going there?"

"I got family in Salt Lake City, I can spot a believer a mile away."

"What are you gonna do there?"

"Look for my sister, she was in a wagon train attacked by Indians."

The pistol lowered. "I warn you, I got nothing to steal."

"My name's Jed Marchion."

"Crisp here, Lloyd Crisp. My horse is back in the trees, didn't want him shot if you pulled a gun." Lloyd grinned sheepishly. "We'll go on up to camp if you'd like."

His outfit consisted of two wagons, one other man, two women, and several children—the oldest a boy of maybe thirteen or fourteen, the youngest just a toddler. The wagons and oxen looked to be in good enough shape, unlike the other man. His leg was wrapped in strips of red flannel and he leaned on a crutch.

"We got us a deal?" Jed asked softly, studying the camp.

"Yes, sir," Lloyd stuck out his hand, "we got us a deal. From here on out just remember we're Saints, not Mormons."

# TEN

*"...freely and fully pardoned for all treasons and seditions heretofore committed..."*

SUNDAY, JUNE 6. Brigham's manipulations pay off, Washington has indeed bowed down. The proclamation rushed across the face of the continent puts an end to the war that never was, all that remains are the amenities.

Bishop Harris was ready. His weight was up, he looked fit as a fiddle. Late the afternoon of June 10 a long line of carriages reached GSLCity from Provot. American Peace Commissioners Powell and McCulloch, along with Governor Cumming, were already in the city, having arrived under escort of Mormon soldiers. That evening, their own hearths dark, the First Presidency of the Mormon Church dined informally with the American officials in the Globe Restaurant.

With time to spare before supper, George strolled up South Temple to First Street to visit the temple, wishing the building done, thinking how very pleasing that would be to God. Walking along, recalling Brigham's ravings about American soldiers destroying the sacred places in the city, the bishop smiled mirthlessly. What if the American soldiers should decide to burn the President's splendid palace? Now wouldn't that be a shame.

As he drew close to the scrawny locust trees lining the con-

struction site, his heart sank. Where were the low walls and
granite foundations? Closer still, hurrying now, he could scarcely
believe his eyes. The handsomely dressed red sandstone walls
had been knocked down and hauled off, as had the granite foundations. A scattering of loose dirt covered the torn earth.

A black rage filled the bishop to the brim. It had been
necessary to tear down nothing. NOTHING! For Brigham to
stoop to this monstrous chicanery was the last straw, *the very last
straw*. The bishop could not have felt worse if he had returned
to find his own home destroyed. His heart began to pound and
he walked away, stuffing his rage back behind the crates of
succeeding days and nights where it grew like mold.

The formal meeting convened the next morning at 9 a.m. in
the Council House on the corner of Main and South Temple.
Before leaving the city the previous April, Brigham had ordered
the windows removed and cached and boards nailed over the
openings to forestall vandalism by the American Army. In their
haste to replace the windows, the workmen had badly damaged
the window casements. George stared at the splintered wood,
remembering the desecration of the temple grounds.

The President seated himself on the floor and invited the
brethren to join him, leaving the bench on the platform to the
American authorities.

Governor Cumming read the Proclamation of Peace aloud,
after which Brigham, taking his time in getting to his feet,
replied,

> I thank President Buchanan for forgiving me, but I
> really cannot tell what I have done. It is true that Lot
> Smith burned some wagons containing government
> supplies for the army. This was an overt act, and if
> it is for this that we are to be pardoned, I accept the
> pardon. The burning of a few U.S. wagons is but a

small item.... What has the United States government
permitted mobs to do to us?

One by one various church officials rose to accept Old Buck's
pardon and to point out that they, too, could not possibly
imagine what crimes they were guilty of.

The Peace Conference lasted two days. President Brigham
concluded his final remarks with,

> Now let me say to you, peace commissioners, we are
> willing those troops should come into our country,
> but not to stay in our city. They may pass through if
> it needs be, but must not quarter less than forty miles
> from us. If you bring your troops here to disturb this
> people, you have got a bigger job than you or President
> Buchanan have any idea of. Before the troops reach
> here, this city will be in ashes, every tree and shrub will
> be cut to the ground, and every blade of grass that will
> burn shall be burned. Our wives and children will go to
> the canyons and take shelter in the mountains; while
> their husbands and sons will fight you, and as God
> lives, we will hunt you by night and by day until your
> armies are wasted away. No mob can live in the homes
> we have built in the mountains. That's the program,
> gentlemen, whether you like it or not. If you want war
> you can have it; but if you wish peace, peace it is; we
> shall be glad of it.

All of which Commissioners Powell and McCulloch meekly
agreed to. The empty streets and brush-piled doorways spoke
eloquently of the churchman's determination to destroy his own
city.

On June 13 the dignitaries loaded their baggage and departed.
Commissioners Powell and McCulloch, at Brigham's urging,
rode south with the President to Provot and on to Lehi to speak
with the people. Governor Cumming returned to Camp Scott to

get his wife, leaving the Kingdom once more in the hands of its Danite guards.

Dawn the morning of June 26 the American Army, on the road since July of the previous year and forced to endure the winter cold in the high desert south of burned-out Fort Bridger, passed unchallenged through the abandoned Mormon fortifications in Echo Canyon and entered the Valley.

By 8 a.m. General Albert Johnston was marching his troops, banners flying, drums beating, down South Temple Street past Brigham's mansion. A band of sappers and miners rode in the van to prepare the bridge over the River Jordan for the crossing. Except for the music of the military bands and the monotonous tramp of boots, the city itself was silent. The only citizens to be seen were the heavily armed guards standing in front of the more prosperous-looking buildings. The day grew intensely hot, still the American soldiers came. Once across river, they leaped into the cool waters for a bath before pitching their tents on the west bank.

Behind the soldiers came a vast line of baggage wagons, driven through the city at a full trot, the hurried cadence raising dense clouds of black dust, coating man and beast with dirt and sweat.

It was well after sunset when the last wagon, followed by loose stock, followed in turn by one last band of mounted soldiers, reached the other side of the river. A *Deseret* reporter counted 3,000 men, 600 wagons, roughly 6,000 cattle, horses, and mules.

The bridge was closed, the angry stares of the heavily armed Danite guards fading in the dusk without having once revealed their admiration for the smart snap of the military bands, nor surprise at the size of the immense army.

Three a.m. the morning of July 1, the leader of the Mormon Church returned in triumph to his city. Raising a languid hand pope-like, he blessed the small crowd of Danite guards who greeted him. Behind the churchman came his wives and children, and behind them the First Presidency—the column more resembling a weary assemblage of late-night revelers than a grouping of celestials. A *Deseret* reporter kindly dubbed it "The Provot Parade."

In the days that followed, ghost-like figures began to filter through the city. Bellies slack with hunger, clothing in rags, eyes encrusted with mucus from the acrid dust. Those too weak to walk rode in wagons or were dragged Indian-style behind emaciated livestock.

An American soldier, writing home, described the scene.

> Old women driving cows, feet bare, scanty dress, scarcely enough to hide nakedness; bleary-eyed women holding sickly looking children to their breasts and men with vice & hate mingled in their faces.

Another wrote of

> …wretched-looking beings—men, women, boys, and girls, old and young, halt and blind, without shoes or stockings, ragged and dirty, though some of the young girls had endeavored to make as respectable an appearance as possible, by making garments out of corn sacks.

George wept to see the rag-tag army queued up at the outdoor soup kettles and sleeping on the floors of the common buildings. Poor unsuspecting red herrings, ripped from their moorings and hurled out into the desert, only to be reeled back when it suited their masters. Thank God these people could be fed and clothed before being sent on up the road to their homes in the northern settlements, but what of the people living in the south, what were they doing for food and clothing?

Declaring himself to be afraid of miscreants sheltered within the American Army, the President ordered the gates of his compound locked and bolted and a guard stationed at the east entrance, where people were admitted.

The wagons of the Gentile merchants lumbered in from the west, the residents of Great Salt Lake City somewhat shyly resuming the necessary intercourse. Governor Cumming and his wife arrived and were moved into a large, most pleasantly furnished adobe house not far from Brigham's mansion. The rest of the newly appointed civil officers to the Territory were also housed as befitting their station.

After three weeks of self-imposed house arrest, Brigham allowed himself and several of his wives a short pleasure trip into Big Cottonwood Canyon. Here he rendezvoused with the First Presidency, ladies and children, and Governor Cumming and his lady at a Pic Nic Excursion. The romantic, shady location chosen for the occasion was further enhanced by the hasty construction of a commodious bowery for those who might wish to dance. The two-day event, enlivened by music, dancing, and song, resulted in much good will.

Returning to the city, the new governor happily declared peace restored to Utah Territory. But the ban on public gatherings remained in place, the Tabernacle of the Lord remained silent.

And no grand jury would indict, and no petty jury convict.

Deep in the howling wilderness that was Kansas Territory, not far from where Sergeant Reeves had earlier camped with the Green Mountain boys, a glint in the water-washed sands of Cherry Creek caught a gold-seeker's eye. The small pocket yielded several hundred dollars.

Across the Missouri River in the States a backwoods lawyer
from Illinois named Abraham Lincoln, running for a seat in
the U.S. Senate, challenged Stephen A. Douglas to a series of
debates on slavery in the Territories.

In Great Salt Lake City the drowsy Sunday afternoon was heavy
with the smell of new-mown hay, a fine mist of pollen lent a
soft glimmer to the air. People were playing catch or throwing
horseshoes, or just enjoying the shade of their porches. As were
George and Ellen and Phoebe.

"Is this the Harris home?" The trail-worn horsemen who
drew rein at the edge of the walk didn't look familiar. But the
voice…that was Jed's voice!

Ellen cried, even Phoebe got teary-eyed. Their dear Jed.
Lean, straight as an arrow, the hollows in his face smoothed over
by rusty beard. The celebration moved inside. George set out
jelly glasses on the kitchen table and waited on everyone with
gooseberry wine and a wonderfully clear whiskey being saved for
Thanksgiving dinner.

"To the yesterdays," George said, proposing a toast.

Jed hesitated, and lifted his glass. "To the yesterdays." He put
the glass down empty, his eyes steady on the bishop, registering,
even as his thoughts turned elsewhere, the ashy pouches under
the faded green eyes.

"Tell me about my sister."

"We think she's alive," George said firmly. "In the south with
Emil and Verity James."

Jed clenched his mouth with his hand. He had feared the
worst, steeled himself for it. "Where in the south?"

"Cedar City, it's on the way to California," Ellen said. "We had some business papers we wanted her to deliver to the James. I have to believe they stopped her from going further."

"So you knew what was going to happen."

"There were rumors."

"And you think Emil knew."

"I'm sure of it."

Jed glanced at Phoebe. Something about her smile unnerved him. "But you haven't heard from her yet."

"No, but the mail's sporadic at best."

"There were men involved who call themselves Saints," George owned, a heavy sadness about him. "No one seems to know what fully happened."

Ellen and Phoebe watched their husband with steady, encouraging looks.

"Why didn't you stop the train?"

"The captain wouldn't listen," Ellen said. "Brigham told him to go south, that the train would be safe, and he believed Brigham."

"So Brigham lied?"

George hesitated. *Yes, Brigham lied! and then he stole everything they owned.* Steeling himself, he merely replied, "Ellen was warned by one of my wives what was going to happen, I thought it idle gossip, I failed to talk to Dinky or Fancher about their leaving."

The awkward silence was broken by Nancy and Jeremy trooping inside followed by several of their friends, the screen door banging behind them.

"My gosh, Jeremy! you sure growed up!" Jed exclaimed, thinking *Ma was right, Ellen could have passed him off as French.* Nancy looked like a young George. Green eyes, curly black hair.

That Yam wore the leather clothing of men who lived in wild places intrigued the youngsters, who, visiting amongst themselves, studied him covertly. Yam's face grew sterner. Periodically he shifted his glance, catching a youngster unawares, setting them to giggling.

Enjoying herself, Ellen stole puzzled looks at Yam. Finally, Jed could stand it no longer. Nudging her foot with his boot, he asked, "Who's he remind you of?"

"Your father, for some strange reason."

"Don't tell him that," Jed said with a grin."He don't believe he's my real brother. I found him in the woods and taught him everything I know. He's coming along, slow but sure."

Yam put his elbows on the table and rested his chin in his hands, he shook his head, he sighed. "It is not like you hear," he said and related a sad tale of seduction—stolen from the peacefulness of the Big Woods and introduced to noisy sawmills and trains and the mysteries of the fork.

Everybody laughed and laughed, except for Jeremy, fiercely aware of his responsibilities as a member of the Aaronic Priesthood.

Shaking hands warmly with his guests the next morning, George said, "Our home is open to you upon your return." And admonished them sternly with, "Now don't forget."

As he rode down State road, Jed glanced back over his shoulder. Against the rising sun the Harris mansion squatted like a broody hen in the shadow of its shrubs. He waved his hat at the knot of people at the foot of the porch, and everybody waved back, even his imperial misery, Jeremy.

Remembering Nancy's words, Jed smiled. What a little cutie she was.

The new day, the peaceful orderliness of the city wrapped itself around him. It was impossible not to feel better about things. Certainly better than when he'd first arrived. He'd ridden into Brigham's city expecting an armed camp. With good reason. On the road south from Fort Bridger the Crisp wagons had been stopped repeatedly by Danites. Were the foreigners Saints or sinners? Reassured by Crisp, the hard-eyed men tipped their hats and backed off.

Not until Crisp reached the city was it learned that the Territory had been open to all traffic since July 1. That was two weeks ago. The road might be open, but intimidation remained the order of the day.

Jed's thoughts turned to Ellen. She'd come to the spare bedroom late. Dozing off, he woke to find her sitting on the edge of the bed, filling the overhead darkness with her urgent whispers. Even if Dinky were with Emil and Verity, she could be in grave danger, so could the James, their actions could be seen as lack of faith. He must be careful who he talked to.

"I'm just saying, don't take chances. The people in the outer settlements are afraid, all they know is what they hear in church." Realizing her worries weren't Jed's, Ellen grew quiet. Life in Brigham's violent world was impossible for an outsider to understand.

"You have a good life?" she asked.

"Yes." The tone sleepy. "You?"

"Yes, George is very good to me, he stopped his religious hectoring years ago. I've grown to love him very much. *Jed, you must listen to me! Don't attract attention!*"

She smelled of lilac talc. Earlier in the supper candlelight she was so achingly beautiful Jed could scarcely take his eyes off her. He found her hand on the bedcovers and squeezed it, wishing she were in bed beside him.

"The American Army is in Cedar Valley," Ellen said softly. "They'll know if the road is open."

"I wondered where all the soldiers was, I never saw any coming in."

"Brigham won't let them in except on business. He's afraid

foolish women will try to smuggle letters out, the way they did with Lieutenant Gunnison's men. Gunnison was here surveying for the Pacific Railroad, his party was murdered at a camp on the Sevier River, and the letters were found on the bodies. The women died, Jed, for the good of the church. They were taken to the river and drowned with their skirts over their heads."

There was no answer. Ellen kissed the sleeping man lightly on the temple and walked down the hall to her room.

The brothers stayed in the city only long enough to purchase supplies and trade their worn horses for Mormon stock before heading up the road for Camp Floyd, forty-two miles to the southwest. The camp in Cedar Valley was a beehive of activity—tents like a vast field of white cock hats pitched amidst the sand and sage, enormous freight wagons painted "Big Cottonwood Lumber" being unloaded, horse-drawn slips working to clear a parade ground.

General Johnston met with the Americans in his tent. Unrolling a large map, he traced the old Spanish trail south.

"Cedar City's about three hundred miles down this road. Parts of the country are strikingly poor, with little grass and no grain. You could have trouble anywhere or nowhere. Be advised, the Mormons dress up like Indians to do their mischief."

He pointed out Cedar City. "You're pretty sure your sister's there?"

"I got friends down by the lake who think so, that's all I know.

The general traced the sharp turn of road into the west, to a large X. "The massacre took place here, toward the desert. A Mormon missionary's got some of the children, we don't know their names yet."

"I heard it was Mormons did it."

The general gestured open-handedly. "We'll make a thorough

investigation as soon as possible, that's my official word. Unofficially, it looks as though Mormons were running the show with help from the Paiute. The Mormon farmers are talking, but the church is stonewalling." He looked chagrined.

"I strongly recommend against your going there ahead of the army, but I can't stop you. If you come across Matthews and Tanner wagons going that direction, your best bet's to link up with them. They're a salty bunch of Mormons, but honest. Be advised, you show up missing, no one's going to come looking in time to do you any good."

He nodded toward Yam. "Riding with him might save your bacon, Mormons claim to love Indians. You speak English?" he asked Yam.

"If I got to," Yam replied.

The general grinned. "Let's hope you figure out when that is."


On the general's orders, Jed stopped by the quartermaster's tent to leave Dinky's name.

"They'd like to make that train plumb disappear," the quartermaster groused, searching through the paperwork on his desk, "like they did the emigrant ledgers."

"I heard they got the Fort Kearny one."

"Fort Laramie too. Yep, they've had that Fancher train in their sights a long time. Old Brigham issued an order, d'you know that? telling his people not to sell those emigrants a damn thing.

"It'll be next summer before we can field units in the south, by that time, there won't be any papers left, no diaries, no supply lists, just buttons and bones. The Mormons'll comb the site looking for anything that proves one of their own disobeyed orders. They find it and…" the official slashed his throat with his finger.

"Hell, we ought ask the Mormons for an inventory sheet, save ourselves the bother."

He found the listing of people reported to be traveling with the Fancher train. "What's the name?"

"Editha Miller and three kids."

"Got her. Mrs. Editha Miller, born August 1834, and three children, daughters Anne and Emily, twins, born September 1852, and son Lymund, born February 1855. Reported by Mrs. Jean Paul Marchion out of Troy, New York."

Jed stared at the quartermaster. Hearing the litany of his family's names made a fist in his stomach.

The official shook his head at the other's shock. "Don't do anything crazy, they'd just soon kill you for God as look at you."

Before leaving the camp, Jed chanced across a newspaper correspondent traveling with the army. The *Cincinnati Herald* correspondent reported that Mormons within a hundred miles of the camp were sending their butter, milk, and eggs to the soldiers.

"The Mormon people are poor and the soldiers pity them, paying as much as twenty-five cents a quart for the buttermilk," the correspondent explained. "Let me show you what I wrote." He unfolded his most recent column, awaiting dispatch by the next mail carrier.

> ...the sympathizing kindness of that army to this people can never all be told. General Johnston has the confidence and good-will of the people. Their officers are, in all respects, well-bred gentlemen, and with a refinement purely American they vie with each other in doing good at every opportunity. But the soldiers—the private soldiers—those Irishmen and others—what shall be said of them? They would almost give the clothes off their backs, and then empty their chest, to clothe the naked people; sometimes they sell them for a trifle, but more frequently they give them away.
>
> Ladies of America, ladies of Europe, will you pardon the

communication of a revolting truth, in vulgar English? You need not pronounce the words with audible voice when you read them, but ponder them well in your hearts. The truth is this: There are among this people, at this hour, hundreds of females who have not a shift to their backs, and in instances not a few their outer garments (alias tatter and rags) are insufficient to conceal their nakedness as they go about the house. Men and boys are in the same condition. The causes of this lamentable distress may, perhaps, be found in Brigham's cruel despotism, in Governor Cumming's puerile administration, and in the suspension of federal protection and aid.

# E L E V E N

CRUELTY AND DISTRESS were certainly no strangers to Daphne Lafitte. The 600-mile journey from the banks of the Sacramento to the City of the Saints was not at all as advertised. Instead of a coach-and-four, she rode in a mud wagon pulled by mules.

Six passengers, including the driver and messenger, rode outside; nine more inside. Unable to anticipate the rough places in the road, the inside passengers kept their feet interlaced, dreading the bumped heads and thumped noses that accompanied being cast into a neighbor's arms. A stifling dust blew incessantly through the open windows, bugs flew in and out at will, fine pebbles kicked up by the passing commotion pinged against the casements. The wind never stopped, whereas the mud wagon stopped way too early—sometimes at one o'clock in the afternoon, sometimes at two—refusing to start again until the next morning, leaving the passengers to sit for hours at a time conversing in stale tones in shacks that were utterly without comfort. Adding to the torture of the abysmally-spaced mail stations was the overcooked food and mossy-tasting water.

The viewing, described as "enchanting" in the brochures, never ventured past dreary shades of grey and brown. Even the sky was grey. "The only time this road is pretty is when it's dark," she complained loud and often, surveying the dead countryside.

Then, like a bolt out of the blue, a glimpse of the magnificent castles that awaited her. The mules were laboring through the sulfurous countryside east of Chokop's Pass when towers and battlements fronted by a long lagoon of light blue water emerged from the mist over the Humboldt Sink. The desert was littered with ghostly mirages, but this was different. The buildings were too grand, people were walking about, carriages moved back and forth.

"I was beginning to think there was nothing out here for my hundred-dollar ticket," Daphne cooed to the one man awake in the wagon, a toothy young druggist on his way to open an apothecary in the City of David.

July 20, on a slight rise in elevation ten days inbound from the Gold Coast.

"Now that does appear to be a real lake, doesn't it. Yes." Nathan pointed at the distant silvery sheet.

Daphne studied the view to the north through jeweled opera glasses—a gift from a long-forgotten admirer. Her lower lip stiffened. "I am not stopping until I reach the castles."

"I promise, darling, we won't be disappointed."

And they weren't. At least Nathan wasn't. Great Salt Lake City was a jewel on the end of a long, dusty string. Civilized trees and sparkling brooks, bright flowers, squared-off gardens and orchards. Unfortunately, the buildings themselves were remarkably dull, being a sort of slate white and rather plain, but solid-looking. Peaceful.

Daphne didn't see any castles, and Nathan thought they were probably further out. Would it be too much, he wondered, given the cleanliness of the streets, to hope for a pleasant boarding house as well. It was not.

Announced by a large signboard on a tall, gibbet-like flag-staff as the SALT LAKE HOUSE, the building was the very apogee of comfort, boasting as it did a long verandah supported

by newly trimmed and painted white posts, and pots of red
geraniums in the deep window sills. That the depth of the two-
storied, pent-roofed affair was greater than its frontage was of
itself reassuring, given the western predilection for false-fronted
buildings with puny one-story appendages.

Behind the house, secured by a *porte-cochère*, was a large yard
for corraling cattle. Off to one side in the lacy shade of young
elms, women dressed in light pastels were taking tea at small
rustic tables in the warm afternoon light. At their feet dusty-
colored dogs of mixed parentage draped themselves with the
insolence of Afghan hounds.

*How very inviting* thought Nathan, warmed by the pastoral
civility.

Alighting from the wagon, Daphne smiled fatuously at the
rough-looking crowd gathered on the verandah—hips swathed
in revolvers and bowie knives—and whispered over her
shoulder, "This place smells like a dead mouse."

"I think it's wonderful, certainly a far cry from the wretched
hostelry usually encountered on western roads."

"Wonderful compared to nothing." Even so, she was not
entirely displeased. There was money here, she could feel it,
even if there were no castles.

As could Nathan. They seemed to have reached a veritable
Kubla Khan. The heavily armed men ogling his fair companion,
he hoped and later found to be true, were merely jehus and
friends of the drivers.

The proprietor of the Salt Lake House was a Mormon from
Maine by the name of Townsend. With the obsequiousness
afforded the very rich, Brother Townsend assumed the
responsibility for transporting the Lafitte trunks inside. Nathan
registered in the guest book on the bureau and glanced about for
the usual array of bottles and decanters.

Ascending the stairs, the new arrivals were shown a Gentile

ballroom, a tolerably furnished sitting room, and a rather small bedchamber. Mrs. Townsend, an Englishwoman in the highest degree civil and obliging, offered her services to Daphne, and the two set off to explore the public areas of the house.

Nathan's explorations took less time. Confirming his earlier suspicion, that there was no liquor to be had in the lobby, he set off briskly up East Temple Street. Alas, there was not a dram house to be found, and very little of anything else. Most of the buildings were boarded up, apparently awaiting the long lines of freight passed en route to the city. The day had grown agreeably cooler, and there was a tantalizing scent of rhubarb pies in the air. *Rhubarb, rhubarb, everywhere,* he mused regretfully, *but not a drop to drink.*

Eventually he found himself outside the offices of the *Deseret News*. The presses were clank-clanking, the air thick with the smell of printer's ink.

Was there anything that better stirred the senses?! He bought a copy fresh off the press and happily settled himself on the bench outside the door.

Later that evening, bathed and powdered, the Lafittes took supper in the Globe Bakery and Restaurant where, handing out his card to the more prosperous-looking diners, Nathan let it be known that he represented Goupil-Vibert and Company of Paris and was looking to buy quality paintings.

Immediately he received several notes directing him to the Council House at the corner of Main and South Temple. The LDS works that adorned the walls when welcoming the newly appointed American officials into the city were still on view. The next day Nathan bribed the caretaker of the locked Council House with a small donation and was allowed inside, but found no Phoebe Taggarts.

That same day Daphne took the air, with predictable results. The men were *so* nice, *so* take-charge.

"I was in and out of carriages more times than a conductor. As soon as one Mormon returned me to the hotel, another took me out. I know this city backwards and forwards. Where the important people live, in their very large mansions. Where all their pleasure resorts are...NOT! *Because there are no pleasure resorts here! there are no boating facilities of any kind! You know why? I'll tell you why, that damn lake is full of salt!!*"

"Patience, Daphne."

"Oh, shut up!" She was lying on the creaky iron bed with a wet cloth over her face, occasionally lifting the cloth to breath deeply of a lemon-scented sachet.

"Any leads on the Taggarts?"

"No. If this Phoebe's so good, how come no one knows her?"

The next day being Sunday, Nathan decided to go to church, or what passed for church. Caught up in the crush of the faithful, he sat manfully through the long service.

Too large to be termed "quaint," the tree-lined bowery was certainly out of the ordinary. Birds flew about, depositing their offerings. Swarms of tiny flies, hatched in the clumps of manure fallen off the boots of the faithful, had to be brushed away from the face. The speakers for the most part were inconsequential and illiterate. Numerous in number, they papered over their ignorance with profanities and obscene gestures. The more indecent the harangues, the more impassioned the audience— the severe faces drawing down into frozen howls.

"One would have to experience it," he told a disinterested Daphne, "to believe it."

The following day he tried the public library. It was closed. There were no book-stalls, no art galleries, no gift shops. Most surprising of all, there was no public market-place. He decided to use the newspaper.

> Messr. Nathaniel Lafitte of Paris is in the city looking to buy fine art. He will be contacted at the Salt Lake House.

"Why so secret?" Daphne asked. "Why not just come out and say we're looking for Phoebe Taggart?"

"Let her find us, we won't have to pay so much."

That afternoon, making himself comfortable in the downstairs sitting room of the Salt Lake House (although not as comfortable as he might have been with a decent bottle of Heidseck), Nathan viewed a constant parade of pleasant, undemanding oils—some quite good, much better than he remembered the Taggarts being. Occasionally he jotted down a name as a hedge against returning to San Francisco empty-handed.

That same afternoon, traversing the crowded boardwalk with a light, elegantly shod step, Daphne accepted a supper invitation from an uncommonly handsome man with a handsome black and gold carriage the size of a meat wagon.

"Look for me by ten," she told Nathan, sailing out the door that evening. She was back before nine.

"We went out to supper," she looked slightly dazed, "and were served by his wives!"

"How do you know?"

"'The help is very good,' I said. And he told me they were his wives!" Her voice trebled, and Nathan put a warning finger to his lips. The rooms, they discovered when a snorer was housed next door, were rather thinly partitioned.

"I thought we were in a lodge or something, it was so big. What was he thinking of, taking me to his house?!"

"I would say, considering where we are, that he was thinking of marrying you."

"I have never...I mean *never* had anything like this happen! I'm flattered, of course...I think. But what do you say to a man who's being very sweet one minute and the next minute introducing you to his wives, of all people?! Tomorrow we meet his young brother, he calls him 'brother young.' I suppose the next day it'll be 'brother old.' This is a very peculiar place."

"He's talking about Brigham Young, the high priest of this whole shebang. Ask him about Phoebe."

Brigham always had a few minutes for a new convert. And could certainly see, he added warmly, eyeing the shimmering blond hair and cameo face with its striking violet eyes, why the good elder was so taken. Unfortunately, the church leader didn't know a Phoebe Taggart, but would be glad to inquire around.

Afterward, on a hill overlooking the city, the courtly suitor declared his love for the fair angel.

"This is a little sudden isn't it." Daphne playfully parlayed the straying hands. "We hardly know each other."

"You know everything there is to know about me, and I soon shall know everything there is to know about you." The elder's hand was on her bodice, undoing the ribbons. "But only after we are married and only if you are willing. You have nothing to fear, I will do nothing ungodly."

He really was a most respectful dear. Daphne relaxed. Now her blouse was off and the wind cooling her skin. She was thinking how the new white cambric corset trimmed with linen trochon edge must look to her lover, and how the city below resembled a chessboard. The further mountains beneath the brush strokes of cloud looked like cardboard cutouts...now that was interesting...

Distracted by the large hand sliding up her leg beneath the pale pink skirt, Daphne told the top of the balding head, "I think we shouldn't go any further, don't you?"

"We will be sealed before God as soon as possible," the aroused elder promised solemnly, and quashed the ruby-red lips in a fierce kiss. "I will arrange everything, rest assured my wives share in my joy."

"Share in your joy?"

It was a long ways back to the city over a dusty bumpy road. The carriage horses took their time. The driver, the gentlest of lovers, made no more demands except for frequent kissing and hugging.

"I'll see you in the morning," he promised earnestly.

"No, that wouldn't be a good idea. I did tell you I was married?"

"That's no problem."

"It's not?"

"Send me a note," he handed over his calling card, "as soon as you're ready."

"He thinks we're already engaged."

"He won't be the first man that's got that far."

They were dressing for dinner, Nathan in a grumpy mood and longing mightily for an iced claret. "D'you see Brigham?"

"Oh yeah. He was nice enough. He doesn't look rich, he's doesn't wear any rings. Kind of portly, kind of plain, like the food." Daphne turned her back, wanting her stays tightened, and sucked in her stomach. "He never heard of Phoebe."

She relaxed. "I can hardly wait to get back to the coast. Clear, delicate food, fresh fish, meat that is *not* dripping fat or bread crumbs, or both. And a bed with springs. What *are* they using? She started to lift the mattress and stopped, remembering something.

"Oh, by the way, you know that painting we sold to that sweet Mr. Uergin, the one with the children? Remember the mountains? I saw them. The artist must of been on the same hill."

"Well, at least we know she's here. Or was."

Immediately after his audience with Daphne, Brigham sent

George a note ordering Phoebe's paintings destroyed. The bishop went straight-away to see what the problem was.

"There's a Gentile in the city passing herself off as being interested in Brother Smoot," Brigham explained curtly. "And the simpleton brought her here, he thinks I have nothing better to do. She inquired about paintings done by your wife."

"My wife?" George said, confused, thinking of Ellen.

"Sister Taggart's scribbles are unworthy of a Saint, destroy them."

"But..."

"...immediately!" Brigham's face settled into its bulldog stare.

Ellen was astounded. "Destroy Phoebe's paintings?! He's gone mad, there's nothing in her paintings that's offensive to anyone."

"He thinks there is. Either that or he's getting even for something." The bishop sounded a weary note. "I made inquiries. The woman's staying at the Townsends with her husband, they came in from California. Apparently our would-be Rembrandt's paintings made their way to the coast. I never felt good about Phoebe's entering the church contests."

"It's the church's idea to sell everything that doesn't win. I think it's wonderful someone likes them enough to inquire after more."

"There won't be any more and that's final. I can't argue with Church Authority over this."

George returned to work. Ellen finished kneading the bread, thinking not so much about Brigham's tantrum as about the buyer in the Salt Lake House. Who could have ever guessed such a thing would happen—not in a thousand years, not in a hundred thousand.

Phoebe came home, thumping up the stairs. Covering the dough, Ellen climbed the stairs to find the artist standing in front of an unfinished painting—another boat.

*She probably wishes she could sail away,* Ellen reflected, admiring the quick, bright, light-filled strokes. *That's why she keeps painting boats.*

Phoebe unrolled a newspaper given her by a friend and pointed to Nathan's advertisement. "What do you think?" She turned her attention to the paintings. "I think I should take this, and maybe that one."

Agreeing mindlessly with Phoebe's evaluations, Ellen studied the room. Boards salvaged from old furniture were stacked against the walls. There was more wood out in the barns.

"Phoebe, there's a problem, but I think we can work it out."

"So what are we doing after we eat?" Daphne was studying the idle street out the bedchamber window, "besides being miserably bored. Have you noticed the women have the prettiest way of braiding their hair. But I don't care for the men's beards, they look glued on, they probably take them off when they go to bed."

"I thought you had plans with Mr. Sheik and his forty wives."

"Smoot, Mr. Smoot. Not tonight. He's kind of...you know, pushy. He does have a lot of paintings hanging around on the walls, but they didn't look smeary, besides, he has a bad haircut. Tomorrow there's a lovely gentleman who works in Walker Brothers Mercantile who wants to show me the beaches." She wrinkled her nose at the thought of visiting the polluted beaches.

"Maybe they'll fight a duel," Nathan observed with a half-smile. His lovely accomplice might have scrambled eggs for brains, but she had a lion's heart.

"Oh Nathan," Daphne threw up her hands in mock horror, "you are *so* old fashioned." But what if they did? where should she stand?

"Let's take a stroll before bed," she suggested.

"Jolly well," Nathan agreed, donning his hat with a flourish. Daphne, he knew, hoped for soldiers. Having seen Camp Floyd from the Chorpenning mail wagon, she was eagerly anticipating hoards of young dragoons cantering through the streets. That the American soldiers were banned from the city, he didn't think necessary to mention.

It was dusk, in the distance a plume of smoke rose. Making their way toward the conflagration, the Lafittes saw a crowd of several dozen people inspecting a bonfire. A tall woman was feeding the flames. Drawing near, Nathan saw that the wood appeared to be painted with figures.

"What are you doing?!" he cried.

"Burning the pictures painted in error," the woman answered loudly. "Cleansing our home. God has given us a new direction. Hallelujah! praise the living Jehovah now and forever." Wheeling about, she grabbed another board and threw it at the fire, the crowd shouting encouragement.

"Here! let me help you!" Nathan picked up a panel portraying a ghastly caricature of what looked to be a devil, turned the back of the panel to the light and read the words Phoebe Taggart.

"Wait!" he cried frantically, holding the wood against his chest. "I have a better idea! I'll buy, you can make some money."

"We'll buy!" Daphne joined in. "Here, here's a dollar."

Jerking the panel free of Nathan's grasp, the woman cast it into the fire and reached for another. As she did, she bent close to Nathan, and under the sounds of cracking wood, under the noise from the crowd, he heard quite clearly the words, "Are you the man staying at the Townsends?"

The Townsends? Nathan's mind went blank. "Yes," he said firmly, hoping he knew what he was about.

"Go to the back door and wait in the shadows."

Nathan craned his neck around, the woman nodded and heaved another painting at the flames.

Dragging Daphne away through the darkness, Nathan made for the back of the house. A kitchen lamp threw a feeble light onto the nearer yard, but not enough to prevent Daphne from tripping over a drainpipe and falling headlong into a bush. She squealed loudly, and Nathan clamped a hand over her mouth and pulled her to her feet. The small porch outside the back door was dark, the screen door propped open. There was a light under the kitchen door.

"Aren't you going to knock?" Daphne asked.

"She said to wait."

They waited sixty seconds, breathing shallowly, listening for they knew not what. The shadows from the fire in the front yard danced crazily off to the side, sporadically revealing a further barn.

"I don't care what you say," Daphne squeaked. "I'm knocking. Maybe the right hand doesn't know what the left hand's doing." She leaned around her cowardly companion, hand upraised, and came face to face with an abruptly opened door.

# TWELVE

"O
H!" A STARTLED PHOEBE shut the door. Or would
have, had it not been for a well-placed boot.
"The tall lady in the front yard sent us," Nathan
whispered through the crack.

The door opened wide. Nathan stepped quickly past Phoebe,
spun a chair away from the kitchen table, and seating himself,
fished a card from his vest pocket. "Nathaniel Lafitte. And you
are...?"

"Phoebe."

"Ah, the elusive Phoebe." Had the hefty woman with the
black paint under her ear been the Madonna, Nathan could not
have been more enraptured. "I have come to make you rich, very
rich."

"Oh?"

"Your paintings, I want to buy your paintings."

"I ain't got any," Phoebe replied sternly. "Ever'thing I got's
burned." Ellen had warned her about the church's checking to
see if she'd burned everything. She dumped the potato peelings
gathered for the slop bucket back into the sink.

"But you can paint more," Nathan said soothingly.

"No I can't."

"How much money would it take to change your mind?"
Nathan scarcely bothered to keep the laughter off his face.

Phoebe's expression reminded him of a puppy waiting for the rag to be pulled the other way.

"Are you tricking me?"

"*Pardonnez-moi, mademoiselle.* I never trick a beautiful woman."

Daphne looked around restlessly. Kitchens did not interest her, not when the stove was cold and the only smell in the room was that of turpentine.

The woman seen in the yard came in. Ignoring Nathan's attempts at introduction, she led the way quickly upstairs to a large bedroom where she placed the lantern, wick turned down, on the dresser.

Phoebe dragged a sheet-wrapped bundle from beneath the bed and unwrapped it to reveal paintings separated one from another by pieces of cloth. Now she was spreading the paintings, ten in all, across the bed and against the headboard.

In the poor light the splashes of color suggested the strident, table-cut jewels the gypsies were fond of wearing.

"We were taking these to you tomorrow," Ellen said. "Since you're here, choose what you want and go."

"Well…" Nathan hesitated, put off his game "…this is certainly serendipity."

"Choose what you want and go," Ellen said sharply, unable to keep the nervousness out of her voice. "And whatever you do, don't show them around in the city, they're…very sought after," she finished lamely.

Daphne's lip curled.

Invigorated by the delightful cloak-and-dagger atmosphere, Nathan lowered his voice conspiratorially. "I'm sure we can work out a plan." He produced a second business card and wrote a San Francisco post office box on the back. "I'll buy all of these and take future deliveries on consignment, mail them to this address and give me an address to send the money to."

He didn't wait for an answer, but moving with alacrity, restacked the paintings, carefully replacing the cloth squares.

"What are your prices?" he asked Phoebe.

The question elicited such a wistful smile that it was all Daphne could do to keep a straight face. Those thick glasses! holy shit! no wonder the art was out of focus.

"Ten dollars apiece," Ellen said.

"Ten dollars it is." Nathan opened his purse and pulled out a hundred-dollar bill.

Phoebe was speechless. As was Nathan when he made out the address on the scrap of paper Ellen handed him.

Ellen stripped the bed pillows and helped Nathan work the paintings into the cases. Immediately she was on her way back downstairs carrying the lantern, the dim light being of little use to her followers.

"Don't lose my address," Nathan whispered as the kitchen door closed behind him. There was no reply.

Keeping to the outside wall opposite the fire, the Lafittes made their way around to the street. The crowd gathered at the fire was thinning. Nathan caught a glimpse of the women coming out of the house carrying water buckets and felt sorry for them. Poor besotted beings. What a strange exorcism to have been caught up in. He could have paid less, they would have taken less, but that would not have been right.

Congratulating himself for not being a greedy man, Nathan lugged his treasures confidently down the street to the boarding house.

The meeting with the rag committee lasted until ten o'clock. Ordinarily, George did not bother with these minor committees, but Brigham wanted the church's call for a new rag mission underscored with his bishop's presence. Ellen and Phoebe were waiting in the kitchen with warm milk and cookies. Not a good

sign, George told himself, signaling as it did a kind of deception.
He sat down decorously, as if attending yet another meeting,
waved off the cookies and sipped on the milk. He was bone tired
and a little dizzy.

"I trust, Sister Phoebe, that you destroyed the paintings as
agreed?"

"Yes, sir."

"And that you will restrict yourself to other activities in the
future?"

"Yes, sir."

She was altogether too docile, no wailing, no gnashing of
teeth. George nodded, too tired to explore the matter further.

"I want you to know, Sister Phoebe, that God does not dislike
what you do. The church does not always speak for God, much
as it may want to. This was a human error on the President's
part. We're all human, and we all make mistakes. The President
has a lot on his mind right now."

*And he likes to turn the screws.*

George pinched off the thought and concentrated on
Phoebe's full-jowled face, brimming with a goodwill that had
nothing at all to do with church upbringing. She was twenty-six
years old, they'd been married twelve years, and there was not a
line of worry, not a grey hair. He should spend more time with
her.

"God is not mean, he loves you and he wants you to be
happy." The bishop paused, gagging on the mish-mash of
words. "I'm sure something good will come of this misfortunate
understanding."

There was really no need to keep trying, he couldn't even
talk straight. Getting to his feet, he took himself upstairs. He did
not check Phoebe's room. Shamed by the thought of the naked
walls awaiting his inspection, he never again looked in on the
room.

That night in George's bed, Ellen considered the strange twists of fate that surrounded Phoebe's art. First it was Constance, refusing to teach Phoebe to read, and Phoebe's deciding to draw instead. Then it was the church, holding contests and selling off the losers. And now it was Mr. Lafitte, all the way from the coast, wanting to buy more paintings. Something was going on that wasn't meant to end in a bonfire.

Unable to relax, George concentrated on the house's sounds—the creak of wood, the clock's voice, Phoebe's faint snoring down the hall, Ellen's deepening breath in his ear. Come morning she'd be back in her own bed. A lock of her hair lay across his neck, he stroked it gently. How well he knew his wives. He supposed he should thank Joseph that he had such women. But he didn't want to think about the dead prophet any more than he wanted to know why Phoebe wasn't upset. What he wanted to do was wake Ellen and make love to her. Wouldn't that surprise her. Wouldn't it surprise him!

*I wish I had more children, but what would be the point? I don't have enough time for the children I already have.*

Early the next morning, Daphne busy making her toilette, Nathan took a last stroll through main street. Walking along, minding his own business, he encountered a drunk navigating the boardwalk in uncertain fashion and slowed his steps to avoid a collision. In doing so, he was jostled by two men who looked like cathedral doors loping by.

"You're the husband of Daphne Lafitte?" one of the men asked the drunk, drawing an enormous hog leg from his waistband.

"Could be." The drunk looked around foppishly. "She lookin' for me?"

Now the second man was waving his pistol and saying

something about a vagrancy law. The next thing Nathan knew, the foolish drunk was being hurried away, legs swinging futilely.

Open-mouthed, Nathan glanced up the street, empty except for a few merchants sweeping off their stoops. Down the street the same. Whistling a careless little tune, he turned carefully on his heel.

The Lafittes were the first passengers in the mud wagon. Nathan sunk down into a corner, hat over his eyes.

His pathetic cowardice embarrassed Daphne. It wouldn't be the first time he'd been thrown in jail by one of her lovers. Distancing herself as best she could, she struck up an animated conversation with a boot salesman with whom her feet were soon entangled.

Not until the Holy City passed from sight did Nathan allow himself to relax. Too soon, as it turned out. The riders who closed the road ahead were the same large men who had accosted the drunk. Now a third man was driving up in a buggy.

"Won't keep you," one of riders assured the driver. "Just need to pick up the Missus Lafitte for a little unfinished business."

"Whose business?" the jehu asked his team. He wore wide-cuffed leather gloves and nursed a sizable wad of tobacco. As a King of the Road he received many gifts from his grateful passengers. Cigars, silver-mounted cigar cases, boots, gloves, gauntlets. He specially liked the wintergreen peppermint candies made up on the wharf in Sacramento, candies which Mr. Lafitte thoughtfully brought with him.

"Church business," the rider answered.

The Wells Fargo messenger weighed in, shotgun trained lazily on the riders "Well, then, I suppose we could sure ask." The messenger stroked his beard and raised his voice. "Anybody down there wants out?"

And heard nary a peep.

"Must have the wrong coach," the jehu allowed, still

addressing his team. "Now this here's enough monkey business." He gathered up the reins.

"Hold on! hold one!" the man in the buggy shouted. He seemed to be writing something. "You are hereby under church orders to…"

Cracking his whip the jehu drove off.

"Oh, dear," Daphne lamented. "I can't marry Mr. Smoot today." Sticking her arm outside the window, she waved her white silk neck scarf languidly at the knot of people disappearing in the dust.

Shortly after this incident, two inbound freight wagons pulled aside to let the mail by. Glimpsing the words SONOMA VINEYARDS on the high sideboards, Nathan moaned audibly.

Back in San Francisco, unpacking the paintings, Nathan told Daphne that the name given him by the tall woman was none other than that of Conrad Uergin himself.

"It's a small world, Nat, it truly is!" Daphne squealed. "Now whatever shall we do about this?"

"The first thing we do is collect for these paintings."

"Yes!" Daphne announced as if laying down a royal flush on a potful of money. "But what will you tell him?"

"Nothing. We'll have to find another buyer, is all."

"That dirty rat!"

The next morning Nathan left his calling card at the Lucky Lady Gaming Establishment with a message requesting the honor of paying his respects to Mr. Uergin at 2 p.m. Then he went shopping. At 1:30 he was ready. His frock coat, rather too heavy for the August weather, sported the latest in wide lapels and fabric-covered buttons. Wide, red suspenders over a sparkling white shirt held up his neatly pressed black trousers. Fashionably understated accessories included a narrow bow tie and silk knit gloves.

Daphne thought the costume laughable. Most of all the shoes. Black-dyed leather heels and soles, black wool uppers fastened with ties. "And you make fun of me. Where on earth did you buy those shoes? They don't even look like shoes. You have the queerest ideas."

"What I have, Daphne, is a fondness for the niceties of formal behavior. The results of which I shall shortly demonstrate." And he hurried off, looking exactly as the emissary of an important client should look.

"I have ten of Mrs. Taggart's paintings." The conversation was taking place at a round table in the corner of the crowded drinking establishment. "Five she will sell, and five she is sending off to France for consideration there."

Uergin looked amused. "That her idea?"

"No, mine. She's very good. New Modern, it's at the very edge of what's coming. She has no idea how good she is, being self-taught and all."

The saloon keeper ordered a drink and gestured toward the lawyer, but Nathan declined.

"You tell her who's buying 'em?"

"That's not my place. If you wish me to, however, I shall."

"No, s'not necessary. I think I know her."

Nathan nodded as if it were of no import.

"What's her house look like?"

"Large, one of the larger houses there. Wooden. Most are clay. Beautifully tended yard and gardens."

"You was inside?"

"Yes, it's very comfortable."

"D'you see anyone else?"

"One other woman, quite beautiful, tall, dark hair, who did not introduce herself." This last with a faint client-protective brusqueness.

"Everybody pretty happy, huh?"

The easy talk could have been the whiskey, but Nathan knew better. "I would say so. Probably."

"Probably?"

"It's not my place to speculate, but I think that financially they are in a bit of a bind. The five paintings I'm taking to Europe, Mrs. Taggart would have sold here. I strongly feel they need a European audience."

"Yes, by all means."

"You may have your pick."

"By all means."

Nathan brought all ten paintings to the saloon the next day. Daphne, to her immense disappointment and comforted but barely by a box of French chocolates, waited in their rooms on Sacramento Street.

"I haven't got him yet, my little *romantique*," Nathan told her.

"Did you tell him what we had to go through to get them?"

Uergin didn't know what he wanted. Several included the children in the earlier painting. At least that's what Nathan said, and Uergin didn't argue, although Nathan himself really didn't know how anyone could tell for sure. None included the woman he'd seen with Phoebe.

Uergin kept the artwork overnight and the next day separated off five paintings and offered Nathan a thousand dollars apiece. "What's your commission?"

"On this amount, one hundred dollars per painting."

Uergin counted out another five hundred dollars.

That he was pleased for his client showed in the small smile Nathan allowed himself as he pocketed the money. "I hope this is a sign of things to come overseas."

"Tell 'em what they're bringing here," Uergin ordered. "And let me know what happens. When are you leaving?"

"Soon," Nathan assured him. *Very soon.*

From where the Lafittes lolled on the broken-down couch, a flock of sailboats could be seen lazily surmounting the swells on the open harbor beyond the rotting ships. Scattered on the coffee table beside Nathan's hat and gloves was three thousand dollars in bills and a bouquet of travel brochures.

"I think we should go to England," Nathan said pensively, stroking his chin, nose in the air.

"I can't believe anyone would pay this kind of money." Daphne swept the bills back and forth with her fingertips, savoring the ecstasy.

"We'll rent Lord Lovat's Castle at Beaufort, one of the finest castles in Scotland, for the autumn shoot, and spend Christmas on the continent, say the Chateau de Canisy in Normandy?"

"Why didn't we sell him everything?"

"After that, I favor the Adriatic coast of Italy between Bari and Brindisi. What is your pleasure, my sweet?"

"Why didn't you just sell him all ten?"

"I can't attract new buyers if I have nothing to show them, now can I?"

"Nathan, you are so baaaad!" The word of the moment. She loved saying it, dragging it out.

"What is the meaning of goodness, if there isn't a little badness to overcome?" Nathan asked, flushed with happiness.

"Just as long as we never have to go back to that lake full of salt."

"Never."

"Did I tell you, there's something spooky about that place."

Nathan turned his attention away from the window. His little camp robber's intellect was as empty as a shallow August well, but her instincts under fire were uncanny. "How's that?"

"All the men wanted to talk about was going to church."

Alone with his outlandish collection, Uergin toasted the painter. "You must be happy, my good Sister Phoebe, to splash so much color about. And blind as a bat. But it works, I can see what you're talking about. That must be Jeremy. And whose little girl? Yours? Ellen's? Won't the beautiful mistress sit for a painting? I shall commission one and we shall see her then."

He smiled at his foolishness. "Ellen Wausau Marchion Harris, holed up in your big house in your big valley happy as a clam. I bet my bottom dollar you was the *last* wife George Harris took."

And thinking about Utah Territory, tasted the dust and the emptiness.

# THIRTEEN

THE BISHOP ARCHED HIS BACK and tried to appear attentive, thinking about what he would say if called on. It was hard to keep his thoughts inside the room. The world outside was so beautiful, the trees bowed low with fruit, the little fields thickly covered with flowing wheat. His heart hurt with gratefulness.

Maybe he should talk about the ban on assemblies. True, the ban was a blessing in that it halted the endless roll call of church meetings that thieved so much time from the families. But there needed to be a middle ground. People needed to be able to worship together in order to anchor their faith and give it nourishment. That sounded pretty good.

The room was awash in the smell of new paint. Someone got up to open a window, and George, his concentration broken, heard Brigham say,

> …as soon as the time arrives, when this people have been proven sufficiently to satisfy justice, mercy will interpose, peace be fully restored, and the valley of the mountains resound with the joyful voices of the Saints. Until then I am perfectly willing that the people do without preaching.

Such a mean-spirited jackanapes. George loosened his coat. It wasn't fair that the President indulge himself as he was today. Utilizing the large upper room in the Apostle George A. Smith's new home as a prayer room for his counselors and The Twelve, while denying the same opportunity to the faithful.

He was still too warm. He removed the coat altogether, and that's when God spoke to him. The bishop could not believe his ears! Not once in all the years of claiming to know what God wanted, in all the endless hours of prayer, had he ever heard God speak. But here was God's voice! *telling him to rise and go forward!*

He got up stiffly and walked toward the front of the assemblage. As he walked, he could feel the expression of deference, so carefully cultivated over the years, dissolve. A board creaked underfoot. He paused to rock back and forth, as if locating the board for the carpenter, then walked over to where Brigham stood. Standing there beside the President, he told the men in the straight-back wooden chairs,

"I have a vision for the Saints, and it is this. We are capable of great, good things, but we must have courage. We must stop purging ourselves with this senseless Reformation. We have been working like coopers, driving the hoops down with great force, but people can only stand so much ranting and raving. We must stop teaching fear and start teaching hope, or the hoops will burst and the people will go their own way.

"We need to separate the church from the state, and let the economics of our situation work. We take too much from the people. Very few are able to buy the ground they've made improvements on. They go without food for their tables just to pay their tithes. Their eyes are dull and they are too thin, they must be allowed to keep more of their goods."

The bishop turned toward his Prophet. He could see the sweat beads at the edges of Brigham's thin, sandy hair, the greyish, slightly bloodshot eyes wide with disbelief.

"Therefore I urge you, sir, I beseech and implore you, to

ennoble yourself by stepping down. Let the Saints remember you by the good you have done in bringing us this far. We have a glorious destiny before us. God loves the Saints, we will prevail. We are a sweet, good church. But you must step down and let us be whole again, so that we may love and trust each other as God meant us to."

Such a beautiful speech. George breathed deeply. He'd never felt better in his whole life, as if he'd scrambled over the sheer lip of a high rock and now stood on the rock's warm, broad surface with the sun in his face.

Ellen was in the back yard, trying to coax a hen from its nest in the rabbit brush beside the barn, when she heard the hurry of hooves on the street. Then she heard someone cry, "Sister Harris! Sister Harris!" She backed out of the brush and started running. The buggy horse was young and inexperienced, and the driver had to dismount and turn it around by hand, then the buggy was flying back the direction it had come.

The bishop lay in an upstairs bedroom in the Smith home. The walls of the room were lined with people watching, faces drawn.

"George, can you hear me?" Ellen eased herself down on the bed. Lying there coatless, his shirtsleeves rolled up, he looked rather boyish, as if caught having a nap. "George?"

He opened his eyes and smiled at her.

"Are you alright?"

For a split second she thought he was, and then he was gone.

"He was delivering himself of the Spirit," Heber revealed, helping the shocked woman down the stairs, "when he fell to the floor, and now he's flown away, up to the heavenly heights. Here, watch your step."

Actually, what Heber was doing, in looking after the widow,

was buying himself time. Brigham heard only what Brigham wanted to hear. A comment on an outburst that didn't happen would definitely not be a good idea.

Edward Tullidge hurried up just as the apostle finished helping Ellen into the Kimball buggy. Hoisting himself up on the foot rest, Edward embraced the widow warmly and said softly, "Don't let anyone near George's desk until you've had a chance to go through it."

"Your husband had great courage, Madame," Heber remarked as they drove out State road. "Great courage." Which was the plain, unvarnished truth. To tell the Prophet to his face that he had become a serious liability to his church was the bravest act of courage Heber had ever witnessed.

Ellen didn't hear him. Leaving the Smith house, and later at home, she moved as if in a great void, putting her arms around the children and Phoebe, hearing neither their words, nor hers in reply. Everything just motions.

The church clerks came, murmuring their regrets and seeking the contents of the bishop's desk.

"He's put the key somewhere," Ellen said, seized not by Tullidge's warning, but by her own revulsion at having the clerks in her home. "I won't allow you to break the lock. Come back tomorrow."

She shut the door and retreated to the dining room to clear the table bought years ago to accommodate all the Harris sisters. A stout pine table, painted and grained to resemble hickory and inlaid with hardwood-box parts. Upon marrying George, she'd restricted the large dinners to special occasions. Remembering that, stacking the children's papers aside on the bookcase, she realized it had never once occurred to her that George might someday lie on the table under the candles.

The bishop's body was brought home and laid out on the

white-sheeted table. He wore the suit coat that he had earlier removed, and someone had straightened his tie. The casket maker came, quietly took his measurements, and left.

The outside wives came, wearing austere faces and dark clothing, and sat silently along the edges of the room. Neighbors, bringing food, visited in low voices in the kitchen.

Flanked by their mother and Phoebe, Jeremy and Nancy sat on the front porch, the soft rain of condolences from the mourners moving them inexorably toward acceptance.

The afternoon light thinned away, and with it the visitors. Ellen sent the outside wives home and covered George with a blanket, tucking it in around his shoulders to ward off the evening chill.

The family pulled their chairs close to the table and told "remember when" stories. Like the time George bought Jeremy a pony for Christmas, and Jeremy took it upstairs to his bedroom to keep it warm after everyone went to sleep. And the time George gave Nancy a large nest of painted, wooden eggs for her second birthday, and Nancy, happily opening egg after egg, came to the last one and found a ring inside and ate the ring before anyone could stop her. And the time crossing the prairies when Phoebe layered the bottom of the wagon with flat rocks she'd painted pictures on. George made her throw the rocks away, but he also gave her a big sheaf of paper being saved for Oregon.

Telling their stories, they glanced at their husband and father, their smiles inviting his response, comforted in some small measure by the look of serenity on his face in the flickering candlelight.

It grew late. Phoebe fed the children and took them to bed in her room. Listening to the house chattering in the evening breezes, Ellen felt the shock wearing off. Jeremy was only eleven years old, Nancy was only seven. They were too young to be without their father. It wouldn't do, *just would not do.* At her feet a terrible gulf was opening, the edges fading away, revealing a host of nightmarish realities. She began to sing, and suddenly to cry wildly.

Hearing the tortured sounds, Nancy threw back the covers, but Phoebe grabbed her nightshirt. "No, Nancy, leave her be, she's better off alone." Whimpering, the little girl pulled the blankets over her head.

Jeremy lay rigid, remembering his mother's stories about Indian women cutting their hair and their arms. Having thoroughly scared himself, he slid out of bed before Phoebe could stop him and crept down the hall to where he could see his mother. She was sitting beside the table, curled over against his father, her head cradled in her arms. He watched awhile and went back to bed.

*Think. I must think.* Ellen lifted her head to stare into her husband's still face. *What's the first thing you would do, George? What should I do?*

Casting about in vain for a sign, she got to her feet and carried the mantel lamp through the house to the office. The waiting desk emerged from the dark, the ceiling lantern hanging dark above it. She'd never before looked inside this desk, to do so would have been unthinkable. Doing so now was unthinkable. A sudden spasm of anguish seized her. She set the lamp down and clutched the edge of the heavy ironwood.

*I can't do this, George, I can not bear this!*

Tidy by nature, George had bundled his private business into one drawer. The payment records showing the Harris houses free and clear of church debt. The will leaving the houses to Ellen Wausau Harris with the understanding that the wives residing in those houses be allowed to keep the furniture and livestock. A list marked "Christmas ideas" based on an inventory of unclaimed items placed in hock by indentured immigrants. A small wooden box loosely filled with detailed notes on the tithing process as it affected different households. This last puzzled her until she determined that George had anticipated eventually handing the little epistles over to his successor, should that man prove trustworthy.

The only surprise was the paper under the iron horse-head paperweight on top of the desk. It looked to have been wadded up and smoothed out again, as if the writer, meaning to discard it, had taken a second thought. Full of scribbles and scratched-out words, it was barely legible.

> *power corrupts you*
> *stolen our religion*
> *exhausted the church*
> *place no restraints on yourself*
> *in bondage worse than Pharaoh's*
> *measures utterly devoid of commercial sense*
> *ambition is devouring you*
> *learn to treasure what we have, not what we lack*
> *cultivating a culture of terror*
> *herd us around like cows*
> *a prison of the valley*
> *betrayed our trust*
> *put aside the laws governing a democracy*
> *pay no attention to facts*
> *divided us against each other*
> *lie and say utterly anything*
> *no open debates allowed*
> *tore down the temple*

She read through the strange list several times. Was George closer to leaving than she'd realized? Satisfied there was nothing of a personal nature in the other drawers, she lay the key on top and scooped the contents of George's private drawer, along with the wrinkled paper, into her apron, making a basket of it.

*Isn't this how the thieves do it, George?*

Carrying the lantern in her other hand, she walked through the outer waiting room—the going of the light secreting away the careful ordering of chairs.

In the dining room she placed the small wooden box on the coals in the stove. And sat for a long time staring hollow-eyed at nothing. Eventually she lifted the lamp over the still features and kissed the cold lips.

"I want you to know, my dearest husband, that I never regretted a single day with you. *Tecihila,* my *Cante Tinzo.* I love you, I love you, my brave, brave heart." Her voice died in an ache of sorrow.

It was long after midnight when she blew out the candles and climbed the stairs, the house darkening behind her. How many times had she been the last one to go to bed, the last one to carry a lamp through the house, and never given a second thought to the years whiffling away behind her.

Approaching George's door, she paused...and walked on.

Inside her own room she secured George's papers in a small locked chest. And taking a handful of charcoal from the stove's cold ashes, smeared it across the lower half of her face.

*I'm being too neat and tidy,* she told herself afterward, washing her hands in the basin. *I've grown too civilized.*

Seated at the vanity, she took the pins from her hair and let it fall loose. Next she opened the little rouge tin and traced a red cross on her forehead and daubed a red dot on each cheekbone. As she worked, she chanted softly, the frightful face in the mirror prompting her to smile inside her mouth. Her Indian sister would scold her, complaining that the sister-by-choice painted for war both as a woman soldier and a Bull Soldier.

*Ah but Sasha, tonight I must find my way as both a warrior and a mother.*

Done, she blew out the lamp and sat in the darkness, forcing herself to concentrate on Brigham.

The birds were singing. She straightened slowly, easing the stiffness out of her neck. The house was quiet. She washed her face in cold water, rubbed it with lanolin and washed it again, and rewrapped her hair. Downstairs, making another pass at the desk, she removed the pens and glass inkwell and iron horse-head. The family was at the breakfast table when the knock came at the door. By 9 a.m. the clerks had crated the desk's contents and hauled them away.

"I want you to put something with your father," Ellen told the children, "something to go with him in the casket." Jeremy's gift was a bone arrowhead found while on a fishing trip with his father. Nancy scattered the black suit coat with her father's favorite roses, the pink-striped blooms he called the Brabant Bourbon.

Phoebe placed her painting of Quacker at her husband's feet.

Quacker had suffered an untimely end while crossing the road, and to appease his broken-hearted children, George had the duck stuffed. It stood on the mantel for years until, being moved aside to dust, it fell to dust itself and was replaced by the only painting of Phoebe's ever to take up permanent residence in the living room.

Ellen slipped Constance's wedding band into the pocket of George's white shirt next to his heart. He was never able to forgive himself for his betrayal of his first wife. After he married Phoebe, he threw his own wedding band away and forbid the extra wives to wear rings. When Constance died, he secured her wedding band, a delicate gold ring with tiny emeralds and diamonds, in amongst his most cherished valuables.

That afternoon, riding out City Creek Road to the graveyard on the north bench at the head of a long line of buggies, Ellen was reminded of her return from Provot last April—the lateness of the hour, the cold house. She pressed her bodice, pressing close the wrinkled litany found on George's desk.

*Today my husband rides in triumph through the streets, even if no one knows it.*

After the service, the Apostle George A. informed the widow that the church audit of house contents would be the following day.

# FOURTEEN

THE AUDITORS WERE POLITE and earnest. The wood stacked beneath Phoebe's bed did not interest them. Finished with the bishop's primary residence, they hurried off to inventory the other houses. The next morning Brigham sent the customary note granting the family of the deceased a visit.

The visit took place that afternoon in the Great One's office, the chairs, nine of them, arranged in semicircles to face the desk that faced the west. Brigham did his Washington business at the desk that faced the east and the Territory's at the desk that faced the west, "the better to keep his stories straight," was how George described it.

The windows were open and children could be heard playing in the yard. Seating herself, it occurred to Ellen that when Heber died, Brigham would have to use the Council House to address all those wives and children.

The walls were filled with framed needlework, each with its own bug-like grouping of initials in the corner. Ellen smiled wryly at the familial outpouring, remembering Appella's likening the wives who lived in the Beehive to bugs in a bowl.

Brigham came in, his face somber, and spoke in detail of Bishop Harris as a dear friend of the church, truly a Saint among Saints. By the time the audience came to an end, there was not a dry eye in the room. The family was filing out of the room when the churchman motioned Ellen aside.

"I'll be home shortly," she told Nancy who, lingering, sought to take her hand. Brigham busied himself at the desk.

*Should I sit? should I stand? what do you want, you bastard?*

A brutish, stupid-appearing guard stepped inside the door, looked at the widow with searching eyes, and motioned her out of the room.

Ellen froze. *Good Lord, he means to arrest me!*

The foolish fear passed as quickly as it came. The church fed on ceremonies that both thrilled and frightened the faithful. Whatever it was that she was about to witness, at least her children would be spared. The guard took her arm. She shook him off and followed meekly downstairs into a rabbit warren of musty, low-ceilinged storage rooms walled off one from another with slats and crammed to the gills with crates and furniture.

George had complained about the indentured goods stored privately by Brigham before the Tithing Office was built. About there being no itemized lists.

At the end of the passageway wooden stairs led down to a dirt floor. At this level the rooms were emptier, made more forlorn by less—the steamer trunk all alone in a corner, lid thrown back idly, the scatter of children's alphabet blocks across the floor. The air was heavy with the smells of mold and mice droppings.

The guard stopped in front of a walled-off room. Turning on Ellen, he forced her against the passageway and muttered something in German and tried to kiss her. When she resisted, he opened the door and shoved her inside. A kerosene lantern hung from the center of the ceiling showed a large room filled with hand mirrors—dozens of them strung up by their handles, hanging down the walls like grotesque teardrops.

The door closed, the rusty key scraped its rusty lock. Determined to ignore her reflection in the mirrors, Ellen concentrated on the stuffed dolls beside them, realizing as she did that the dolls were impaled on the prongs of pitchforks that appeared to have been run through the walls.

She grimaced and hissed through her teeth. She'd heard about the scare rooms, the things that were hung there, the things that were done there.

*This is so stupid!* She glanced at the lamp, it was full of oil. Spiderwebs shelved the corners of the room. A rat skittering along an edge of wall disappeared down a hole.

*He won't dare lock me up for long, George's friends won't allow it.*

"You will die and go to hell!"

Ellen jumped. The words sounded hollow, as if spoken through a stove pipe. Looking around, she made out a woman sitting in a recess in the wall. The woman's clothing was dark, her face looked unnaturally white.

"Who are you?" Ellen asked loudly, unnerved.

The hollow words resumed. It wasn't the woman speaking, the voice came from somewhere in the walls. The apostate's life was sinful, she was bound for eternal damnation, only by the Prophet's intercession could she avoid the hell fires. This is what would happen to her in the grave. This is what would happen to her worldly possessions. Her children would curl up and burn away to cinders in the hell fire.

Now the woman in the corner came to life, praising the Lord in soft, prayerful moans. The moans grew louder, flattening in shrieks, like a small animal caught in a trap.

Despite herself, Ellen sank to the floor, sobbing wildly.

The door opened, the guard came in, pulled the sinner to her feet and out into the hallway. Now they were threading the labyrinth again. Ellen began humming under her breath, reassured by the sound. She smoothed her hair and straightened her dress.

Brigham was working in his office. The excess of chairs had been removed, there was but one chair in the center of the room. The windows had been shut, and a rag shoved under a crossing of sticks in the fireplace to hurry a fire. Waiting to be noticed, Ellen watched the flames eat at the cotton, remembering the words of the disembodied torturer. And then something much more practical, George's complaint about women tearing up their petticoats to contribute to the rag committee.

*It must be nice, having rags to burn.*

Brigham looked up affably, ignoring his visitor's swollen face and disheveled hair. "I've been studying the audit report."

Ellen dug a carefully wrapped packet out of her pocket and placed it on the desk, noticing as she did that her hand shook. "I kept out George's mother's rings, George wanted you to have them."

"That was very kind of the bishop." Seemingly pleased, Brigham unwrapped the silk square to expose a ring with a large yellow diamond surrounded by smaller diamonds. A second ring held an opal. "Yes, very kind." Opening a drawer, he swept the rings out of sight. The silk square wafted to the floor unnoticed.

"Have a seat."

The President began by elaborating on his earlier condolences. He thought Nancy very bright, bright enough to attend the school he had for his children. As he spoke, he nodded periodically, agreeing with himself, his fingers steepled.

Remembering what George had said about Brigham's burying hooks deep in innocent conversation, Ellen uttered only monosyllables.

"Some people say I'm not a patient man." The warmth in Brigham's voice slid away. "I've been waiting for this day for a long time, so you see, I can be patient." He glanced at the paperwork on his desk. "You've been at war with us since you got here. If you say different, you are a liar, yes, the damnedest liar that lives!" He looked up, his lips bunched tight.

"That's not true."

"Of course it's true. You remember the Fancher party, entertaining them with your stories. As a result, three wagons turned north. That going against Authority will cost you three houses and their contents. You will be notified which ones."

*You miserable thief! strutting around, hiding behind God.* Ellen bowed her head, hiding her loathing. "I can make you more money if you leave them under my care."

The Prophet clapped his hands together as if shaping air. "Very good. Yes, I can see why George found you interesting. No talk of God, of right or wrong. Simply of money."

He leaned forward, hands splayed on the desk as if he were going to throw himself across it. "Well, I am not afraid to talk about God. You've lived very well here. Servants, carriages, food, clothing. But you have not heeded the whisperings of the spirit, and now you will pay the piper. God will not be mocked.

"YOU WILL DO AS I ORDER! YOU WILL BE THE FOOTSTOOL UNDER MY FEET! NOT UNTIL I FORGIVE YOU WILL GOD FORGIVE YOU!"

He looked deranged. But then he relaxed and said quite conversationally, "You have not been a good steward of Sister Phoebe's interests, she's clearly in need of moral guidance. The colors she wears are immoral. She does herself injury, and the public who are obliged to look upon her. A strict husband will correct that."

Ellen gasped.

"BOW YOUR HEAD, WOMAN. BOW YOUR HEAD! I will not see your face or hear your words. You are not to leave your home for three months. After that you may go about, but only in black. I haven't forgot your running away at Fort Laramie. Should you try again...look at me!...I have only to crook my little finger and you will die." He held up a fist of hand, his little finger sticking out, and with his other hand slowly closed up the fist.

"Mr. President, I'm a respectable woman. And you've said many times that you never refuse any respectable woman who asks you to marry her. Will you marry me?"

Brigham stared, doubting his ears. "Will I marry you?" He bared his stained teeth in a huge smile that contained no mirth whatsoever. "You should have been born a man, you might have amounted to something. Good day, Sister Harris, the poor grieving widow of our much-beloved bishop. I'll have my eye on you."

# FIFTEEN

THE EVENING STAR WAS out, a warm wind trembled the flat leaves. Walking home, Ellen remembered with shame her arguments with George over leaving the Valley. It was her fault they were in this mess. Now Brigham would have his revenge, and there was no one to stop him. She'd entered the land the Indians dreaded—the dark land without sun or flowers.

*How do I live without you, George?* she asked silently, flayed with sorrow. *How do I breathe?*

The next morning she ordered the buggy brought around and drove herself to Appella's. George had liked this stableman— neat, quiet. She couldn't remember his name, but it probably didn't matter. The men who lived in the barn in exchange for work came and went like snow birds. As soon as they got themselves established in the city, George was interviewing someone new. Now she would be the one doing the interviewing, depending on what Brigham left her with.

The kitchen on Second North smelled pleasantly of cherry tea. Ellen was describing her visit with Brigham.

"Jesus! Mary! Joseph!" Appella squealed merrily. "I can't believe you proposed to him!"

"George always said he wasn't a fast thinker, that he hides it by getting belligerent. I think that's why he was yelling at me, he'd run out of things to say."

"Well, *you* sure didn't."

"I was trying to confuse him."

"What if he takes you up on it?"

"Better the tick bird on the back of the hippopotamus, than the one under its feet."

"Maybe *I* should check him out," Appella batted her eyelashes, "see if he's got a bedroom for me."

"Do it! He's got so many wives, he'd never bother you."

"Who are we kidding? We don't want to be part of his crazy game of musical chairs. I'm going out to the American camp, we'll go together."

"You're leaving?!"

"What choice do I have?"

"Stay at least until I find out what Brigham's up to."

"I don't dare, the soldiers will be gone. We have to get out while we can."

"This is Jeremy and Nancy's world, the only world they've ever known. To lose their father, then their moorings, it's too much too soon. Where will you go?"

"Indiana, I've got family there."

"Take Phoebe. Brigham's licking his chops at the thought of giving her a strict husband."

"Fat chance." Appella puffed her mouth and squared her shoulders, and collapsed in laughter. "She's built like a Prussian soldier, I doubt anyone's going to get too ornery with her."

"Why doesn't he just leave her alone? doesn't he have anything better to do? What is it about those funny paintings that he hates so much?"

"Just that, they're funny and bright and happy. He doesn't like bright colors or happy women. I would love to have Phoebe with me."

"You mustn't go out there alone, something could happen. Let Joseph take you."

"Joseph would betray me." Appella's usually mellow

disposition vinegared. "Remember that, Ellen, when Jeremy gets older. God loves children who spy on their parents. Anyway, I've already got it planned out. The new governor's wife has a lot of time on her hands and likes to tour the countryside, I'll suggest we visit Camp Floyd. Do you really think Phoebe will leave the Valley?"

"In a heartbeat, she's wanted to for years." Ellen fiddled absently with the salt and pepper shakers, a jolly ceramic Dutchman and woman. "George wanted us to leave and he'd meet us. I wouldn't do it, I wanted it all—the money from the houses, and George. I couldn't imagine living out there without him."

She got to her feet. "I better go begin my exile. I'm restricted to the house for three months, I shouldn't even be here."

"Oh, I wouldn't worry. It'll take Brig awhile to get the new list of do's and don'ts into his spies' hands."

"At least it keeps me out of church. That is, if His Holiness ever gets around to having church again. I do believe, if God's a bully, Brigham must be the holiest of men."

"Hallelujah, Sister Harris!" Appella laughed and clapped her hands. "The devil is among us." Appella enjoyed church, Brigham's strutting and posturing, Heber's crazy antics, the lesser speakers taking their cues from first one then the other, swimming madly back and forth like schools of fish.

"Take my advice," she wagged a warning finger, "when your three months are up and you do go out, look very unhappy. It's just possible Brigham will decide he's punishing you by *not* letting you marry anyone. He's so damn sure that all of us want to be married, particularly to him."

When Ellen arrived home, the stableman told her he was leaving. "I got a job moving dirt downtown starting tomorrow. I can still do a little around here 'til you get someone new."

"That'll be fine."

That evening after supper she told Phoebe, "Appella's leaving. She's placing herself under the protection of the American officials. I want you to go with her."

"Appella's leaving! Where's she going?"

"Indiana."

"I wanna see the ocean."

"Phoebe! one step at a time. You'll get there eventually. This is a start."

But Phoebe was adamant. She was not leaving without an ocean waiting.

"I know it's scary going off by yourself…"

"…I ain't scared."

"Well then, GO!"

"Write and see if we got any money for my paintings, and we'll all go together."

Many were the times they'd cheered themselves by imagining what the carefully wrapped packages addressed to Mr. Nathaniel Lafitte in care of the Wells Fargo will-call box in San Francisco were bringing in the free world. By now the money left with Uergin was sure to be a tidy sum.

"I've got enough money to get you settled."

"Why can't we just write Uergin?"

"Good Lord, you know why we can't write Uergin! for the same reason he can't send money here! the post office might open it! We've been over this before! When you get settled, *you* write Uergin. Send him your address."

"I can't write."

"Appella can write for you."

"We oughta stick together."

"I don't know if we can, the church doesn't like single women."

"They can't make us marry just anyone."

"And what happens when we run out of food and the cow dies?"

"They ain't gonna let us starve."

"They're taking three houses from us, that's good income lost." Ellen bit her tongue, she hadn't meant to tell Phoebe.

"What houses? why?"

"I don't know what houses. Why is because Brigham is getting even for Dinky. I tried to stop her from taking the southern road."

"We can rent some rooms here, we got ten."

"Yes, that's true if we get to keep this house, which is unlikely, it's the nicest one."

"I'll start selling my good paintings here in the city again, there's lots of new people around."

"It was never the bishop's idea for you to stop painting, it was Brigham's, and he's still around."

Poor Phoebe. She was so sure if she just kept tap, tap, tapping at the mindless rules, that somewhere a crack would open. After George made her stop painting, she painted in her bedroom, hiding the bright canvases under the bed and behind the wardrobes, not knowing that George never looked in on the room anyway. In the meantime, ever stubborn, she carried her easel outside and painted plain, muted landscapes which she sold unsigned at church events in the Social Hall. These drab acts of defiance she called her mushrooms.

"Nothing's changed, Phoebe, and nothing will, not as long as Brigham's in power. You simply can not paint your good pictures out in the sunshine, or someone will report you."

"Well, ain't that bird shit." Red-faced, hands plopped on hips, mouth screwed down, Phoebe resembled a mad pumpkin. "Some people sew, I paint, and I'm tired of being picked on."

"My dear little sister." Ellen brushed a straggle of hair off the broad forehead. "Back in the States you'll be free to paint whatever you want. You *must* go!"

"Oh, I'm going alright!" Phoebe exclaimed angrily, bug-eyed. "I'm not staying where I'm not wanted, just sweep me out the door, just sweep me out the door and rent my room to someone else, that's what's the problem ain't it, you want my room."

"That's not true, and you know it. You know I'll miss you terribly. I just think it's such grand opportunity, and Appella will be much safer traveling with you than alone. It isn't like we'll never see each other again. I promise I'll come when the children are older, in the meantime I'll write every day."

"Oh, that's just dandy! I CAN'T READ!"

"Appella can read the letters to you, everything will be fine."

Four days later Ellen received Appella's cryptic note. "Will be stopping by first thing tomorrow morning to pick up my things."

Grey dawn. Phoebe upstairs packing and repacking. The children still asleep. By sunup a fat little sack bursting at the seams, drawstrings pulled tight, waited by the front door.

"Remember," Ellen warned, working a pencil and a rolled paper partially into the sack's opening, "you're going out there to sketch the camp."

Eight o'clock. Phoebe sat by the window in the front room. The children, leaving for school, wanted to know where she was going. "Nowhere," Phoebe answered without looking at them. Ellen didn't say anything, hating herself for acting on Appella's words.

Ten o'clock. Governor Cumming's carriage was out front, and Appella was hurrying up the walk. But what had once looked so easy was not to be.

"Elizabeth's gathered up some of her friends," Appella explained, her face full of disappointment. "There's no room.

I feel horrible about it, but I dare not wait, she may not go out there again."

Phoebe was weeping, fat tears running down her cheeks. She had put it in her mind to leave, to see new things. She would learn how to read and write, everybody would be so surprised. But now she had to stay home and give up her big, bright bedroom to strangers and live downstairs in the dark basement.

"At least you tried," Ellen told Appella, tears in her eyes. "Good luck, dear friend, travel well, be careful."

Appella kissed both women and hugged them, and walked back to the carriage.

"Oh, stop crying!" Elizabeth Cumming exclaimed sharply, spying Appella's wet cheeks. "I don't like crying women. We see so many among the so-called happy women of Zion that it is really a shame and a disgrace. Tell me whatever is the matter now."

"There's just a lot of sadness in that house," Appella murmured, dabbing at her heartache with a handkerchief, "what with the bishop gone and all."

Appella did not return from Cedar Valley and was officially branded an apostate. Shortly afterward, Brigham confiscated Appella's house on Second North, Sister Zilpha's house out City Creek Road, and the house occupied by the youngest of the bishop's wives, a vestal virgin whom George had enjoyed visiting prior to his marriage to Ellen.

That the President did not take the mansion on State road left Ellen giddy with relief. The remaining houses, two small adobe rentals previously occupied by two of George's wives, now deceased, were sold and the money, eight hundred dollars, secreted in the hole in the wall behind the kitchen clock.

Suitors bearing fine gifts appeared on the front stoop. The Harris widows were not hard to look at. Only one had children, and mostly grown at that. But the women proved extremely hard to court.

Both took tea together with their visitors, neither one having the good grace to withdraw and leave the field to the other. This insensitiveness was seen by the suitors as an eagerness to be chosen.

"With him you won't have a cold bed," Ellen remarked after a jolly, tub-shaped fellow made the widows the gift of a slab of pork ribs wrapped in butcher paper.

"I don't now," Phoebe replied. "That's what my bricks are for."

An elderly furniture maker carted a large, finely made pine rocker up the walk. He left promising to call for the rocker in a few days and suggesting the women try it out.

"He's too old," Phoebe said later, rocking happily away. "He probably has a dozen wives."

While suitors were quick to mention their prospects, they never mentioned the wives waiting at home. And Ellen never discussed with Phoebe what those wives would mean to their own sheltered household.

A suitor with glasses thick as Phoebe's brought a large wheel of goat cheese and spoke of houses in Provot and Virgin. A nice looking man with a soft southern drawl.

"I wouldn't mind living in Provot," Phoebe said after the suitor left, promising to call in a week when he was back in the city. "If my husband has a nice house."

The small kernel of hope caught the light. Ellen could hear it reflected in the wistful tone. Phoebe was becoming seduced by the thought of having her own husband, someone who would actually love her.

*Oh no, Phoebe!* she cried silently. *No, no, you must stay here in the city so I can help you. Your husband's not to love and cherish you, he's to be your jailer. Brigham would never allow you a lover.*

## SIXTEEN

CROUCHED WAITING FOR WINTER, the Southern Corridor is a harsh, colorless land. The fog eased in, hanging up on the mountaintops as if caught on briars. Broomed off by an occasional updraft, it settled back like an old cat pushed away from the hearth. Noiseless little rains came and went.

Down by the creek below Cedar City a large train of Matthews and Tanner freight was camped beside a row of empty pole shanties. The shanties had been thrown up for the Utah War refugees who had since returned home, a sadder but not necessarily wiser people.

Jed and Yam unloaded their pack horses outside an empty shanty with a partially collapsed roof, and Jed rode uptown looking for Emil. Cedar City was a grey and melancholy place. A dreary cross-hatching of muddy tracks occupied the main street. In the puddled ruts, crowds of tattered sparrows flew up at the horse's passage and returned to their labors with sordid patience. The foot traffic shuffled silently along, turning sour, distrustful faces on the stranger in their midst. In a small eatery, the cookstove belched black smoke, leaving a depressing wrapper of soot on dishes and tables.

Jed ordered a piece of squash pie and told the serving girl, "I'm looking for a friend of mine, Emil James."

The girl came back with the pie, her face blank, collected

fifteen cents and busied herself elsewhere. Crossing the street to
an armorer, Jed tried again.

"Out the California road," the armorer said. "Big hog farm,
can't miss it."

"Why, Jed!" Verity James gave her visitor a warm hug. A
small, wiry woman, peppery as ever. It'd been twelve years since
she'd seen Jed. Back in '46 in Independence, when he hired
on with the Harris train. She said as much, and added "What
a special surprise! First we got your sister, and now we got you.
Everyone's moving west."

"So Dinky was here." Jed could have hugged her again. "Ellen
said you'd stop her."

"Well, she stopped herself. You don't look anything like your
sister, she had the brownest eyes." Verity's soul puckered and
she busied herself at the stove. "A good two weeks she was here,
before leaving with another train.

"What was that party's name, do you remember?"

"Why no, I never paid no attention. Here, have a seat."
Verity poured a cup of coffee and slathered a chunk of bread in
applesauce. "She made her own arrangements. We was sorry to
see her go."

The plank table was no higher than what the James needed.
Jed pulled his chair alongside and stretched out his legs. "You
realize, Verity, my family is deeply indebted to you. You didn't
get in trouble for taking her in, did you?"

Verity pressed both hands against her chest as if pushing it
back in place. "It's a very hard thing to talk about. I wish I could
tell you more. Emil surely took a shine to that little family."

"Because if you did, if there's anything I can do to help…"

"…no! we don't need nothing!"

"Alright, just so you know." The James were an interesting
pair, Emil always puffed up, ready to take offense, Verity fiercely

defending him. That having decided to protect Dinky, they would do so at any price, was sure no surprise.

Verity's eyes welled over and she dabbed at her face with her apron. "It was hard for your sister, don't you know, this farm smelling so of hogs and her not knowing us. Them twins is something else, ain't they." She smiled through her tears. "Regular Mexican jumping beans. My, my, could those children eat. I loved to sit and watch them. Indian pudding was their favorite. They'd eat anything, but they liked that best."

Jed brushed the loose bread crumbs into his hand and licked his palm. "Where's Emil?"

"Gone to Harmony with a load of hogs He'll be back today, you just make yourself to home.

The sun came out, the wet earth steamed, smelling of fermented peaches and hog waste. Poking around outside, Jed checked the hens' nests. He found the initials AM and EM carved in the wood railings in the cow barn. He found little roads lined with rocks. The cow came in on her own, and he milked her.

Emil got home. A bald-headed, raspy-voiced rooster with a large crop of whiskers shot through with grey.

"You join up?" the hog farmer asked, vigorously pumping Jed's hand.

"Gonna wait 'til I get bald like you." Jed patted the top of Emil's head. "Just checking on my sister."

"She was here, but she didn't stay long. Too bad." Emil grinned. "I could of used those kids, they was better at finding eggs than Verity."

"If ever I owed a man anything, Emil, I owe you. And I told Verity, too, if there's ever anything I can do for you, you just say."

"Here, you can stop jawing and help me with this horse."

It was when he threw a scoop of ground corn in the manger

box that Jed happened to look into the adjoining stall. Surprised, he leaned over the partition for a closer look. The clutter of boards in the unused stall had been worked aside to allow for a narrow corridor that ran the length of the partition.

And there, under the unused manger, was a field of white chicken feathers—hundreds of them stuck upright in the dirt. To someone not tall enough to see over the partition to the floor, the strange army would be invisible. As it would have been anyway, without the lowering sun shining through the knotholes.

Supper was rice and pine nuts dressed with shredded pork and long green chilies on the side. Jed talked about Julia, about J.C. and the Achilles tendon, about timbering in Maine. What he didn't mention, although he started to several times, was Yam. The same with the feathers. The same with the massacre—the elephant in the room.

Verity pointed at a row of crooked pots on a shelf. "The kids did those, I fired 'em in the stove, they painted 'em. They used hog's blood for paint."

"Where you headed from here?" Emil asked.

"Julia and ma are writing me at San Bernardino. They should of heard from Dinky by now."

"Well, I wouldn't worry one way or the other," Emil said. "That sister of yours, she knows how to take care of herself. You best scoot on home, winter gets in here, you won't go nowhere."

Jed grimaced. "I wish I was home. So where all's everybody who come out with us?"

"Most of 'em's in Salt Lake, 'cept that Fruthwirth woman. Her and her husband, they liked that Oregon country, I think they left the church." Emil tore off a piece of loose fingernail with his teeth and spit it on the floor.

The house darkened, water could be heard dripping in a bucket somewhere. Wondering why he didn't just mention Yam

and rustle up a dry place for the night, Jed worked himself free
of the table and pulled on his coat. "Better go while I still got
daylight."

"You're sure welcome to stay."

"I'm set up with the freighters. I won't forget you, I owe you,
my whole family does, real big, for what you done for Dinky." He
shook hands with Emil and gave Verity a hug.

"I don't wanna hear any more about it," Emil said firmly. "A
nice little family."

A crazed wind through the open doorway carried the sting of
rain. The table lamp flared wildly.

Back in shanty town Yam had the horses penned in the
three-sided shed behind the commandeered shanty and a fire in
the clay fireplace. The warmth made a cozy cave of the lop-sided
shanty. Propped against their saddles, bare feet toward the fire,
the brothers chewed on a front quarter of fried goat that Yam
wheedled from the freighters.

The flames danced blue and green above the wood. Jed was
thinking about Julia and J.C. She would be hot, Dinky all safe
and sound and him still out there in the West. But not much
longer. His little sister was something else. She'd cheated death
by a whisker, but that hadn't stopped her from catching another
train and pressing right on.

Somewhere in the night a fiddle sounded a lively note, and
he wished aloud for a little whiskey. Yam said the freighters
might have some. It was pleasant to contemplate, but neither
man checked.

"Tell me about the hog place again," Yam said.

"That's it."

"About the feathers."

"Ahhh, well, kids like secrets. Didn't you have ever secrets
when you was a kid?"

"Yes, this might be true."

The way the Indian said it reminded Jed of their father. Of his own pouncing on solid truth like a cat on a mouse. *Yes, indeed, this is a mouse!* And his father answering, *possibly.*

"What do you mean 'might'?" Jed asked over a yawn.

"I think," now Yam was yawning, "they were counting."

"Counting what?"

"We don't know that, do we."

By the next morning, Yam was adamant. One more day. "Perhaps you will find someone who saw her," he argued. As for himself, he was going out to the massacre site alone. The freighters had two Paiute herdsmen in their employ. Out away from the camaraderie of the cooking fires, the Paiute told of a great amount of sign in the meadows. Bones, hair, pieces of clothing and metal, broken dishes. The Mormons guarded the area, routing white traffic around it, but let the Indians roam freely over it.

"Cedar City don't strike me as overly friendly," Jed observed. "But there could be someone around remembers Dinky and who she left with. Be careful out there alone. The Mormons say the Indians are their friends, but don't push it. There ain't no army gonna come looking for a missing redskin."

"You will, my brother."


Jed turned up nothing in Cedar City, except the suspicions of its inhabitants. Toward noon he picked up a shadow—a man walking with a limp. Late afternoon, returning to the hitch stable, he passed his saddle horse and kept going to the other end of the stable, where he swung up a ladder into the loft. Sure enough, here came his shadow, shuffling down the walkway.

Rolling out of the loft, Jed tackled the man, knocking him down. A glass eye popped out and rolled into the hoof shavings scattered about the floor. Jed twisted an arm back. "What are you following me for?"

"I ain't…following…you…get off me!"

"When I get some answers."

"I can't breathe!"

Jed cuffed an ear with the flat of his hand. "Why are you following me?"

"Got orders."

"Whose orders."

"Church's…we don't like…foreigners around."

"I'm an American citizen, what are you?"

"I can't…I can't breathe!…American citizen."

"That's right, we all are." Jed got to his feet. "Let's go talk to this here church."

Bad Eye rolled over and pulled a pistol from his waistband, Jed kicked the weapon out of his hand. "Get up!"

Wincing, working his bad leg around to where it took his weight, Bad Eye stood up. "Look, sonny, all we want you to do is just get out of town, and there'll be no trouble."

"How 'bout I make the rules." Hooking a leg around the man's good leg, Jed upset the apple cart again. "Let me know when you're ready to go to church."

The yard smelled of coal smoke. At a table in the darkening kitchen several women quilted by lantern light. In the meeting room roughly a dozen men sat on chairs arranged in a circle.

Bad Eye hesitated in the doorway, and Jed shoved him inside.

Twisting in their chairs, the churchmen stiffened, eyes fixed in a hard squint.

"Hello, the room," Jed said evenly. "This fellow says he's got orders from the church to follow me around. I was wondering why."

The men stared at the one-eyed man in ugly fashion. "Those orders never come from us," someone said.

"He's one of the Dogs," said another.

A man with a rutted face and badly wrinkled coat walked over to study Bad Eye. "Where's your glass eye?"

"Bastard here knocked it out."

"You got no family in Cedar City," the churchman answered. "No reason to be hanging around. Now you go on back to Lee's, you tell him this thing with closing the city is over. You got that? it's over." He turned toward Jed.

"You can be about your business, sir, with our apologies. Where'd you knock his eye out?"

"In the hitch stable."

"If you can find it, step on it."

When Jed got back to the shanty, Yam was waiting, the pack-horses loaded.

## S E V E N T E E N

WHAT YAM HAD DONE with his day was mosey out the road to the west. Passing the hog farm, he considered the bare yard and upland buildings. When he was little, he used to measure time with rocks.

Toward afternoon the gun-metal skies gave way to sunshine and sudden warmth. In no particular hurry, Yam rested and ate hard bread and currants and took up the road on foot. A little-used wagon track opened in the cedar forest and wandered off to the southwest, and he followed, floating now, pulled by his instincts. The trace reached an edge of overlook. In a brushy basin a mile distant were several log buildings and a patch of cleared ground, a cow grazed on the cleared ground.

The damp weather had taken the noise out of the ground, he never heard the riders approach.

"HALT! UNITED STATES SOLDIERS!" one shouted, waving a gun and galloping wildly about the intruder.

The other rider started to follow, but broke off to stare. "Are you my uncle?"

"Yes!"

Dropping her horse and gun, Emily jumped on the Indian, followed immediately by Anne. Their blonde hair had been whacked off at the ears. A multitude of colored patches foxed their pants and shirts.

"How is it you are here?" Yam asked when he could.

"Where's our mother?"

"I don't know, Emily. Do you?"

"I'm Anne."

"Anne. You live over there?" Yam pointed in the direction of the basin.

"We're just visiting." Anne hugged the Indian again. "We live in Cedar City, we're waiting for our mother. Then we're going to California to be with our father. We had a real horse once, but it died."

"We don't really want to arrest you, Uncle Yam," Emily said, and pulled on his braid. "Do you know your braid's coming out?"

"Get on your horses!" Yam barked. "Do you wish to see your Uncle Jed?"

"Yes! yes! yes!"

"You must do as I say! do you understand?"

"Yes! yes! yes!"

"Stop yelling! Go back there and stay." He pointed toward the basin. "Do not tell anyone your uncle is coming. Do not tell anyone you saw me."

"Why not?"

"Go and do as I say!"

"When is he coming?"

"Soon, but not if you tell."

"We're both sergeants, Uncle Yam," Emily explained and picked up her horse and gun.

"So we can't give orders to each other," Anne added.

Yam scowled fiercely and pointed. The twins saluted and galloped from sight sounding the trumpet charge.

The well-used California road was easy to pick out in the star shine. When Yam reached the landmarks lined up earlier—three tall pines standing alone against the skyline, followed by a watercourse washed into the road—he crowded his horse against the deep shadows to the south. Blowing over the ground, the brute picked up the wagon track leading to the overlook and beyond to the basin and settled into a steady walk.

The largest of the log buildings was full of light and noise. Jed had to knock twice before hearing a man say, "Hold on, missy. Better let me get that."

A hulking shape with pistol drawn opened the door. Several children, three-year-old Lymund among them, peered out owlishly past the man's legs.

"I'm Jed Marchion from…"

Pushing their way out the door, the twins jumped on their uncle, followed by Lymund. When their tall visitor stepped into the light, the woman at the stove gave a shriek and flung her arms wide. Of a sudden, the whole room was full of children shrieking and jumping up and down higgledy-piggledy.

To Jed's astonishment, Yam had found not only Dinky's children, but the home of Patience Ballard, one of the extra wives who made the trek west with George Harris in '46. Her once-thin waist had assumed the proportions of a molasses barrel, her long horse's face hosted a blotch of moles, but her maniacal enthusiasm remained undiminished.

Introducing Mr. Ballard—a huge, red-faced fellow with a toothy smile—Patience gave Jed a slap on the back that knocked the breath out of him. Indicating the extra children in the room, she gigged him sharply in the ribs. "He *did* have another wife! I told you he would."

Mr. Ballard looked a little sheepish.

"But *she* didn't know about *me*, and when she found out, she just up and run off it made her so mad. Left her kids *and* Mr. Ballard, which was a good thing." Undone by exuberance, Patience grabbed an older girl and squeezed her. "Because I can't have any. That was the barrenest clutch of women! I never saw the beat. Constance, Verity, Phoebe, me, that Fruthwirth woman, none of us got any kids. So how's Verity feeling?"

"Good, so far as I know. Where's Dinky?"

"Why, Jed, she's not here!"

"How come her kids are?"

"Verity's sick, that's why Emil brought 'em over."

"How long ago?"

"Oh, how long you been here, kids? Kids! answer me! How long you been here? Day before yesterday I think." Patience looked askance at her husband and then at Jed, a slow realization dawning. "Oh-oh. Emil didn't send you?"

"Nope."

"How'd you find us way out here in the boonies?"

"Luck. Where's my sister?"

Patience sucked the air loudly over her back teeth. "This is really bad. I can't believe you don't know anything. You kids go outside and play, watch Lymund. Don't let him wander off." She fed the wood box and scraped the contents of several bowls into a skillet. "First let's get you fed."

"I got someone with me."

"The more the merrier," Mr. Ballard said. He'd been standing off to the side, slightly stooped, hand cocked on his hip as if to prop himself up. Now he lifted the lid on a seat bench and produced a clay jug and three little clay cups. "It's good corn," he nodded in self-agreement. "Takes the nip outta the air."

Over a hash of goat meat and beans, the brothers learned what little the Ballards knew. Dinky Miller left Cedar City right after the massacre to visit the survivors. She had two guards with her, the Indians killed one and wounded the other and took her. Search parties went out until the snows came, and again the past summer, but never found a trace.

"No one's told the kids, yet," Patience said.

"I always thought the Indians'd know something." Mr.

Ballard glanced at Yam. "I don't know if anyone ever asked 'em, maybe you fellows oughta."

"Why would the James lie to me?"

"That is sad," Patience said.

"Sad!" Jed exploded. "Is that the best you can do?! My sister stops in Cedar City and disappears. I show up and Emil hides her kids out here. What the hell's wrong with you people? Is that what you do, kill emigrants and steal kids?!"

"We don't know nothing about the massacre." Patience's loud voice got a notch louder. "We wasn't part of it, and we never knew Emil'd lie to you!"

Mr. Ballard pushed his hands against the air. "Calm down now, everybody just calm down." He tilted the jug over the clay cups. "This wasn't the church's doing, none of it. I don't know what's got into Emil. Verity wanted to keep them kids, I know that. If he lied to you…"

"…he told me Dinky left last fall with her kids!"

"Well, that was wrong. I can't put a good face on it, won't even try. This is a hard land. The church tries to make it right, but there's bad and good everywhere, and we don't lack in that department either."

Stalling out, losing his train of thought, the master of the house hesitated and started up again. "A man's got to believe in something, he can't just up and jump ship every time it springs a leak. He's got to hold fast. Might have to adjust the jib a little," he grinned in the direction of his wife, "but I believe…"

"…I don't give a rat's ass what you believe!" Jed took a deep breath. "Long as you help me get these kids out of here. I need a buggy and a team, I'll pay good money."

"Well." Mr. Ballard's mouth made a thin, flat line, and then he said, "I don't have a team or buggy in that good a shape, but there's folks around that do, and I think the Lord would have me help you. What do you say, Mrs. Ballard?"

"I say we all go," Patience hooted in her big, cracker voice. "Get Hogan's boy to do the chores. We'll find you a regular wagon, Jed, one with room for everybody and a good team, but you gotta put your money where your mouth is."

"Dammit, Patience," Jed said with a grin. "I don't care."

Early the next morning at the hog farm. The air cold, the hogs huddled in piles waiting for the sun. And someone banging on the door.

Emil peeked through the shutters. An Indian was standing in the yard holding two horses. The hog farmer couldn't see around to the door, but it didn't matter, he knew who was there.

He lifted the latch and looked into the chiseled, angry face.

"Where's my sister?" Jed asked, stepping across the threshold. Emil was wanting to shut the door. "Leave it open," Jed told him.

The cookstove, crammed full of starter, was belching smoke around the lids. Emil opened the firebox and blew on the wood, coaxing a little lick of flame. Verity emerged from a back room. She was clutching a grey blanket shawl-like over her night dress. "Shut the door, Emil," she said, ignoring Jed.

"Leave it alone, Verity. Where's Dinky?"

"We told you what we know, Jed!" she snapped. "Come inside, you're letting in the cold!"

Emil sat down heavily at the table and washed his face with his hands. One of his eyes was closed tight.

"Where, Emil?"

"I don't know."

Jed waved his hand out the open doorway. A rifle sounded, a hog squealed. Emil knocked down the chair getting to his feet, but Jed blocked the doorway.

"Where now, Emil?" The words soft as snow falling on ice.

"I told you I don't know!"

BANG!

"Jed, you goddamned sonofabitch! that my living!"

"Where is she?"

"I'll tell you what I do know, stop the shooting. She was here with the kids. She wanted to see the survivors of the massacre."

"They brought the wagons to the church." Verity hunched herself down on a chair, as if afraid whoever was shooting would train the rifle on her. "We walked to town that day, that's how she learned of it."

"Two men took her out," Emil said. "We never saw her again, that's the God's truth."

"What men?"

Emil hesitated.

BANG! Another hog died.

"STOP THAT!!" Emil looked around wildly, as if considering reaching for his own gun. "I was at a meeting at Tellus' place. Bishop Haight, Higbee, Shirts, Lee, a bunch of others was there. I told 'em we had a woman and kids with us, they'd of found out anyway. They picked the men. The Indians jumped 'em, killed one and took her."

"What was their names?"

"It's against Authority, I can't help you!" The words were squeaky. "The church won't have it."

"I ain't never been that religious, Emil."

BANG!

Frantic, Emil jumped to his feet. Verity was squawking like a chicken.

BANG!

"I dunno know their real names," Emil keened. "Never did know."

"Where the one that's alive?"

"Gone up north."

"So there's no way I can trace what you're telling me."

"I can take you to the grave of the one."

"There's a lot of graves in the West."

"Look," Emil cried. "Ask anyone in town, we searched and searched. Nothing turned up."

"So why'd you lie to me?"

Emil glanced at Verity, and forgetting himself, studied the floor.

BANG!

*"Alright!!* We wanted them kids. I know it was wrong, it was wrong." He was crying openly, mashing his fists against his eyes.

Jed shoved the table hard with his boot, tilting it over against the wall. Tin cups and a bowl of sugar went flying. Verity screamed.

"You're lying again, Emil," Jed said. "You see, I'm learning. I think Dinky wanted to see the survivors alright, and I think you're the reason she didn't come back."

*"That is not true!"*

"What is true?"

BANG!

A hog squealed and kept squealing.

BANG!

Maddened, Verity shrugged off the blanket and jerked the table upright. "True?" she asked, made fearless with anger. "I'll tell you what's true." She snatched the cups off the floor and slammed them on the stove.

"Bad things happened to that company. Things so bad," she leaned into the words, "that everyone had to be killed, everyone eight years and older. Poor little tykes." She twisted around to look at Emil and kept looking at him—hitting him with her words.

"Them that was younger was farmed out to different families, so's they couldn't talk to each other, couldn't even have that little speck of comfort. The Survivors of Sevastopol, that's what they're called, ain't they, Emil. Tell him, Emil."

She looked at the floor. "I never told anyone where Dinky came from, I knew better." With a loud cry of anguish, she attacked the spill of sugar, scooping it up and throwing it at the table.

"When they come for her, the guards, I asked Emil, 'was those men at the meadows?' and he didn't know. But I heard later they was with the Dogs in Hamblin's meadows. That's what folks around here call the men who killed the emigrants, Mountain Meadow Dogs. We know most of 'em, don't we, Emil?

"I knew when they took her, she wasn't coming back." Now Verity was whispering. "I knew, but I didn't tell her. I let her go." She stared at her husband, and unwilling to accuse him further, prowled the kitchen, picking up dishes and putting them back in quick bird-like motions. Then, abruptly, she was at the window, throwing open the shutters and screaming, "Shoot all them hogs! Shoot 'em all. We deserve it. That girl come here looking for help and we let her go!"

Face cradled in his hands, Emil was moaning, wrestling with his demons.

But Verity, seizing the truth, had seized strength. Wheeling, she stood chin up, eyes steady on her husband, daring him to punish her for disobeying.

"We lied about the kids, Jed, because Authority told us to. They said they give the American Army a count, and that's all was going to be turned over. Bishop P. K. Smith, he's got a girl that's not counted. John Lee keeps one at Harmony and Jacob Hamblin's got three, I don't know if them kids was counted or not. And I guess the Indians found some hiding in the woods.

"It was easy to lie to you. She's dead, your sister's dead, what does it matter?" Verity scratched her neck, pulling at the collar of the night dress as if burned by it. "It's like those kids is my kids. Don't take 'em away, I'll do right by 'em and love 'em so much. Please. This is their home now. Please."

Jed leaned against the doorjamb, waiting for the storm to pass. And said when he could. "Yesterday in town someone was tailing me, a man with a glass eye. Who was he?"

"That's the guard who lived." Suddenly mindful of Emil's words, that this guard was supposed to be gone up north, Verity hesitated and then plunged on. "Bad Eye, he calls hisself. He heard you ask about Emil and come told us."

More silence.

"You got anything else you wanna say, Verity?"

"They was starving, that train was starving. Nobody would feed 'em. They was so thin, their faces all burned and empty. I seen 'em outside Cedar City. It was a death march is what it was. Their animals was starving, nothing but bones and hide stumbling along. The same with the people, all bones and hide.

"I fed your folks up good, I never stinted. They ate all the time, ate sugar cookies in bed, but I never fussed. They climbed trees and shook down green peaches, there was no holding them back. They like to scared little Lymund to death with ghost stories. He'd come crawl in with us, sleep on our old pokey mattress, and he's got his own goose feathers. So do the girls, and each got their own slate tablet, they don't want for a thing."

She paused, her expression anxious. Jed didn't say anything, and she moved as if to put her arms around him. He shoved her away.

Sniffling, she retrieved the blanket and clutching it against her chest stood rocking from side to side, her eyes closed.

"You got anything to add, Emil?" Jed asked.

The hog farmer, his fist clenched over his jaw, didn't look up. The cookstove had given up the ghost, a river of cold air poured through the open door. Even so, there was a sheen of perspiration on his forehead.

"Emil?"

"Don't listen to that old woman." Emil drug his hand off his face and down his neck. "It was Injuns that took your sister, there's a man dead for god's sake! The church runs the show, and they're plenty mad. They don't know where she is."

"How come you didn't want me talking to Bad Eye?"

"I got enough trouble without you stirring up more." The unfairness of it all set the hog farmer to crying again, he felt like he'd been beat with a whip stock. "I wish I'd never laid eyes on her or them kids, I could lose ever'thing I worked my whole life for."

Jed hunkered in front of the distressed man. "Look at me, Emil James, I want you to hear what I'm saying. I'm the one you gotta worry about now. I'm going looking for Bad Eye. If your stories jibe, I'm leaving and taking the kids back to the States. If they don't, I'm burning you out, then I'm leaving. In either case, I will be back, and you and me will go hunting for Dinky together."

Verity was watching her husband, all worry for his hogs and his church gone out of her empty face.

Jed walked outside. The yard was full of dead hogs, but he wasn't any closer to Dinky.

# E I G H T E E N

BAD EYE WAS NOWHERE to be found, but his absence proved no great loss. Folks were more than glad, learning who Jed was, to share details of the long, fruitless searches for his sister. As to where she was, they had no idea—maybe dead, maybe with the Indians. He asked about Mun, if Mun had been there, but no one knew anything about the woman's husband.

What he didn't ask about, not wanting to bite the hand that fed him, was the massacre itself. And Yam asked no questions at all until…

"Our God loves everybody," the eatery girl confided warmly in the Indian. "The missionaries even marry squaws to save them."

"To save missionaries?" Yam asked.

Mr. Ballard located a stout team for $250 the pair, and a plank-sided spring wagon for $185. Jed was watching when the twins went to load their horses. "Can't load horses in the back of a wagon," he told them. "Even if you get 'em loaded, they won't stay."

Sensing a worthy opponent, the twins looked to their Uncle Yam for an answer.

"Cover the eyes," Yam advised.

Mr. Ballard wasn't surprised to hear that folks in Cedar City had gone out of their way to distance themselves from the treachery of the massacre by discussing the loss of Jed's sister.

"They feel real bad, and they don't know what to do about it.
It's like when you fall hard on ice, it takes a while to figure out
what happened and where you hurt the most."

It was a grey journey north, the mantling sky cold and still.
That the ground stayed dry and the team made jig time of it,
Mr. Ballard took as a sign of the Lord's approval. In twelve days
the party was eating ice cream in glasses in Godbe's apothecary
for twenty-five cents a glass. Jed gave Mr. Ballard the team and
wagon, and then the Ballards were saying good-bye and pushing
on to visit relatives in Ogden.

"When you come back looking for your sister, look me up,"
Mr. Ballard said. "And bring this Injun with you. Is he really
your brother?"

Jed offered his hand to Patience, but she grabbed her Oregon
Trail sweetie and bussed him good on the mouth and gave him
a hug that like to broke his ribs. Once upon a time, a long time
ago, they'd danced under a powder-sugar sky and he'd kissed
her. Thinking back on that hungry kiss, feeling his beard on her
lips now as she climbed back into the wagon, Patience smiled
wistfully. It was funny how the pieces that didn't fit together
anymore still warmed the heart.

Embittered by the constant need for diplomacy in his
dealings with the Mormons, Jed didn't revisit the Harris
mansion, but sent a note instead, saying he had Dinky's children
and was taking them home.

With a room rented in the Salt Lake House and the saddle
horses sold, it was time for the finer things of life. The shaving
saloon for the men, where Lymund got lathered up like
everybody else, and from Messrs. Hockaday and Burr's general
store four hair bows for the twins.

And for supper, the Globe Bakery and Restaurant. Steak
and new potatoes fried, spinach sprinkled with pearl onions,

chocolate cake topped with peppermint ice cream. For Jed, trying to square the civilization they'd reached with the massacre in the south, nothing made any sense. It was as if Salt Lake City was in another country. Or maybe it was Cedar City and the Mountain Meadow Dogs that were in another country.

The next morning, buying tickets in the crowded express office, he was asked for his permission slip.

"Permission?"

"Anybody going east or west's gotta have permission from the church." *Everybody knows that,* the clerk's tone said.

"I ain't no member of any church." Jed had to fight to keep his anger down. "I got my sister's kids, she was with the Fancher train."

The information meant nothing to the official. He started to say as much, then shrugged and counted out five tickets. Being the church's policeman was becoming a thankless job, what with all the foreign traffic in the city.

Waiting out on the street with Lymund and the twins, Yam fell into a little unfinished business of his own. A group of boys just out of school walked by, moving in fits and starts like colts out of a pen—one minute talking and shoving each other, the next minute strolling along indifferent and far away.

One of the boys looked familiar—taller than his friends, not so heavy in the face, with a high forehead and strong nose and a solemnity to his expression that had nothing to do with his actions. *That was Jeremy,* Yam told himself, absently fingering the cross under his shirt.

The twins ran up to the boy, who paused briefly and bounced away, but not before they gave his bright yellow suspenders a tug. Watching the group move down the street, Yam—in an expression common to his own youth—heard the whistle pig.

"Go get the one called Jeremy!" he ordered the twins.

"Why?" asked Emily.

"Now!"

Jeremy returned, and Yam handed him the mystery wood. "This wood travels a long way to find you." Yam made his own face as long as possible. "It has great power. Take it, you do not have a choice, and do not be afraid."

Embarrassed and acutely aware of his loitering friends' dislike of Indians, Jeremy nonetheless responded as a true bishop's son—courteously thanking Yam for the gift and placing the leather string with its old wooden talisman around his neck.

Drawn by four mules, the mud wagon rolled north up East Temple, the street called Whiskey Street by the Gentiles. Lymund was soon asleep, Anne and Emily were polishing off the last of the hard candies purchased in Goddard's confectionery and hatching plans to ride up top with Yam.

Jed was remembering Dinky's having come down this very same road a year earlier, all her plans for a new life in California in her old kit bag. What a cruel thing had happened to her. Traveling north with the Ballards he'd considered leaving her children with Ellen and going back to Cedar City, but he didn't want them out of his sight, not in Utah anyway, and he had a family of his own to tend to.

The passengers, Gentile businessmen, spoke mostly of their troubles in putting the wheels of commerce back in motion in the Valley. The massacre in the south never came up. Jed was wondering why, when the truth dawned on him—the stolen emigrant registers. Whoever stole the registers from Forts Kearny and Laramie knew the value of the Fancher names not only to the army, but to the reading public.

Back in Salt Lake City he'd posted letters saying he was on his way home. Reaching the new telegraph line at the edge of the States, he sent wires: To his mother,

HAVE NOT FOUND DINKY YET STOP BRINGING CHILDREN
HOME STOP JED

And to Julia,

TAKING DINKY'S CHILDREN TO NEW YORK STOP BE HOME
SOON STOP ALL MY LOVE STOP JED

## N I N E T E E N

WALKER RETURNED HOME TO a hero's welcome. A community dinner served in his honor in the First United Presbyterian Church of Troy. An invitation to speak to the United States Agricultural Society at their meeting in Syracuse about agricultural prospects in the region immediately west of the Missouri River.

And everywhere he went…

"What happened to your arm?"

"My brother knifed me."

"Your own brother! why?"

"Didn't want me finding our sister, I guess. Just jealous. He was at Fort Kearny waiting…"

A horrifying tale told out of earshot of Christina, who thought her son crippled by Indians. Poor Walker, blindsided by his own brother! You could tell by looking at him that he was hurting.

Why there wasn't a man ever called on Walker Marchion for help, that he didn't oblige. Never cheated anyone, never went back on his word, not a profane man, nor a drinker. Went to church regularly and paid his full tithes. Poor fellow.

For his wife Walker had a slightly different story. Jed had urged an Indian to attack him. Katherine clucked sympathetically. There was no way to ferret out the truth, no point in even trying.

Aged by worry, Christina grew increasingly frail. Katherine pressed her mother-in-law to move to the farm at the mouth of the Mohawk. But Christina refused. When Jean Paul died, it was as if her right hand had been ripped off. But she just kept stitching right along, and that's what she'd do now—stay in her own house on the Batten Kill and take care of her chickens. Everything rested on Jed. He was the only one with any business out there in the Indian lands, the only one who knew how things worked. In the meantime she would wait right where she was.

Uergin was eating breakfast in the Auction Lunch when he read a headline in the *Chronicle* picked up from the August 26, 1858, *Journal of Commerce*.

### THE NEW ELDORADO!!!
### GOLD IN KANSAS TERRITORY!!
### AND THE PIKE'S PEAK MINES!
### FIRST ARRIVAL OF GOLD DUST AT KANSAS CITY!!!

He didn't read anymore. Lousy damn gold. The empty land between the rivers wasn't made for white men. They didn't know to treat it. Jesus Christ!

Later, drinking his first brandy smash of the evening, he couldn't shake the lingering melancholy. His new singer had a haunting, bell-like voice. Across the room, through the cigar smoke, she looked radiant as the evening star over El Paso del Norte, holy as the lighted candle in the church window at La Mesilla.

The saloon was filling up, it was getting hard to hear the music. Bags of gold dust and piles of doubloons and Mexican dollars were changing hands like water at the monte and roulette tables. Glancing around, Uergin exchanged nods with several fruit growers and merchants.

*Our father, hear us, and our grandfather…*he looked at the floor, surprised to find the Arapaho prayer in his thoughts…*all those that shine, the yellow day, the good wind…*

The Indians said it over food. He walked outside, wanting to remember the rest of the prayer before it slipped away. The wind was corkscrewing through the man-made canyons, bringing with it the smells of rain and sage

> *…the good timber, and the good earth…let there be long breath and life…we are going to eat.…*

He had to go back to the desert, back to where rivers disappeared in the sand. He had to walk on the dim, lonesome paths furrowed into the crumbling moss on the forest floor and find his way on the hardpan. Now, before he forgot how. Lousy damn gold!

A sudden, thick fog tangled itself in the gas lights and blurred the rhinestone sparkle of the lighted buildings on Washington Street. The street was full of foot traffic—Mexican, Chileans, Europeans, Chinese—intermixed like stray cattle in a pound. Horses pushed their way through the crowd, drivers yelled, whips cracked. A fire-hose wagon clanged its bell, demanding immediate passage. Newsboys screamed. A street urchin scissored through the crowd to hold out a tin cup, and Uergin dropped a silver dollar in.

"The luck of the Irish to you, sir."

"And to you, son."

A crowd of Chinese surged past, their high sing-song voices, the slap of their slippers on the redwood planks, momentarily cutting off Uergin and the street urchin from the greater confusion. The urchin studied the portage of wagons, waiting for an opening.

"I'm part Irish," Uergin said, as if to claim something for himself.

"We all are, sir," the urchin replied and was off like a sparrow hawk.

Uergin took a deep breath, making a bellows of his mouth, and eyed the Miners Exchange Bank. *We all are.*

He owned a piece of that building, fancy Moorish tower and all, and by god, he wasn't jumping ship yet. He went back inside the Lucky Lady and fired his lambent-eyed Angel of the Brazos.

# T W E N T Y

G OD IS GOOD. How else to explain what was happening in the Southwest.

The natives were growing restless.

Runners moved regularly between the Nations carrying messages that called on leaders to make common cause against their enemies. Aided by their Ute brothers, Jicarilla Apaches stepped up their harassment of settlers and patrols. The Mescalero and Gila Apaches joined in with their own brand of hit-and-run misery.

The Navajo drove cattle onto the green fields near Fort Defiance. Soldiers chased off the cattle and shot several in the process. Then the Navajo shot the Negro boy owned by the fort's commander with a steel-pointed arrow. Now the army wanted the killer punished, and the Navajo wanted restitution for their dead cattle.

For a provident horse trader anxious to tap the American market, this was very good news indeed. Thanks to the loco *indios*, the prospects for war in the Southwest were hotter than a *habañero* chile eaten ripe off the vine, more soldiers would come, the market for horses would go through the roof.

And who had the best horses around? Señor Alfredo Perez Luna! And why not? He bought his colts from Edwardo Ledyard up on the Mora, who covered his Mexican mares with a Morgan stallion. Smaller than the emigrant horses and not as clean-

limbed as the Thoroughbred, these crosses had the endurance
and the quickness of the coyote.

Alfredo did not consider himself a lucky man and so did not
count on that. In its place he said his prayers regularly and went
to mass when he could. And moved his operations north to the
Gallinas River below Las Vegas, a poor country of itself, but near
the American outposts, to wait for further developments.

Sure enough, it wasn't long afterward that the powers that be
in far-off Washington earmarked one hundred thousand dollars
for the Military Department of New Mexico—not for soldiers,
but for the things soldiers need, including horses.

Riding into Albuquerque that hot August day with over
one hundred head of good horses, and spying men in American
uniforms, Alfredo made another prayer.

When he was twelve years old, he traveled from his home in
Santa Fe all the way north to the Laramie River with his uncles
who were whiskey peddlers. After the uncles were murdered at
Fort Laramie by Indians, he made his way back home walking
beside an American bull wagon as far as the pueblo on the
Arkansas. From the pueblo he walked alone to Santa Fe carrying
his uncles' whiskey money.

Many were the stories he told of those early adventures and
of the kind, red-headed *americano soldado* whose *bueyes* he
drove.

He penned his animals in the army corrals near the plaza and
was walking toward the Quartermaster's office when a rugged,
bare-faced man in uniform, wolfing down a can of sardines,
stepped into the sunlight.

"¡*Sargento Carlosito!* ¿*es usted?*"

"Whaaa…who in the…"

The Mexican standing in the road wasn't very big, a stocky
fellow with thick black hair pulled back and caught in a little

strip of cloth. Coffee-colored eyes and strong white teeth. A black *bigote* that covered the upper lip and came down around the sides of the mouth, a soft, trail-away voice.

"...*soy tu amigo! Alfredo! El que trajo los bueyes desde Fort Laramie. ¡Buenos dias!*"

"Jee-sus Christ! what are you doing here?"

"You forget, this is my country." Alfredo shook with laughter.

"Yeah, that's right," Charlie replied, hugely pleased. They'd had exactly the same conversation back in '47 on the Camino Real de Tierra Adentro when Alfredo was caught hitching a ride in the sergeant's wagon.

"Come here, come here!" Alfredo hollered at the nephews who had ridden in with him—an older boy maybe fifteen and three younger boys.

"See, here is my friend, the señor who lost the beautiful woman to the *indios* and found her in Albuquerque and hid me in his wagon when the gringos stole the money from St. Francis! Here!" he slapped the dusty hat off a nearer head, "take off your sombreros!"

The nephews' dark eyes were round as saucers. Many good things had come to their uncle as a result of knowing this gringo, and now the *compadre* stood before them in the flesh.

"They are with me all the way from the Mora county," Alfredo explained. "Emmanuel, Rafael, Jorge, Laureano."

"*Con mucho gusto, señor.*" One by one the boys stepped forward to shake hands with the sergeant.

"Well done, gentlemen. As you were. Where are you dropping these..." the sergeant started to say "miserable crowbaits," but the beaming youngsters changed his mind, "...*caballos buenos?*"

"Fort Defiance," Alfredo said.

"Hot damn!" The sergeant grimaced. "Ain't that the drizzlin' shits." He studied the little *muleros* and shook his head sadly.

"Canyon Bonito. That's Navajo country, Hell's Gate. Hope you boys can handle 'er." That he was leaving Albuquerque in three days with a security detachment assigned to civilian wagons destined for the same drop-off point, he didn't mention.

The sergeant ordered the heavy uniform jackets and caps of his men stored, and two blue flannel shirts and a felt hat procured from the sutler for each man. That done, along with the necessary provisioning of the detachment, the wagons set out. The August sun was a hot iron pressed to the skin, limiting the marches to the early morning and late afternoon hours.

The days plodded by. The wagons reached the high ground west of the Middle Valley and set sail on a vast blue-green ocean of meadow grasses. The grasses were higher than the saddle stirrups and gave off an iridescent shimmer in the idle breezes.

Late afternoon. A lone peak, rising sharply to the north, was smudged with heat and haze.

Alfredo spit out a grass stem and reached for another, trying to decide what it tasted like.

"Jicama, tastes like jicama," the sergeant said. One of the *muleros* galloped up, asked Alfredo a question, and galloped off.

"Those boys think you walk on water. You got any kids of your own?"

"Nobody wants un *mercader de caballoes. Soldadoes y rancheros, sí*, but a smelly old un *traficante de caballoes* gone most of the time…" Alfred shook his head "…*muy pronto* my wife would be gone."

"You gotta clean up, pick 'em a flower."

"If you are born to be a *pinche* horse trader, you can't change your *destino*."

Another *mulero* galloped up, this time Alfredo left with him. The *mulero* had found a human skeleton on the prairie.

"I had a woman once," Alfredo explained on his return. "The kind you marry. We walked to the square every Sunday and ate tortillas and boiled eggs. I was so happy, I painted my *palizada* all different colors, everything was *muy* beautiful. Everyone says, 'Alfredo the horse dealer lives here.' But my wife-to-be and her mother and her family, they say 'why is Alfredo putting on the dog? does he think he is better than us? he is just a *madereado*.' That is the way with some people, they do not want anyone to be *rico* and have *buenas cosas*."

"So what happened?"

"I say her brother and his family can live with us, and each have a fine horse, and she marries a *ranchero*. And that is my life."

"So she give you the gate. You ain't even lived half your life yet, how old are you?"

"Twenty-four. My life will not change. *¡No madera!* If I tell you that the donkey is grey, señor, it is because I have a handful of the donkey's hair and it is grey."

Throughout the day, the *muleros* punctuated the silence with long whistles that snaked around their horses like ropes. At night the civilian contractor and his teamsters kept the loneliness at bay with gourd banjo and squeeze box and Jews' harps.

A melodious journey indeed.

Sunday, August 15, Navajo country.

Seven days and some one hundred eighty miles west of Albuquerque the train made Fort Defiance. Alfredo's contract called for one hundred horses. Of the eight extra head he'd started with on the Gallinas, he'd lost three—not bad for such a long drive. Did Major Brooks want the remaining five? But the fort's commander took only what he had authorization for.

"*Quien no se arriesga no pasa el mar*," Alfredo agreed with a smile. The customer was always right.

"Our interpreter's sick," the commander told him. "You speak Navajo?"

Alfredo rattled off something.

"It's worth five dollars a week and regular quarters," the commander said.

Five dollars a week was not so much for a *hombre* already as rich as a freighter, but the goodwill of the *americano soldados* was important. Alfredo left the contract payment—a draft for ten thousand dollars drawn on funds held by the Albuquerque Paymaster—locked in the commander's office and and went on the fort's payroll. The *muleros* he shooed back down the road to Albuquerque, but held onto his extra horses with the promise to pay for their keep. Who knew but what thieves would come in the night and steal the fort's horses and open a market for his horses.

The timid nephews did not wish to leave by themselves.

"*Quien tiene tienda que la atienda*," Alfredo scolded. "He who has a store must watch it."

But the red-headed sergeant who brought them to Fort Defiance was also staying at the fort. A short-timer returning to Albuquerque was taking over the security detachment. Who should the boys answer to?

"*¡Basta, buey!* Yourselves, of course. In Albuquerque stay with the *tíos* and take such work as you find. I will be along *cuando Dios quiere*."

On Friday the third of September a Ute runner, stopping at the fort, was made welcome with food and medical attention for an injured eye.

That same afternoon Charlie came in off patrol duty at Zuni. Filed his report with the major, threw extra hay in the stall for the big roan gelding called Nig, left an order for the shoes to be pulled and the horse to be turned out in the morning. And after

drinking his tod at the settler's, sank down for a nap under the
*ramada* behind his quarters.

Of the fifteen thousand sheep stolen from the *rancheros
mejicano* below the Zuni villages, the patrol had located eight
hundred. The little sheep, all head and horn, were exhausted
and took considerable time to return. As for the raiders and the
balance of the stolen sheep, they'd vanished like smoke in the
hand.

"*Buenas tardes, señor.*" Squatting on his heels, Alfredo
nudged the sergeant's shoulder. "It is me, Alfredo."

Charlie surveyed the tip of his boot and wondered what
was in the shadow. He could feel the horse moving under him.
Damn thieves, where were they?

"Señor, wake up."

"Christ almighty!" Charlie said with a jerk. "Alfredo! what
d'you want?"

"*Guisqui,*" the Mexican answered softly. "A runner on the
way to the mountains is resting in the Indian house. He has a
story."

The sergeant yawned deeply and rubbed his eyes. "Dream on,
cat shit, someone'll cover you up."

"*¿Qué¿*"

"It's against regulation."

"It is not often that a runner will tell his stories."

"He just wants hooch."

"*Sí,* it is a trade."

Charlie yawned again, this time loudly, trying to wake up. "In
the tin box under my cot. Hide it away 'til after dark and give it
to him slow, or you won't get squat."

Alfredo lifted his eyebrows. *Squat?*

Dawn. The log barracks creaked in the wind. Charlie was

shaving, squinting into a little mirror hung on a nail over a basin. The soap smelled of lavender.

Alfredo plopped on the cot and hugged himself. "Oh, such a beautiful smell. Oh, tell me, *señor,* where is your honey bear?"

"Was it worth my good whiskey?" The words twisting around the razor.

"You say. The Mormons are with the Moqui."

"Great. We ain't fighting the Moqui." The sergeant swished the razor through the basin water. "The Holy Joes got as much right in this country as we do. You got shystered, amigo."

"The missionaries are using the Paiute chief Naraguts to guide them. The missionaries go up on the Kaibab. Now they are with the Moqui to tell them about God. But not all. Some stay behind to look for a white women who lives with the Paiute."

"White women do that sometimes."

"Naraguts tells she ran away."

"They do that too." Charlie dried his face and mopped the inside of the basin with the towel.

"From the wagons the Paiute helped the Mormons steal, and kill all the people. You don't know this? the news is in Socorro."

Charlie stared at his friend. "Yeah, I do. What else did he say?"

"When the Mormons find the woman, they will bring her to the Moqui village. Naraguts thinks they mean to kill her."

"Why's he care?"

"*¿Quien comprende indios?* She is blind."

The commander's office was cool and dark. Water in *ollas* hanging from the rafters gave off a rusty smell of rain.

"It's unheard of for runners to stop," Major Brooks told the sergeant. "I suppose he could have been spying, they're full of tricks. Or wanting whiskey. My guess is a little bit of both, he has a bad eye and a good story. Let's talk to him."

The runner, a small, dark man of the desert, didn't have anything to add to his story. The right side of his face was badly scratched, his right eye was swollen shut. At Alfredo's signal he emptied a small leather sack on the desk. The bloodied claws of a lion too young to know how to finish off its prey.

"Give him what groceries he wants," the major instructed Alfredo. "Tell him he did a good thing by coming here."

The room's rusty smell of rain was gone, replaced by the smell of camphor salve. Alone with his sergeant, Major Brooks upended a small barrel of rolled-up maps, remarking as he did, "One thing about those boys, they don't lie, they haven't learned the art yet."

He unrolled a map on his desk. "Alright, let's shake the bushes and see what falls out. Take three men, a hundred rounds each, grain and rations for four weeks, and some trade cloth and trinkets. I need my scouts, but there's a renegade Zuni living at Laguna Negra the Zuni say is damn good.

"We only have a little time at best, so don't monkey around. Miles and Loving will be taking the field in another week, and we can't get replacements."

Studying the map, finding what he wanted, the major used a dry quill to indicate a wavery line labeled *C River*. Circles indicated the tops of adjoining plateaus.

"The Moqui are this way from the river, south and east. The Paiute are across the river, over here on the Kaibab and to the north. The Paiute are timid little people, the poorest of the tribes, if they steal your horse, they eat it. The Moqui live a little better, farmers for the most part, peaceful. But that doesn't mean they'll make you welcome, they've been sending the Jesuits packing for years.

"This is the only crossing in the canyon." The quill paused at an X followed by the words *Ute Crossing*.

"Our regular interpreter's due back in a couple of days, so we

won't be needing Mr. Luna's services. Tell him he goes along
and I'll buy his extra horses, that'll give you another rifle. If you
find the woman and she resists, do what you can with her, short
of going to war. At the very least, get a statement as to what
happened in Utah."

Led by its Zuni guide, the patrol pulled out two days later.
North and west up Bonito Creek, over Defiance Plateau, and
down through the dry washes at the head of Chinle Valley—
everything draining off to the north. Through a break in the
rim of Black Mesa and across those deeply corrugated slopes—
everything draining off to the south now, into an immense paint
box of stirred colors. Averaging some twenty-seven miles a day,
weather hot, no rain to speak of. The hot desert wind blowing in
fits and starts, pulling on the clothing, whipping the horses.

In the more sheltered places the ancient trail worn deep in
the red rocks was beautiful to behold. But most of the time it
was Mato-ayuwi, following the maps he was born with in his
head, that the soldiers followed. For these soldiers, 1st Dragoons,
Company A, fresh from a firefight outside Bear Springs, New
Mexico, where twelve enlisted men, along with their captain
and twenty-two Mexicans, took on three hundred Navajo
warriors, the patrol was a walk in the park.

The sergeant kept his men spaced one hundred feet apart and
posted a guard at night. During the day the sergeant's shoulders
ached with tension from studying the bleak, bare-knuckled
land, knowing the Navajo could well be standing in plain sight
watching him.

He had a fifty-caliber Sharps carbine with metal cartridges in
a saddle socket under his left knee, a forty-five Colt revolver on
his right hip, a ten-inch Bowie knife on his left hip. And a good
Missouri horse under him that hadn't been ridden in over two
weeks. But they didn't do much for his peace of mind. He felt

like a little bitty pebble rattling around over the hot rocks and sun-torched sands.

A comet of surpassing splendor appeared, growing so bright that even during the day it could be seen—an eerie pretender to the sun.

# TWENTY-ONE

**T**HE MAN BESIDE HER slipped away, and Dinky reached for her clothes. A row of stones leads to where she relieves herself, and from there to the cooking fires. Her stick waves aimlessly, her feet having memorized the uneven path. The voices around her sound of shore birds. A few of the words she recognizes, having married them to what she experiences, but she has no language of her own, except that occasionally she sings something so strangely beautiful that Dancer is reminded of the painted-wings that flutter up at the river's edge.

After breakfast she will walk with the children, letting them lead her about by the stick. Later she will sit with them in the shade.

This day starts no differently than all the rest, but it will not end the same.

Far out on an arm of plateau that thrusts itself into the canyon of the Colorado three riders draw rein. To either side rise majestic temples and buttes. A fire in the piñons on the far south rim sends up tiny spikes of smoke. In the deep distance beyond the south rim is the clear outline of snow-capped peaks.

The horses stand head down, eyes closed against the sting of fine gravel in the forever wind. A hungry dog rests, tongue lolled out, in the shade of the scrub brush. A colorless dog big as a loafer wolf.

On the bench below, a dozen pole huts and a scatter of pole

lattices shimmer in the heat. That their Ute guide has been able to thread his way through the dense timber to come out above this camp amazes his employers. This is the third camp the guide has located on the Kaibab. The other two, small bands of Kumoit and Paguit further to the north and lower in elevation, contained no white woman.

Hopefully this camp will be different. The high rim of the plateau, with its spooky cliffs and canyons dropping off into thin air, frightens the white men, as does the possibility of snow. The nights whisper snow, there is already some snow in the trees.

Dinky, braiding grass and humming, hears the clink of shod hoof on stone and an unfamiliar voice. Holding her breath, head cocked, she sorts out the sounds.

The Ute is talking to the *naiv*. He tells the chief that the foreigners with him are Moronies. They have come a very long way, they are searching for a white woman.

The dumpy, dusty woman pointed out to the Moronies is the color of tobacco spittle. She wears a skirt of mountain sheepskin with the hair on. Soapweed sandals lace over her feet. A basket hat sits cone-like on her head. Her ragged blouse, a white woman's blouse, is closed in front with a knot.

Mock and Bishop study her intently. Is this the woman who ran away from Cedar City? If so, the news heard from the friendly Indians at the good spring far back on the tableland, that of a white woman living with the Paiute, harkens of divine intervention.

The Cedar City runaway is the only adult to survive the Fancher massacre, and that's only because she left the train before the meadows. The diaries of the murdered emigrants have all been collected, but the runaway woman knows the stories. It won't be good for the church if that woman ever makes her way back to American hands.

Which explains the large reward on the woman's head, and why Jacob Hamblin, the leader of the mission to the Moqui, sent Mock and Bishop off with the party's Ute guide to investigate.

"If this is her, I wonder what we'll get named after us," Bishop said with a sly grin, referring to Jacob's naming the good spring on the tableland after himself.

"Are you the mother of three children in Cedar City?" Mock asked the woman.

Dinky rubbed her eyes and squinched up her face.

"Did you run away from your children?" The words harsher. "Your children cry for you, you should go see your children, poor babies."

Dinky's answer was a Paiute child's song.

Made uneasy by the anger in the words, Dancer told the *naiv*, "Send them away."

But the foreigners would not leave. When the woman refused to reply in English, they spoke through their guide. What was her name? where did she come from? how did she get here?

Dinky's dark eyes darted about as a bird's. She worked her thumb along a strip of grass, flattening it.

The avalanche of words and smiles frightened Dancer. The only Mormons he knew were the ones who used Indians to kill white people. He told the Ute this, but the guide merely shrugged.

The loafer dog, tiring of fighting the camp dogs, flopped in the shade of a hut, a bloody gash on his flank. The white men unloaded their pack horse and spread a red cotton sheet on the ground. They insisted the blind woman sit at the edge of the sheet.

It wasn't until now, watching her led to the sheet, that they realized the woman was blind. That could have come later, they told themselves.

Colored beads appeared on the sheet, followed by little tin

mirrors and metal buttons and beaded jewelry. Speaking through their guide, the white men pressed gifts into the woman's hands. The gifts were presents from the family of the blind woman. Her family wanted her to come home.

The *naiv* nodded, not sure what to do with the information. The children helped themselves to treasures, the older people holding back with indulgent faces. The visitors motioned at Dancer, but the boy shook his head. Finally the *naiv* came forward to gravely select a string of blue glass beads, and now everyone was crowding close. Dancer helped his wife to her feet and tried to lead her away, but the white men prevented it.

Emptied, the red sheet was rolled up and handed to the *naiv*, who called a meeting of the camp's men. The visitors sat quietly through long recitations of why Dancer loved this woman, why the children loved her, why the old people loved her.

From the recitations, although Dancer himself gave no details, the visitors learned the woman had been with the Kaibab band for about a year, that she became blinded while with the Indians.

When the visitor's turn came to speak, they concentrated their efforts on the woman's Paiute husband. What good was a wife that couldn't see? Wouldn't a man want a wife that could see? The white doctors could make it so.

"The spirits leave their tracks on the deep black too," Dancer argued. "She will find her way."

The *naiv* had the last word. Everyone but Dancer should now go to their blankets. The decision as to what to do with the woman rested with the boy. The *naiv* added wood to the fire and sat waiting, hunched under his thin robe. Dancer stared silently into the flames. It had never occurred to him that the white men would come all the way up to the top of the earth after his wife.

He had a fine winter home over a shallow pit. The spaces between the posts were filled with wild rye grass, the posts themselves were held in place with bark and willow boughs. He had two warm blankets fashioned from rabbit skins. In the camp were large caches of wood and pine nuts. His wife wanted for nothing.

But he couldn't bring her soul back. The *puagant's* dried lizard blood and burnt crow feathers hadn't worked, and he worried, particularly when she was sick, as she was occasionally and without warning, that the spirits would take her. Perhaps the white man's magic could make her whole.

"Use the quills," he told the *naiv*, who, stiff with cold, made his way to his hut and returned with a slim leather-wrapped bundle. Dancer selected three quills. The *naiv* fashioned a little tent stuck together at the top with a dab of mud and poked a live coal inside. "If the first quill to fall points to the north, I will send her with the Moronies," Dancer said. No sooner had he spoken than the spirit who lived in the fire made it so.

When Dancer joined his wife under the rabbit blankets, he held her close and murmured endearments until sleep came. Early the next morning, he piled the clothing she had worn from the north near their blankets, and packed her soapweed sandals and sheep-skin skirt in a leather sack. He also packed his sandals, he would go with his wife. All this he explained to her, convinced she understood.

His decision pleased the foreigners immensely. Not to have the blind woman's care was a great relief. Immediately after breakfast they took their leave.

Dinky rode on a travois pulled by the white man's pack horse. Dancer rode the pack horse. It was pleasant seeing the rumpled countryside from the back of a horse, something the boy had never done. But the animal, being young, wanted to go too fast. When Dancer tired of arguing with it, he got off and led it. But then the horse was constantly bumping into him. By far the most enjoyable travel was where his wife walked holding onto his shirt, the travois horse untended.

An occasional park, opening on the sky, gave way to deep grass and sometimes a spring. But most of the day was spent burrowing through forests of towering ponderosa pine, spruce, and fir, intermittently set ablaze with yellowing aspen. Now and again, Dancer called a halt and took his wife off where she could not be seen. His wife was his only concern, that and the horse which pulled her.

And the strange curve of light in the sky that could be seen even at noon on the brightest day and at night shone like a brilliant feather dragging through the stars.

By noon of the third day the party reached the large *tinaja* where the Mormons and their Ute guide had earlier parted company with the larger party of missionaries. After a short rest, the Ute led out to the east. Dancer thought the guide confused. The Moronies lived to the north. But no, the white men explained. They must go to the river, there was a boat at the river.

The ground that in the higher elevations felt spongy underfoot, under the rim of the Kaibab grew hard and dusty. Away to the southeast rose the high walls of the Mystery River. Across the river, up on the long mesas, was where the Moqui lived.

The downward path settled into a wide, shallow trough curving between the Pahreah and Kaibab plateaus. Here the grasses were so deep the running wind caused them to ripple like water. The white men talked excitedly about what fine farm country it was. The Ute told Dancer and laughed to see the Paiute wrinkle his nose and spit, and then the Ute spit.

An afternoon rain drove the party to take shelter under a huge block of sandstone fallen from a cliff. By the time the rain stopped, dusk was coming on and the cliff faces were full of the acrobatics of white-throated swifts and cliff swallows hunting for insects. Dancer loved this trail. The colors on the red cliffs after a rain, the purple mists that filled the clefts and canyons, the water breaking out of the ground.

He killed a large frog crouched above a spring that flowed from a seam in the sandstone and fried the meat for his wife. Contenting himself, as did the others, with jerked deer and hard bread. Afterward he made a little pile of the frog bones and scraps of hard bread for the dog, who would not come near until the camp slept. The men liked having the dog with them, but Dancer was the only one who always made sure there was something left.

When Bishop passed around a little sack of dried berries, Dinky said. "They taste like raisins."

The strange utterance did not surprise Dancer. This happened. But the white men were very pleased.

"Slipped up, didn't you, lady," Mock said with a knowing smirk. "You the one killed Snyder, ain't you."

The Ute's ears perked. It was the first he knew of the woman's having done anything more than just run away.

"Come on, sister, come on, tell us more." Bishop held a pinch of raisins under the woman's nose. But the flash of comprehension, like a lightning bolt, vanished into the darkness from whence it came.

The trail wandered toward the red slopes of the Pahreah, and the grey shoulder of the Kaibab retreated behind a welter of wrinkled foothills. Reaching the stone forest, Dancer described for his wife in painstaking detail the thick stumps and fallen trees that decorated the hillsides and how the ground was all awash in beautifully-colored splinters.

"You'll reach for a stick for the fire before you know it is a stone."

Ninety miles east as a crow flies, the valley below the north rim of Black Mesa contained running water and a good trail. Some twenty miles down this trail into the southwest the patrol reached the first Moqui village. The peaceful-looking *rancherías* boasted the usual scatter of dogs and goats. The fields were dotted with orange pumpkins which the Moqui were busy bundling for winter use. Seeing the horsemen, they ceased their labors and gathered close. Mato-ayuwi rode amongst them as a conquering hero, announcing himself and ordering that the chief be sent for.

Watching the guide, Charlie's instincts caught something. "I wonder if Mato's gonna haul ass on us," he told Alfredo.

"*¿Qué me dijo?*"

"Run away."

"*Lo qué se aprende en la cuna, siempre dura.* He has a Paiute wife. She lives with the Koosharem."

"I wonder where that would be," Charlie said.

A Moqui spokesman saluted the sergeant with "God damn my soul eyes. How de do! How de do!" repeating himself to every man in the patrol. Women and children brought presents of *mezquitama*, and Charlie spread out his own presents. The Moqui tossed the gewgaws high in the air one at a time, loosing a frenzy of laugher and scrambling about. There had been no recent sightings of missionaries.

The village was at the confluence of several drainages, one of which translated from the Moqui as Sour Water Wash. Charlie dug out the map copied for him at Fort Defiance and added the wash, together with a dozen circles indicating the grass huts, to his other legends,

> lam horse, water washe, chock carries, long canyon, heden spring, red redge, bad trail, ratill snack bed, wild schash, deep sand, bunch of cedar, deep ne/sw canyon

From the village a well-traveled trail climbed west,
breaching the rim of the Kaibito Plateau between two peaks and
unraveling in a patch of cedar. Keeping to the high level ground
above Kaibito Creek, Mato-ayuwi led the way straight as a string
into the northwest through a strange land awash in sand dunes
that lent distant rocky outcroppings the queer appearance of
stranded ships. An easy-journeying land.

*Too bad I ain't Injun,* the sergeant told himself, his head
pounding from arguing the question of whether to stay on top
and swing around the west rim or drop down into the canyon
lands. *I need a sign. Like that little quail there, hunkered in
the brush, now what's she trying to tell me? Or that rock,
pointing just so. Or them two turkey vultures hanging up there
motionless. Damn! I need a sign.*

"How far to the river?" he asked Mato-ayuwi at the noon
stop.

"For white eyes?" the guide said with a smile, "two sleeps."

*"Es un grano de anís,"* Alfredo said, and added, "He is joking,
he tells me we are only a day away."

That the Zuni would joke with the sergeant told Alfredo
something else. Although the Zuni was afraid of the mysterious
light in the sky, he was also becoming happy. He no longer
searched about for campfire smoke or cross travel, he seemed to
have made up his mind to stay on the good trail.

"He is going home," Alfredo said, and sergeant agreed.

The tableland was falling under the spell of lengthening
evening shadows, the red-rock country off to the north deepening in color, when the sergeant made up his mind. He could
always search the plateau, but he might not be able to find the
crossing without Mato-ayuwi, not without wasting valuable
time.

On the verge of calling a halt for the night, he heard a faint clink-clink and saw a belled billy goat walking through the sage, followed by a boy and a crooked old man. Seeing the soldiers, the boy wanted to run away, but the crooked old man could not. The old man introduced himself as Tau-gu and the boy as Pickyvit. Entertaining himself with the white man's tobacco, he told that the Moronies were in the village to the east. Seven of them. There was no white woman with them.

"Tell him we ain't going to the village," Charlie ordered Mato-ayuwi. "Tell him he didn't see us."

On learning this last, Tau-gu turned cloudy eyes in Charlie's direction. "We hope the Moronies will go away, so it is well you do not come either." He cupped his eyes with a hand deformed by arthritis and said with a wide grin, "I do not see you, they will not see you. Wait here until dark, and my son will take you across this open ground to a little water. The sheep have spoiled what water is here."

The sun slid down the sky, turning the lofty northward sweeps, together with animals and men, a lurid orange. Dark came, and the old man and his goat were alone beside the small juniper fire.

Dancer's party had long ago stopped for the night. Much to Mock and Bishop's chagrin. The party had reached the Mystery River and was traveling upriver under the late-afternoon shadows of the Vermillion Cliffs when a gathering of stones looking remarkably human blocked the way, stopping the Ute and Dancer in their tracks.

Flung here and there by the hand of a giant, some of the stones were balanced on slender necks as if protruding from bodies beneath the sand, others resembled skulls with eye sockets where desert rats made their nest, still others offered shelter in large cupped hands.

This was the holy earth that in the long shadows belonged to the silent men of the dead land.

As Dancer worked to make his wife comfortable beside the fire, she became very sick, vomiting and holding her head. Her moans continued long after dark, the white men remaining unsympathetic and aloof. But then Dancer decided she would need at least two sleeps to recover.

Mock poured whiskey into a cup and handed it to the boy.

"Drink it," Dancer ordered his wife, repeating what the Ute told him. "It will make you sleep."

The Ute wanted whiskey too, but Bishop told him to wait until they reached the camp on the Pahreah.

Moonlight was a cool white sheet thrown over the canyon lands. Although the moonlight blotted out the stars, it could not blot out the comet passing overhead. Bivouacked in a shallow depression on the north side of the Kaibito Plateau, the patrol made a cold camp. The next morning the soldiers descended into Kaibito Creek and crossed at the point where three steep ravines come together. Gaining the further height of land, they trailed west, downhill toward the desert river.

# TWENTY-TWO

THAT'S THE THING about desert country. Mile after mile, hour after hour, silent, eerily empty. And all the sudden, *KA BOOM!* something happens as if it was always there, bubbling just beneath the surface.

Racing out of a nearer arroyo in a boil of dust the Navajo came face to face with the soldiers. Veering their ponies aside up a nearer slope, they vanished as quickly as they'd come, leaving in their wake three horses dragging picket lines.

The soldiers caught up the horses and continued toward the river. An hour passed and they could hear it. Then, at last, they were in the bottom. A wide lick of muddy water eased its way past the further wall. The riders stopped, unnerved by the enormous depth of the canyon. Alfredo especially, the hungry brown swells touching a chord deep inside him, the Indian before the Spanish yoke.

Directly ahead was a park occupied by a white tent. The men camped in the park watched the soldiers' approach with mixed feelings. God had returned their horses, but in the hands of the American Army. The shortest of the men, a pleasant-faced fellow with blue eyes and graying, curly hair, introduced himself as Brother Roundy.

"We thank you for your trouble, sir. This is not a place we'd care to be afoot in."

"Sergeant Reeves out of Fort Defiance," the sergeant said and gave the order to dismount. "I understand you're here looking for a white woman. Any luck?"

"Not yet. How'd you hear?"

"Man at the Moqui village. You three the only ones here?" Roundy nodded.

"How many you got in the field?"

A second's hesitation. "Two and a scout."

Charlie frowned, hiding his relief that the Mormons were still looking. With luck, they just might save him the trouble of finding the woman. "Let's hope they get in soon, the Navajo are building up for something. We'll stick with you boys a couple of days, rest our horses."

Solemn-faced, the Mormons didn't say anything.

Old cottonwoods, gnarled and spreading, blanketed the little park with shade. Bleached cattle bones and the remnants of old campfires were everywhere. Grass looked to be adequate, along with a sizable amount of driftwood. While Charlie was surveying the situation, Mato-ayuwi approached. The army mount had been stripped of its saddle.

"My way is north," the Zuni spoke in his own language. "We settle this with honor, with this horse as my wages."

The sergeant didn't understand the words and didn't have to. "Always hate to lose a good man," he said, extending his hand. "Don't take any wooden wampum."

Watching the guide ride away, Alfredo could not believe his eyes. Why give the runaway a horse?

"You dropping the lip on poor old Mato?" Charlie asked.

"His work was to take us and lead us back."

"He got us to the crossing, let him go home while he's got a home to go to."

Later, in a quiet aside, the sergeant asked Roundy, "What's the deal on the woman?"

"Stolen by Indians. Some buck wanted a white wife."

Downriver at the mouth of the Pahreah, inside a newly
built cairn standing off by its lonesome, was a letter from Jacob
Hamblin. He wrote that his Paiute guide had become confused
and brought the party down the wrong canyon. To get to the
right canyon, he would have to climb out of the Pahreah and
cross over the top. He would mark his path.

The message filled the Ute with scorn. Chief Naraguts knew
exactly how to get to the crossing. For this reason the chief had
argued against going up on the Kaibab if what the Moronies
wished to do was visit the Moqui. But the missionary called
Hamblin wouldn't listen. Having heard about the sweet grasses
down the long trough off the Kaibab and the pretty park at the
mouth of the Pahreah, he wanted to see for himself.

Now he was blaming Naraguts for having to climb the cliffs.
White men lied all the time.

When Dancer learned of the change in plans, he was aghast
and decided to go back home. No promise was worth risking his
wife's life for.

The Ute hesitated to translate Dancer's words. The white
men wanted this woman, they would not let her go. The boy was
no match for them, but the boy's friends were. The Ute had seen
neither hide nor hair of the Paiute who followed them, but the
wind whispered their nearness.

"The white men will kill you if you stop now," he warned
Dancer. "They want this woman, they will take her no matter
what you do."

The party moved three miles up the Pahreah to where
Hamblin's men had wrestled a line of rocks around to point
toward a sandy incline. Crestfallen, Dancer stared at the wall. To
carry a loaded travois up there couldn't be done, not if his wife
were on that travois. It was too easy to fall and let the travois
fall.

Feeling a sheet of flat rock underfoot, Dinky let go of her
husband's shirt, shaking herself free as might a child. On these
places she liked to walk unaided.

She began to sing, and Dancer chided himself for being a
deer mouse.

The slope steepened abruptly.

Dinky was put on the travois and secured with ropes. Pieces
of goat trail and hollows long ago chipped in the rock led the
way over the perilous ledges. Higher and higher the ledges,
hotter and hotter the day. Dancer covered his wife's face with
the piece of hide she used for a pillow. He wanted to pour water
on her face, but there wasn't enough.

Early afternoon, some two thousand feet above the Pahreah
River, the exhausted men reached the top of the cliff. Here, the
pack horse ran away with what was left of the water, and the
men were reduced to dragging the travois by hand. Over the
crest and down through the rocky arroyos and deep red sand—
the passage of Hamblin's men easy enough to follow in a land
long without rain.

The pack horse was waiting by the small creek called the
Wahweap, packs all in disarray from the brute's fruitless attempts
to dislodge them. Camp that night was comfortable, with the
Wahweap's potable water and good pasture, much better than
the white men had expected to find. Across the creek were little
mesas and peaks of red earth resembling the ruins of a fortress.
Dancer had explored these places with his people and found
broken pottery and a very good spear. But exhausted by the day's
demands, went to sleep without sharing the stories with his wife.

Down by the Colorado River the insects sounded a cadence
unusual for the desert, and the passing water growled agreeably.
The American soldiers played cards and made music and, after
some hesitation, the Mormons joined in. They told stories of the

Navajo driving stolen cattle down through the narrow feeder canyon that opened at the head of the sandbar.

"The crossing's no good without that sandbar," Roundy explained. "High water, forget about it. This is the only crossing in the canyon, anywhere else, you can forget about that too." He told of coming off the top into the wrong canyon and being forced to climb back on top and travel cross-country to find the right one. "Horses had to make out like goats, we wasn't the first ones, the hollows was all chipped out, a long time ago too."

One of the soldiers asked the youngest of the Mormons how many wives he had.

"None yet," the boy admitted defensively. "But I come of good polygamous stock."

Which set everyone to laughing.

The next day the sergeant took two men with him and entered the river, the horses getting little more than their feet wet before reaching the wide, sandy road up the middle. Near the top of the sandbar, around the bend from the camp in the trees, was the narrow feeder canyon shown as *Padre Cr.* on the map. A short ways up the Padre, the sergeant found the weathered steps coming down from the top, and fresh scarring on the rocks.

Returning to the park he posted Alfredo to watch the canyon entrance.

Following the intermittent strands of stones that meandered back and forth along the high edge of the canyon wall cost Dancer's party two nights on top of the plateau. These wanderings told the Ute that Jacob Hamblin no longer trusted Narraguts.

At last, some forty miles from the Pahreah River, the tell-tale stones pointed to step-like grooves leading downward.

Emerging from the canyon entrance the dog splashed through the water, losing the bottom and swimming lazily about. Alfredo got to his feet. When Dancer's party appeared, he slipped into the brush and headed downhill. There was only one Mormon in camp, the others having gone fishing. Alfredo signalled the sergeant, and the American soldiers were in the water before the Mormon realized what was happening. When he did, he took to his heels after the other two.

The sun on the little peaks and rifts sparkled invitingly. A branch draped with rattlesnakes floated by. Passing within yards of the last horse in the line, a huge diamondback whipped itself free and went for the shadow in the water. The soldier waited until sure of his aim and, with the rattler little more than a yard away, pulled the trigger.

Ignoring the riders in the river, Dancer studied the downstream bend of the river. The boat would be down there in the trees. Hopefully it would be a nice, big boat. One with shade for his wife to lie in.

The apron of sand at the canyon entrance was not very wide. With hard faces, Mock and Bishop pulled their horses aside to let the Americans ride through. And then...

"Hey, what are you doing?!"

The sergeant had dismounted and was walking over to the travois.

"She's sick," Bishop said sharply. "Leave her alone and go on about your business."

"Leave her alone," he said again, this time to Dancer. But the Paiute, wanting his wife to walk around, had already loosened the travois ropes and was helping her to her feet.

Dinky screamed and held her head and weaved about in halting steps. Dancer ran to the water and dipped his shirt in. And returning, tried to pat his wife's face with the wet leather.

"Tell the boy I'm putting the woman on my horse," Charlie ordered Alfredo. The horse dealer tried, mixing up Spanish with sign, but Dancer didn't understand and moved to keep himself between his sick wife and the soldiers.

The Ute got into the act. "Let them take your wife across the river," he warned the boy. "She can not stay here."

Dinky was on her knees, beating the ground with her fists.

"Tell me where you hurt," Charlie told her. "So I don't hurt you again."

There was no answer. Gritting his teeth, the sergeant lifted the woman into the saddle and swung up behind her. Dinky fought back weakly, and Charlie eased the horse into the water. Behind him, Dancer was arguing with the Ute. Bishop and Mock were yelling about theft. Now the entire patrol was in the water, leaving Dancer's party reduced to bringing up the tail-end.

The Mormon soldiers were in the park. Roundy wanted the woman taken to his tent, but Charlie ordered her placed on boughs in the American campground.

"We went to a lot of effort to find this woman," Bishop argued shrilly. "This ain't your jurisdiction out here. She goes with us to Utah."

"She goes with me to Fort Defiance," Charlie replied. "I got a doctor there."

Bitter accusations ensued. The woman was a Saint with family in Cedar City, she had to stay with the Saints. Anything else was out-and-out kidnapping. "If we wasn't Saints," Mock accused, getting in the last word, "you'd be leaving us alone!"

Dancer was beside himself. There was no boat tied up in the trees. He tried hard to get someone to address its whereabouts, but the Ute brushed off his questions and no one else could be made to understand.

That night Charlie pulled Alfredo off the hill and put an extra guard on the camp. The next morning, with the Mormons keeping to their own side of the campground, Dinky became sick again. But not so sick as the day before. Her patient husband cleaned her face and clothing with his wet shirt, and afterward she sat quietly, eyes closed.

It was always like this after the headaches. First she got sick to her stomach and vomited. Then, for a very short time, her mind was clear. She knew who she was and that she was lost from her husband and children. The awareness evaporated as quickly as it came, and she settled once more into her surroundings, in much the way a dull-colored moth settles against a tree.

Sensing that his wife was listening to the unfamiliar voices around her, Dancer held her hand and spoke softly, careful to keep the fear out of his assurances.

Nevertheless, the Paiute was very much afraid. There was no boat to take his wife to get her soul, and no way to get her back home.

When he could do so unnoticed, the Ute told Dancer the woman was to go with the blue shirts. Dancer closed his eyes and shook his head, snorting like the buck deer when cornered.

"Do not be afraid," the Ute cautioned. "This thing I know for sure, the Moronies do not mean you well. The blue shirts say they have a doctor, send your wife with them. Do as I tell you if you want your wife to live."

Charlie led the way out of the park, Alfredo behind him leading the travois horse—this time a U.S. Army pack horse. Dancer walked behind the travois, the loafer dog at his heels. Behind Dancer rode the soldiers, rifles at the ready.

Leaving the river's voice, entering a land which he had only looked upon from across the river, Dancer wanted desperately to run away back to Mountain Lying Down. But he kept walking, determined not to go home without his wife.

Alone in the park, the Mormons went about the business

of breaking camp with dark hearts, by now convinced that the woman stolen from them was the same woman the church was offering one thousand dollars for. One thousand dollars! It was hard to lose that kind of money, times were hard.

Mock and Bishop were particularly angry, keeping to themselves, tight-lipped. Left behind on the Kaibab to search for the woman, they'd prayed long and hard for God's help. Now that help was being made mockery of.

"We're lucky the Americans come along in the first place and we got horses to get out of here with," Roundy told them. "Just calm down. She's pretty sick, she might not make it."

"She's to be brought in alive or left for dead," Mock answered. "That's our orders."

"I never heard nothing about killing her," Roundy said, surprised. "Where'd those orders come from?"

"High up, it's secret."

The words drove a pointed stake between the Mormons—the loathing bottled up inside Roundy and the men with him seeping into their faces.

Mock and Bishop were Mountain Meadow Dogs. In Cedar City, Pinto, Parawon, and far up the Corridor, such men were shunned and hated, their families pitied and walked around.

Filled to the top with shame soured to bright, bitter hatred, the Dogs stared back at the lily-livered men, their own faces flushed.

The Ute slipped out of sight into the trees. White men liked to shoot each other too much.

"That massacre was ordained by God!" Mock cried, knowing better than to indict the church's priests in the heinous crime. "If you let that woman go, you're turning your back on Joseph and all the men who died in the faith. You're wicked and filled with the devil!"

In the answering silence, the Dogs loaded their horses and rode out the trail to the east.

"Now, you two go on up on the Kaibito like Jacob ordered," Roundy yelled. "And leave that woman alone!"

When Dancer and the travois left the park, the half-dozen Paiute resting on a ledge across the river kept to their high overlook. Their friend would be easy to find, and it was pleasant there in the shadows. But when two more men rode out, traveling the same trail and hurrying their horses, the curious Paiute worked their way down to the river and crossed out of sight of the trees.

A soft, autumn light filled the sky. Studying the countryside, the sergeant put together what he could see, and what he couldn't. From what all he'd heard about the Fancher massacre, the Indians refused to kill the women and children. They must have taken pity on this woman and hid her away. In the hands of the American authorities, her mind restored, she could do the Mormons a lot of damage. No wonder they wanted her dead.

A steep upthrust drowning in its own shade waited just ahead. Charlie eyed it warily. It wouldn't happen there, the little butte was too isolated. In the distance a rise of ground edged with high slabs of ancient rock formations crossed the trail.

In the shadows of the butte, the sergeant called a halt, rested an hour, and led out. The trail swung toward the broken rock, the sergeant riding hunched over, dozing. Behind him, Alfredo and Dancer rode double on Alfredo's horse. Next, the travois horse, some 20 yards out on a long lead. Further back rode the soldiers.

The marksmen waiting in the rocks were good. Both bullets hit the travois. The sergeant and Alfredo jumped their horses into a run. The soldiers broke formation and took up defensive positions.

A mile out on the open ground, the sergeant drew rein and

gently worked Dinky's hands free of his saddle horn. Dancer and Alfredo eased the woman to the ground. The rock that weighed down the travois was rolled off. The soldiers cantered up, and the patrol resumed its eastward march, headed, though still a long ways out, for the Moqui village at the bottom of Sour Water Wash.

Congratulating themselves, Mock and Bishop made their way down through the warm rocks toward their horses, their guns empty. The waiting Paiute readied their arrows.

# TWENTY-THREE

THAT NIGHT Dinky was sick again. After Dancer cleaned up his wife, Charlie sat on his heels beside the woman and promised, "We're gonna get you to the doc, he'll fix you up." And heard quite clearly the words, "Please God."

Leaning close, he asked "Who are you?"

"Dinky."

"What's your last name?"

"Marchion."

"Where do you live?"

"Up from the school about a mile."

"What's the name of the school?"

"Just the valley school."

"What valley?"

No answer.

"What city do you live near?"

No answer.

"What state?"

"Hmmm." The woman's features were becoming slack, her head lolled to the side.

"Hold on!" Charlie ordered, taking hold of her hands. "Hold tight. Don't let go. Tell me the city."

"I can't, I can't." Now she was talking Indian.

"You live near…" the sergeant prompted. "Where? What city? NAME A CITY! ANY CITY!"

More Indian. Then, "TROYTROYTROYTROY!"

Charlie let go of her hands, aware he was holding them harder than he meant to. It didn't matter. She was asleep or unconscious, he couldn't tell which.

At Fort Defiance the blind woman was examined by Dr. McKee. After the examination, Dancer was told by the fort's interpreter that his wife was to go further away and that Dancer could not go with her. This information caused the Paiute great consternation, and he ran off and hid. But later he was seen in the shadows near where the woman had been taken, and persuaded to spend the night in the Indian house.

Long before dawn he went outside and sat against the wall. He should not have brought his wife to this place. Many times, crossing the desert beyond the river, he asked the foreigners where they were going, but no one would answer. The strange light in the sky had tried to warn him, but he didn't listen. He began to weep, alone as never before. What would happen to his beautiful wife? Who would care for her?

The morning star appeared, the night began to pale.

"I send my wife to your bed," Dancer whispered. "Every morning you will see me watch for her to return. Tell her that. Make her see what you see." A long, graceful vee of geese approached the star. At the precise instant the star hung out ahead of the lead bird, Dancer closed his eyes, holding the picture in his heart.

That morning the Paiute was given a little burro which had strayed into the fort. The burro was packed with food and blankets, and Dinky was led into sunshine to say good-bye. Standing beside her, Dancer looked the very picture of despair.

"Where she goes to live, she will be like a grand lady in a carriage," Alfredo explained in a vain attempt to cheer the boy. He held his nose in the air.

The gestures left Dancer's face blank.

One hand behind his head, the other on his hip, Alfredo sashayed toward a nearby wagon, climbed up in the seat, and shaded himself under a make-believe parasol.

The sergeant grinned, so Dancer grinned too.

"Tell the Indian that his wife can come back when she gets well," Charlie told the interpreter.

"She will come back," Dancer told the interpreter. "Her name is Icamani. The wind will not know her name in a different place."

He walked off, the little burro in tow. Determined to do otherwise, but unable to help himself, he glanced over his shoulder. There she stood, his treasure, so lost and all alone, surrounded by strangers.

"*Alouette, gentille Alouette,*" he sang cautiously, walking back toward her. "*Alouette, Je te plumerai.*"

Surprised, Dinky looked that direction and broke into song. "*Je te plumerai la tête, Je te plumerai la tête.*"

An unstirred silence followed. Then Dancer was walking away, and the thing between the lovers was done.

Charlie spotted the loafer dog in the shade of a wagon. "Quarter says the dog goes with him."

Alfredo cranned his neck, scratching a stubble of beard. "No, *señor*. He is not dumb, he can smell the kitchen."

The loafer dog waited long enough that Alfredo held out his hand, then got up and trotted off in the direction the Indian had taken.

With no work to keep him there, Alfredo left Fort Defiance shortly after this.

"It's a good thing Major Brooks never needed no Navajo translated," Charlie told his friend. "You might of gone down the road sooner."

"Oh, no, *señor*, I'm very good at Navajo. It's Paiute I don't savvy."

"So, say something in Navajo."

Alfredo grinned widely. "It is a very hard language to master, *señor*, even for the Navajo. The next time I see you, the gods willing, I will teach you. I hope that time will not be long."

"Me, too, amigo. And don't forget, get yourself some kids. By the way, doc says the blind woman's four months pregnant."

"That is too bad." Alfredo crossed himself. "*Carretita, carretón, los que se valen al compadre, y a la comadre y se desvalen, se les pare el corazón.* If she does not come back, both will die of a broken heart."

While at Fort Defiance, Dinky lived in the quarters of one of the fort's laundresses, the officers' wives having been removed to Albuquerque. The sergeant spent what free time he could with her, taking her on walks and sitting with her in the shade. "How's my pretty lady?" he would ask.

At first, if Dinky answered at all, it was in Indian. Gradually, she flirted more and more with English, quoting poetry in disjointed fashion and once asking out of the blue, "Do you know the difference between a buffalo and a bison?"

No, the sergeant didn't know.

"You can't wash your hands in a buffalo," she replied archly.

The previous February, during the festivities for Edward Beale in Albuquerque, Charlie had emptied his pockets to buy a three-inch toad carved in jet. The street vendor said it was the work of the ancient ones and would bring good luck. The next morning, sizing up the warty little talisman with its bulging turquoise eyes, the sergeant wished real hard he'd kept his money in his pocket. It was the work of grifters is what it was.

Now, on a whim, he dug the toad out of his pack and gave it to the blind woman. She turned the stone over and over and rubbed it against her cheek. He never afterward saw her without it. Even asleep, as she was much of the time, dropping off unexpectedly and settling into herself like a sack of meal, she held onto the little toad.

She did not again recall anything of importance. The doctor thought the laudanum, which kept her from having seizures, also kept her from remembering. The sergeant was sorry. He'd like to have asked about that name "Marchion," if she ever heard of a fellow called Jed Marchion.

TWENTY-FOUR

THE FLAT WALKWAY STONES glistened in the cold December rain. Ignoring the road box, the postman unfolded his umbrella and made his way to the front porch.

"It's from Washington," he told the woman who answered the door. "The War Department. Could be it's your sister-in-law."

Rain patterned the paperboard with dark streaks. Numb with apprehension Katherine stared at the packet. Beneath the large black government seal were the words "Marshun, in care of the Postmaster at Troy, New York State." At the bottom of the packet was scrawled

*In haste!*

The ink was blurring. She signed the receipt and shut the door. "Walker, Walker!" Her hands were shaking so that Walker, hurrying out of the kitchen, had to undo the knotted strings.

> To anyone by the name of Marshun in the area of Troy, New York.
>
> A blind white woman taken from the Indians has been brought to the Post at Albuquerque. She has mentioned the words troy and marshun. If this information is of interest to you, please contact Major James Longstreet, the Post at Albuquerque, New Mexico Territory, United States of America.

The letter had been forwarded from Colonel William W. Loring, Commander, New Mexico Department.

"She's alive!" Katherine cried, breaking into tears.

"If it's her."

"Who else would it be?"

"The woman's blind."

"Why would that matter?" Her voice rose. "You don't think it's her?"

"Maybe she just knows Dinky."

"That's good enough for me, Walker." She drifted away, savoring the sweetness. Jed was on his way home with Dinky's children, and now she would be going after Dinky. She recalled the jump rope at school, how she would jerk it to get Jed's attention, and he would jerk back, red-faced. But when someone started jumping, how carefully they made the rope swing, never hurrying the cadence, never positioning the rope too low or too high. That's what they were doing now, holding both ends of the jumping rope, bringing home both Dinky and Dinky's children.

The Marchions left their farm at the mouth of the Mohawk on Thursday, December 16, traveling downriver on the train through a storm, the passengers warming little holes in the window frost to watch the countryside, the great trees bowed low, the shrubbery along the river like risen loaves of snow. The gloomy weather added greatly to Walker's distress at being so far from his children and the farm at Christmastime.

"You never want to leave anytime," Katherine scolded. "Just buck up, there'll be more Christmases."

A week later, at the old Marchion farm on the Batten Kill.

Expecting to find Dinky's children ravaged by grief and mistreatment, family and friends gathered near as soon as they heard of Jed's return. Their own children cautioned not to talk of the aborted California journey, all manner of sweets prepared.

The welcoming went on for several days, people arriving with long faces and leaving with best wishes for what they couldn't very well spell out—not with Lymund and the twins so oblivious to the dangers their parents faced.

Anne and Emily shared stories and arguments that ran the gambit from having their very own horse to seeing Jeremy in Great Salt Lake City.

*GREAT!* Salt Lake City, they liked to say, and *boring.* They'd walked all the way across the prairies in one direction (they couldn't ride the horse, and it died anyway) and rode all the way back the other direction in a wagon, which was very boring. And more boring and more boring. They liked dragging it out. Borrrrrring.

They lived on a hog farm, and it smelled…a lot…so that was really boring. Their mother was still in Utah Territory…no! Mexico…not Mexico! *New* Mexico. Uncle Walker had gone to get her, and they would start all over for California again. Over the boring desert. There was nothing to see. That would be the worst. Maybe there would be a train. The trains were alright, yes—a sudden burst of enthusiasm—trains were definitely alright.

Lymund greeted the curiosity seekers with his brow furrowed, as if suspecting their motives. He never mentioned his father at all, and his mother only in passing. He was into hogs, the names of hogs, the troubles hogs got into. Hogs and playing kick-the-can with the Ballards.

Christina put Yam up in Walker's old room and went out of her way to make the savage feel at home. What choice did she have? According to Jed, this was the man who found the children.

Julia Cordelia Marchion was delivered of a healthy baby boy
January 10, 1859. In Maine for his father's funeral, Sigvald
Proulx, Julia's cousin, waited downstairs throughout the ordeal
and afterward visited briefly with the mother. Learning that
the infant was to be named John Paul filled Sigvald with sweet
elation. Paul was Sigvald's middle name. With tears in his eyes,
he accepted the honor of being the baby's godfather.

Delayed by heavy snows Jed reached Houlton ten days later.

"I've got someone who wants to meet you," Julia told him,
leading the way to the bedroom.

And there was Paul.

Jed whooped and scooped up the little boy. "I didn't even
know you was pregnant!"

"I didn't know it either. Would you have stayed if you'd
known?"

"Damn right I would have."

She didn't believe him, but it didn't matter. All that mattered
was having him back safe and sound.

That Saturday Julia and Bettina hosted a combination
welcome-home and coming-out party for both father and son.
The ceiling was an upside-down forest of cardboard silhouettes.
Pilgrims and turkeys left over from Thanksgiving joined toma-
hawks, Daniel Boone caps, toy drums, and ponies. Sitting inside
a matchstick fence in the center of the table were two, large
layer cakes, one decorated with the words, "Our Hero Jed!" the
other with "The Hope of the Future Paul."

The clutter added considerably to Dr. Clare's enjoyment of
the afternoon. "Bettina never disappoints," he told Jed, rolling
his eyes.

With his toast, Jed thanked all who came and added, "If

anyone's got any notions about going out West, talk to me first."
His words bought a genial round of laughter.

Julia graciously called on her cousin to say a few words about
the news from the Capitol, and Sigvald graciously obliged. Such
charming, well-bred people. That came down from the Putnam
line, their mothers were sisters.

"Sigvald is an aide to Congressman Fuller in Washington,"
Julia said warmly. "Our home-town boy made good."

Wavy ash-blonde hair, deep-set Norman blue eyes, the stance
of a Viking, the face of a hero. The audience clapped, the young
girls swooned. And wouldn't every mother in the room love to
have such a son-in-law, talented yet modest, well-mannered,
robustly healthy and bright.

Sigvald's brilliant smile faded. The drumroll of Southern
States threatening to secede from the Union was growing louder.
Southern sympathizers were threatening to tar and feather Sam
Houston, Governor of Texas, for calling the notion of secession
"hogwash." A Confederate States of America was sure to be
organized if Abraham Lincoln were elected, one could already
hear the boom of the guns.

In the warm room the chocolate letters on the cakes oozed
into the white frosting. Bettina shored up what she could with a
toothpick.

Paul's loud squall put an end to the speech.

## TWENTY-FIVE

FEBRUARY 1859. Albuquerque. Miles and miles of absolute nothing, and then this! My, my, my. Adobe buildings tinted in soft washes of peach, huge terra cotta tubs bursting with greenery, a sea of tiny courtyards and gardens.

At the Post the Marchions learned that the white woman brought from Fort Defiance had been taken to Los Pinos near Peralta. She was staying in the home of Dr. Henry Connelly and his wife, Dolores Perea. Dr. Connelly was not a physician, but a wealthy American merchant and member of the Legislative Council. This information pleased the Marchions, indicating as it did that Dinky was healthy despite her loss of memory.

The pretentious Connelly hacienda sprawled in a grove of immense cottonwood trees. Wind-bells large and small hung everywhere. In the center of the courtyard a water fountain made its own pretty melodies. Katherine was enchanted, she absolutely loved traveling about seeing new things.

The hacienda's large front room was as primitive as the outside surroundings were enchanting. The dirt floor was covered with a kind of rough material that looked to have been glued down. Bleached muslin tacked to the overhead beams served for a ceiling. Faded strips of figured calico made a peculiar kind of wainscoting for the whitewashed walls. The furniture resembled the poor offerings of farm sales—a handful of wooden chairs, a horsehair sofa, a bureau and an unpainted pine table.

The room reeked of garlic and roasted peppers. Katherine asked Walker if the smell made him hungry, but it didn't.

A short figure approached down a dim hall. Giddy with anticipation, Katherine hugged herself.

The woman who walked into the light would have walked on through the room had not Dolores Perea stopped her. Her face was blotchy, as if an old sunburn were giving way. Her clothing was bright and clean, her feet were bare. A long braid of dark hair hung down her back.

"Dinky?" Walker asked uncertainly.

The woman's face was blank, her eyes hooded.

"That's not Dinky," Katherine said sharply, unaware she'd spoken aloud.

Walker was on his feet, putting his arm across the woman's shoulders. "Dinky, can you hear me? it's Walker. Don't worry, everything's fine." He nuzzled the rough cheek. "Katherine's here too, we've come to take you home."

The only sound was that of the jubilant fountain in the courtyard.

The drive back to Albuquerque was a portent of things to come. Dinky sat quietly for awhile and abruptly began digging frantically through the canvas bag Dolores Perea had placed on her lap. Finding the little stone toad, she abandoned the search, and Katherine repacked the clothing and toiletries.

The American officer who escorted the Marchions to Los Pinos and returned them to their rooms in the Colony Hotel asked that the officials at the Point be notified at once if Mrs. Miller's health improved. "We'd like to know how she came to be with the Paiute."

"By all means," Walker said briskly. "I expect you'll be hearing from us soon."

Most of the time Katherine found her husband to be very dull. It was impossible to engage him in a conversation having to do with the temperance issue or the ramifications of secession. Farm business was all he cared about, most recently the possibilities of using steam to maximize the output of the sweep in grain threshing.

"By the seventies the horse will be seriously challenged." That was Walker's idea of a ringing manifesto.

But still, there were times she *so* appreciated him. Like now, bracing up her world with small talk, as if his own heart weren't breaking in two. Dinky was twenty-five years old and looked older than his mother.

The long journey home to New York State was difficult in the extreme, especially for Walker, who, while a compact, muscular man, nonetheless suffered terribly from the strain put on his crippled arm. Dinky weighed what he guessed to be two hundred pounds and moved with a halting, old woman's gait. Guiding her up and down the stairs of the various conveyances was all he and Katherine could do. Fortunately, there was usually someone nearby to lend a hand.

Unfortunately, once seated, the disoriented woman was liable to stand at any time. Katherine thought this due to leg cramps, but there was no way of knowing for sure. Dinky's speech, although occasionally perfectly clear, was never in context and more often than not resembled that of a rooting hog. Needing to relieve herself, she uttered an incoherent cry the meaning of which her fellow travelers learned only after several unfortunate accidents.

Katherine cut back the twice-daily dosing of laudanum prescribed by the Post Surgeon in Albuquerque, believing it to muddle Dinky's thinking.

At Fort Osage Dinky was seized with a terrible headache unlike anything the Marchions had ever witnessed, and the journey was delayed a day. Forced to spend the night in the abandoned fort, the Marchions paid a pretty penny to local squatters to sleep under hide blankets and eat boiled rattlesnake meat for supper and breakfast.

Katherine increased the laudanum.

The only thing that made the misery bearable was its consistency, there were no disappointments because there were no gains. Problems solved simply made room for others. The time, for instance, Dinky dropped her little black toad on the floor of the stage. Nothing would do but that the passengers get up and search for it, cracking their heads and mashing each other's toes. Katherine tied a ribbon around the toad's neck and made a second loop for Dinky's neck. But Dinky didn't like the ribbon.

Oh well, she didn't drop it that often.

That she resembled a peacock in her loose, brilliantly colored Mexican clothing added unpleasantly to the attention the party drew. At the edge of the States in Independence Katherine was able to purchase two civilized grey dresses with suitably boned bodices and short flaring sleeves. Another, much larger gain was made in St. Louis when the the railcars were finally reached.

In New York, Dinky lived for a short time on Walker's farm before being moved downriver to Troy. In a small white cottage near the east bank of the Hudson River in the northern section of the city, she lived quietly with her children, a day caretaker, and two nieces who were enrolled at the Troy Female Seminary.

The twins saw their mother's condition as a challenge and spent hours hatching plans to engage her in various pursuits. Lymund, on the other hand, seemed content with her silences. Drawing close, he would listen intently, as if hearing something no one else could hear, before running back to his playmates.

Such a sad situation.

Doctors came regularly to the house, sometimes whole

classes of nurses and doctors to sit in a circle and discuss various diagnoses and treatments. That their patient suffered from compression of the brain was the only thing they agreed on.

One day, while engaged in a cheery one-sided conversation with her sister-in-law, Katherine's gaze happened to fall on the kitchen windowsill—on the bottles—all sorts of bottles short and tall. Imperial drops, dyspeptic cordials, liver pills, cathartic syrup, headache drops, sulfate of quinine tablets, laudanum.

Jumping up, she swept the useless medicine into her apron and emptied the apron in the trash. And taking a second thought, returned the laudanum to the window sill.

In April Dinky gave birth to a healthy boy named Stephen Abraham Miller by the twins in honor of the presidential campaign being studied in school. Dinky was a gentle mother, if careless in opening her gown to nurse, and the baby thrived.

The caretaker, her hands full with the baby's arrival, began administering the prescribed laudanum to herself. Its absence had no obvious effect on Dinky.

That fall Katherine and Walker were in Troy on business when they passed an Indian woman peddling fish.

"Maybe we should ask her who she uses for a doctor," Katherine said.

Walker threw his arms wide in disbelief. "Absolutely not! use your head!" Like his mother, he hated Indians for the time his father had spent with them.

"Your father believed in Indian cures."

"He didn't have any choice, there weren't any doctors around."

"Don't be silly, there were always doctors around."

Katherine paused in front of the cart. The woman pulled the paper cover off the day's catch. Walker shoved his hands in his pockets and studied the skyline.

"I want to hire a doctor," Katherine explained slowly and rather loudly. "An Indian doctor, to see my sister-in-law. "

The fish peddler recovered her wares. Katherine started to explain again what she wanted.

"Let's go," Walker snapped.

But then the peddler asked, "Where?"

"In the white house across the river from the lumber mill," Katherine explained painstakingly. "The mill upriver on the north end of town."

"He will come tomorrow."

"Tomorrow," Katherine repeated.

Walker was furious, Katherine had never seen him so angry. Still, she stuck to her guns, convinced she was onto something. Dinky's doctors had determined that their patient—because she did not walk *into* things, although she might *bump* into them if below eye-level—was able to discern light and dark. Didn't it follow then, that in some fashion or other her mind was working?

Jean Paul used Indian medicine when Christina was in labor with Jed, so the story went, and kicked out the settlement doctor. If the Indians saved his wife and his son, maybe they could save his daughter.

Walker returned to the farm, Katherine stayed the night in Troy, sharing a bed with one of the nieces. It helped that she did this occasionally. The twins were like rat terriers, the slightest deviation could raise their suspicions. Fortunately, the next morning everyone was off to school by the time the caretaker showed up and was herself promptly sent back home with Stephen.

Midmorning the fish peddler was at the door accompanied by a very old man bent over with age and reeking of rancid fish. Using the kitchen stove for an altar, the shaman built a tiny fire on top of the stove lids and fed the flames with burned feathers and little chunks of material that looked to Katherine to be dried dog poop.

Chanting unintelligibly the shaman blew smoke in the blind woman's face, periodically lifting first one eyebrow then the other to study the pupil, and waved a lighted stick wildly about (worrying Katherine that it would catch the curtains afire). Tiring, he plopped himself down on a kitchen chair.

The first time he fell into the chair, Katherine thought the visit over. Countless plops later, it was. Without warning the shaman upended what was left in his bag on the kitchen table and walked outside and down the street.

"A very bad thing happened," the fish peddler explained, making a little pile of the bag's contents. "The spirit inside is hiding. Burn one piece every night and blow the smoke in the woman's face so she can smell it."

*That won't be hard,* Katherine told herself wryly. *You can smell it clear out to the street.*

Neither the smoke nor the smell seemed to bother Dinky, who sat quietly throughout the treatment, almost as if a spectator. Arriving home from school and learning what was expected of them, the twins were delighted. Could they start that very night?

"Oh, definitely," Katherine replied, and having written out the instructions in detail for the nieces, who were sure to object, beat a hasty retreat, laughing all the while.

It took a week for the medicine, which cost ten dollars, in addition to the ten dollars charged for the ceremony itself, to all go up in smoke.

And Dinky saw.

Christina called it a miracle. Katherine, unwilling to call it a miracle, had a hard time believing a pile of old, cold turds had anything to do with it either.

An intern at the hospital ventured that Dinky's eyesight had been returning for some time, but not her comprehension. "The primitive ritual may have cleared her thinking, reminding her of her captivity and triggering a natural inquisitiveness that in turn led to heightened awareness."

No one knew, nor knowing would have cared, that the mosquito which bit Dinky above her eye the morning the miracle occurred, raising quite a lump, had been dispatched by Lymund with a sharp blow.

Along with her vision, Dinky's mental acumen also improved.

Shortly after regaining her eyesight, Dinky was sitting in the front yard—Lymund whistling here and there as he played— when a group of mill workers accompanied by fife and drum came down the street. The marchers were headed for the Navy schooner *Enterprise*.

Lymund whistled along as best he could. And Dinky broke into song.

> *Brother, will you meet me by...Canaan's happy shore? Brother,*
> *will you meet me by...Canaan's happy shore? Brother, will you*
> *meet me by...Canaan's happy shore?*
> *To watch the Jordan roll.*

"You got your whistle from your father," Dinky said and hoisted her son into her lap. "He whistles all the time, you're named after him."

Lymund wriggled free and strolled off after the fife and drum.

That June the Millers moved home to the old Marchion farm to live with Christina. Walker had his brother-in-law declared officially dead and applied for the widow's stipend. This stipend, along with pasture rent received from adjacent neighbors, enabled the household to get by. Dinky took walks and planted a big garden and came gradually to look the very picture of good health. She remembered clearly growing up on the farm, bringing up old stories that warmed Christina's heart.

She even agreed, in the face of her family's insistence, that she remembered them. Still, sorting through the words, Christina had to admit that her daughter's memories did not go past childhood. Her poor broken-winged chickadee saw the elephant and something terrible happened.

August at Walker's place on the Mohawk.

Everyone was there for Walker's birthday party, and now they'd all gone home and the house was full of flies. Katherine was standing at the screen door in the half-light of dusk letting the flies out of the darkening house when a canned dog went yowling down the lane.

*Dinky reminds me of that dog,* she told herself. *We just can't hear her, that's all.*

Surprised by the thought, Katherine busied herself with supper with unaccustomed vigor.

"Dinky's not well."

Walker finished washing up. He took the little metal comb from its place on the shelf, parted his hair, and sat down to pork chops and potatoes fried with scallions.

"Why all the fancy food?" he asked.

"We need to talk about Dinky. She's not getting better, I can feel it."

"Yes, she is," Walker bridled. He hated to talk about Dinky. Every time they got together, he had to introduce himself all over again.

Katherine helped herself to more potatoes. Potatoes were pretty good this way, all lathered up with onions and cheese, but such a lot of work.

"I know it's not easy for you, but I thought if we could talk about it, that we might hit on something."

"I told you, she's getting better."

Katherine sighed. "I hope so. Maybe it's all this wind, maybe that's what's bothering her. It's been blowing so hard, like it did on the prairie."

She was fond of drawing such comparisons. It was as if some primitive chord were still resounding from her journey to the Southwest.

"Nobody feels good all the time." Walker pitched a bone at the dog and licked his fingers. "Maybe she's beginning to remember unpleasant things, like where Stephen Abraham came from."

# T W E N T Y - S I X

*Deaer Sera, we are campt outside farfax headed for richmin
and have the rebs on the run we are folowd by larg camps of
prolitishons and well wishers a lot of the boys are short timers
and will leveve seen but we will stil be in good numberrs most
are note uset to travelling on foot and complane a good deel
lots of fress water and fruit and everything ells most of it stolld
we are close to the reb line tonite and will give theme a good
thrashing if they stop i wood be glad to have you with me to nite
i wood be glad to hear from you but the mail can not catche us.*

SERGEANT CHARLES REEVES was commissioned from the
ranks and breveted a first lieutenant shortly before
the brief and deadly fight at Blackburn's Ford, July 18,
1861. This engagement at the downstream crossing of Bull Run
between Union and Confederate troops would become known as
the first Battle of Bull Run.

In Magdalena, trailing horses through the settlement, Alfredo
spied a soft-eyed *palomita* in a row of school girls standing at a
pump. Roping a gentle yellow horse, the horse trader waited for
the girl to get her drink and led the animal over to her.
"Would you hold my *caballo?*" he asked, offering the rope.
She was very pretty, the eyes of a saint. Her long dark hair

was pulled over her shoulder and caught with a string before falling to her waist. A red paper rose was tucked under the string. She wore a pink blouse and a blue-checkered skirt and her feet were bare.

"Now, what would I want to hold your *caballo* for?" she asked. "Tie it to the fence there." Nevertheless, she took the rope.

"It is very gentle."

"That's none of my concern. How long am I to hold it?"

"I'll be back in two days." He rode away laughing over his shoulder.

"*¡Qué batalla!*" The girl dropped the rope in the dirt and puffed up indignantly, hands on her hips.

That Alfredo Luna happened to be in Magdalena had to do with the decision to move his horse operations south out of Las Vegas toward Fort Bowie in the Chiricahua Mountains. Out here, he could better supply the American soldiers protecting travel along the Tucson-Mesilla road.

Skittering with the tumbleweeds through the dusty New Mexico *rancherías*, avoiding the scrubby Indian stock and buying only suitable crossbreds, he traveled as far as Socorro before turning back west to collect what he had found. On the day he passed through Magdalena he had an older yellow horse purchased to accommodate his friend in Socorro. The horse had little value otherwise. Until now.

After meeting the girl, he returned to Socorro.

"*¡Amigo!*" the friend shouted to see him come. What happened to my *caballo?*"

"I went to Magdalena," Alfredo said. "And left it there with a *muchacha*. I need a new shirt from the *sastre*, then I am going back.

School let out, and here came the girl. "You like the *caballo?*" Alfredo asked her.

*Sí*, she liked it. A lot. She rode it, she fed it apples. Alfredo smiled at her, she smiled back. The yellow horse was in the pen under the trees. Alfredo and the girl walked that direction.

When she graduated, she would move to Santa Fe where her uncle, the stonemason, was working on the new cathedral of St. Francis. She would meet Bishop Lamy and then enter the convent of the Sisters of Charity. It was all arranged. She hoped to be called María Francesca.

Alfredo, who said his prayers regularly and went to church when he could, knew differently. His bright blue shirt had small silver conchos for buttons. He brushed a speck off the sleeve.

"You would ride out with me on the High Plains of San Austin?" he asked, his eyes warm.

Yes, she might. Her name was Theresa.

In Great Salt Lake City that October, in the Harris mansion on State Street.

"I do.

"Then I hereby pronounce you man and wife. You may now kiss the bride."

The widow Harris lifted her veil and closed her eyes and leaned forward.

Jack Straw, forty-one years old, in the city but a few weeks, dutifully pecked the proffered cheek and breathed a deep prayer of thankfulness. To live where people were thriving and making it after the dangerous crossings of water and sand, to marry a fine, strapping girl with her own roof, filled him with worthy resolve.

Phoebe had found herself a husband.

It happened when Ellen advertised an upstairs sleeping room for ten dollars a month. A small, disheveled man inquired about the room, and Ellen sent the fellow packing. His clothes were dirty, he stank, and he appeared simple-minded. If she had to suffer strangers in George's old room, they were going to be clean.

Later that same day she was showing the room to a young couple from England when Phoebe planted herself in the doorway.

"The room's already rented."

"No, it's not, Phoebe," Ellen said.

"Yes, it is," Phoebe stepped aside, "to Mr. Straw here."

Poor Mr. Straw. His gapemouthed stare only served to strengthen Ellen's resolve to have nothing to do with him.

"What in the world are you thinking of?" she asked, drawing Phoebe down the hall out of earshot.

"If anybody's gonna find me a husband," Phoebe replied firmly, "it's gonna be me."

"A husband!! good lord! Phoebe, this man…"

"…is just who I want."

"You can't be serious!"

Phoebe bristled up like a porcupine. Jack Straw had approached her as she came home from Hooper's clothing store and asked if she knew of any rooms for rent. She thought him rather sweet. Walking along together, visiting, there were a lot of things about him she thought rather sweet.

"He's my pick."

"Phoebe, listen…"

"…Mr. G.'s friends can explain how things work here and get him all lined up."

"Get him all cleaned up, you mean. Listen to me! We don't know anything about this man."

"It ain't for you to say who I marry, you ain't sleeping with him."

"You don't have to settle for bull's wool, you can…"

But the determined bride-to-be was already marching back to her prize.

Jack's most important assignment, as described by his patriarch, was to report any unseemly or unsanctioned actions on the part of the sisters in his household to the ward clerk. Accordingly, shortly after abandoning his small upstairs rental for the large room at the end of the hall, he asked Sister Ellen what "unseemly" and "unsanctioned" meant, thereby saving himself the embarrassment of asking the holy Mormon of the Melchizedek priesthood himself.

"Phoebe is to paint every day," Ellen explained. "But you are never to mention it, less you be looked upon as a braggart."

"Oh, I would never do that," Jack promised earnestly. And with a humility both genuine and tender, confided only in his loverly wife his admiration for her loverly paintings.

In granting permission for the marriage, Brigham had fallen into a trap laid by Tom Stenhouse. The same trap that caught Jack Straw.

Visiting with the President on another matter, relaxing, Tom engaged in a bit of gossip having to do with a newly landed Saint from northern Wales.

"Apparently a mean-spirited fellow, kind of dull-witted. He's rented a room in the Harris home, and Fanny tells me the sisters are having a fit. He doesn't work and is there at the table for every meal wanting to talk scripture."

"The Harris sisters find this objectionable?"

"Well, George's wives were never the most pious of women."

"Perhaps God is trying to tell them something."

"Fanny thinks they're afraid of him, that he's stealing from them."

"Hmmm." Brigham smiled, remembering his promise to find

the widow Phoebe a husband. "I should meet with him, in the meantime I'll pray on it."

The big day came. Ellen thought Jack should borrow a Sunday suit for the meeting, but Tom advised against it. "Clean, but ragged, that's our boy."

Jack was all that and more. He was scared to death and very unhappy. Despite assurances to the contrary, he knew that to meet the king of the city was an honor he did not deserve, something very bad was going to happen. Afraid to go, he was even more afraid not to go.

At the very last minute, as the Stenhouse carriage was passing in front of Brigham's mansion, Tom wondered aloud if the Prophet might think Jack wished to marry Sister Phoebe.

"But I don't, sir! no such thing! I just want a room."

"Would you ever want to?"

"Oh, no, a woman with property would never look at the likes of me."

"Even a woman with property needs friendship."

Jack scarcely heard the introductions. Directed toward a chair he sat gazing in rapt wonder at the heavy, dark furniture, the stacking of worn ledgers, the massive, ornately decorated safe, the saintly pictures on the wall. At anything but the great man himself.

"Our good Brother Straw here wishes to marry the widow Phoebe Harris," Tom explained.

Jack's jaw dropped wider.

Brigham huffed and puffed. Did Brother Straw have a job?

Tom looked at Jack encouragingly, and realizing that Jack was completely stuck, answered, "Yes, he's just taken work on the new theatre at the corner of State and First South."

"And has he a cow?"

"Sister Harris has a cow."

"He can't speak for himself?" Brigham sounded amused.

"Apparently not."

"Hmm. Do you know the Lord, Brother Straw? Will you love him and serve him for as long as you live? And see to it that your wife does the same? and all those who live in your household?"

Catching Jack's eye, Tom nodded.

Totally befuddled, Jack nodded.

Brigham grinned against his hand. "I can't imagine why Sister Phoebe wouldn't agree."

"I do love the Lord," Jack said. "I do do that."

"Sister Ellen is also to be under your care, you understand." Brigham paused, his face grew stern. "But you are in no way to think of Sister Ellen as your wife."

This admonishment so horrified Jack that he was finally able to find the right words. "I don't want a wife."

"Brother Straw knows that he can only support one wife," Tom said, jumping in, "and that Sister Phoebe is to be that wife."

Later, describing the meeting to Ellen, Tom laughed so hard his stomach hurt.

Happily for all concerned, Jack Straw was not so much dull as shy, and loyal as a dog.

It was reassuring having him in the house, particularly with the succession of strangers that came and went in the barn and the upstairs sleeping rooms, Ellen having moved downstairs into a pantry. Taking his place of an evening at the head of the dining table, Jack reviewed the day's business and mediated his family's disagreements. They manipulated him shamelessly, and divining this, he would scold them, and they would laugh, and he would laugh.

The credits Jack earned at the Tithing House with his labor on the theatre kept the wolf at a comfortable distance, and his gratitude for being clasped to the bosom of such a fine family was returned full measure.

"Remember to look sad if you see Brigham," Ellen regularly reminded the good brother on his way out the door. "Be ever suspicious of pleasure."

Forewarned, the little Welshman, while at his labors on the Great Salt Lake Theatre, made sure to keep his face dark and brooding. Although in his heart he had never been happier.

Saturday afternoons Jack borrowed his sheepskin portmanteau from the church's storage room, where items hocked to secure passage for the migration were kept behind a padlocked door. Inside the portmanteau was Grandfather Straw's violin. Sitting in the kitchen of his new home Jack would wrap his arms about the instrument and saw madly away, eyes closed, tears streaming down his cheeks.

Phoebe thought the church took too much of Mr. Straw's time, but wouldn't change her lot with a king's queen. That's what she told Ellen, who answered,

"You *are* a king's queen, Phoebe."

# TWENTY-SEVEN

"You've got to get out more," Fanny Stenhouse warned Ellen. "Get involved in the community."

"I loathe and despise meetings, nothing's ever decided, it's just busywork."

"Brigham likes busy women. You don't want him asking Jack what it is you do all day. Lord knows what Jack would say. It doesn't have to be meetings, just don't offer your services as a seamstress. I worked up thirty-three bonnets for Amelia, and Brigham had Tom deduct the cost from our tithing. I never saw a penny."

Considering the possibilities, knowing Fanny was right, Ellen decided to throw in with Eliza Snow. Sister Snow was Brigham's most socially prominent wife. As High Priestess of the women's section in the Endowment House, she was busy reviving the old Female Relief Society of Nauvoo.

Ellen proved a good soldier—three times a week attending afternoon tea out and once a month hosting her own afternoon tea using her best patterned china and managing to lose herself in the chitter and the chatter.

That spring, shopping in Brown's Mercantile, Ellen glanced up to find Verity James staring at her through the window.

"Verity!" she cried, startled.

But Verity was gone, hurrying off down the boardwalk and dodging into a lumber yard.

Ellen found her hiding in a upright stacking of shovels, cringing like a child about to get a haying. "What's wrong, why are you running from me? I am so glad to see you, I was afraid to write."

"Leave me alone! we don't owe you nothing."

Ellen's eyes widened. "You saw Dinky! she gave you the note. What happened to her?"

"The Indians killed her."

"Oh, dear, I'm so sorry. Jed was here with her chil…"

Without warning Verity swung a shovel at her tormentor, striking a glancing blow on Ellen's shoulder and fleeing the store with her ghosts.

The neighbor across the street from the Harris mansion, a palsied greybeard, gave his wife a list of names to consider in enlarging the household. Two of the names were those of the Johnson twins, Nancy's friends.

Ellen was horrified, and there was no one to turn to. Extra wives, the young girls in particular, were symbols of money and power. That was life in the Valley.

"What would you think about me leaving?" she asked Jeremy.

"The city?"

"The Valley. I've got to get Nancy out of here before the old men start following her around."

"That's not going to happen for a long time."

"She's already eleven. The Johnson girls are only thirteen."

"Yeah, but they're…whew." His hands carved the air.

"They're still little girls."

"I can take care of Nancy."

"No, you can't, Jeremy. Sooner or later you'll be sent on a mission. Make a nuisance of yourself, and it'll be sooner."

"She's gonna squall like a scalded hog if you make her leave."

"That's because she doesn't yet understand the problem. But

you'd be alright with us leaving? you wouldn't be going, you'd stay here with Phoebe and Jack."

"Where will you go?"

"Oh, probably San Francisco. Uergin's there, he'll help us."

"When?"

"Not this year, it'll take a while to get my ducks in a row."

"I thought you was getting to like it here, you got lots of friends."

"Friends?" Ellen shrugged. "Fanny's the only friend I have outside my family. Women don't trust me, I'm not married, and they can't understand why. They're afraid I'll pick their husband, or their husband will pick me. They spend most of their time complaining about how difficult the other wives are to live with, so I won't get too interested.

"Did you know? of course not, how could you, the whole purpose of Sister Snow's society is to *prevent female extravagance!*" Her tone became a whiney monotone. "'The human form and the human face are to be adorned, but only with the workmanship of Saints.'"

She made a slurring sound. "It's not a relief society, it's a school for slaves, so the husbands can give more to the building up of the Kingdom. We instruct ward teachers on how to make hair ribbons out of old petticoats, so women won't buy new hair ribbons. And how to make dresses so as not to use one inch more material than necessary, the President does not approve of long, flowing skirts and full sleeves, except on his latest love.

"And at every meeting, every single meeting, as soon as the business is done, Sister Eliza entertains us WITH HER POETRY! 'Arise my infant muse, awake my lyre…' Agghhh!!"

Jeremy laughed. His mother was funny when she got rolling. "What do you care? we have everything we want."

This was true. Things forbidden under the new moral laws were easily purchased at the back doors of the Gentile

merchants after dark. They called it "greasing the log" after
Abraham Lincoln's likening the Mormon problem to an old, wet
log on the forest floor.

Ellen studied her son speculatively. Jeremy hadn't mentioned
any concern for her safety, he and his friends must have already
figured out what she suspected—Brigham's iron-fisted rule was
weakening, the cruel Reformation was receding, leaving behind
a thick residue of guilt. The Twelve, if gossip heard at the society
meetings was to be believed, were bitterly divided over what
to do with the President—some calling for his removal, others
fearing attention from federal officers investigating the meadows
massacre.

"Do you realize, Jeremy, if it wasn't for women, this whole
damn church would fall apart?"

"It's not so bad," Jeremy said. The city was livelier than he'd
ever seen it. There was more traffic, the railroad and telegraph
line were coming in, new stores going up. It was too bad his
father wasn't here, his father could protect Nancy.

"You mustn't tell anyone I'm leaving."

"I'm not telling anyone." He sounded annoyed.

"I thought," she ran her fingers through the loose hair at the
back of her neck. "I mean, I thought…"

"Well, don't think."

George used to say that when she got herself mired in words.
She looked at her son, smiling through her tears.

The following occurred shortly after Jeremy's fifteenth
birthday, which was celebrated on May 10, that day being picked
by Ellen as her best guess.

A deacon in the Aaronic priesthood, Jeremy was now old
enough to become a priest. He was at the Endowment House
early for the ceremony, dressed in his new suit, hair neatly

barbered, black shoes shined. The tallest of the boys, with a prominent nose the teachers were fond of likening to Joseph's.

There were seventy boys in all, rough-housing in the back of the Appointments Room, waiting for the signal. At the approach of the President's counselors, the boys, hair hastily smoothed, took their seats on the straight-back wooden chairs in the center of the room.

Listening to the preliminary speeches, Jeremy thought about his father, wishing his father were sitting there at the back of the room instead of Jack Straw. Afterward they would go home and have lemonade and cake, and his father would stay home the rest of the day and play some ball and sit on the porch and tell stories about his own youth. Jeremy felt his eyes burn, and turned his thoughts aside.

Jack Straw was a nice man, and Sister Phoebe was very happy. Kind of like Jack Sprat and his wife in the book of rhymes.

Bored, Jeremy put his elbows on his knees and his chin on his hands. He very definitely needed more than one wife. His father never held with multiple wives, even though he himself had eight. But he always felt guilty, probably because he grew up in the States.

*I wouldn't feel guilty. Do Indians take more than one wife? Did my real father?* He should ask his mother. He didn't know much about his Indian father, except for the strange name. Whonow. A word dreamt up by his mother because she couldn't understand the language.

One of the Apostles was talking about how many Saints there would be on earth by the end of the century. That was a lot of Saints. The boy next to Jeremy was snoring. Jeremy gigged him in the ribs. "Hey, they called your name."

The boy jumped to his feet and looked around sleepily. The row twittered.

Who should he marry first? could he have two women in bed with him at the same time? would they take off their temple garments? did the men do that, or was it a sin?

"Jeremiah George Harris."

It was the clerk from his ward standing over to the side. Jeremy worked his way along the shifting row of knees to the aisle and followed the clerk into the hall and down the stairs. Outside in the sunshine the opening bars of the "Missionaries Camp Song" wafted through an overhead window.

"You can't take orders." The clerk had a foxy face, sharp pointed nose, and yellowed, buck teeth crowded one over another. His black suit smelled of mothballs. "You got the curse."

"Leave me alone, you crazy old fool," Jeremy said. The city was full of wild-eyed fanatics overflowing with the Spirit, gathering on street corners and lurking in the stores, making a general nuisance of themselves.

He started back inside, and the clerk grabbed his arm. "'And their curse was taken from them, and their skin became white like unto the Nephites,' 3 Nephi 2:15, but yours ain't white enough yet."

Jeremy jerked free and kept going.

"Don't go up there!" the clerk brayed. "President Young said not."

Upstairs, Brigham had taken his seat at the speaker's desk, clerks were placing rolled-up papers tied with white ribbons in front of him. The boys about to be ordained were standing, waiting to work themselves to the front. Watching the President from the hallway, Jeremy thought about his father, about how difficult Brigham must have made it for his father to care for his family.

*You wanna see Indian blood, white man?* Jeremy asked in his eyes. *Hide and watch.* And he returned to his place and stood with the others in his row.

Lemonade waited at home, along with warm chocolate cake. Celebrating, Jeremy's family speculated as to where he'd be sent on his mission.

"You should go to Ireland," Nancy said. "That's where I'd go."

"You should go wash your face," Jeremy told her.

Nancy stuck her chocolate-smeared face in Jeremy's and revealed a mouth full of mashed cake.

"Yuck! Go away!" Jeremy shoved her chair with his boot.

Later, alone in the kitchen with his mother.

"I think it's a bitch that mothers can't go to the ceremonies in the Endowment House."

"Jeremy! don't say that word. You have to be a member of the priesthood to enter the Endowment House, men have to have their secrets."

"What secrets?"

"That's a silly question, the secrets that enable them to make the rules." She kissed the top of his head. "Women would point out how stupid the rules are, like temple garments."

The one-piece white cotton undergarment, which she refused to wear around the house, was one of her biggest complaints. She was convinced that Brigham just got tired of his wives wanting more wood and made them put on more clothes instead.

"Brigham shook my hand." Jeremy cut himself another piece of cake, his movements deliberate. "He said I was my father's son."

"There's no doubt he misses your father. They've hired three men to do what your father did in the Tithing Office." Ellen poured hot chocolate sauce over the cake.

"He was talking about my Indian father."

"No, he wasn't, Jeremy. I don't think he even knows."

"He knows. That weasel-faced Hawkin said I couldn't go forward because of my Indian blood."

Ellen stared at her son in disbelief.

"I did anyway. Brigham never batted an eye, just shook my hand and handed me my certificate like everybody else. You know what I told him? I told him 'I accept this on behalf of my fathers and their fathers before them.' And I said it loud enough for the whole room to hear."

The kitchen grew quiet except for the steady drip drip of water in the pan under the ice box. Noticing the evening bread bumping up under its cloth, Ellen punched it down, wishing she were punching Brigham.

They had talked about this, she and George. The doctrine of the Lamanites gradually becoming white and delightsome through repentance. George called it one of those foolish phantoms that bedeviled the church. "It will never be used against Jeremy," he'd insisted. "Jeremy's no darker than any Englishman burned black by the sun in this desert."

Nancy yelled through the back screen for Jeremy to come outside.

"He'll be out in a minute," Ellen yelled back, and sat down. It never ended, just never ended. "I should have known something like this would happen. Your father always said Brigham nursed old grievances like a Greek."

"So what's he mad about now?"

"About my running away at Fort Laramie."

"That is a long time. Are you going to ask permission to leave?"

"I'd never get it. I'll just hold my cards close, and one of these days when he's off visiting the settlements, I'll ease on out."

Jeremy grinned. "I never told you this before, but sometimes you sound like the card players down on Whiskey Street, except for the swearing."

"I didn't know church boys hung around the saloons."

"Actually…it's kind of fun, we hear lots of jokes. I've been thinking, maybe I'll leave too."

"Is that supposed to be a joke?" Ellen was unprepared for the alarm that flooded her senses. "You can't leave the safety of the Valley. Life is different here for men, and your friends are here. Brigham's a nuisance, but he won't live forever. This will pass like wind on water."

She learned that saying from the Indians, Jeremy knew. He grabbed his mother's hand and held on briefly, affectionately.

"He's after me, Jeremy, not you," Ellen breathed softly. "He knows I'm not a believer."

"Well, guess what."

They didn't discuss it further, Ellen fearing her son might be serious, and Jeremy more than a little overwhelmed with the possibility.

Autumn lingered long into November. Jeremy was allowed to read the priest's prayer over the silver trays of broken bread and little cups of water. Ellen said nothing more about leaving.

Despite Brigham's warning that he would have his eye on her, the churchman continued to ignore her. He had long ago, even before Jack appeared on the scene, pulled off the guard assigned to watch the house when Appella ran away. As for the house itself, he could take it anytime—designate it as a public building in George's honor, unearth a bogus unpaid note.

Fortunately he had business elsewhere.

The California volunteers, some 750 strong, on their way to the States to fight for the Union, had halted in Great Salt Lake City to guard the Overland trail and the telegraph line.

Ignoring Brigham's orders to stay at the abandoned Camp Floyd, the volunteers marched through the heart of the city and set up Camp Douglas on a site overlooking the city. Federal appointees housed in the city made the volunteers welcome, as did the merchants—affording Brigham no small opportunity to rant and rail from the pulpit.

Another, and infinitely more pleasing distraction, was Amelia Folsom, a new arrival to the city. The President's carriage could be seen parked all hours of the day in front of her parents' home, his dress became more stylish, his beard trimmer. That their sixty-one-year-old Prophet should make such a spectacle of himself over the twenty-five-year-old girl amused the Saints, as did the lavish bestowment of gifts (including, Ellen noticed, the rings that once belonged to George's mother) and the promise of an elaborate mansion all her own if Amelia would but consent to marriage.

It first happened in the kitchen while moving the chairs aside to mop. Ellen was pulling back a chair, and the next thing she knew she still had hold of the chair, but something was different. A little snippet of time had disappeared. Several days later it happened again, outside, sweeping snow off the porch. Wondering if she might be working too hard, she rested for awhile by the kitchen stove. After that, it happened about once a week.

She decided to send for Uergin, ask him to take her to California. Even so, she delayed. What if he wouldn't come? She should have told him years ago.

Several days later, on the heels of another episode, she again set out pen and paper.

> *Dear Uergin, I am writing to you for help. George is dead,*
> *please come. I want you to know Nancy is your daughter, I*
> *am sorry for not telling you sooner, we need you, love, Ellen.*
> *Please come.*

She glued a second sheet together to make an envelope, and afterward ordered the buggy brought around.

As he did for many in the community wishing to avoid the prying eyes of the Lord's post office, the Wells Fargo agent in the Salt Lake House secreted the letter away without comment.

## TWENTY-EIGHT

THE CITY BY THE BAY, 1863. The new owner of the fire-gutted lot across the street leaned against a convenient lamp post and laughed out loud. Oh, to be dancing at the edge of the ocean in the merry month of May or June or whatever in the hell month it was. Damn, it was queer what people won in poker games.

Most of the bricks had been hauled away, leaving behind a ghostly litter of burned looms surrounded by charred bolts of cloth and sacks of feathers. He should leave the ground empty, let it grow some grass. That'd be pretty.

He sat for awhile on a convenient stoop, considering the possibilities, and started back up Sacramento Street. The early-morning air was minty with the smells of salt water, the streets empty except for the gutter sweeps and the occasional hurry of a coach homeward bound from a late-night assignation.

Turning the corner at Battery Street he plowed square into a man in a terrible haste.

"Oops! I beg your par…why, Mr…ah…Mr… fancy meeting you here!"

"Yes, extraordinary, isn't it."

"How was Europe? You sell all them paintings?"

"Every one," Nathan said, cursing his bad luck.

"And they did good as you thought?"

"Considering the artist is unknown, jolly well."

"Gonna get more? If you do, look me up."

"I'll do that, sir, yes, thank you." And the art dealer hurried off as if late for an appointment.

In an upstairs room of the Rassette House Daphne played with her jewelry, sliding the baubles in and out of their ornately carved wooden box.

"How many'd we get?" The words had a syrupy edge.

"There seems to be a problem." Nathan worked a shoe off and ruefully surveyed the hole in his stocking. "The post office has added a new wing or some such thing, and the bins have been renumbered. That's apparently why so little was forwarded. They offered me a new number, but weren't holding any mail. I spent most of the day looking through their unclaimed junk." He pulled off his suit and arranged it over a chair. "I feel as though I've been working in a coal mine."

"'Junk' is right."

"We need those paintings, they're our bread and butter."

"That isn't what I call bread and butter," Daphne said.

The five paintings they'd hauled off to Europe hadn't done so well. Three hundred dollars from the *Kunstmuseum* in the Moselle Valley in southwestern Germany, two hundred and fifty dollars from the *Musée d'Art* in the Bordeaux region of France, lesser amounts in other places. Hardly the spill of cash they'd hoped for. Adding to the disappointment were the meager shipments picked up in Dresden—two measly packages containing two paintings each.

Prowling about in his drawers, Nathan located the half-empty bottle of burgundy and poured himself a glass. "I ran into Mr. Uergin this morning while taking my walk."

"Ooooh," Daphne simpered. "Mr. Uergin. And just when we don't have any paintings, wouldn't you know."

Nathan closed his eyes, resting his forehead on the rim of

the glass. "We can't deal with him, Daph, we're supposed to be giving him the artist's share of the money, remember?"

"He is soooo handsome."

"Hardly. He has a paunch and a red nose, he obviously drinks too much."

"You're just jealous. You weren't wearing that dreadful costume, I hope."

"No." Nathan dampened his handkerchief in the basin and gingerly brushed down his suit. "We should probably dine further out this evening."

"You are *such* a coward. We have reservations. Besides, that restaurant isn't anywhere near Mr. Uergin's saloon."

They were sipping cocktails in the quiet, dark Rue de Paris when who should walk through the door but Uergin, with a most beautiful young woman on his arm.

"Why, Mr. Uergin!" Nathan exclaimed. "We were just talking about you."

Daphne smiled sweetly, trying not to stare at the enormous diamond stickpin in the saloon keeper's white silk scarf.

"Mr....?"

"Lafitte," Nathan said, wishing he could say Smith.

Uergin smiled wickedly at Daphne. "And the lovely Mrs. Lafitte." He motioned the waiter toward the nearby table. "So when you going back to Utah?"

"In due time."

"Let me know." Searching his pockets with some difficulty, Uergin extracted a roll of bills from his clothing. "I'll take 'em all."

Daphne gasped.

"I have appreciated your business in the past, sir," Nathan said primly. "And I'm sure I shall again. But this is hardly the time or the place."

Uergin nodded agreeably and poked the money away. "Me too, ain't that the shits."

Nathan tucked his coattails closer as if to distance himself.

"It's a terrible place," Daphne curled over her plate to whisper, and felt Nathan's warning boot connect with her toes.

The waiter brought two servings of *petite marmite*. Determined to ward off further conversation, Nathan attacked the soup. Uergin squinted at the little iron pots. "We'll have whatever these good folks are having."

The next thing Nathan knew, Uergin was helping the waiter slide their two tables together.

"That's better," Uergin said. "Now, what's the problem?"

"With Utah?" Daphne cooed. "Well..."

"...there is really nothing to tell," Nathan said firmly. "I never divulge details about a client. Now if you'll forgive us, please, sir." He turned his attention back to the soup.

The waiter brought two more pots.

Uergin smiled invitingly at Daphne, who, keeping her feet a goodly distance from Nathan's, pronounced Great Salt Lake City pretty only when compared to the surrounding countryside. "The men are followed around by all sorts of women, young and old." She fiddled with her earring, a tiny waterfall of pearls. "They're the wives, and the men always have an eye to acquire more."

The young woman with Uergin looked bored.

The bouillabaisse came.

"What's that?" Uergin asked, eying the large plates.

"It's *la bouillabaisse*, the fisherman's meal, a native of Marseille and quite the favorite child of the whole Côte d'Azur," Nathan explained, inviting the beautiful woman's response. But she only had eyes for Uergin.

Conversation dwindled. The waiter came back with two more plates. Nathan relaxed. And heard Daphne say, "It's the queerest place. The morning we left the city? someone tried to arrest Nathan for no reason at all."

Uergin's companion looked properly horrified.

"Why is that, Mr. Lafitte?" Uergin asked, sorting through the little chunks of fish for something edible.

"I have no idea," Nathan said, and in a last-ditch attempt to silence Daphne, launched his own description of the city.

Dessert was a large *savarin* decorated with candied fruit and a drizzle of rum syrup. Nathan requested a chilled Sauternes, Uergin waved off the wine glass in favor of a whiskey sour.

As soon as he could, Nathan snapped his fingers for the *billet*. "We must be going, I have all sorts of important commitments."

"I understand, me too." Uergin leaned back in his chair and waggled his empty glass at the waiter. "Tell you what, let's all go visit that goddamned salty lake in the middle of nowhere. Why not? I pay for everything."

"Impossible," Nathan snapped.

"Ahh, Mr. Lafitte, nothing's impossible." Uergin raised his eyebrows impishly at Daphne. The waiter approached, Nathan reached for the *billet*, but Uergin beat him to it, spilling a fresh whiskey sour in the process. "It's a long trip alone."

"Oh, you won't be alone, dear," Daphne assured the saloon keeper. "All kinds of people go there, some not so nice if you catch my drift."

"In that case," Uergin looked alarmed, "it's a damn good thing you got me."

"Mr. Uergin, I fear you've had a bit much to drink. I apologize for my wife's having unduly alarmed you." Nathan glared at Daphne even as his thoughts tumbled. He needed those paintings. They may have simply stopped coming, in which case Mohammed would have to go to the mountain. As for Uergin's knowing that he himself was to be the recipient of the painter's share of the money, that letter seemed not to have arrived.

"It does so happen," Nathan conceded reluctantly, "that we do plan to go there, and there is a certain safety in numbers."

Daphne stared at Nathan flabbergasted. "That's a terrible long drive," she squeaked.

"Not if you know what you're doing," Uergin assured her.

"You know another way to get there?"

"I'll handle the arrangements," Nathan said, making it obvious he wanted the chore done correctly.

Daphne objected strenuously. *"You handled them last time!"*

Careful not to look into Uergin's face, Nathan pushed back his chair. "We'll be in touch."

Outside the Rue de Paris, unable to immediately hail a carriage, Nathan hurried off up the dark street, determined to be out of sight by the time the saloon keeper staggered outside.

"Don't run, Nathan, it's unbecoming. Did you see that roll of money? it was big enough to choke a horse." Daphne was having trouble keeping up on the uneven cobblestones. "My umbrella!" She stopped abruptly. "I left my umbrella in the corner."

"Never mind, dear." Nathan took firm hold of her elbow. "Where we're going, you won't need a brolly."

"You think he'll bring that woman with him?"

"When he's got you to look at? Don't be ridiculous."

By George he'd done it! Indeed he had! His chances of dragging Daphne back to Utah Territory hadn't amounted to a snowball in hell. But with the saloon keeper along, it was a different horse race.

Uergin leaned back against the carriage seat. The shod hooves on the cobblestones sounded a familiar lullaby. He liked the sound in the half-deserted streets, he liked horses. He had several out on pasture at San Pablo, but he never rode them. Too busy. The sweet young thing under his arm cuddled close, fingering his tie. She was wearing Pearl of Savoy, it reminded him of new mown hay. His mind wandered, the carriage swayed and seemed to lift off the ground.

The next morning in the rooms above the Lucky Lady, the young woman collecting her things and seeing the man on the bed watching her assumed the obvious and began undoing her newly fastened hair. But Uergin waved her off.

"It don't cost nothing to look," he told her warmly, wishing he were one of those fresh-faced kids full of piss and vinegar strutting off the gangplank down on Front Street. The first thing he'd do is go back to the desert, it followed him like a black dog. Someday he would.

That's when he sat bolt upright. Sonofabitch! that little pip-squeak of a dealer had called his bluff.

# TWENTY-NINE

UPSTAIRS IN THE RASSETTE HOUSE. "According to this, the roads are far superior to those we encountered back in '58." Nathan was reading the brochure taken from the rack in the Overland station. "Instead of a mud wagon we'll be traveling in a Concord Coach pulled by horses. Once we leave civilization the stations will be every twenty-four miles, an easy day's journey. In less than fifteen days we'll be at Temple Square. The last stop before the city will be Camp Floyd, where over four thousand federal troops reside."

He looked up. "You are right, an opportunity neglected never comes back."

"I didn't say that."

"And it *will* be a lovely jaunt, green rolling hills, wild flowers merrily blooming, all thanks to you, my brave companion. I could never do it without you."

"Are you absolutely sure about Mr. Uergin?"

"Absolutely. The die has been cast. We shall arrive well and rested on that golden shore and fling wide our nets!"

On the nineteenth of May, some twenty miles east of Sacramento in a rude settlement called Placerville, Uergin was having breakfast with Daphne in the Miners Restaurant, commiserating with her concerns about the wind rocking the coach, when he missed Nathan.

"Oh, he's running." Daphne waved her hand airily.

"Running?"

"Ever since we went to England. They have some sort of sport called English cross country, and he's all taken by it. He insists I do it." Daphne tapped her forehead. "There he comes now."

Uergin looked out the open door just as Nathan trotted by wearing dark green long-johns cut off at the knee and a sleeveless purple shirt.

"Well, I'll be go to hell!" Uergin said.

The bell sounded for departure. Nathan trotted in, his flat shoes clicking queerly on the planks.

"Nathan, what in the samhell are you doing?"

"What I'm doing, Mr. Uergin, is what you should be doing, toning my muscles."

"A nervous tic," Uergin told the onlookers. "Can't help it."

Later taking his seat in the coach suitably attired and feeling fit as a fiddle, Nathan sighed happily. "No leg cramps for this chap."

His fellow travelers grew accustomed to the show, having determined the Frenchman harmless enough, a performer of sorts no doubt and needing to practice. One afternoon late, sunk in the shade of the Carson Valley station, Uergin saw an Indian ease out of the brush and trot after Nathan.

Uergin yelled, and Nathan put on an extra burst of speed, shooting out of sight around a far corral. In no time at all the two were back, running neck-and-neck. Approaching the station corrals, the Indian veered away into the sage.

"Did you see that?" Nathan yelled excitedly at Uergin. "How about that! He was actually racing me! I think I acquitted myself jolly well, don't you?"

"Nathan," Uergin observed stonily. "You're a jackass."

Five miles east of the station on the Muddy River a hub

broke, tipping the coach into the dirt. The team was unhooked, the women made themselves comfortable in the shade, and Uergin volunteered to ride back to the station. Nobody noticed the team disappear. One minute they were there, and the next minute they were gone.

Flailing himself for his carelessness, Uergin immediately set off on foot, Nathan at his side. They'd gone less than a mile when, growing thirsty, Uergin realized he carried no canteen.

Another mile.

"Sit here and rest a minute, Mr. Lafitte, before you have a brain stroke."

"Ah!" Nathan exclaimed, sinking into the shade of a piñon. Two minutes later was on his feet again.

Uergin looked up. "Easy does it, Mr. Lafitte. You gotta learn to pace yourself in this heat."

Five minutes passed. Uergin checked his timepiece. "Now, Mr. Lafitte. "

By the time they raised the station, wavering in the heat, Uergin was done. He waved Nathan on and sat down at the edge of the road. Eventually a wagon drawn by mules showed up headed for the wreck. Seated beside the driver, Nathan hoisted a canteen in the air triumphantly.

The next evening before supper, at the stop on the Virgin River, Nathan ran circles around the corrals and station, and Uergin walked. Periodically passing the saloon keeper, Nathan slowed his place to call encouragements. "What jolly good fun." "What a pair we make." "You're looking spiffy." "A pity you don't have grippers."

And off he would go, dirt flying from his spiked shoes.

And so it continued day after day.

Uergin's mellow forbearance of his fellow travelers vanished completely. He had little to say and on the road spent his time brooding out the window. In honoring his drunken promise to the Lafittes, he'd uncovered an ugly truth. He had all the advice and all the answers, but no one was listening anymore. Not even himself.

Camp Floyd, their last night out.

Daphne envisioned strolling in the shade of a large, tree-lined parade ground, young men cantering past casting admiring glances. Sadly, there were no trees, no young men. The Overland station was outside the camp, her hair was a fright, and her best dress was packed.

After supper Nathan called his companions to sit on a convenient rock beside a dry arroyo. Removing his tie, he spread the ribbon of fabric on the rock.

"There are those who travel and those who travel well," he observed, fishing three small, long-stemmed glasses from one coat pocket and a flask from the other.

Moving cautiously so as not to spill a single drop he filled the glasses with the last of the cherry herring.

"To Mormon town," Uergin said and drained his glass.

"To Mormon town," Nathan took a small sip, reluctant to proceed too quickly, "for weal or woe."

THIRTY

THE CITY WAS BIGGER than he remembered. He walked down main street to a saloon and sat in the cool darkness smoking a cigar. It'd been thirteen years. They weren't the same people, as least he wasn't. Ellen would do the right thing, invite them for dinner, George would get in his licks with a little sermon at grace.

Recalling the preacher's sermon on the Laramie about the evils of drink, Uergin ordered another whiskey.

With Daphne upstairs resting, Nathan cooled his heels on the ground level of the hostelry. In the last five years a goodly number of saloons had sprouted up and down the main street, but the Salt Lake House itself remained dry as the surrounding desert. When he could stand it no longer, he straightened his back, screwed up his courage, and slunk out a side door, coming first to a print shop where he paid the atrocious price of six dollars for a newspaper. And next to a spirits shop.

On his return, happily settled behind the headlines in the Deseret News, a flask of rum at his elbow, he learned of President Lincoln's intention to draft American men for the war. A Mr. Gatling had invented a gun that fired better than four shots a second. A large tabernacle 65 feet high and 232 feet long was being built in the city. On the back page a church sermon compared the United States to a Cartesian vortex.

Ah, yes, where would civilization be without a newspaper.

The next morning the trio took a street hack to the neighborhood where the women who burned the paintings lived. Seen in the glorious sunshine surrounded by flower bushes, the large wooden house stained a dark brown didn't look so ominous.

Receiving no answer to his knock at the open front door, Nathan led the way around back. The women were there, hanging clothes out on the line. Their excitement at seeing Uergin was enormous.

"I'm here looking for a little girl called Phoebe," Uergin said.

"She's right here." Phoebe patted her chest. "Where'd you come from? where'd you get all that grey hair?"

"Worrying about you!"

Phoebe giggled, undone by surprise. Nathan introduced himself, and Phoebe asked "Did you bring my money?"

With a flourish Nathan whipped an envelope out of his inside pocket and said grandly "There it is, every penny!"

Phoebe was speechless.

"Unfortunately," he added quickly in a scolding tone, "when I returned from Paris, there were no paintings whatsoever being held in the San Francisco post office, which is why I am here."

"I send paintings every month," Phoebe insisted with child-like sincerity.

"I see. Well, I was afraid of that. I'll take what I can with me and give you a new address for future shipments, you do have more artwork?"

"Everywhere, I got it everywhere."

"Well, let's go see it."

"Right now I'm painting a tree through the open barn doors," Phoebe said. "You wanna see that?"

"I want to see everything!" Nathan exclaimed, poised on a spiderweb of contradictions, and hurried toward the barn. The last thing he wanted to do was give Phoebe time to count her earnings in front of Uergin.

"You get prettier all the time," Uergin told Ellen, holding her at arm's length.

"Oh, go on. It's you that's stayed young." She hesitated, momentarily losing herself in his presence. "Let's go inside, I know what the barn looks like."

Uergin was silent, his apprehension at seeing Ellen vanished by his concern. The dark, molasses hair, now silvered at the temples, had lost its luster. A faint spiderweb of veins shown though the translucent skin over her cheekbones. She was still beautiful, in an eggshell sort of way, but thinner than he remembered.

Displaying an unfamiliar giddiness, jumping from one subject to another—the garden, the weather, the cost of buttons—she set cups out for coffee.

The Lafittes were returning, preceded by their bright laughter.

"I have to talk to you alone, it can't wait," Ellen said and abandoned the kitchen.

The small room in the downstairs corner of the house held only a narrow bed and a dresser and an untidy stacking of household linens against one wall.

"Sit down." Settling herself on the bed, she plumped the blankets. "I had to give up my room upstairs, but I don't mind, it's another ten dollars a month."

"What's going on with you?" Uergin asked, remaining by the door.

"What do you mean, what's going on with me. What's going on with you?"

"Are you drunk?" Uergin asked.

"No."

"What's wrong with you?" Realizing she was fighting back tears, he sat down beside her.

"I am so glad you came! just so glad!" Ellen's defenses crumbled, and she threw herself against him, clinging to his coat, crying wildly. "I'm sick, Uergin, I need help. I'm sorry I didn't tell you sooner about Nancy."

He could smell the liquor on her. "Who's Nancy?"

"You didn't get my letter?"

"No."

"Then why are you here?" She straightened, brushing away her tears with her hand.

"Where's George?"

"He's dead. You never got my letter, and you're here anyway? I can't believe that! are you clairvoyant?"

"So who's Nancy?"

"Our daughter." Ellen turned aside to stare at her hands, thinking how white and bony they looked. "She's got to get out of here."

"Why? what'd she do?"

"Grew up. We can't leave on our own, this is a prison, this whole Valley's a prison, nobody knows that, nobody who's not in the church knows that."

"I don't understand, you want me to take Nancy somewhere?"

"Before the old men start following her around. Both of us, as soon as possible, but we have to wait 'til Brigham leaves. That won't be long, he travels a lot, then we'll get on the stage and go like thieves in the night." She laughed. "It won't be night, of course. Stages don't leave here at night.

"California's where I want to go, but I've been sick in the strangest way. I think I better go to the States instead, that's where George's family is. They're in Lawrenceville in Illinois, you think we'll be safe traveling there, what with the war going on?"

"I can get you anywhere you want," Uergin said. "Have you seen a doctor?"

"They think it's heart trouble, it's getting worse, I keep losing pieces of time. The other day I was in the garden, and the next thing I knew I was looking at the sky wondering why it was in front of me. I didn't even remember falling. Uergin, you mustn't tell anyone she's not George's daughter."

"Who?"

"Nancy! Are you listening to me?"

"Whose daughter is she?"

"Why, yours of course."

Uergin stopped breathing. Nancy was *his* daughter? Ellen was pregnant when he left her in Utah?

"What about Jeremy?" he asked when he could.

"Oh, he's fine, he's not going with us. We keep our boys in school a long time, but not the girls. Oh, no, can't do that. By the time Nancy's fourteen, she'll be done with homemaking classes and there isn't anything else. 'A little education has spoiled many a good wife.'" This last mockingly.

"Where's your brandy?"

She pointed at a jar beside an upturned jelly glass on the nightstand. "Jeremy buys it after dark from Clements."

Uergin filled the glass and handed it to her. "Go to sleep."

Leaving the room, he heard her say, "You'll have to...." and closed the door on the rest.

He was so angry. *So angry!* To think she'd cheated him out of his own daughter to trap a rich man. He wanted to yell at her, or worse. And now she was wanting him to take his daughter back to live with George's family? To hell with that noise!!

He walked through the house and out into the back yard, calling her names in his thoughts, vicious, foul names. Hating her as much as he'd ever hated anyone, wishing her dead.

Returning, he told Nathan in a soft aside, "Go back to the boarding house and and stay there until I find out what's going on."

Mr. Straw came home and wanted to know—but not in an argumentative way—what Uergin was doing there.

"Am I not my daughter's keeper?" Uergin replied sharply and reined himself in. There was no point, no point at all. The Straws looked back at him, their faces blank.

"This here's my husband," Phoebe said, wondering where all the joy went.

"I need to talk to Ellen's children alone," Uergin told her. "Some place quiet."

Seated in George's darkened office, Uergin stared into the shadows. He would dress his daughter in silks and send her to the finest schools and not let her marry any scum, and not let her come to the saloon, except to meet him for lunch. Maybe he should get out of the saloon business, buy an orange grove or something.

Hearing voices in the outer waiting room, he took a deep breath and walked out to where he could see clearly in the window light.

She was beautiful. A beautiful little apple-cheeked girl. Twelve years old, that's what she'd be. She didn't look like her mother, she must look like his side of the family. He wanted to hug her. Instead, introducing himself, he shook her hand as with a perfect stranger. And wasn't she a stranger? and whose fault was that? whose goddamn fault was that!? He fought off the anger and concentrated on Jeremy.

A handsome fellow, Cheyenne to the bone. Chiseled, slightly arrogant expression, tall. Jed's family had wanted Ellen to pass him off as French. Yes, that would have worked.

"I'm taking your mother out of the city," Uergin told the boy.

"Are you a friend of our father's?" Nancy asked.

"He's a friend of the family," Jeremy said. "He helped mother and me come here from New York."

"You're not taking my mother anywhere," Nancy said.

"Nancy," Jeremy said softly, "she wants to go, she's been wanting to go for a long time."

"She didn't tell me, and I don't care what you say, Jeremy Harris. You always act like you know everything."

"She wants to leave, Miss Nancy," Uergin said. "That makes it the right thing to do." Such a pretty little girl. Her hair was curly like his, she had his eyes.

He forced his attention back to Jeremy. "She wants to leave when Brigham leaves."

"It'd probably be safer, she's supposed to have his permission. And…" Jeremy hesitated, choosing his words, feeling disloyal for sounding the warning "…we can't tell Jack." (He refused to follow the family's example of calling Jack "Mr. Straw," thinking it silly.)

"He would tell, he'd think it was the right thing to do, and you could get locked up. That's why Sister Phoebe don't know."

"And me, why don't I know?"

"Because you can't keep a secret."

"I can keep a secret as good as you can!"

Uergin fell silent, thinking about the world Nancy lived in, the world that looked so perfect. What a shame it wasn't, that what went on inside the houses couldn't be as peaceful as the brook-lined streets.

"I'm staying in the Salt Lake House," he told Jeremy, who nodded.


Knowing Jeremy wouldn't show until after dark (it was funny, the odd feeling of being hunted, so peculiar to this city), Uergin spent the afternoon on Whiskey Street. Ellen was too sick to ride any great distance in a coach. He needed a wagon, and he needed Jeremy, whether Ellen wanted him along or not.

He wasn't the only one confronting his demons. That afternoon Jeremy rode up Mill Creek alone, putting together what saying good-bye meant. He waited until after dark to visit the Salt Lake House.

Uergin was sprawled in a leather chair, his feet on the ottoman. He looked tired. Seeing Jeremy, he put on his hat and walked outside and down the street.

"We need a wagon."

"A wagon?"

"A light wagon in good shape and six mules, Mexican mules. You know good mules when you see 'em?"

"Yes, sir."

"When's Brigham leaving the city?"

"I'll find out."

Uergin pulled a fold of paper bills from his pocket. "Get yourself two saddle horses."

"I already got two."

"Young? sound? good teeth? good straight legs? good feet?"

"Well, sir, they're kind of pets."

"Quit with the sirs." Uergin handed over a wad of paper money. "Get yourself two horses, make sure you get 'em shod, ask Nancy if she wants a horse."

Nancy didn't. "I'm not going."

"Grow up, you're the reason mother's going. Either get a horse or ride in the wagon."

"She's going in a wagon!"

"Shush, don't talk so loud."

"If I do go (she could take a lot of things if they went in a wagon), which I don't know yet...ahhh...it has to have black and white spots."

Jeremy looked pained. "Just take what you get."

"I don't like horses, dummy, in case you didn't notice."

"You can learn."

Sleep didn't come easily that night.

Staring into the darkness Uergin ransacked his memory for a picture of the mother he hadn't seen in over fifty years. She was a pretty woman, as he recalled, his daughter probably looked like her. *His daughter, his very own daughter.*

Jeremy wrestled with getting his hands on a team and wagon. Not rousing the attention of the ward clerk would be damned near impossible, he should have told Uergin that.

Nancy made mental lists of the belongings she could not live without, adding to the list until it became clear she could not possibly move anywhere.

Only Ellen slept well. The first thing she did the next morning, saucering her morning coffee, was to tell Phoebe that she and Nancy were leaving and going to the States.

Evoking a terrible storm.

"Phoebe! calm down! I've never seen you like this!"

"Then don't leave, damn it!" Phoebe wailed.

"Listen to me!" Ellen begged, but Phoebe stomped outside into the grey morning. Returning with the eggs.

Watching the heavy hands gently candle the eggs against the lamp light, Ellen thought, *Sasha called me her sister-by-choice, that's what you are, dear Phoebe, my sister-by-choice, I am leaving all my sisters.*

Bracing herself, she began anew. "This is Nancy's opportunity to see more of the world. The Valley's no place for young girls, that awful, all-seeing eye everywhere, no bright clothes, the silly underwear..."

Ellen stopped abruptly. The *last* thing she wanted to do was talk Phoebe into leaving! "Uergin can keep us safe, that's why we're going now."

"What about me and Mr. Straw and Jeremy?!" Phoebe's voice clawed. "I suppose it's alright for us to stay, we don't matter, we ain't cow shit!"

"Jeremy is sixteen, all his friends are here, he doesn't want to leave. Maybe he'll come later, maybe you all will. But right now you have this good house and a good milk cow, just stay put and enjoy your life."

"But Nancy gets to go!"

"You're not listening to me! I will *not* raise Nancy here to be pawed over by old men, and you can't protect her! None of us can."

"How do you know you even can get out? What about that woman who asked the emigrants to take her out, and they left without her? she was killed down at the lake, remember? and what about poor Mr. Landon? they chased him all the way to Nevada, that was horrible, he didn't have no food, no shoes, no shelter, that was horrible, that could happen to you!"

"That's just idle gossip cooked up to scare people from leaving. We'll get on the stage, no one'll bother us, people do it all the time. But you mustn't tell Mr. Straw."

"Oh no! Mr. Straw ain't good enough to know! he ain't trustworthy! he can work like a whipped dog and give us all his money, but when it comes to telling him anything…"

"…Phoebe! for god's sake! we all love Mr. Straw! but it's not fair to ask him to keep a secret, it would worry him. That's why we don't tell him about mailing your paintings to California, remember? He would worry. He *is* a dear man, the day you met Mr. Straw was a good-luck day for all of us."

"But he can't leave, and me and Jeremy can't leave, we gotta stay and take care of the goddamned milk cow!" Phoebe fell into a fresh tide of swearing and weeping and would not be solaced.

About this time Jeremy was standing with Enoch Kepler in the churned-up dirt of the Kepler corrals. "There's a fellow in the Salt Lake House wants a good, clean, six-mule hitch." Jeremy said. "Them little Mexican mules."

Enoch gave the boy a steady look. He and Bishop Harris had

been friends. They visited after dark, whispering outside the back door of the Harris mansion. Jeremy must have discovered who he was, why else would the boy trust him now. "You working for the Gentiles?"

"Ain't we all?" Jeremy asked.

Enoch smiled depreciatingly. "We are if we wanna eat. It's a new day, sonny, but it'll cost you plenty, mules are bringing upwards of three hundred dollars."

Jeremy smiled and shook his head. "Not me."

"Give me a couple of days. There's folks around got mules right now," Enoch said, curious to see if he was reading things right.

Jeremy didn't bite.

Well, that settled it, somebody was running. "You got a wagon?"

"Not yet, need a harness too."

"I got both, ain't much for looks, but they'll get you far as the Salt Lake House."

Nathan visited the Harris mansion every day, packing up various paintings to be shipped by Wells Fargo to a new box in San Francisco, instructing Phoebe in what subjects had the greatest appeal. That there was very good brandy to be had in the house spared him the risk of shopping for it.

Uergin went back to the house only once, to tell Ellen they were taking a wagon.

"Oh, no, Uergin, it's too slow."

"Who's skinning this cat?"

"I need to get there as soon as I can."

"You'll get there." He'd made up his mind to that. Nancy belonged with her mother, but he'd have a say in things. They could travel overseas together, that would be a good idea.

Daphne spent her days between the Salt Lake House and the Harris mansion. At the mansion she spent hours describing for Phoebe ad nauseam the ocean and the European countryside. At the boarding house, except for brisk walks out to the restaurant or the print shop, she stayed inside playing board games and dominoes with Nathan.

Serving as Nathan's nanny (the little coward went nowhere without her, fearful of encountering Mr. Smoot) was bad enough. But having him rat-hole money for the artist, now that was just plain wrong. Two hundred dollars, he said. He must have pawned her jewelry, there did seem to be ear drops missing.

This betrayal aside, she remained bewitched by Uergin's stoicism. Sensing an old love affair with Ellen, she saw herself as part of a grand conspiracy. This insight enabled her, but barely, to forego livening things up a bit with the holy men of the city.

A very smelly city when the wind blew from the north, bringing with it the odor of rotten eggs from the hot sulphur springs behind Ensign Peak.

Nancy asked her mother how to address the Lafittes. Ellen told her to ask Daphne, who replied waspishly, "Call Nathan 'uncle,' it'll make him feel grown up, but just call me 'Daphne.' 'Aunt' sounds too old."

Next, Nancy wanted to tell her friends good-bye. Forbidden to do so, she shrouded herself in sorrow.

"Your father asked us to leave, remember," Ellen told her.

"That's when we were all going. I don't even know my grandparents!"

"Well, we have their pictures and their letters. You know them that way. Besides, we won't live *with* them, we'll just live nearby, so they can help us settle in."

"You're not making Jeremy go."

"Jeremy's older, maybe he'll come later."

"Maybe he won't, they're not his grandparents."

"Nancy Jane! They're his grandparents the same way George is his father. And they love you both the same, you know that."

"I hate them!" And off she'd go.

If Ellen despaired of reaching her daughter, it was the only thing she despaired of. She grew increasingly sanguine, throwing caution to the wind and confiding in Mr. Straw. Afterward coaxing him with, "Now remember, you can't tell anyone."

Mr. Straw didn't say a word, just sat there in the kitchen staring at the floor. That evening in the meeting in the Council Hall, he was still struggling with what to do. At the end of the meeting, when his patriarch approached, Mr. Straw took it as a sign.

"There's something I need to tell you." He had no choice, he was responsible for keeping his family safe. "I need to talk to you about the widow Harris who lives with us." He hesitated, checked one last time by his promise. But what Sister Ellen wanted to do wasn't safe, she wasn't well.

"And I have something to tell you, good brother," Elder Park said jovially and offered the cushion tucked under his arm. "Would you like a cushion? my wife's sister made it."

"Why, yes, yes, I would like that." Mr. Straw repositioned himself on the cushion. "Now about Sister Harris…"

"…she's come here from Missouri," the elder said.

"Oh."

"You only have one wife."

"Yes, that's true."

"You should consider a second wife," the elder confided warmly. "My wife's sister would be a great help to Sister Straw, she's a good worker and of the marrying age."

"Why don't *you* marry her?" Mr. Straw asked. Uncharacteristically so, it wasn't like him to question authority.

Elder Park puffed out like a pigeon. "I do my duty, Brother Straw. I have married two of her friends, who are exactly like her. Very godly. I have a small house. You have a large house, larger than most."

"Yes, that's true."

"Come around in the morning after breakfast." The elder beamed with goodwill. "You're a righteous man, a righteous man is pleased to spread the wealth. Come tomorrow and see what you think. If you wish, you may have the upstairs bedroom to yourself to visit. I promise you, you won't be disappointed." He squeezed Mr. Straw's shoulder and walked away.

Mr. Straw sat for awhile thinking, but not before sliding off the cushion and pushing it away.

# THIRTY-ONE

"WE'RE GOING WITH YOU."

"No, you're not!" Ellen was lighting the stove. Distracted, she forgot to shut the firebox door. Phoebe reached past her and shut the door. "Elder Park told Mr. Straw he has to take another wife." She sounded amused, unmindful of the brink she teetered on. "He's madder'n hops, but it don't bother me none, that's the way it's always been."

"No, it hasn't, Phoebe, not at all. Joseph wanted someone besides Emma in his bed, so he made it a church law. George married us because of the church. It's what killed Constance, she'd be alive today if we weren't here. If Mr. Straw takes more wives, they'll live right here underfoot, you'll have to share your husband and your privacy."

"That's what I saying, we're going with you. Mr. Straw…"

"…Brigham can not force Mr. Straw to take another wife, he doesn't control the church the way he used to."

"Well, that's alright, it'll be nice to live somewhere different."

"Not when you don't have any money in your purse, and have to live in a rented house and go to work as a domestic. You don't even know that Mr. Straw can get work elsewhere."

Phoebe had an answer for that, but Ellen was done being conciliatory. Mr. Straw came downstairs to breakfast. He looked rumpled, unslept.

Ellen poured him a cup of coffee. "I want you to talk to Brother Stenhouse."

"I don't wanna talk to no one," Mr. Straw muttered into his cup.

Jeremy came in from the barn with the milk, and Ellen hurried him off to the offices of *The Daily Telegraph*.

Tom Stenhouse and Mr. Straw talked alone in George's inner office for an hour. Afterward, dinner pail in hand, Mr. Straw went off to work. But not before explaining to his wife that calling a bad thing religious did not make it good thing. He would stand on his convictions, the God who brought him to the Valley would sustain them both.

Cold comfort to a woman primed to set sail for the new world.

Alone with Ellen, Tom said, "You look tired, you should get some rest."

Ellen handed him a sheet of paper. "This puts the house in their name, it's a copy of what I gave Phoebe earlier. I need you to record it for me."

The editor studied the deed overly long, perhaps thinking of the disentanglement his own leave-taking would involve, and folded the paper away in his coat pocket.

"Both Fanny and I believe you're doing the right thing. As long as Brigham is allowed even the trappings of power, he will be very hard on his weaker enemies. There's something else we should talk about. Fanny says Phoebe secretly sends paintings to San Francisco. If that's so, it must stop."

"There's never been a problem, I pay the agent extra and that's what Phoebe will do, we've got it all worked out."

"And she receives money for them?"

"Nothing through the mail."

"Funds she's not paying tithe on?"

"No. I mean, yes, that's right."

"The most dangerous place in Utah is between Brigham Young and a nickel. If he discovers the deception, he'll take the house."

"He won't."

Tom looked dubious. "Brigham keeps track of apostates, he'll be watching Phoebe very carefully to learn your whereabouts."

Ellen smoothed the tablecloth. Finally she said, "If Brigham confronts her over her paintings, she could easily do something very stupid—accuse him of being ignorant, or jealous, or worse, whatever crosses her mind."

"I think we can scotch that," Tom said with a chuckle. "No matter how well deserved. Tha auld church is going, there are new forces at work, strong forces that will gie us our opening. Ha Sister Phoebe paint tha new theatre. I'm on tha theatre committee, we'll sell tha painting to raise money and advertise tha sale in tha *Telegraph,* that will do tha trick."

Ellen smiled, remembering George's amusement in hearing the Scotsman, when excited, given over to brogue.

Nathan stopped by with Daphne, and Ellen enlisted his help. Nathan was heartbroken. His wonderful golden goose was cooked.

"I've come to the conclusion," he later explained to Phoebe, mustering as much enthusiasm as possible, "that the paintings will have wider appeal if they have a provenance."

"A what?"

"A recognized place of origin, so to speak."

Phoebe was dubious. "How was they advertised before?"

"Well, they weren't, and that's the problem. Yes, no advertising."

"I don't know how."

"Get Sister Ellen to help you."

Ellen's help consisted of sending Phoebe to Brother
Stenhouse, who explained the plan to have the newspaper
handle the artist's sales and collect the money for same.

"Which will then be forwarded to you minus the tithes."

Phoebe's disposition, considerably soured by not being able to
leave the Valley with Ellen, took a sudden jump for the better.
The tithes, however steep, were nothing compared with being
able to sit out in the sunshine again with a tray of bright paints.

It rained and rained some more, splicing the dry wasteland
to the west with rivers. A subalpine fog blanketed the Valley.
In church that Sunday Brigham announced plans to visit San
Pete, going by way of Nephi to Manti and returning by the road
through Spanish Fork Canyon.

On Tuesday the President's entourage left the city. Nathan
immediately bought tickets on Friday's stage for Sacramento and
secured one last painting—two women at a clothesline in the
wind, their white skirts puffed out like a disjointed sail. He did
not mail this painting, which measured roughly twenty by fifteen
inches, and instead packed it in his trunk.

Jeremy didn't have the outfit yet. Uergin gave him until
Friday.

Thursday morning a rider from the Deep Creek mail station
reported the inbound stage hung up at Egan Canyon. The San
Francisco road was closed. Nobody knew for how long.

The news was posted in the boarding house.

"We should take a stroll," Nathan said with forced
cheerfulness. "Clear our thinking."

"Clear our thinking to do what?" Daphne snapped. "Build our
own stage?"

Nevertheless, for want of something better to do, outside
they went. The brown air felt sticky, as if the mist and chimney
smoke were congealing. Daphne tied a handkerchief over her
nose and met all attempts at small talk with stoney silence.

A little row of unpainted outhouses stuck up stovepipe-like near the post office. Beside these conveniences was a large pile of waste paper. Nathan secured a scrap, and waiting in line, noticed the words, *Dear Fran, We are in the / who dress very planely but everything is / not dangereus but very long and / which are favored so by the foriegn....*

He stared at the paper in utter amazement, the line moving around him. The very letter Daphne had written to her friend in San Francisco! He remembered seeing her bent over the crude desk in their room and cautioning her not to say anything that might cause them trouble. He retrieved another scrap, someone was wanting money sent them in Sacramento.

The discovery flew in the face of all Nathan knew to be right and civilized. The post office was tearing up mail to use for lavatory paper! How absolutely reprehensible! If he hadn't seen it with his own eyes...!!

Later that same day.

"Mr. Uergin, I think, under the circumstances, seeing as how the roads to the west are washed out, that Daphne and I would do well to travel with you so as to render what service we can."

He had ventured out on the streets alone, skittering from one drinking establishment to the next, finally locating the guide in the Pioneer Water Hole.

He spread the refund from the stage company on the counter, $151.30.

"Well now, that's mighty kind of you, Mr. Lafitte." Uergin had to work to keep his face straight. *Welcome to my world, Mr. Lafitte, now you're gonna find out how the boar ate the cabbage.*

That evening, upstairs in the Salt Lake House.

"We're going east...into the desert...in a wagon?! Are you out of your mind?!"

"No, my little wild rose, I'm saving your skin. As of tomorrow we'll be alone in the city, hardly a pleasant prospect."

"I'm perfectly capable of saving my own skin, thank you, Sir Idiot!"

"Don't whinge. You get along jolly well with Mr. Uergin and Mrs. Harris and her daughter."

Daphne plopped on the bed and stared into the chipped mirror across the room. She wanted out of the city. They'd been there two weeks. The air was hideous, the food was foul, and there was no entertainment whatsoever.

"Why can't we just wait and go the right direction."

"Number one, we don't know how long that will be. Number two, Mrs. Harris is leaving without Brigham's permission. Having spent a great deal of time in her home, we could be under suspicion."

"Oh, phooey! I never heard of having to get pemission to leave a city, it's just nutty!"

"Nevertheless…"

"I know, I know." Daphne waved her hand dismissively. "We have to stay inside the boarding house."

"Which is owned by a Mormon."

"Oh, Nathan, you drive me crazy! I do not get along well with wagons that go two miles an hour…"

"…at least fifteen with horses…"

"…bugs, dust, eating on the ground!!…"

"…we'll have folding chairs and velvet-covered camp stools."

"Who's going to cook?"

"Why, Mr. Uergin, of course."

"And wash the dishes?"

Nathan lifted his chin. "I shall."

"You're lying to me, Nathan."

"You have only to attend to yourself. You may visit as you wish and rest whenever you so chose. We will, of course, be

staying at the military encampments. Fort Bridger, the Platte
Bridge Station (he ticked them off on his fingers), Fort Laramie,
Fort Kearny, Fort Atkinson, where you shall have ample time to
shop and dress for dinner."

Nathan smiled approvingly inside his mouth. That should do
the trick. She had a thing about soldiers, all those brass buttons
and chevrons. It was all she could do not to swoon when they
rode by.

"My clothes will be wrinkled."

"And you," Nathan tickled her cheek with his little finger,
"will solve that problem with your usual style and grace. I swear,
I have no idea how in the devil you do it." This last with just a
slight touch of awe.

Daphne was silent. "No," she said after a time, shaking her
head. "I'm going home to San Francisco, your magic's no good
anymore."

"Utah is a very dangerous place, my little prairie pansy, you
will never guess what I discovered today near *La Poste*."

"I don't care."

"They're taking letters for which people have paid perfectly
good money to be mailed, and tearing them up for lavatory
tissue!" He held up the scraps.

Daphne glanced at the scraps and did a double take. Her
mouth dropped open.

Horrified by the perfidy, the couple could only stare at each
other.

Late Thursday afternoon Jeremy drove a covered spring
wagon pulled by six clean-limbed, smallish mules to the back
door of the Harris mansion and loaded what looked to be
bundles of bedding. A neighbor asked what he was doing, and
Jeremy said his mother sold the goods to a party of gold seekers
for a smart profit.

"I didn't figure that for your outfit," the neighbor observed. "What d'you think them mules cost?"

"I'll find out."

"Don't bother."

Jeremy returned to the Salt Lake House and secured the loaded wagon in amongst several other wagons and turned the mules loose in the corral.

That night after his mother went to bed, he told Phoebe and Jack he was leaving with Uergin "I'll be gone before you're up, so I'm saying my good-byes now. Don't tell mother or Nancy, I want to surprise them."

Jack nodded. "We heard the Lafittes was going with them on account of the western road's being closed. With a mob like that, who knows what'll happen when they get loose in the desert."

"It's right that you go," Phoebe agreed. "You got no choice."

"That Nathan won't be no help," Jack said. "He don't know how to team, you can tell by looking at his hands." With that, the good brother's stern resolve dissolved in tears. What if something bad happened?

Jeremy tied the family dog in the barn and rode out of the city before the roosters crowed. Those who noticed saw nothing unusual about a boy's riding out bareback on an old wagon horse early in the morning, a rifle across the horse's withers. How could they know that in a little sugar sack in his coat pocket the boy carried his mission money, all $43.27, saved ever since he knew what money was.

That same morning Nathan traded his good wool suit for two red hickory shirts and two pair of pepper-salt cloth pants. And Daphne bravely surrendered her best dress, a black silk manteau trimmed with velvet bands and fringe.

Surveying each other at the front of the store, the couple broke into laughter.

"No one but you could wear that…" Nathan's voice trailed off. "What in the world is it?"

"A Bloomer dress, it's practical and fetching at the same time." Daphne pirouetted and the blue, obscenely long bloomers tied at the ankles flared prettily, as did the short puffy skirt with its edge of white piping. "Not everyone has the figure for it. But you can take those god-awful pants back."

"Trust me, no one is going to notice my pants."

Noon. The cold, foggy weather was retreating, State road steamed under a listless sun. Mewing like a lost kitten, Phoebe watched Ellen and Nancy drive away from the mansion. All week she had courted good luck for the travelers by avoiding bad luck. But visiting the silent rooms—beds shorn of their blankets, dresser tops bare—she could not stop her poor heart from breaking to pieces.

Reaching main street, the buggy horse reached a blockage of a sort—wagons and people all scrambled together. Ellen attempted to escape down a nearer side street, but a line of heavy freight wagons was turning ahead of her. Standing on the buggy seat, Nancy could see men hastily erecting a platform in front of the express office. Then she spotted Brigham's buggy.

Ellen was dumbfounded. What was the President doing back in the city?! Thinking more quickly than was her wont of late, she left her buggy in the street and gave the butcher's boy in a nearby shop two quarters to take the buggy back to the Harris mansion as soon as the traffic cleared.

It was the photographer's lucky day. He'd hired workmen to build a little platform in the street near Walker Bros. Bank, the better to photograph the commerce of the busy city, when he learned that the large assemblage of buggies approaching were those of the great man himself.

In an absolute dither, the photographer urged the workmen to top speed and shinnied up the rickety ladder, equipment in hand. That's when he spotted the tall woman in front of the Pacific Hardware Store.

And sent his assistant to draw her into the street.

"That won't be possible," Ellen told the assistant angrily. "I'm not who you think I am." She was often photographed in public and suspected the photographers confused her with Amelia Folsom, who was also tall. People were staring. The assistant, having no idea what his employer thought, refused to go away.

"Stay here," Ellen told Nancy and joined the crowd gathering about the platform, where she learned that the President, in his travels south, had been taken with a severe cold, and fearing he would not recover in time to properly address the faithful, had returned to the city.

Brigham liked having his picture taken with crowds of the faithful. He did not like having his picture taken with his apostles, least of all with the Apostle George A. Smith, who lumbered up from a further buggy to stand beside his Prophet.

The Brigadier General of the Nauvoo Legion was a vain man whose preposterous girth, well over three hundred pounds, prevented him from mounting a horse. His outlandish clothing resembled that of a carnival barker, his ill-fitting red wig looked, as usual, to be on backwards.

Brigham turned his bloodless face on his footman. "Would you get me some water to drink, Brother Smith."

George A. glanced around for someone to give the order to.

"I prefer it come from your hand," Brigham said.

Ellen felt herself growing faint and wished Nancy were beside her. George A. waddled off. Brigham squared his shoulders and lifted his chin. The photographer took four pictures, moving so as to catch different backgrounds. After what seemed an eternity, Ellen heard him say, "Thank you, sir."

She walked away, her ears were ringing and the ground seemed far beneath her feet. Then Nancy's hand was in her own.

"Are you sick?" Her mother looked so white.

"No, I'm alright, keep going."

On the back porch of the Salt Lake House a different problem had arisen. Sitting next to the Lafitte's leather trunks were pillows, folded air mattresses, a tent, and blankets.

"Good Lord, Nathan!" Uergin stared in disbelief at the pile. "We'll have to buy another wagon!"

Nathan grimaced. "Maybe I did go overboard."

"Overboard! You sank the goddamned ship!"

"Wait, I have an idea."

"Treat it kindly, it's in a strange place."

"Load everything," Nathan begged, worried less about what to leave than what to tell Daphne. "It'll be a shakedown, we'll see what fits and what doesn't."

Uergin didn't have time to argue, and so they loaded everything. That done, Nathan hurried off to fetch the women. They strolled leisurely downstairs, stopping to adjust their hats in the front-room mirror, before making their way outside around to the tables under the trees, and to the back of the house.

Where Daphne took one look at the small wagon and mules and stopped dead in her tracks. Ellen walked around her, stepped up on the bench behind the wagon and folded herself away under the canvas. Nancy followed.

Nathan took sharp hold of Daphne's arm. "Get in *now*."

"I am not getti…" The next thing Daphne knew she was being propelled onto the step and into the wagon.

The canvas over the end-gate was cinched tight. The wagon jerked and creaked, Uergin at the reins. Daphne could hear Nathan urging the led horses on and wondered if he might actually be riding one of them.

*I hope you break your goddamned neck!*

The wagon swayed gently. The muddy road stretched across Big Field and climbed the further terraces. Shapeless wool hat pulled low whenever meeting anyone, Nathan walked briskly along, enjoying stretching his legs. The clean air smelled sweetly of sage. He never used to think of sage as smelling sweet, but that was before suffering through two weeks of far more odious vapours.

Uergin, too, was feeling good. That Jeremy'd done alright. The box was badly weather-beaten, but the running gear was solid. Mules were a little long in the tooth, but healthy. Harness was pieced and patched, but not dried out. Not bad for two thousand dollars, not bad all.

Seated with little more than a foot of space between her head and the canvas roof, Daphne was miserable. On pins and needles waiting for Nathan's signal, she'd overlooked her own needs. Now she was going to have to crawl back outside and hunt up a damn bush!

Nancy peeked through the tiny opening in the back canvas. Leaving the boarding house, she thought she'd seen a black and white pony. And sure enough, there it was tied with the other horses, even a saddle on its back.

A rising tide of freedom filled Ellen's chest, then her throat. It was time to leave. She'd buried a fine husband in the Valley and left a fine son there, a son who would go far in the church. It was a man's church anyway. All she had to worry about now was Nancy, Uergin would help. Almost twenty years she'd known him. Whatever in the world had he come to Great Salt Lake for, if he didn't get her letter?

"Tell me before we leave sight of the Basin," she told Nancy.

The wagon reached the highest overlook. The women worked their way to the ground. Unstirred air overspread the city, leaving the tops of the taller buildings perched like ducks on a smooth, brown pond.

A lonely bell sounded in the distance. Ellen picked up a rock and hurled it at the sound as hard as she could. Unheedful of the large number of horses secured to the rear irons, she returned to the wagon and lay with her face against the canvas.

# THIRTY-TWO

THE JOURNEY BEGAN but several hours earlier halted well before dusk, much to Nathan's disappointment.

Jeremy rode up, surprising no one.

"He rode ahead to clear the way," Nancy explained to Daphne with a show of disgust. "He likes to pretend it's the old days."

Uergin wanted the wagon emptied out. The humpty-dumpty pile grew and grew. Clothes, groceries, bedding, tools, trunks, tents. A lovely silver ewer Ellen couldn't bear to part with. Several sacks packed by accident containing quilt scraps and clothing meant for the rag committee. Gifts purchased for the stage never taken (always carry gifts, Nathan explained, one never knew when one might need a friend). Numerous pairs of shoes, including a spiffy new pair claimed by Nathan to custom-fit the left and right foot. Dozens of smaller cases holding Daphne's cosmetics, jewelry, gloves, perfumes.

And last of all, a pine rocking chair!

Uergin positioned the surprise, made fancy with a foot rest and a tall back, on even ground and offered it to Ellen with a low bow.

Next, he doled out flat rubber packets and ordered the boxes and trunks discarded. Shook open, the packets were as large as barrels and reeked of mildew. Daphne sprinkled a bottle of White Heliotrope perfume inside her sack, closed the sack firmly, shook it, took another whiff, and reached for the perfume bottle again.

Watching her, Nancy laughed and laughed.

Helter-skelter into sacks went the contents of the trunks and little boxes. Ellen was going to leave the ewer, but Uergin shoved it under a wagon bench.

Refused a second sack, Daphne wheedled enough space from Nathan to pack her silk plush cape trimmed with dyed-pink marten fur. Unfortunately, she had to leave all her hats.

"Why, what do you know," Uergin would say, bringing forth yet another box. "Now, I wonder what we'll find this time."

"That's none of your business," Daphne would reply, snatching the box away. But she did have her day in court, albeit briefly.

"Now, who's laughing, Mr. Smarty Pants?" She held the brown cambric coat and walking trousers toward Uergin. "They're certainly wide enough, but too short. Wasn't there a mirror in the store?"

Nathan closed his eyes, grimacing.

"Are they *yours?*" Daphne asked, turning on Nathan.

Everyone was laughing, but Daphne.

"Nathan!" Daphne bellowed. "These are mine? you bought these for me? just how big do you think I am?!!"

Nathan came across a leather roll that turned out to be a bear hide.

"Jeremy!" Nancy cried, reaching for it, "You're giving me your bear hide! That is so unlike you."

"I ain't giving you nothing!" Jeremy grabbed the hide away. It had belonged to his father. The bishop shot it while with a hunting party near the San Pete cliffs, and tanned it himself. It was a beautiful hide, thick, deep black.

"Well then, what's it doing here?"

"'Cause I'm here, stupid."

"Are you staying?"

"No, I'm leaving in the morning, are you staying?"

"Oh, yuck."

Ellen shook her head. "I thought you came to say good-bye, you can't go with us, we don't have anything packed for you."

Jeremy upended the sack thought to be full of rags. A few rags fell out, followed by clothing and a bedroll.

Ellen was aghast. "But your schooling! you belong here, your friends are here."

"How about my schooling and my friends?" Nancy asked.

Ellen was shoving the bedroll back in the sack. Jeremy pushed the flat of his hand against the air. A familiar gesture. Ellen dropped the sack and walked away from the wagon, and Jeremy followed. There was an angry exchange out away from the wagon, but it didn't change anything.

"I *knew* that old, beat-up saddle on that horse looked familiar," Nancy said. "Jeremy's always up to something stupid."

Taking advantage of the confusion, Uergin hoisted a leather bag out of the pile and walked away from the fire. Not, however, before a familiar clink caught Nathan's ear.

"Why, Mr. Uergin! you brought along something with which to christen our journey. I commend you."

All eyes were on Uergin.

"He wasn't going to tell us," Nancy said.

"Oh no, dear," Daphne cooed. "I'm sure he was just going for glasses. Now Nathan," she eyed the pile uncertainly "where *are* your glasses?"

"Right here, my little cactus flower." Burrowing a bit, Nathan triumphantly produced a small black satchel.

Uergin glumly fished the whiskey bottle out of his possibles sack. Nathan waited until Ellen and Jeremy returned to the fire and poured two fingers of dark liquid in each of six small glasses.

"I do not drink alcohol," Nancy said.

"In that case…" Uergin reached for her glass, but she beat him to it, taking a mouthful and spitting out what she didn't swallow. "Aggg, that's awful!"

"To the road!" Nathan said, hoisting his glass.

And everyone answered, "To the road."

The wagon was repacked without the supper fixings and bedding. Uergin scooped a hollow inside a ring of rocks and lay unhusked corn in the hollow and built a fire over the corn and lay rods across one side of the fire and an iron tripod over the other side.

"May I hand you something, Mr. Uergin?" Daphne inquired sweetly, watching him position an iron skillet on the rods and hang a coffee pot on the tripod.

"Nope, I'm ready. Here's your grease and meat."

Daphne sputtered and threw up her hands, but Uergin was off and gone. She scooped out a spoon of grease and dropped it on the skillet, where it slowly melted. She poked at the stack of steaks. "Nathan!" But Nathan was helping Jeremy move the mules. Nancy wandered up.

"Don't we put flour or something on these?"

"We can do it either way." Nancy eyed the clutter of groceries and winced. Her mother was sound asleep in the rocking chair. "Let's do it plain."

The steaks were burned, and no one thought to add coffee to the water in the coffee pot, but the corn was delicious. After supper Nancy washed the dishes, Ellen and Daphne dried, and Nathan looked long and hard for the tent-pins, finally locating them in a side tray in the wagon box along with the poles. Next there was the hammer to find. Struggling thus, he decided that Uergin didn't know how to travel overland in a wagon.

But Jeremy read things differently. By not setting up the tents before dark, Uergin was teaching them the hard way the penalties of not knowing where everything was kept. Considering the long road ahead, they couldn't learn too soon.

In the clear night air the sky was a bowl of stars. Nancy was amazed. "I never saw the sky so beautiful! Did you, Jeremy?"

"Sure, you have to get out of the Valley to see it."

It had been Uergin's plan to sleep the women in the wagon and Jeremy and Nathan in a small tent on the ground. With the addition of Nathan's large tent, the women slept there instead. Jeremy meanwhile ignored the small tent to unroll his blankets near Uergin's.

Before retiring, Ellen apologized to Uergin. "I had no idea about Jeremy's coming with us. He's so quiet, I never know what he's up to."

Daphne certainly wanted an apology from *someone*. Lying on the cold rubber air mattress under the smelly rubber blankets, she addressed a long litany of grievances beginning with the missing folding chairs and velvet-covered camp stools. "Did you see a folding chair anywhere, Nancy? Or a camp stool?"

She worried about her nails. She worried about her skin. And remembered the parasol! *Her good black Gloria silk parasol left behind in the room!!*

Nancy covered her head to hide her laughter.

"There must be a sheet here somewhere," Daphne muttered, feeling along the edges of the bed. She suspected Nathan of hoarding the sheets. "He has a taste for the finer things of life, apparently he's forgotten that I do too. We're going to smell rubbery all day long! this is impossible, whose brilliant idea wa...good god! what's crawling up my leg!"

Nancy laughed so hard her stomach hurt.

"Nancy...Nancy!"
"What!"
"It's time to get up."

"Go away, Jeremy."

Daphne opened her eyes. It was pitch black. She lifted an edge of canvas. It was just as black outside. Nancy was burrowing through the covers to the foot of the bed for her clothing.

Daphne closed her eyes and retrieved a corner of the blanket. This couldn't be happening. Then Nancy found a mouse in her trousers.

"Why do that?" Jeremy asked, watching Uergin blindfold the mules.

"A mule's a funny critter," Uergin explained. "One end bites, the other end kicks. You say they're out of a pack string? More'n likely they was blindfolded before being packed, and they had a bell mare. Mule never forgets. Might as well do it their way as best as possible. And you always wanna carry a blindfold with you in case they get in trouble. Blindfold works real good."

He eased the harness down, the blindfolded mules standing perfectly still. "It's when they hear a noise they don't expect that you got trouble. Smartest thing then is to get away 'til they finish kicking their fool heads off and settle back down."

"Why didn't we just get horses?"

"'Cause we don't want any more trouble than necessary. Mule'll take care of hisself where a horse won't, he's a real sophisticated little guy."

The day that started at three a.m. under a quartering moon, by mid-afternoon was overcast. There was a soft rustle of rain on the wagon canvas and a sudden roll of thunder. Uergin halted in a sparse shelter of tattered willows and unhitched the mules. A thick fog closed in, set aglow with lightning strikes that shook the ground. Anticipating hail, Uergin threw a heavy canvas over the mules and lashed the canvas to the harness.

But the thunder rolled away taking the promise of hail with it. The fog lifted and a fine, steady rain fell. They built a fire in the shelter of the wagon using a stash of dry wood carried from the previous night's camp, and coaxed it along with much huffing and puffing. Ellen pulled a black dress from the wagon and ripped off a sleeve.

"I never packed my black dresses to save," she explained, feeding the material to the fire. "I was going to wear them out on the road, but I'm tired of wearing black."

Daphne served up a skillet of half-cooked, burned potatoes mixed with eggs poured from a jug and a large helping of murderous looks in Nathan's direction. A wind came up, changing the rain to sleet and making a blizzard of it. The party huddled close to the fire for warmth, but the wind stole the warmth.

Bedtime. The ground under the tents was wet, but the bedding stayed dry. The next morning Uergin produced rubber cloaks and caps and wading boots from his now magic stack of rubber goods.

Their third night out, skies overcast and fresh snow on the grasses. Hungry and cold, Nathan threw in the towel. The result was crisp bacon smothered in gravy made from the grease and poured over stale bread.

"I can't eat this," Daphne complained. "You didn't use enough flour."

"The starving Chinese would be glad to have it," Nathan answered.

"Or the Indians," Nancy said.

"Ha!" Ellen exclaimed. "Don't fret for the Indians, they always have meat."

"Young dog's the best," Uergin allowed. "Turned on a spit."

"With the hair scraped off," Ellen said.

Nancy made a vomit face.

"It's good, isn't it, Uergin. Buffalo blood jelly on the side, maybe a little meal made with corn and kidney fat."

"What's really good is raw kidney sprinkled with green gall juice," Uergin said with a whistle. "Just enough for a little zest."

That night he put a guard on the camp, taking the first watch. Jeremy took the second. More than once the boy fell sound asleep. It took several nights, but eventually he taught himself to stay awake until dawn and catch a little shut-eye on the back of his horse.

Nancy named her pony Pal and rode him everywhere. The first time she saw the pony roll on the ground after being ridden, it scared her.

"Sometimes you just gotta let a horse be a horse," Jeremy told her. "You know what I mean?"

"You're a big help, what if he rolls on me?"

"He ain't gonna roll on you deliberately, did you notice how he looked around making sure there was no rocks?"

In time Nancy grew tired of the saddle and rode about like an Indian. She also grew tired of Jeremy's advice and relied on her brother only to catch up the pony.

For her part, Daphne preferred viewing the countryside out the back of the wagon, the flaps having been left open, except for storms, since leaving the Basin.

When Ellen rode in the wagon, Uergin drove. Something about her wasn't right, something in the way she moved. She told him she wasn't sleeping well, that she had nightmares—the Apostles arguing with the all-seeing eye, babies crying and men praying.

She worried about her garden and the roses and Phoebe, and buried her disappointments in anger, but there was no naysaying the dreams—Brigham sitting on an upended barrel collecting his tolls at the Eagle Gate and shaking his fist at her, Dinky dragging her moldy trunks south into the eye of a buffalo skull.

When Ellen walked, Nathan drove the wagon. Why this
dangerous chore fell to him and not to Jeremy he never did
figure out. His very first day he had two runaways for no reason
at all that he could see. Two days later the mules shied at a
rabbit. Each time Uergin and Jeremy rode the brutes down.

"They're funning with you," Jeremy explained. "Mules get
bored, they wanna do something different."

Cold comfort to a man whose stomach tied in knots every
time he took the reins. "I don't think I'm cut out for this," he
would argue, but to no avail.

At supper-time Uergin told stories. The elephants on the
Oregon Trail. Trapping beaver on the Powder River, named for
the fine sand blown over the surface by the wind. Exploring the
Yellowstone, named for the yellow cliffs that lined the river.
Cooking fish in the hot springs up in the Madison River country
and seeing columns of water shoot up high as a flagpole.

West of the Bear River divide they had the prettiest day since
leaving the Valley, the air soft as sheep's wool, fragrant with the
lingering perfume of the evening primrose.

That afternoon Ellen wore her red dress. She'd made it to
wear on picnics in defiance of Brigham's ban on the color red,
along with a red dress for Nancy and a red shirt for Jeremy. She
called the clothing their picnic clothing. George never would
bend. His shirts always had to be white. Just the same, he liked
the bright colors bobbing around in the green meadow, he said it
made hide-and-seek easier to play.

She felt so good, so good, better than she had in years.
Determined to be loud and light-minded she put a red comb in
her hair and whistled at the birds. She wouldn't worry about
Phoebe anymore, the Lord would take care of Phoebe. Tonight
she'd talk Nancy into sleeping out under the stars, they'd have
so much fun. She'd show Nancy where the dipper was and the

bear. Maybe they'd sit out with Uergin awhile, and he could tell her some stories.

*All we have of childhood is just a glimpse,* she would tell him, *and then it's gone forever.*

Watching Ellen, Uergin fell in love all over again. What a picture, and wasn't Nancy pretty, chattering away like a little monkey. His very own daughter.

*I should of been the one raising her, I could of raised her and Jeremy both.*

But not as good as George, he knew.

That night Ellen lay down to rest before supper and never woke up.

# THIRTY-THREE

*Adios, mi corazon*

ELLEN WAUSAU MARCHION HARRIS, mistress to the Great Scout, wife to the Grizz, was laid to rest in a shallow grave on a lower slope of the Bear River divide June 18, 1863, and covered over with stones. She was forty years old. Her bed was Jeremy's bear robe. Tucked under her arm was Edward Lear's *The Book of Nonsense*, the only book Nancy carried from home.

Sunshine flooded the sky, a light breeze cooled the grave diggers. Nathan performed the service regretting he had no bible to read from. It didn't matter, there was no way to soften the blow.

Daphne stood with her arm tight around Nancy. "Don't you be feeling bad about your momma, she's not there in the ground, she's up walking in heaven in a brand new dress."

Camp was broke. It was time. Not seeing Nancy, Uergin went looking and found the little girl seated beside the grave. Fastened around her neck was the blue-stone necklace he'd given Ellen the night she left him for a rich man's bed. Uergin stared and jerked his head away. Taking his seat on a convenient rock, he studied the countryside, worn to hardscrabble by the passage of thousands of wagons.

After awhile Nancy removed the necklace and cupped the stones against her mouth to warm them before carefully laying them on the grave. "It came from the Indians, maybe the Indians will come along and take it back, my mother wouldn't mind. She never said anything bad about the Indians the way some people do. That's what Jeremy's father is."

When she was ready, Uergin offered his hand, and together they made their way back to the wagon.

A storm blew up, making the road slick. Uergin and Jeremy rode hunched against the wind, hats pulled low, collars turned up. In the wagon, shivering under the feather comforters, Nancy talked to her mother, straining to hear her mother's voice in reply. Nathan and Daphne huddled on the wagon seat, a blanket around their shoulders, another blanket across their knees.

Daphne wiped the wet hair off her forehead. "I'm going to die out here too, Nathan, and it's all your fault."

Nathan didn't answer. His fingers were stiff on the reins. Damn his decision to buy pitiful silk gloves instead of mittens!

They crossed Bear River using a new bridge, paying fifty cents, and stopped to fish on the far bank, catching several fat speckled trout. Every day the weather was the same—mornings breaking clear and cold, then clouds rolling in. At Bridger's, camped on a flat near the shallow stream Uergin called Blacks fork, they lay by two days and washed their clothes and slept like old rocks. To Uergin's disappointment, Jim Bridger was gone off into the Bitterroot country.

The old trading post was full of American soldiers and emigrant traffic. The first edition of a newly minted newspaper, a single-sheet affair called *The Daily Telegraph,* was out on the street. Making his chair against a rock Nathan read of a General Connor's putting an end to Indian attacks along the California Trail with his defeat of the Shoshone Nation. God bless General Connor. General Meade stopped General Lee at the Battle of Gettysburg, the military draft had gone into effect, Vicksburg had fallen to the North. A Turkish bath was being built in New York City, and the author of "Dixie," a northerner and Union sympathizer, was surprised to find his song sweeping the South.

An exciting world out there.

Jeremy sold the pet horse he'd ridden away from home, and kissed it good-bye on the nose. Nancy paid a squaw a penny for a large, brown eagle feather and tied the feather in her bridle.

Uergin told stories about the fort before it was a military encampment, and the traders and Indians who stopped there. The original buildings fell down, he explained, describing them as old poles with a dirt roof that the first good snow caved in. Stouter buildings were then erected a little ways off to take advantage of the emigrant traffic, but the Mormons burned those buildings out in 1857 to stop the American Army from using them.

Daphne found the history talks excruciatingly tedious. Who cared if Jim Bridger couldn't read or write, or if the Indians called him "Blanket Chief" and the trappers called him "Gabe." Then there was that really dumb story about a Crow chief called "Long Hair." The chief's hair was eleven feet, six inches long. He did it up in a braid and doubled the braid until it was about eighteen inches long and six inches wide, leaving it to hang down his back in a big club. Now wouldn't that be a dandy conversation piece!

Her own observations were much more fun. Starting, and ending, with the handsome young men who occupied the fort. Lamentably, by the time she felt rested enough to air out the proper clothing and call on the officers' wives, Uergin was wanting to move on.

No one talked about the alternatives—that here at the crossroads with the Oregon Trail, where stages routinely pulled out westbound for Fort Hall and eastbound for the States, it was possible to part company. That's because everyone knew the real crossroads were in Lawrenceville.

Further up the road, at a noon stop in a poplar grove south of Hams fork, Jeremy remembered the rum and burrowed in the bowels of the wagon to where a false board concealed a case of pale golden brew.

"It's a surprise from mother," he explained to Uergin. "She said she owed you, she was saving it for when we got to Bridger's. I just now remembered it."

Holding a bottle against the light, Uergin could hear Ellen laughing.

"So why'd she owe you?" Nancy asked.

"If I tell you that, then I'd have to tell the rest of the story."

"That's right!" his listeners exclaimed.

"It come from California, the distillery right down the coast from where I live," Uergin teased.

"That's not the story," Nancy prodded. "C'mon, tell us everything."

So he did, the whole long story, not just the short of it. After first helping himself to a healthy swig of rum and handing the bottle to Nathan, who painstakingly wiped the mouth of the bottle with his tie.

When drinking rum, Nathan preferred the dark rum. Hot and sweetened with sugar and flavored with a pinch of nutmeg, there was nothing more worthy of the name.

"Nathan, if you're not going to drink it…"

"When in Rome…" Nathan said regretfully, and took a fastidious sip.

Uergin took another slug and made himself comfortable against the wheel.

"It was in '46, I was working for your pa. We got to Bridger's, and I got to gambling and lost a good horse. That *was* a good horse, I called him Bunny.

"So I felt pretty bad, and I was a leetle worried about your pa. I needed another horse, but I didn't need a sermon, which put me in a bit of a bind. Preachers can work up a real lather over liquor. So I bought a horse from Bridger on the cuff for ninety dollars and a bottle of States rum. It was a good horse, called him Eagle, a big, red sorrel.

"After leaving your pa's wagons in Oregon, I went on to California, then down to Mexico. I could tell you stories about that, too. In 1850 I hired on with a fellow called Hedrick to take him out West, now there was a Scotsman for you, never took his hand off his purse. Tried a hundred times to fire me."

"Why?"

"He was smarter'n me, knew everything there was to know about that road, read it in a book. He'd figure out where we was and try to chop off the rest of what he owed me, kind of like buying a donkey but only wantin' three legs."

Uergin paused to squint at his listeners. He looked around for the rum and held it up against the light. "Nathan, our bottle's got a hole in it."

What happened next?" Nancy asked.

"I'm going, I'm going, I'm just tryin' to put a good face on it. Like I say, your family has got me in a whole lot of trouble over the years. Like sittin' here right now with you yahoos, 'stead of back in Frisco enjoying those cool ocean breezes. Now where was I?"

"With Hedrick."

"Right. Ornery old rooster. The last thing I did, leaving the Westport Landing, was buy that bottle of States rum I owed Bridger. Well, it wasn't to be. Your ma was on that train, and she up and traded my good rum for information on a little Indian girl she took a liking to at Fort Laramie."

"That was Ruth," Nancy said.

"Something. Then your ma owed me, which leads us to our

good fortune today. Hand me what is left of that, Mr. Lafitte, if you do not mind."

Yes, sir. The whole story, right down to how Ellen bought Taos whiskey, the whiskey the traders called Mexican mule, to replace the rum, and how the Mexican mule made Bridger sicker than a dog. Well, that last was kind of a fabrication, but it was funny.

Better than the truth. Uergin's eyes went out of focus.

Gabe wasn't at his fort when the Hedrick party got there, so he traded the whiskey to a squaw for the blue-stone necklace.

He told Ellen to wear it the night she left him, and she said it was too gaudy, but she changed her mind and sat down on the bed for him to fasten it. She was all excited. Then she was gone, like now, just flat gone.

"Are you going to sleep, Mr. Uergin?" Nancy asked.

"I've got to lie down," Nathan said to no one in particular, and crawled under the wagon. Uergin got to his feet and wandered toward a convenient tree where he spent the rest of the afternoon catching flies.

Jeremy unhitched the mules and put them on pickets. The graze was poor, but at least they got a half-day's rest.

Daphne went down to the creek and took a bath behind the bushes. She wasn't worried about treacherous Indians, there weren't any around, or Uergin wouldn't be drunk. He was smarter than that. Not only did he know everything there was to know about wilderness travel, but if it hadn't been for him, they wouldn't have rubber bedding and rubber clothing in the rain.

And Nathan wouldn't know how to cook hot pone and dundy-funk and slap jacks and squaw bread. Not that he was any good at it, but she didn't want the job.

What Daphne didn't know, which was just as well or she would have teased him unmercifully, was that Uergin talked to himself. Jeremy knew because he rode with Uergin.

And Jeremy knew that Uergin wasn't talking to himself, but to his horses. This funny little habit afforded Jeremy the perfect opportunity to talk about his favorite subject.

"Some folks work these horses and don't like 'em, some folks like 'em but don't understand 'em. In this business you gotta like horses."

"What business is that, Jeremy?"

"Like you and me right now, leading the way to the States and watching for Indians. If we sell out on these horses, they'll sell out on us. You gotta ride 'em quiet. Some people get on a horse and the first thing they do is get real noisy, horses don't like a lot of noise, they don't know what to do with it."

One bit of philosophy led to another.

"If a horse likes you, he'll partner right up with you. But if he don't know you, he's got to be careful. A horse can sense if you like him...

"...horses would be better off if people didn't wind 'em so tight. They're like clocks, they get wound too tight and they don't work right. They look around and say 'this is just too much.' A horse is not a dog, you know what I'm saying?...

"...treat 'em decent and they're not scared of you, that's the way you want it. People think you gotta hurt 'em or scare 'em, now that's just plain stupid...

"...they don't ask much of you, they don't ask for Sundays off or nice smooth roads..."

"...when a horse is watching you, he's asking you what you're gonna do...

"...a problem with a horse is like an itchy place, you better scratch it 'til it gets solved...

"...the thing about a good horse is not that you can ride him, but that anybody can. A good horse knows how to take care of hisself and take care of you. Why, I've knowed horses who dance around and have a gay old time when somebody's on 'em that knows how to ride, but you put a kid on 'em, and you see how quick they shut down…

"What do you think, Uergin?"

"Well, that's about what I think."

"Tell me about the Indians, about my people."

"Tall like you, good-looking people. They get all fancied up for dances, they're something to see. Coils of silver around their arms and hanging from their braids, lots of beads, lots of bright paint."

"You know what I think?" Jeremy said. "I think they must be real good horsemen, they'd have to be. That's one thing white people don't realize coming into the mountains–horses that ain't used to rough ground worry about getting tippy. They got to learn how to go, you force 'em and you can get in a terrible wreck."

Around the campfires, wishing to distance himself from the empty chatter, Jeremy was a man of few words. But truth to tell, he liked to talk. He liked to think too, studying the countryside. These welcome periods of drought were invariably followed by monsoons.

"A man's got to walk the line between the ten commandments and the laws. They ain't always the same. You got to use common sense and try to be kind. You got to let the water run downhill, you know what I mean? There's no downside to being honest and being kind."

"You got to appreciate the kindness in a horse's eye and put a little sugar on the words when you talk to them, pet a horse with your heart *and* your hand."

"Your ma said you was real quiet," Uergin observed mildly.

"Yes sir," Jeremy agreed.

When Uergin wanted to rest his ears, he'd send Jeremy back to ride drag, even though they weren't pushing cattle and the

horses—long ago left loose to follow the wagon—needed no
encouragement.

Sometimes he'd interrupt with, "Be quiet, Jeremy, I want you
to hear what I say." And he'd point out a nearly-invisible trail
and talk about spotting trails. Or point out plants and explain
what to eat of the wild foods and what to pass by.

They crossed Green River on a ferry run by a ferryman well
into his cups. It wasn't yet ten o'clock, leading Daphne to
wonder what kind of a job the fellow would be doing by late
afternoon. Thirty miles later, in a hard wind, they reached
Big Sandy. The ground grew increasingly more arid, the grass
thinner. Slowly but steadily the Rocky Mountains were lifting
them up. The next day they watered at Pacific Springs, but
were forced into the hills for grass, and poor grass at that. At
least it got them out of the wind for awhile, an unceasing wind
determined to make a kite of the wagon.

The only real bad trouble they had, and that depended
on who was doing the telling, came at the top of the pass
through the Rocky Mountains, high on the headwaters of the
Sweetwater, when both a leader and a swing mule lamed up on
the stoney road.

"It's a good thing we're on the downhill slant," Jeremy
observed. "It won't matter if we shorten the team."

To which Uergin replied, "Jeremy, you're a worry to Christ."

Working with Jeremy, he put the good swing mule on the
lead team, moved up a wheeler, and filled in the blank places
with the extra saddle horses.

And walking behind the team, shook out the ribbons.

The horses kicked over the traces and tangled themselves like
sled dogs twisting in harness, and it took awhile to get the hitch
lined out again. Eventually off they went, mules kicking, horses

humping and bawling, Uergin following on foot, geeing and hawing. And singing.

> There is a tavern in the town, in the town, and there...whoooa, whoooa, whoa!...my true love sits her down, sits her down...HEY! that's enough! stop that!...and drinks her wine with laughter free...stop that!...and never, never...whoa, boys, back up...thinks of me, fare thee well, for I must...step up now, step up... leave you, do not let this...whoa, HO! HO!...parting grieve you, just remember that the best of...calm down, calm down now...friends must part, must part, adieu, adieu...EASY THERE!

Twenty minutes and several songs later, he hitched the team to the wagon. The horses tried to run away, but the mules, obstinate as usual, wouldn't go anywhere and kicked when crowded.

Poor horses, wall-eyed and forming at the mouth, ears laid back. Jeremy was horrified at the rough, humpty-dumpty spectacle.

Eventually Uergin was able to pull the wagon up and down the road without a fight. "The problem," he explained, crawling out of the wagon, "is mules is real clannish, they don't like partnering up with someone new, but I think we got a handle on it now. They're all yours, Mr. Lafitte."

"Surely you jest," Nathan squeaked, but Uergin was walking away.

Jeremy soothed the distraught animals as best he could, whispering in their ears and rubbing their necks. Nathan climbed into the box as if mounting a keg of dynamite. He was talking to himself. "Up we go, absolutely, of course, a man must do what a man must do, mustn't he." Daphne thought him incredibly brave. Uergin laughed so hard he like to busted a gut.

As it happened, things turned out alright. The mules knew their business, and both horses and mules were tired of arguing.

But poor Nathan. Departing his perch at the evening stop, he could hardly walk from having been braced stiff as a board for hours.

That night Jeremy slathered the cut hooves on the lamed mules with grease and wrapped their feet in burlap. "You can't just wrap one foot," he explained to Nancy, who was helping him cut the burlap. "Or they go to favoring it and lame up on another."

"Hurry up, Jeremy."

The next day Uergin stopped at what he called the ice slough, and digging down less than a foot beneath the overburden, withdrew chunks of ice clear and beautiful as ever seen. Daphne rooted around in the food box and found the sugar and the cups and poured sugared water over the ice, calling it lemonade. And Uergin told how the Sweetwater got its name from a pack mule falling while crossing the creek and spilling its load of sugar in the water.

Some three hundred miles from the salt lake Uergin pointed out his name, scratched on the Independence Rock. The date was 1826. Scratched nearby were the words, "H. Scott '26."

"That there's your ma's pa, your grandpa," he said. Jeremy and Nancy stared transfixed at the letters. "You wanna hear the story?"

And so there he was, telling the old story again, but never before to such a grand audience. How he came to meet Hiram, what a good person Hiram was, what a wise person, kind to people and to animals. Yessir, Jeremy came by his love of horses honest enough.

One hundred and forty miles further down the road at Willow Springs Uergin put the recovering mules back in the hitch—a good many days after the brutes had stopped limping it seemed to Nathan.

A large group of horse soldiers approached.

Daphne was clumping along in the ugly boots purchased for her by Nathan in Salt Lake City. A hateful exercise, but one that got her out of the jouncy wagon for awhile. She was tasting warm buttered biscuits spread with warm maple syrup and little finger sausages on the side. And a cup of black tea with a delicate peppermint flavor in a delicate china cup decorated with tiny red roses, and the sugar spoon the same. Or perhaps silver. Filagreed. And a bowl of thick cream. She didn't care for cream, but it should be on the table.

The officer touched his hat as he rode by.

Daphne almost fainted. Behind the officer trooped a glorious parade of young men. She combed her hair with her fingers and smiled at the beautiful, tanned, resolute faces. She was still smiling when all she could see was the dust settling back to earth. Smiling through her tears. Not one of those brave boys looked her way! not with a glance that lingered. And why should they?! Her hair was frizzled, her ugly cambric trousers were filthy, her skin was burned.

She would never forgive Nathan, never! never, never!!!

# THIRTY-FOUR

ORT LARAMIE. With Nathan in charge of the camp, Uergin and Jeremy crossed the river and rode up the hill to the fort. The cool darkness of the sutler's store was awash in the smells of tobacco and spices and fresh ground coffee.

Uergin lit a cigar and handed it over, and Jeremy took a deep drag, put the cigar down and didn't pick it up again. The whiskey tasted worse than hard cider wrung out of wormy apples, but he kept his face straight and emptied his shot glass.

Two old men sat in the corner counting out their coins. They wore white men's clothing, but they were Sioux. Uergin joined them with the whiskey. They reported no squaws around the fort, the camps were out on the prairie. The soldiers visited the white squaws living in tents in the trees.

Returning, Uergin upended what was left in the bottle over the glasses. "Might be forced to get us another bottle," he said with a foolish grin. Damn! life was good.

"Jeremy, my boy, it's time you went down the line."

Jeremy frowned, wondering if he were being sent back to camp.

"Used to be the whiskey came in casks," Uergin said. "A jug'd cost you a dollar, or you could fill a tin cup for a dime." Remembering, he fell silent.

A buck wanting whiskey would trade a squaw for a jug, a pretty squaw that'd been to the river.

When the fur company men came to the fort with their Indian wives and dogs, now that was a parade to see. Those squaws were downright beautiful. Bright red blankets over their shoulders, soft leather dresses embroidered with ribbons and corals and beads, silk kerchiefs on their heads. Their horses all decorated up with ribbons and beads and little bells that jingled when they passed by.

Those squaws couldn't be bought for whiskey, but their favors could be won in a card game with an unlucky lord. Remembering, Uergin tipped his head back laughing.

That's when truth walked in the door. It sat down beside him and blew against the back of his neck and grew and grew until it filled the room.

*Oh Jeez! oh, Jesus Christ!*

Uergin emptied his glass and stared at Jeremy as if from a great distance.

"I'll be right back," he said abruptly, making a pushing motion with his hands. "You just stay put."

The room washed pleasantly around Jeremy. That was interesting, watching Uergin with the Sioux. He didn't know Uergin could use hand talk, he bet his mother could too.

He decided to buy another bottle and fished in his coat. He had a quarter. He sat for awhile, considering what to do, and settled for carrying the glasses up to the bar. The sutler refilled the glasses and gave him a nickel change. Pleased with himself, Jeremy sipped the whiskey and considered the room. Most of its occupants looked to be soldiers. He wouldn't mind being a soldier, as long as he could ride a horse.

Uergin returned. His attitude hadn't improved any. He led the way outside and around behind the barracks to the Quartermaster's office. There in the map room, on a big map smudged and worn with use, he ran a forefinger down the line marked *Council Bluffs Road.*

"If anything goes wrong, stay north of the river 'til you reach Fort Kearny, that's the easiest grass and you don't have to fight Ash Hollow and the south fork. Fort Kearny's right here above Grand Island, you'll see it across the river, there'll be a ferry here, use it, even if the water's low.

"Once across, some ten miles down the Platte, you pick up the Independence road turning south, can't miss it."

Uergin paused, the trails to the Missouri River and the edge of the States coming together in a slow waltz in his thoughts. There was no point describing the shortcuts to Jeremy, no point at all.

"The Independence road follows down the Little Blue and crosses the high ground to the Kansas. There'll be a ferry on the Kansas. Some forty miles upriver of the ferry crossing you hit the big trail junction with the Santa Fe, that's where you turn north to Independence. At Independence you're in the States."

The map ended, Uergin's finger kept going, tracing an invisible road.

"Follow the Missouri east to St. Louis, Lawrenceville is east of St. Louis, your ma's map shows where. There's lots of people on the roads, you won't have no trouble."

Jeremy stared down his nose at the map. "How 'bout that."

"Sober up and pay attention!" Uergin snapped.

Jeremy squinted his face and pretended as best he could. The map moved gently back and forth.

"You got any questions? you following me?"

"Sure am."

"Let's go then," Uergin said and stepped out into the bright sunshine.

"Let's just have another drink." Jeremy made a beeline for the sutler's store. "Nathan's got it covered."

But Uergin stopped where the horses were tied and crawled on his horse, so Jeremy floated after him.

"Your ma said you was supposed to be in Utah," Uergin explained as they rode through the gate. "It was like you had some destiny to go there or something 'cause the Indians said so. But I don't figure it that way, never did. Your people, the Cheyenne, got no history in Utah and no business there.

"The way I see it, your people knew you was going to the land of the Ute, alright, and wanted to get you back safe. Indians know things, there's no accounting for how they do it. That place where your grandpa died, that's way south of here, down on the Vasquez on the Arapaho trail. That trail runs north of the river into the mountains. Your grandpa went there to protect you, now that's how I heard it. Your people and the Arapaho are friends, but that there's a dangerous place for you for some reason."

Jeremy knew the story. It was interesting. If he ever got to meet a real honest-to-god Cheyenne—not that there seemed to be much chance—he'd ask about that trail.

Uergin's words cut into the fog. "Talk to the men at Fort Kearny, find out what's going on ahead, talk to people coming up the road, remember what I told you."

Jeremy agreed, although he didn't remember squat.

They were approaching the Platte. Jeremy wrapped his hands around the saddle horn and considered the possibility of falling off. Crossing rivers made him dizzy, and he was already dizzy.

"Listen to me!" Uergin barked. "I want you to hear what I'm saying. Ever' time I mess with that dirty old river out there, *every single time*, whether I'm outbound or headed for the States, I got to have one good bout of trouble. *Got to.* It's the rule…Jeremy, you listening?"

"Yes sir."

"Quit with the sirs. Remember when we crossed the Platte below Devil's Gate at Richard's Bridge and then crossed back on account of the grass? remember? and we never had no trouble, did we? ...Jeremy?"

"No."

"That's right, you *are* right, we never had no trouble. And that means big trouble. There's gonna be a terrible wreck, it's out there waiting for us."

Jeremy was silent. Uergin grinned despite himself. "To give you credit, son, I did notice if we ain't talking about horses or Indians, you ain't got much to say. Just remember, anything happens out there, don't let your hummingbird brain overload your alligator ass."

Jeremy groaned, but not too loud, and heard Uergin say, "But if you gotta be a bear, be a grizzly."

Two girls wearing Shaker bonnets were walking up the road toward the fort, the wind hiking their skirts mischievously. Jeremy smiled broadly, and the girls smiled back.

They reached the scatter of wagons north of the river. Uergin was talking to his horse, something about there not being a damn thing he could do.

An emigrant working a shotgun free of a pile of goods dropped the weapon on the ground. The charge caught Uergin square in the chest, knocking him off his horse. The last thing he did was pull something out of his shirt pocket. A shredded piece of blood-soaked paper. And handed it toward Jeremy, who bent over him white-faced and shaking.

N

W ◇ E

S

# THIRTY-FIVE

THEY PLACED THE BODY in the shade of the wagon awning and covered it with a blanket.

"We need to make arrangements for a proper burial," Nathan said, eyeing the blanketed form. "Jeremy, hold my horse." And he climbed on Uergin's horse and followed Jeremy back to the fort.

That night no one mentioned Uergin's name, so great was the void that yawned at their feet.

The next morning in the hard dirt on a chilly hill long abandoned to the dead, the man who led Elder George Harris across the wide prairies in 1846, and who seventeen years later buried that elder's good wife on the Bear River divide, was himself buried by his friends. He was fifty-one years old.

Soldiers took the blanket-wrapped body to the graveyard in a mule-drawn cart, the little knot of mourners following on foot. One of the soldiers blew taps with a silver bugle, and the detail lowered the body with ropes into the hole dug earlier. As the soldiers worked to refill the grave, an uneasy wind brushed gritty dirt over the mourners in a kind of baptism. Then the soldiers went away, leaving the desperately lonely graveyard cloaked in silence.

"We have to say some words," Daphne said, her arm tightly around Nancy. "I'll start. Lord, he doesn't look too good right now, but he cleans up good, and he got us here. That has to be worth something."

"This was a good man with horses," Jeremy said forcefully, hearing his father's church voice in his ears. "That's the finest thing I know to say, Lord, because you made the horse. And, Lord, you must of needed him up there pretty bad to take him away. Don't be sending him anywhere else, because he doesn't belong anywhere else, don't think that for a minute. Just because he has a drink once in awhile or swears a little. He's a man you can count on, Lord, a man on the square." Jeremy breathed deeply and looked at Nathan.

"This man was my friend," Nathan said. "He invariably acquitted himself well under the most trying of circumstances. I never once saw him do anything small or mean, I certainly recommend him to your care. Forgive him his trespasses as he forgave those who trespassed against him. Amen."

"Amen," everyone said and hesitated, as if waiting for a signal to leave.

Nancy held her arms wide. "Tonight the wolves in the desert will call Uergin's name, they will make their music just like we make ours. Now everyone sing 'Wayfarin' Stranger.'"

They sang one verse and the chorus, that's all they knew, but that was enough to set the heart weeping.

"What you said was beautiful," Daphne cried, drawing the girl away down the hill. "Just the right thing."

"When my mother died," Nancy sobbed bitterly, her face hard against Daphne's shoulder, "I was mad at her for making me leave the Valley, and we made up, but I never said I was sorry, I never did! and then she died, and we never sang, and she likes songs so much…I feel so horrible…so horrible!…and I just made up my mind to do it right this time."

Poor baby. Poor little girl.

Nathan wanted to meet with the Quartermaster to discuss conditions on the road east.

The Quartermaster reported minor Indian outbreaks north and west of Fort Kearny. The problem, he explained, was the withdrawal of soldiers from the frontier to fight the war in the States.

"Where you headed?"

"St. Louis," Nathan replied, studying Ellen's map.

"Most direct route's down the Independence road. Your best bet's to cross here at the fort, grass is worse, but road's safer. What are you using?"

"Mules."

"That's good, mules is easier to take off the road. Here at Ash Hollow," the Quartermaster ran a finger down the long wavy line marked *N. Platte,* reminding Jeremy of Uergin's futile gestures, "you turn south away from the river and get up on the bluffs. You're headed for the upper ford of the south fork, there's no ferry, you gotta cross as cross can. Ever cross a big river before?"

"No."

"The thing to remember is don't get in a hurry. If that south fork's up, you're looking at water over a mile wide running faster than the Missouri. Watch someone else cross, see how they do. Any military wagons going across, hook up with them.

"Caulk your wagon water-tight and raise it to the top of the standards and tie it down. Soon as you hit the current, follow it up or down at an angle, depending on your shallows, but don't get sideways and don't stop anywhere but on dry ground."

Embarrassed that he could point to nothing familiar on the map to ask about, Jeremy was silent. Uergin had said something about Fort Kearny and Ash Hollow, but he couldn't remember what.

A small circle centering a tangle of fine lines toward the
middle of the map caught Nancy's eye. "What's there?"

"That's a mining camp, Cherry Creek."

Breaking camp they took the government ferry across the
Platte, waiting several hours in line behind government wagons
hauling rock. At the fort Jeremy sold one of his horses and
one of Uergin's. The money bought grain and groceries and
postponed the need to root through Uergin's things.

Late afternoon, across the creek called the Laramie and lined
out for the States, Jeremy rode up front alone, following his
shadow east. Nancy walked beside Daphne, the large Mexican
hats purchased at the fort making puddles of shade. Nathan
drove the wagon. The one extra horse and Nancy's pony trailed
behind.

The wind took up with them, blowing as hard as it had on
the top of South Pass, but steadier, as if rolling downhill it'd got
up a head of steam and couldn't stop. Standing in it was like
standing in a river.

"It's very hard on the complexion," Daphne said, smoothing
her cheek. "I feel like a piece of hemlock." To her constant
sorrow she'd left her chamois-skin face masks in the Salt Lake
House. "Try this, Nancy." She pulled her hat ribbons, which
were no more than wide strips of bug netting, across her face and
Nancy followed suite.

"If we can figure out a way to pin the strings over our face
tomorrow, the bugs won't get us. That is, if the wind stops
blowing. It's either bugs or wind, take your pick. I'd like just one
day with no wind and no bugs and nothing to do but walk on a
beach and watch the ocean break on the shore. It's so beautiful,
and no two waves the same, and the noise rolling in, building up
ahead of it."

Less than two miles down the road the front axle snapped.

They'd arrived at Fort Laramie having no extra axles left and meaning to restock, but forgot. Jeremy rode back to the fort while the others made camp on the open sage, building a fire of twigs and dead sage in the lee of the crippled wagon. There was no grass, but the animals had eaten well enough earlier.

Nathan took them to water, and dusk was coming on by the time Jeremy returned dragging a new axle and a spare. Supper was a dismal affair. Nobody spoke, just sat staring into the flames.

"It's time we went through Uergin's things," Daphne said briskly, her voice on the quiet ground making the others jump, "Give ourselves something to do."

So that's what they did, making a ritual of dividing the contents of what Uergin called his possibles sack so as to blot out the feeling of thievery.

Folded in a metal clip was six hundred and seventy-five dollars in paper money. Nathan put the money in his purse and gave the clip to Jeremy. A deck of playing cards from the Lucky Lady along with a pair of black dice went to Daphne. An extra shirt and pants looked closest to fitting Nathan. At the bottom of the sack, wrapped in a clean kerchief, was the blue turquoise necklace.

Astonished, scarcely knowing what to make of the find, Nancy fastened the necklace around her neck.

Jeremy wanted the leather sack itself and found inside, caught on the hide, a braided horsehair bracelet. The bracelet was too small to get his hand through, so he poked it in his shirt pocket for good luck.

The fire burned low. Nathan said he'd take Jeremy's guard shift. The thought of sitting out alone in the dark with a gun listening to the wolves and the owls with their terrifying howls was distressing to say the least. But no worse than leading the mules down to the river, snakes slithering here and there, the ornery mules pushing at him. That's the way life was now, what choice did he have.

Puttering around, getting ready for bed, he realized Jeremy had gone sound to sleep by the dying fire. *At least I won't have to get up in the middle of the night,* Nathan told himself ruefully, covering the sleeping boy with his blankets, *I'll already be up.*

There was a meteor shower going on. The shooting stars looked like sparks scattered from a hot fire on a windy night. Nathan considered waking Daphne to watch the brilliant display with him, but knew she would recognize his cowardice for what it was.

A coyote yipped in the direction of the river. Was it a coyote, or an Indian recruiting his friends? The minutes ticked by—a veritable Chinese water torture. Surrounded by the muffled footfalls of dreadful catastrophe, Nathan resigned himself to spending the night in the open. He couldn't very well wake Jeremy, that would be shameful, the boy had his hands full as it was.

Jeremy woke him. It was bitterly cold. Nathan stumbled to his tent wishing he had Daphne to warm himself against.

Half-asleep, leaning against a wagon wheel, Jeremy heard a distant rumble. His first thought was for buffalo and the stories heard from Uergin. But before he could warn the others, he saw to his amazement an Overland coach drawing near. In absolute silence, except for the dull munch of wheels, the coach glided by—a dozen horses in the hitch, three shadowy figures on top— and disappeared against the stars to the southeast.

Early the next morning everyone walked out to study the ground. Sure enough, there was a road through the sage. Not much of a road, just two strings.

"It wasn't a ghost after all." Nancy sounded disappointed.

"I never said it was a ghost, that was your idea."

The mule called Repeat kicked at its belly, moved a little ways off and kicked again. Now he was pawing the ground. He stopped, grabbed a mouthful of cracked corn, and chewed furiously.

"What's wrong with him?" Nancy asked.

"Colic," Jeremy said. "Just what we need."

"Can he be fixed?"

"Not with what we got. The best I can do is buy time enough to get him back to the fort." Which Jeremy did, mixing soda and laudanum in water and pouring the concoction down Repeat's throat.

Next, he laid the poorest set of harness across the mule's back and and headed out. The journeying took awhile, the attacks growing in severity despite the laudanum.

At the fort the colicky mule brought twenty dollars, the harness fifty dollars. Jeremy bought a sack of hard candy and a wheel of cheese. Back at camp, working with Nathan to refit the axle, he realized they were missing a bolt and walked off into the sage kicking at the dirt.

The day was half over, and they hadn't moved an inch.

"Something's wrong, Jeremy," Nathan said when the boy returned. "There's something we're supposed to do different."

"Yeah?" Jeremy said. "Well, you just tell me what the goddamn hell it is, I'll sure fix it right up!" And he stomped off into the sage again.

Nathan found the bolt and struggled alone with the axle.

Something *was* wrong. He'd learned years ago that unforeseen obstacles falling one after another across his path were meant to turn him aside. It wasn't something he wanted to believe, it was just the way things were.

First it was the axle, then the mule. Were they being cautioned against traveling alone? They could wait at Fort Laramie for a government train, Daphne wouldn't object to that.

Or should they be taking the stage? leave everything behind but their clothing?

He pondered so hard he got a headache and decided the only thing to do was wait for the next event to unfold.

Midafternoon, down to four mules in the hitch and Repeat's partner running loose, they lined out again. But when Nathan reached the lonesome rabbit track through the crowding sage, he stopped the team. "Is this the road you saw the coach on?" he asked Jeremy.

"Yep." At least Jeremy thought so, in the afternoon light it looked different. Glancing around, he spied a long hank of horsehair caught on the sage. "Yep," he said again.

Nathan nodded. The hank of hair wasn't much of a sign, but to a man watching for signs, it was enough.

Nancy and Daphne came up.

"Down there somewhere is Cherry Creek," Nancy said.

"That's a pretty name, Cherry Creek," Daphne mused.

"Prettier than Lawrenceville," Nancy said through her nose.

"Why do you think the stage was running at night?" Nathan asked.

Everybody had an opinion. Indians maybe. But then Jeremy remembered seeing a lantern hung on the coach. There wouldn't be a lantern if the driver were worried about Indians. Maybe it was to take advantage of the cool night air and get away from the bugs. Maybe to get out of the wind, Daphne didn't think the wind blew as hard at night.

"We're going to Lawrenceville," Jeremy said firmly, as if anyone had suggested otherwise.

When he could do so without being overheard, Nathan spoke to Jeremy. "I strongly believe there's a reason we've suffered two delays since leaving the fort and before passing this road, this road's the stickler. It could well be a sign of a sort. I'm not a superstitious man, but I have learned there is generally a reason for the little roadblocks, little nudgings you might say, that come one after another. We may well be meant to continue our travels eastward by way of Cherry Creek."

Jeremy didn't think so, but Nathan persisted. "There is more we don't know about how things work, than we do. Ride down that road aways, see how it makes you feel."

It didn't make Jeremy feel any different. But studying the bone-dry world under the southern horizon, he did recall his mother's telling him how hard it was not to leave the Hedrick train and go south into the desert when she left the States the second time. She said the Cheyenne, she called them "the People," would find her.

His mother said there were ghosts at Fort Laramie, that she could hear them in the night. Was someone trying to tell them something?

The lonesome track wandered off, hiding itself in the sage.

Jeremy glanced back at the wagon with its little knot of people anchored in a sea of sage. Duty called loud and clear, but the siren song of curiosity is what got him. He pulled the pistol from his coat pocket and shot a hole in the sky and yelled, "What are you waiting for?"

# THREE

# THIRTY-SIX

NEEDED ! !
22 BRAVE MEN AND BOYS
TO DEFEND THEIR COUNTRY.
THE CONSCRIPTION ACT
HAS NEVER BEEN APPLIED HERE.
DO NOT LET IT BEGIN WITH YOU.
> Sign posted on courthouse door,
> Houlton, Maine, August 1863.

ONLY TWENTY-ONE MEN VOLUNTEERED. No surprise there. If President Lincoln's generals would fight, the war would be over. Meade, Burnside, and McClellan, what a bunch of rabbits. Grant was the only commander worth his salt.

Thinking about the men who'd already walked away from wives and sweethearts and farms, the mill supervisor at the Cary Lumber yards decided to sign up. Why he did this made no sense to his devoted wife.

"You are not going off to war, you idiot! what in the world is wrong with you?! You know Shep Cary isn't well, he depends on you, for what little good that does. We all depend on you. You have a wife and two sons, and all you want to do is run away, just like you ran away five years ago!"

Untended, the pan of pudding popped, splattering pudding across the hot lids.

"I been putting it off for two years," Jed said, moving to slide the pan back.

But Julia, distraught with fright and anger, swept the hot pan onto the floor. "You just keep putting it off, you hear! Let them have their slaves, who cares!"

"It's going to split the country."

"Mr. Lincoln's who's going to split the country! It's one thing to leave me, if you're tired of living with me, it's another thing to leave your children, there's plenty of men without families, they're the ones to be taken if the enrollment's low." Down on her knees, wiping up the mess, she ticked off the names.

Jed bent down with a towel to help her.

"Not that! that's not a rag!" She grabbed the towel out of his hands. "Just go away and leave me alone!"

In the end the couple made up. Julia determined to wear black until her brave soldier came home, Jed promised to write as often as possible and send souvenirs for the boys.

Cary was running two mills day and night. Bringing on his replacement, Jed moved the foreman in the Red Dog Mill into the front office and filled the foreman's job with a ratchet setter from Gordon's Falls.

Two days later the new foreman reported the boiler leaking. Jed shut down the Red Dog and shipped the boiler down to Hodgdon, where the iron works put a plug in it and pronounced it safe.

Monday the boiler was put back in service. Jed was standing there watching it when he noticed a small leak. He stepped on the footboard of the engine and signaled a stop with the whistle, and reversed the lever. And stooped down to scrape out the fire.

The roar was deafening. A cloud of dirt and steam engulfed the mill. The giant engine sailed twenty feet through the air to land with a ground-jarring thud. The boiler turned inside-out and shot through a wall and across the yard, slamming into the coal shed and splintering it to pieces. The long drive belt, writhing like snake, wrapped itself around the man working the gig, cutting him severely on the head and arms.

The fellow who, hearing Jed's whistle, had jumped on one of the tables to turn the water into the batteries, found himself awash in planks and timbers. A skid man standing some twelve feet behind the engine was knocked down by the steam and water, his face and hands badly scalded.

The most amazing escape belonged to Jed. Stooping to scrape out the fire saved his life. Instead of being hit by the engine, he was blown through the opening in the roof over the saw pit, landing a good hundred and forty-two feet away under a wagon. He was unconscious for the better part of a day, during which time Dr. Clare removed a six-inch piece of iron embedded in the bone below the knee, but was unable to right the dislocated shoulder.

A week later, hating Yam, hating the world Yam represented, Julia watched the Indian and her crippled husband ride off into the woods together.

In the Malicite camp on the Tobique, deep in the North Woods, Jed lay in a sweat lodge with two rows of warm, flat stones down his back and a large stone on his pelvis. Cooling, the stones were replaced with others.

Half-asleep, he felt hands on his shoulders and tried to relax. This would have to work. There was a sharp crack, a wash of pain. He moved gingerly, testing the result.

A month after the accident he was back at work, the Aroostook Seventh regiment having long ago marched off to war. At the last minute three more volunteers boosted the total recruitment to twenty-five, but not before Shep Cary paid the three-hundred-dollar exemption to keep his foreman at home.

⬧

One year later. September 1864. The Walker Marchion farm at
the mouth of the Mohawk, New York State.

"We've got to try *something!* we have a problem we're not
facing."

"*You* have a problem, Dinky's doing just great."

"Walker! she's dying!"

"We're all dying."

"Don't be dramatic. I'm telling you, the light's going out of
her eyes. She won't talk about California, she won't talk about
what happened."

"Katherine." The tone sounded a warning note.

"I don't try, Walker, it's her children. They bring up
California. They talk all the time about going there, but she
never remembers anything they tell her from one day to the
next. And that's my point. She helps them with their lessons,
she reads to them. She talks about the farm, but not about Mun,
or California. Don't you think that's odd? I think that's odd."

"It's nothing we can fix." Walker was sopping his bread in the
soft eggs on his plate. He didn't much like eggs in the evening,
or boiled fish anytime. Helping out the neighbors, he never got
fed meals like this. In fact, there wasn't anybody he knew didn't
eat better than he did.

"I think there *is* something we can do," Katherine argued.

Walker shrugged. "What's for dessert?"

"There isn't any."

That night, undressing for bed, Katherine pressed her
concerns again. Dinky's headaches were returning, along with
a growing malaise. She was not eating well. According to
Christina, she was not sleeping well either, prowling the house
and the yard into the wee hours of the morning.

"You and I are the only ones who *can* do anything, Walker."

Shivering under the cool covers, Walker worked his feet against the warm, towel-wrapped stone. Last week it was the Soldiers' Aid Society in Troy. Next week it would be the Union War Bonds Committee, and the week after that the Constitutional Amendment Committee. Today, apparently, was Dinky's turn.

"Desperate problems call for desperate measures," Katherine said.

"Come to bed, dammit, it's cold."

Which Katherine did, lying there wide awake, Walker drifting off to sleep against her.

A sudden rush of wind in the trees rattled the shutters.

Comforted, thinking *I'd rather hear the wind than you anyway,* Katherine recalled the desert. What a wonderful journey, the coach flying over the rough roads, the countryside unfolding in slow-stirred colors.

The next morning over breakfast she told Walker she was canceling her commitments for the rest of the year and taking Dinky to visit New Mexico. Stephen and Lymund would go too.

Walker couldn't believe his ears. *Simply could not believe his ears!* Was she losing her mind? NO! There was a war going on! He felt the blood pound in his temples and took a deep breath. "Why not a few days in the Adirondack? You haven't been there in years."

"I just think the desert air would be good for her." Katherine hesitated—it was so obvious, but it was so harsh—"Why not let Stephen's father look after him for awhile?"

"Good Lord, Katherine! you're talking about Dinky's *son!* You can't just tear a family apart."

"Dinky is dying! Stephen needs to be with his father."

"His father is a savage, you wouldn't know him if you were looking at him."

"Dinky would know him."

"And how is that? she doesn't know us. And we don't know when she got blind, maybe she never saw Stephen's father."

"Now hear me out. The other day when I was up at the farm, the wind broke a branch out of that old apple tree near the house. I was sitting on the porch with Dinky when it fell. There was this big crash, and just for a minute, less than that really, Dinky knew me, I mean, really *knew* who I was. And when she looked at me, I could almost hear her say, 'I have to go back.' It was very unnerving."

"Oh shit!"

"And the only place I can think she has to go back to is where all her troubles started."

"No, and that's it."

"We have the money, and I can make the time. The war's down in the Deep South, it won't affect us, the trains are running west, I checked."

Walker didn't answer and Katherine stopped pushing.

Then came the dream.

She woke early one morning, and drunk with sleep, walked through the house to the kitchen to start the fire. The morning star was up, shining with an unusual brilliance, and that's when she remembered the dream.

She was on the coast watching the ocean white-knuckled against the shore when she saw Dinky walking across the water, then the water was sand, stretching on and on, and Dinky was climbing train steps. She was carrying a large traveling bag, and the train was taking her away. Katherine could smell the coal smoke and hear the engines.

Unnerved by the memory, she walked through the house to the back bedroom and pulled her traveling bag with the jacquard coverlet out of the closet. Yes, that was the one.

She didn't describe the dream to Walker, she simply told him at breakfast that she was taking Dinky to Albuquerque.

"You can't control Dinky by yourself."

"She's much better."

"That's because she's here. You've forgotten what a terrible time we had getting her here."

Katherine slid a big piece of ham onto Walker's plate, followed by hot biscuits.

"Are you trying to soften me up?"

"I guess." Katherine ruffled her husband's hair and kissed his brow, knowing his thinking. As unapproachable as he was for small children, Walker liked them very much. It was as if in them he saw his own missed childhood, the childhood he never talked about. Locating Stephen's father would solve a big problem for the caramel-colored little boy. Small for his age and a half-breed to boot, in school he'd be a sitting duck for every mean-spirited prank that came down the pike.

"Well, don't look at me," Walker groused. "I've got commitments, and I don't sleep well in strange beds."

"It will be difficult without you," Katherine said dutifully.

"Then stay home where you belong." Actually, he was used to her traipsing around the countryside. He supposed by the time his daughters finished Normal School they'd be off too, totally untethered from domestic concerns. Hopefully they'd marry provident husbands, they'd get none of his money for their foolishness.

"Oh, Walker dear," Katherine simpered, "think how well you're going to eat, you'll have an invitation out every night. You'll be round as a bun by the time I get back."

"You better take Lymund along to help."

"That's a good idea."

◈

Far away to the southwest on a high ledge, Dancer made his
usual prayer for his wife's return. For over a week fog and rain
had swept the canyon lands. As Dancer stood listening to the
whispering night, the moon broke through, turning the fog at
his feet into chunks of tallow floating on black water.

The Paiute stared at the scene, wishing his wife could see it. If
she were here, he would tell her that this was the cool moon, the
moon that made the animals put on their fur coats. She should
follow the cool moon across the sky, it would lead her home.

A prayer no more heartfelt than all the other prayers for her
return. Only this night, picking his way back off the rim to his
lodge, Dancer was sure he heard footsteps on the rocks behind
him.

# THIRTY-SEVEN

*I* *THINK SHE'S BECOMING SENILE. She hates Indians and she abhors the West, she nearly lost her only daughter there and three of her grandchildren. I got hurt there.*

Walker was listening to his wife and his mother go on about New Mexico—the scenery, the healthy air, the colorful natives—as if the Southwest were the promised land. They were in the waiting room in Troy, Dinky was inside with the doctor. Walker had insisted on the examination and on securing an ample supply of sedatives.

*She's never liked Katherine. She must be getting senile.*

The doctor joined them with a small bottle of Horsford's Acid Phosphate and a large bottle of Perry Davis Painkiller, and a bill for nine dollars. There should be no problem with the journey, in the very least it would be a good airing for the patient. That afternoon Katherine, Dinky, and the boys boarded the *New York Central* for New York City.

"I wish you were coming with us," Katherine called gaily from the little wooden platform. The boys were already on board, waving wildly through the windows. Now Dinky could be seen taking the seat across from her sons.

"We will next time," Christina promised.

Walker managed a weak salute.

At New York's Grand Central Station the sojourners

transferred to the *Baltimore and Ohio*. In Wheeling they would transfer to the *Illinois Central* for Kansas City—the whole of the train travel to take not more than seventy-two hours and cost less than one hundred and twenty dollars. It was all spelled out on the paper tacked to Katherine's kitchen wall. Not addressed was the cost of the stage from the edge of the States to Albuquerque, and the cost of the lodging while in Albuquerque, those matters requiring a certain latitude.

A woman with a cat got on. Escaping its basket, the cat wandered down the aisle and settled in Dinky's lap with a contented purr. A banjo player worked his way through the cars played a lively tune, his wife followed behind holding out a tin pitcher.

In Virginia an eating car was put into service. The car offered a kitchen and pantries in one end and small tables bolted to the floor in the other. That it would not be necessary to leave the train to secure food was an immense relief to Katherine. Railroad-bound, Dinky was proving surprisingly little trouble.

The nephews, on the other hand, were an endless source of trouble. Wondering how she could have possibly forgotten that, even when Dinky was well, the Miller children ran amuck, Katherine alternated between scolding and bribing Lymund to watch out for Stephen.

"You are nine years old, you know better. Stephen is only four, he doesn't know any better. You *must* set a good example!" But Stephen continued to play hide-and-seek at every opportunity, and Lymund continued to wander off, visiting here and there, totally unattached to his family.

"Lymund, would you like to have a horse to ride?"

"Sure."

"You may have a horse as soon as the opportunity presents itself, if you will keep track of Stephen."

This worked occasionally, but only occasionally.

They caught the stage in Independence, Dinky remaining docile, doing whatever Katherine told her. The Indians along the road were reported to be hostile, but the men in the stage were heavily armed and professed themselves to be crack shots.

Fortunately, there was only one real scare.

It happened in the wild country below Fort Larned, at the noon stop in the middle of nowhere, when Dinky stepped out of the outhouse and hurried off in the wrong direction.

Lymund wandered inside the station. "Mother's taking a walk," he told his Aunt Katherine. Frightened, Katherine ran outside in time to see Dinky disappear through the sage.

"STOP!" Katherine yelled over and over, running as fast as she could. Succeeding in planting herself in front of Dinky, she yelled "RIGHT NOW! GO BACK TO THE STAGE!"

Katherine had visions of having to enlist the men to carry Dinky bodily back to the station, and worse, of being left there, the driver deciding his passenger was too much trouble. But Dinky stopped just short of bumping into her antagonist, turned, and marched back on her own hook, oblivious to the stares of the passengers roused from their meals.

The remaining miles of the old Santa Fe trading trail were uneventful. The weather was splendid, neither too hot not too cold, the autumn prairie colors soothing in a sweet, melancholy way. In Albuquerque the rooms arranged in advance in the Atlantic and Pacific Hotel were more than suitable. More important, the children swarming in the streets were the same hue as Stephen. This is where the boy belonged.

Katherine could not have been more pleased. That first visit with Walker was such a shock, and so exhausting. Back then the little streets with their little shop signs, the open markets, the restaurants—all had to be ignored in favor of getting Dinky home as quickly as possible. Now she was back, and there was time for everything.

After a short rest—it was impossible to rest long anyway, with Lymund and Stephen to entertain—the sojourners strolled through the plaza, stopping in the mercantile firm of F. & C. Huning to buy *serapes* bright as the American flag and black sombreros with silver discs the size of dimes.

Another short rest, and then it was supper. And so they whiled away the days, shopping, strolling aimlessly, taking carriage rides. Why anybody would like Albuquerque, Katherine had no idea. She didn't know why she liked it. The dusty, narrow streets were rank with manure and infested with flies, the hostelry was slovenly despite its being new, the food was too hot and there was no ice for the water. Still, there was just something about Albuquerque, maybe the air, maybe the music after dark.

Not until their fourth day in the city, after instructing Lymund, "you just keep everybody together and I'll buy you a new pair of boots," did Katherine resume her self-imposed task.

The lieutenant in charge of the Army Post at Albuquerque listened intently while his visitor described how her sister-in-law, a Mrs. Editha Miller, had been captured from the Indians and brought to Albuquerque in 1858. He shuffled some papers, as if the needed file were on the desk.

"Mrs. Miller's sight has returned, fortunately, and she has returned to the city with her two sons, one of whom was fathered by an Indian, and is hoping to be reunited with her Indian husband."

"And where is he now?"

"He lives around here somewhere."

"And his name?"

"I don't know his name, but she was brought to Fort Defiance first, so that's where we should start."

The lieutenant looked disappointed, he stopped shuffling papers. "Fort Defiance was shut down in 1861 by the demands of the Civil War. What's his tribe?"

"Do Indians have tribes? I don't know."

"You're familiar with the campaign to remove the Navajo?"

"I'm from New York, I didn't even know you'd been attacked by the Confederacy until I saw a plaque on a building."

That seemed to be a rule with mannish women, to have no idea what they were talking about. "If he's Navajo, he'll be over on the Pecos at Fort Sumner."

"How far is Fort Sumner?"

"Roughly a hundred and fifty miles."

"Well, alright, we'll start there."

Thanking his lucky stars his visitor wasn't the wife of a ranking officer and wanting an escort, the lieutenant got to his feet. "There's a stage leaving here tomorrow, give Colonel Worthington my regards."

Waiting for the Fort Sumner stage, Katherine struck up a conversation with the editor of *The New Mexico Press*, a talkative fellow from Pennsylvania who explained that Fort Defiance, although closed down in '61, had been re-established in '63 for a campaign against the Navajo. Mountain man Kit Carson operated out of there along with a thousand New Mexico Volunteers.

"It's been renamed Fort Canby, but nobody calls it that. Too bad you don't know what tribe you're looking for. Mescalero Apache is what's at Fort Sumner right now, some five hundred of 'em from down on the Pecos. There's not many Navajo in there yet, they're still being rounded up, you think you might be looking for a Navajo?"

"He could be an Eskimo for all I know. I do know that my sister-in-law came from Fort Defiance."

"Well, that's west of here."

"How can I get there?"

"A supply train goes out regularly."

"Who provides the supplies?"

"The Huning Brothers."

Franz Huning was most happy to accommodate the American who had already spent so much money in his store. His wagons would be leaving in two days. For fifty dollars he could provide a buggy and a driver and a suitable tent with bedding.

"A tent?" Katherine said.

"Fort Defiance is a hundred and eighty miles from here, seven days out. There will be no danger, the wagons travel under escort from the Post."

The land through which the road wound was uncommonly fine, covered as it was with a sea of tall grass curing in a silvery, blue-green shimmer. Cedar and piñon appeared like lonely sentinels, slowly gathering themselves into clusters, and at the top of Campbell's pass into a cool, refreshing forest.

Fifty-five miles further, approaching a cleft in a high ridge, the wagons passed by a colony of curious-looking sandstone pillars and cones, some over a hundred feet high. On the other side of the cleft rose an immense mass of trap rock at least two hundred feet high resembling an old cathedral blackened with age. Beyond here were the gardens of Fort Defiance. A scanty rivulet had been dammed to create several respectable traps, but the dams had long ago been breached by heavy run-off and left unrepaired.

Nearing the encampment Katherine noticed a scatter of tents across the nearer slopes, hundreds of them.

"Good grief, there's a lot of soldiers here!"

"Them's Indians," the driver explained.

"Indians?"

"They come in on their own, they got no food or blankets
otherwise."

"What in God's name is that about?"

Watching the carriage disgorge its load, Kit put down his ink
pen. Two boys and two women? where did they come from?

An aide, sent to inquire, was told the women were looking
for an Indian.

Kit stared at the aide is disbelief. "Get 'em in here."

Katherine came alone. The man who introduced himself as
Kit Carson was small of stature, wiry, with a wizened face and
a thin braid of faded brown hair that hung down his back. His
clothing was leather, as were his boots.

*So much for the spit and polish of the military man,*
Katherine reflected, aware of a decided chill in the room, and
explained the reason for her visit.

"You got a tent?" Kit asked her.

"Yes."

"Put it up by the wagons you come with, and leave with them
same wagons in the morning."

"What about finding the Indian?"

"I'll let our interpreters know that Mrs. Miller is here looking
for her husband, that's the best I can do."

"I was hoping she might be able to meet with some of the
Indians, that one of them might recognize her."

The fort's commander looked confused.

"Mrs. Miller was blind when she was brought here, so I'm
not sure she's ever seen her husband, I don't know when she got
blind. I hoped..."

Kit was laughing, a deep, belly laugh.

"...I *hoped* coming here might trigger some little memory.
I thought if I brought her back to the scene of the crime so to
speak..." Katherine smiled deprecatingly "...not that there *was*

a crime that we know of, but back in New York she seemed to be slipping away from us, so I had to try everything."

"Slipping away from you?" Kit could easily imagine wanting to slip away from this woman. He didn't seem to be able to stop laughing.

"We won't be in your way, we'll just walk around...out of the way."

Which they did, strolling about aimlessly here and there.

*I should have married a soldier,* Katherine scolded herself, seduced by the romance of the lonely outpost. *Why did I never ask myself, where do the men go that leave the Point? In the very least I should have visited the western forts. I had friends who married military men, why didn't I visit them?!*

Such a dry land. The bleakness was almost painful. No greenery except what grew near the creek, the fort's flag snapping and popping in the ancient wind. *Only brave women and resolute men need apply here,* Katherine reflected.

She tried to draw out the soldier who accompanied them, he moved out of earshot. She approached a group of Indians sitting on the ground. They looked to be starving. Another group the same, and another, clothing all in tatters, faces gaunt. Several squaws came close, fingering the white women's skirts. The soldier shooed them off.

A toothless old woman crouched beside a curl of wood smoke. Seeing the white people, she got to her feet, speaking loudly. Katherine opened her hands, hoping to convey her ignorance of what was being said. The woman backed away, and Katherine began to feel a slight menace in the air. She looked at the soldier, who seemed unconcerned. "Dinky," she snapped, frustrated, "does your husband look like any of these people?"

Dinky replied with the blank stare she always gave a direct question, and Katherine turned and led the way back to the security of the fort's buildings.

The wagons were parked by a long warehouse, the tent had been set up and a bucket of fresh water placed inside the canvas flap.

*If ever I have to rent another buggy and driver in Albuquerque, I'll be sure to employ Mr. Huning,* Katherine told herself. In the privacy of the tent she washed as best she could and redid her hair, and made Dinky come inside and wash.

And went in search of the boys, who disappeared shortly after realizing what was in store. Avoiding the commander's office Katherine strolled about the parade ground calling the boys and trying not to see the further tents—keenly aware that she'd visited but a tiny fraction of what was out there.

They remind me of trapped mice in a drawer. I didn't see any horses, I wonder if they have to walk where they're going.

A Mexican leading a horse caught up with her. He smiled and touched his hat brim and asked something in Spanish.

"The best laid plans," Katherine answered forlornly.

"Often go astray."

Katherine's mouth dropped open. "How do you know that?"

The Mexican looked at Katherine's hand, at the diamond wedding band. *"¿Esta su esposo aqui?"*

Guessing at the gest of the question, Katherine walked on. But then she turned to say, "It's oft…oft go astray."

"It can be whatever you want," the Mexican said, his warm eyes steady on Katherine's face.

Her own face reddened.

## THIRTY-EIGHT

THE BOYS SHOWED UP at supper, sitting with the teamsters in the lengthening shadows. On the slope the tents made their own forest. The Mexican approached. He'd changed his blue flannel shirt for a heavily fringed leather shirt closed with flat silver buttons. The wide leather belt around his waist boasted a square silver buckle and two pearl-handled pistols.

Would the *señora* care to take a walk? His smile anticipated her acceptance. His name was Henry Chee Dodge, interpreter and scout, and his first question, out of earshot of the others, was to ask what such a pretty lady was doing at Hell's Gate.

Hearing Dinky's story, he thought he could help.

"How's that?" Katherine asked teasingly.

"Oh, there are ways. When do you leave?"

"Tomorrow." He looked Mexican, but not quite. Perhaps part-Mexican. His mustache curved down nicely around the corners of his mouth, his eyebrows were thick, as was his dark hair.

"That is not a lot of time."

"Mr. Carson thinks it is."

He leaned so close, Katherine thought for an instant he was going to kiss her. But he simply whispered, "I'll be back."

The red sky faded into violet. Worn out with play and full of beans and goat meat, Lymund and Stephen fell asleep in the middle of the tent. Katherine made up the beds, dragged the boys to them, and brought Dinky inside from her couch against a wagon wheel.

The day slipped into darkness, and Henry came.

"I should think the Indians would have fires," Katherine said, walking away from tent, filling the awkward silence.

"They don't have wood." Henry drew the woman's hand through the crook of his arm to guide her in the darkness. "They cook in the daytime when they can find twigs, at night they wrap themselves in blankets to keep warm."

"How do you know English poetry?"

"My mother was Navajo, my father was Mexican, he died when I was four. The fort's officers took a liking to me and called me 'Henry' after Captain Henry L. Dodge, an agent to the Navajo at the fort. He didn't have a family here, so I became his family. He died in '56, killed by Apache, and I inherited his books.

"The officers taught me to read, but only in English." He laughed softly.

A full moon floated above the horizon. Katherine pressed herself against Henry's arm. "Do you really think you can help me?"

Henry was very sure he could. He was full of sympathy, his kisses were sweeter than wine, his hands strong and knowing. And if Katherine couldn't hear the anguish in the throaty chants rising out in the darkness, it was because of the wild music in her own heart.

"Navajo's all that's here, along with a few Mescaleros," Henry explained. "If these aren't the Indian's people, he won't be here."

They were walking back to the tent, finding their balance against each other on the uneven ground. Bathed in the glow of the moon the fort looked peaceful, patterned as it was in irregular patches of velvety darkness and yellow dots of welcoming lantern light from the little wooden cabins.

"I think Dinky was happier blind," Katherine mused. "Now that she can see, nothing makes any sense."

"Your friend..."

"...sister-in-law..."

"...sister-in-law, she was blind!? ¡*Chingada!* If this is true..."

"...why would I make up such a thing?..."

"...she is the wife of the Paiute called Dancer! Her name is Icamani, it means 'walks alongside.' The Paiute gave it to her because she was blind."

Perplexed, Katherine stared at Henry's profile in the night light. "You're making this up."

"Of course! I am a great storyteller! Twice a year this Paiute journeys from the Kaibab to this place. Twice a year, with his friends waiting out in the rocks like grey wolves, he walks into the yard to ask if a blind woman is come to the fort. Would you go to Moenkopi springs to meet this man?"

"You *are* making this up."

"The springs are two days below the crossing of the river. The Paiute live north of the river." Henry leaned close, his breath warm. "I am going there, come with me."

The next morning Katherine confronted Kit Carson. "You knew all along who I was looking for."

"One way or the other it don't matter. The Paiute was here three, four days ago, he won't be back 'til spring moon, and you won't be here then, no one will, the fort's being abandoned."

"I understand there are missionaries here at the fort headed for Moenkopi springs, and that Mrs. Miller's husband lives near there."

"In a matter of speaking."

"Then that's where we're going."

"And how do you plan to get back?"

"I've engaged the services of a competent guide," Katherine replied tartly. "He'll make that arrangement."

"Territory's open. Long as the missionaries don't mind, I don't."

"How very kind of you." What a boorish, slipshod man! He should be taking care of the poor creatures on the hill instead of bullying visitors.

Watching Katherine stride across the parade ground, Kit chuckled. Pushy women were like cockleburs, one way or another they had to be dealt with. In this case it'd all worked out—one of those funny, unplanned coincidences Josefa Carson called the things that are meant to be.

The missionaries hadn't asked for a guide, but they would by the time Henry got done with them. As for finding the Paiute, all that was necessary was to put out the word to the fort's scouts—men from the Ute, Zuni, and Moqui tribes—who would tell the runners, those invisible message carriers who were quicker than shadows.

"God has called on me to do this," Henry said earlier, explaining his plan over breakfast. "I know it will be dangerous."

"Very dangerous," Kit agreed. "You're a good man, *amigo.*"

"Brave too, don't forget that."


The first night out from Fort Defiance, the sage bathed in luminous grey light, the wolves so close that Katherine could see them singing, heads thrown back. Henry had carried a *fresada* out away from the wagons and was sucking on her breasts, and it was all she could do, fists wadded in the scout's soft leather shirt, not to join the wolves in their eerie opera.

One hundred and fifty miles of strawberries and cake, sweet cherries and wine—ochre countryside unfolding, distant mountains glazing over with heat, flaming sunsets vibrating with promise—that was the road west from Fort Defiance to Moenkopi springs.

The missionaries numbered nine couples and a half-dozen

children. At Moenkopi springs they would convert the peaceful natives to Christianity and set up a mission for travelers. They talked constantly of the need to do this before the Mormons got their hooks too deeply embedded in the region.

That day after day brought no sight of wild Indians was a great disappointment to the party, armed to the teeth and anxious to test their faith. And an equally great relief to Henry, who gambled heavily on the Indians being too afraid of the "Rope Thrower," their name for Kit Carson, to approach the little column.

Katherine and Dinky rode in the horse-drawn buggy owned by the missionaries. Lymund and Stephen rode Indian ponies purchased at the fort by their Aunt Katherine at a cost of twenty-five dollars apiece.

Periodically Katherine mentioned the name "Icamani" to Dinky, but got no reaction.

A day east of the springs, crossing a high red mesa overlooking a fan of deep draws off to the north, Henry realized they'd picked up an escort—men on foot who watched from a distance.

Six days after leaving Fort Defiance a handful of deserted flat-roofed stone houses lifted themselves out of the sage.

"This is a trading post?" Katherine asked.

"The Moqui live here part of the time," Henry explained.

A squaw stood in the doorway of one of the houses, out in the sage a handful of small, buck-naked men got to their feet.

"There they are!" Katherine exclaimed. "Waiting for us!"

"Aghhhhhh!" Henry spit. "Diggers, they live where they can. Watch your sister."

The minutes crept by. Waiting for Henry's signal, the missionaries studied the farm of the native, noting with surprise the large number of cultivated plots laid out in terraces on the dry slope of mountain and the permanence of the stone structures. There was still much work to be done, but much work had already been done.

The squaw was too much a part of the land to know what the foreigners were seeing. For their part, the missionaries took little notice of her.

Two Indians approached from the east, a large mongrel dog at their heels. Short, stocky men wearing breechclouts. One had a red cloth draped around his neck. Katherine glanced at Dinky. Her hand was stuck in the air, as if caught in the act of brushing the hair off her face, and she was watching the two men.

Walking with Dancer was Rabbit, a member of the UaiNuint band which lived near the Rio Virgin and worked for the Mormon settlers in St. George. As luck would have it, Rabbit was visiting the camp overlooking the Mystery River when Dancer received the wonderful news that his wife had returned with his son. Because Rabbit would know how to speak to his son, Dancer secured his services with a blanket made of goat hides.

*The man wearing red must be the husband,* Katherine told herself. *He looks as if he's seeing a miracle, which I guess he is.*

Henry helped Dinky from the buggy, and the missionaries went to work unloading their gear. Katherine ordered Stephen to get off his horse and stand beside his mother.

Dancer stopped where he could reach out and touch his son, but this he did not do. "Say I am pleased he is here," Dancer instructed Rabbit.

Rabbit had about him an air of pointed kindness. After relaying Dancer's message, he kept his head inclined, inviting the boy to answer.

Stephen hesitated, then held out his hand. Holding the small hand in his own made Dancer shake with happiness. He felt as if he were flying far out over the deepest part of the mystery canyon, swooping and climbing with the cloud bird.

Moving instinctively, Dancer led his family away from the buggy. Rabbit could be seen talking with the boy, but then Rabbit withdrew and Dancer and his family walked on alone. The yellow dog, having avoided the wagons, joined them.

Dancer took the red cloth from his neck and put it around his son's waist. His beautiful wife nodded the way she used to, only now she had her soul. The three of them laughed, and Stephen did an Indian dance, jumping up and down and making war whoops, and they all laughed some more.

# THIRTY-NINE

I N BELIEVING HIS WIFE'S SOUL had returned, Dancer was
partially right. When Dinky saw the Paiute, she remembered
a small river hemmed in by mountains and Dancer coming
up behind her. She remembered a big, red horse and that they
turned the horse loose and walked into the water.

"Where are they going?" Katherine asked, watching Dinky
disappear in the sage.

"Home," Henry answered.

"Oh, no, that's impossible!" she cried. "Dinky doesn't know
what she's doing! go get them."

"Leave them alone a little while," Henry told her. Eventually
he did ride out. He explained to Dancer that the woman and
child must return for their things.

Dancer knew that, yes, he just forgot. He turned his family
around and led them back to the wagons. What was his son's
name, he wondered.

"Come in the morning," Henry told the Paiute. "When your
family is rested for the trail."

Dancer walked away, and Katherine said, "Send the boy with
his father."

"The Paiute will be here in the morning," Henry told her.

"Yes, that's better," Katherine answered quickly, embarrassed
by her coldness. It was only fair that Dinky be made to
understand what was happening.

Dinky didn't want Dancer to leave. "Come back!" she called sharply. "Come back now!"

Which Dancer did happily, understanding the gesture, if not the words. Indeed, all the world was a happy place.

Taking care to allow some distance from the building occupied by the squaw, the missionaries commandeered the soundest of the empty houses, and that night prepared more food than usual. Dancer and Rabbit joined the feast, as did the Diggers, as did the squaw who had watched the wagons approach.

Instructed by the missionaries, Henry told the Indians about God and pointed to where the missionaries would build their church. He described how the church would look and explained that the missionaries would work very hard and that everyone would have enough food. He asked questions. The answers he received pleased the missionaries.

After supper Dancer took up his post outside the stone house occupied by his wife and son.

The boys asleep, Katherine spoke with Dinky about allowing Stephen to get to know his father. "We won't be in any hurry to leave. Perhaps when we do, Stephen will want to stay here awhile. That would be alright with you, wouldn't it?"

In the darkness of the house she was doing all the talking, it was maddening. Dinky could talk when she wanted to.

*I wonder how old the Indian is, not very, little more than a boy. God only knows where he found her, but he probably saved her life, and he's saving it again, no matter what Walker thinks.*

Henry called softly and Katherine slipped into the open. Walking hand-in-hand with her lover under the explosion of stars, she could hear agreement in his soothing words—the boy should get to know his father.

The next morning she woke to all-but-empty rooms. Only

Lymund was there, tangled in his blankets. Dressing as quickly as possible, she hurried outside. The sun was well off the horizon, there was no sight of Dinky or Stephen.

Henry was on the far side of the houses, standing at a small seep of water with several of the missionaries. "Dinky's gone off somewhere," Katherine cried breathlessly. "I'm afraid she's with the Indian, she's got Stephen with her."

"Don't worry, they won't be far," Henry said, walking back with her toward the horse corral.

"He can have his son, he can have both the boys' ponies, tell him that."

Henry nodded. "*Sí*, whatever's necessary."

And what was necessary was that he stay out of sight, but not too far away. The Paiute's friends would be watching to see that no one followed the friend who got his wife back. Late afternoon Henry returned to confirm Katherine's worst fears, Dinky had vanished without a trace.

"I can't believe I let this happen," Katherine wailed. "Why didn't I anticipate this?! What is wrong with Dinky, why can't she just behave herself!"

All day Lymund had watched for his mother. The last time his mother went away, he didn't see her for a long time, and when he did, she wasn't right. Now, hearing the scout's words, he burst into tears.

Henry shook his head, consumed with sorrow, and took Lymund on a ride to the top of a ridge to better see the dark rise of plateau off to the north.

"That is a magic place, only very brave people go there. You, too, must be brave. Listen to the night sounds, they will speak of your mother and your brother, you must know this and not be troubled."

He gave the boy a little bone whistle.

That night Henry comforted Katherine with whiskey from the stash he carried in the buggy. She woke the next morning with a terrible headache, a small price to pay for a night of spinning through the stars.

She wanted Henry to go out again and take the missionaries with him to help.

"And when they get lost, who do I look for then?" he asked with a smile.

He'd done the right thing, warning the Paiute to take his family and leave. The crazy woman was meant to be with her husband, otherwise the spirits that see out further than a man can see would not have found her and brought her here. Who knew why they did, it was a mystery, the earth was full of mysteries.

"Once across the river there are a hundred paths on the back of Mountain Lying Down," Henry explained sadly. "Not even I know which one the Paiute will choose."

Two of the missionaries were returning to Albuquerque immediately to buy another wagon and load it with supplies more fine-tuned to the possibilities of the countryside. That had been the intent all along, it was why the party brought only two supply wagons with them.

Katherine had planned on returning with them. Now, filled with self-loathing and praying for a miracle, she wanted to remain at the springs.

Henry argued against it. What good could be done by staying there, maybe even a year, before another ride came along?

The road back across the desert to Fort Defiance was as long and bleak as it had earlier been short and sweet. The crooked little draws with their crooked little cottonwoods looked ominous, as did the saguaros, arms uplifted in surrender.

At the fort the lovers spent one last night together, the night

winds crying under a razor-faced moon. Dawn came too soon, .
and with it bitter parting. Shortly after breakfast the missionaries took up the well-traveled road for Albuquerque.

Hunched down in a corner of the jouncing buggy, a sniffling
Lymund wiped his nose on his sleeve, ignoring his aunt's offer of
a handkerchief. Alas, he had convinced himself his mother and
brother would be waiting at the fort.

"Your mother did right to bring Stephen here," Katherine
reminded him for the umpteenth time. "She is coming back, she
came back home before, remember?"

But Lymund would only look away, as if remembering
something else.

*Oh, God, please don't let him know anything more.*

All the magic was slipping away, taking with it life itself, she
would never see Henry Chee Dodge again.

*I must send him books. To think he had* Little Dorrit *and* Life
of Washington *here in the middle of nowhere, and that book
of poetry held together with a string. I will send him books and
enclose a token in each.*

Mrs. Jean Paul Marchion was dead of rheumatism of the
heart. Katherine learned the news when she reached the railroad
station in Troy. The nieces had already left, taking the morning
train upriver, the service was to be that afternoon.

Arriving at the Congregational Church in the Batten Kill
countryside with minutes to spare, Katherine explained softly
that Dinky had decided to stay in Arizona awhile. And in the
solemnity of the occasion was able to postpone the details.

And maybe it was the truth. Maybe Dinky, unlikely as it
seemed, did make a rational choice. After all, she did seem to
know her husband when she saw him.

Lymund sat with his sisters during his grandmother's service,
frowning as usual. It occurred to Katherine that she should have

his eyes examined. The preacher was young and really didn't know Mrs. Marchion all that well. He did, however, know a great deal about the road to perdition. Shutting her ears to the sermoning, Katherine concentrated on her own magic journey—the urgency in Henry's hands, his soft voice in the darkness, the smells of tobacco and whiskey.

That evening Walker told Katherine of his mother's recent dream—that Dinky would come back healed.

"She dreamed it twice, she was very sure."

Katherine didn't answer. She was watching her husband undress, neatly laying his clothing aside. He was a nice man, a nice, civilized man. She couldn't really *live* in the desert, it was so…unyielding. It went from hot to hotter, from windy to windier, from dry to drier, it was like living in an oven, and so dirty.

"You say he did appear civilized."

"Very."

"And the missionaries were Presbyterian, not that…"

"…they were Presbyterian."

"Well, I guess if she knows what's she's doing, that's more than she knew here."

"Remember the carving she carried around all the time? the little black toad with the turquoise eyes and turquoise collar? She left it on Lymund's pillow. That was very unlike her, that presence of mind."

Walker blew out the dresser lamp and crawled under the covers, the mattress sagging to one side under his weight, heavier than Katherine remembered.

"Did you enjoy it as much as you did before?" He rolled against her.

"Enjoy what?" she asked, startled.

"The desert. As I recall, you were very passionate." He stuck his tongue in her ear and blew softly.

"It was different this time, dear. Very different."

"My poor brave wife," Walker murmured, the words climbing out over a yawn.

# FORTY

HOULTON, MAINE, 1865. In the home of Susanna and Shep Cary on Garrison Hill a handful of dancers work out the steps to the latest conceit. Among those watching from the sidelines are a tall, lank man with light brown hair and beard trimmed close, and a handsome Creole woman in a elegant, green moiré gown with a sweeping hoopskirt.

"They do catch the eye, don't they," the woman said. "Your wife and my husband."

"Not as much as I would." Jed grinned.

"Perhaps you should learn to dance."

"Not me."

Camille Proulx studied Jed briefly. "A pity." And turned her attention back to the dancers. "Do you ever ask yourself why they didn't marry each other?"

"No."

"You northern boys, you are so cold-blooded. I understand your younger son is named after my husband."

"He's named after my father, Jean Paul was his name."

"And you have an Indian brother?"

"Yam."

"He's not here?"

"He's up north."

"I wouldn't expect him to be here. I doubt there's ever been an Indian inside this house, or a Negro."

"My cup's empty, how 'bout yours?" Jed asked.

Camille was silent, watching the dancers.

Jed eased away. Cousin Sigvald's new wife was every bit as unpleasant as her obnoxious husband. *Serves him right.*

It was a lovely party. Driving home, the dust from the stars drifting down from the skies, Julia was effervescent thinking about dancing, about being beautiful and everyone's watching her. She absolutely *adored* parties.

"I saw Camille cozying up to you. I suppose she was complaining because Sigvald wasn't teaching her the steps, she's very jealous."

"I think she kinda likes all the attention he gets." Jed loosened his tie with sigh of relief. "Like me with you."

"Ohhhh, aren't you sweet. She is so far beneath him. I just can't imagine…it must be the accent, Northerners talk through their nose."

Sunday, two weeks later. Jed was sprawled across the floor playing jacks with the boys, Julia was mending by the stove. Across the room Dr. Clare blanketed himself in a quilt to read. The cold November rain was turning into snow, and the windows were icing up.

"Time goes so fast, next week we'll be gone."

"Gone where?" Jed was running his hand over the rag rug looking for a missing jack.

"You remember, the boys and I are going to Washington for the holidays."

Jed stared up at Julia. "What are you talking about?"

"I told you the night of the party that we're invited to Bettina's for Christmas. Sigvald says she's homesick, she hasn't been home since she married Edwin."

"I can't go to Washington for Christmas." Jed was incredulous.

"No, of course not. But the boys and I can, the bogeyman's not going to get us."

"That doesn't make any sense. It's a long ways to go in the winter, and the roads are bad. And the boys are in school."

"There's all sorts of history in Washington, more than they'll ever get out of books. " Julia paused. Her voice took on the tone she used when explaining school assignments to J.C. and Paul. "Including Bettina's home. Bettina has a lovely home in Georgetown, a Georgian mansion designed by Nicholas King. There's a great deal of history right there, starting with the man who built it, I believe his name was Davidson. He was obsessed with privacy, his dire warnings to trespassers are under glass in the library. And, of course, there's the Capitol."

"Paul's only six," Jed argued. "He won't know what he's seeing."

"Don't be silly. If you spent as much time with your sons as I do, you'd know how much they'd enjoy it."

"We can't both be home."

"I'm just saying, we need to take advantage of this opportunity while we can. Now that the war's over, Edwin expects to be transferred soon. Bettina says Christmas is the best time to come, there'll be all sorts of parties."

"We got all sorts of parties here."

"And every one just as boring as the last one!" Julia straightened in her chair. "Bettina has gone to a great deal of trouble to arrange this, you should have told me sooner you didn't want me to go." She dumped the mending in its canvas sack and stomped out of the room.

Jed felt as if he'd been blindsided by a barge. He pulled on his coat and hat and went outside into the storm, the boys following, wishing for snow.

Frail, blue-veined hands shaking on his cane, Doctor Clare made his way into the kitchen. "Are you two having trouble?"

"Heavens no! I wish Jed could go with us."

The doctor cleared his throat in his handkerchief. "I advise against it, Christmas is a time for families." The voice he used on patients, the final word.

"Well, darling, I'm very sorry to disappoint you, but it's really none of your business."

"It's a serious mistake, Julia. You don't want to be in Washington now, there are a great many unhealthy people there, what with the wounded soldiers being sent to the hospitals. In addition, forty thousand slaves have migrated into the District. It's not a safe place and won't be for a long while, I imagine that's why Edwin is leaving."

"You're just saying that because you'll miss us." Julia pecked at the withered cheek and turned her back so her father wouldn't see her tears. It was alright for Jed to go off lollygagging in the West with that dirty Indian for the better part of a year. But let her make plans, and no, that wouldn't work, wouldn't work at all. Well, it would work!

Julia and the boys left the morning of December 2, going by team the forty miles to Canterbury, and from Canterbury by rail and steamer to Washington. This gave them plenty of time to do Washington before Christmas, and the day after Christmas they would be back on the railcars for home.

Jed was at the mill when they left. That night the house felt like a grave, all the sparkle gone away. Sorry to the point of being sick he hadn't stayed home and taken his family to the station, Jed busied himself with supper. After a quiet meal of warmed-over mutton stew along with bread and butter, the good doctor and his favorite son-in-law toasted the absent family members with the peach brandy being saved for the Christmas cooking.

"The housekeeper won't be happy," Cyrus said, eying the

decanter. "Julia left long lists of instructions, including what we're to eat for Christmas dinner."

"That was nice of her."

"She always was headstrong, it didn't do any good to tell her no."

"None of this is your fault, she's my wife."

"You couldn't have stopped her," the doctor observed owlishly and lifted his glass for another nip. "The last time you tried, you lost."

Jed looked sheepish. "You heard that?"

"I may be getting deaf, but I was only upstairs. Then too, plates make a great deal of racket." The men smiled fondly at each other, liking each other's company. "What set her off? I don't remember."

Jed groaned. "That goddamned Thanksgiving party at Uncle Jimmy's old inn. We was reliving history, remember? I had to take a wagon over to Mars Hill and get enough turkeys to feed an army, and everyone had to come in costume, remember that? No pilgrim costume, no food, that was the rule. You looked sweet in that preacher's skirt, by the way."

"Always was a pious man." Cyrus sucked the last of the brandy out of his glass and turned it upside-down regretfully, ignoring the stain on the tablecloth. "As I recall, your buckskins were a little short in the ankle."

"They was Yam's."

"She hates Yam," Cyrus said.

"She went skinny dipping in front of him, that's why."

"Logical for a woman, I suppose," Cyrus remarked dryly.

"Yep."

"I try to be philosophical, I look at it this way, she gave me two fine grandsons."

"And me two fine sons, and tomorrow morning one hellava hangover!"

On the nineteenth of December the largest of the Cary saw mills burned to the ground, taking with it the nearby offices.

Jed was driving to work that morning thinking how he'd come up in the world. Now he drove a buggy and lived in a fine house, and didn't have a wife to decorate his fine house for Christmas.

Snow choked the woods and stacked itself on the tree boughs. Narrow ribbons of packed snow lined the road. Occasionally a short arc of wheel track showed where a wagon had pulled aside into the deeper, unpacked snow. Game tracks broke through into the open in little explosions of snow. Jed wondered if it was snowing in Washington, if anybody missed him.

The road, turning as the creek turned, grew cobwebby with fog. Of a sudden Jed realized it wasn't fog, but smoke. A mile further, hurrying now, the snow speckled with ashes, he reached what was left of the mill—the charred saw and iron ramp standing strangely naked in a sea of black. The morning crew was sifting through the rubble. They told of finding evidence of vagrants—an iron pot and a case knife alongside smoldering blankets.

Shep Cary delayed rebuilding until after the holidays, and Jed caught the next train out, Cyrus' gifts in his bag. He'd buy his own gifts when he reached the city.

Washington, D.C., December 24. The Franklin address on 28th Street.

The street hack stopped in front of high garden walls where a bronze plaque fitted into the wall read EVERMAY. Entrenched behind the walls and barely visible under a heavy winter-grey mat of vines was an austere, two-story Edwin kind of mansion. The front door was tall and narrow, as if reluctant to admit more than one visitor at a time, the door knocker was a heavy piece of iron in the shape of a swan's head.

Jed opened the door and threw his hat inside the vestibule. A startled servant picked up the hat.

"Your name, sir?"

"Jed Marchion."

"Your coat, please."

The wet wool coat hung on the hall-tree, the servant disappeared down a waxy corridor.

"Jed!"

"Bettina! how are you?" Jed hugged her warmly. "How's everybody doing?"

"Well, this is a surprise."

"Ain't it! Mill burned up, so here I am. Where's Julia?" He glanced down the hallway expectantly.

"Well, wouldn't you know, here we are, thinking we don't have any problems with this house, and Christmas comes along and the roof leaks! We had to close off the guest rooms and take Julia and the boys to the Willard's." Bettina's voice registered both indignation and disappointment. "It's certainly not what we planned."

"Where's Willard's?"

"I'll tell you, but first you must have some chocolate in the parlor, yes, you must! you dear man, and tell me about the fire. Oh, goodness, you weren't hurt, were you? I'll be right back."

It may have been Edwin's mansion, but it was Bettina's home. Clusters of brightly painted papier mâché figures hung from the ceiling in the corners of the parlor, a stack of small, red drums decorated a side table.

Barreling merrily along in his pony cart, the gardener's boy would have made it to Willard's with time to spare had he not broadsided a phaeton and been forced to suffer a fine dressing down from the phaeton's owner.

"Why, I'm afraid she's left," the desk clerk at Willard's told the breathless youngster, seeing over the boy's head a swish of red hoopskirt and the carriage pulling away. "I'll make sure she gets the note when she returns."

He stuck the paper in one of a multitude of cubby-holes behind him, and as soon as the boy was out sight, fished it back out to read, *Jed is here.*

The immense corridors of the city were smudgy with cold, in the early winter twilight the gas lamps along Pennsylvania Avenue were being lit. Stuck in traffic, Jed got out of the street hack and walked toward the hotel. He was standing under a lamp waiting for the traffic to thin, when a carriage, wheeling into a side street, came so close he could have easily touched the door. He looked up to see Julia on the other side of glass—her head back, laughing. The wrap was off her shoulders and she was wearing a red dress.

Jed yelled and Sigvald's face appeared in the glass, looking past him. Then the carriage was gone, the lights bobbing down the street. Jed took after it at a run, but a patch of ice brought him down, giving his head a good thump and spinning him around. When he got to his feet, the street was empty.

# FORTY-ONE

"NAME."

"Jed Marchion, I'm looking for my family."

"I'm sorry, Mrs. Marchion has left for the evening."

"She's staying here with our sons."

"I see." Thinking *You are not at all the sort of man I would have picked for her husband,* the desk clerk moved down the counter to another guest, eventually returning to the bedraggled man splattered with the mud of the streets. "Was there something else?"

"Would you check the room just to be sure?"

There were people waiting up and down the counter, important-looking people.

"I'll send someone up, in the meantime I suggest you wait in the lobby."

Choosing a chair where he could see the front doors, Jed helped himself to a piece of wrapped candy from the bowl at his elbow. The white marble lobby with its high ceiling and overlooking balconies felt like a palace, the stuffed, black leather chair felt like a throne. A uniformed boy armed with broom and dustpan tended to the rugs in the entryway. The large Christmas tree in the corner shimmered with hundreds of candles. Pleasant-faced people in holiday finery swept past, and costumed singers took up their posts inside the front doors, managing to sound joyful despite their cold-nipped faces.

A black man in the red uniform of a porter approached. There was no one in the room assigned to the Marchions. That said, the porter held three fingers against his chest.

Jed stared, but before he could ask a question, the porter was gone. His family was at a party right here in the hotel, the clerk should have told him that. On the other hand, in a fancy place like Willard's, maybe people couldn't be too careful. They didn't know him from Adam's off-ox.

Washed over with relief, Jed waited until the counter was busy to stroll across the lobby and disappear through a wide doorway framed in wintergreens. Potted plants hung with glass-beaded chains lined the hallway. On the walls behind the plants, tall mirrors separated large paintings of horsemen careening through deep woods. A darkly flowered carpet covered the floor.

At the end of the hallway a wide flight of carpeted stairs led up to a second hallway that opened on small sitting rooms identified with gold nameplates and furnished with couches and paintings. Some of the rooms were empty, others hosted small parties.

Another, somewhat narrower stairway led to another corridor. Utterly quiet, the doors closed, bearing numbers instead of names. Kerosene lamps mottled the carpet's dark flowers in yellow pools of light. Listening in vain for a familiar voice, Jed walked the length of the corridor. The next floor was the same. And the next.

*Somewhere there has to be a party going on,* Jed told himself, accounting for the quiet. For some reason he recalled Julia's first party. That night she expected him, this time she would be so surprised.

He stopped short, listening.

Nothing, then a shriek. Children rough-housing, a lot of

children. He spotted a ceiling grate and moved under it, cocking his head to listen. Faintly, ever so faintly, came the thump of feet, then another outburst.

He grinned and hurried down the hall to take the stairs three at a time. At the top he was greeted by a full-sized replica of a knight in black armor holding aloft a tall candlestick. A painting of the same knight decorated the door on the noisy room.

"Merry Christmas!" Jed told the youth who opened the door. "I'm Jed Marchion, my family's here."

Numerous children roved about a large ballroom, some running, others engaged in games on the floor. Spotting his father, J.C. broke off a game of tag, made a detour to jerk Paul's shirt, and ran for the door.

The youth wore a white uniform with the words, STAFF, WILLARD'S HOTEL on his shirt. Checking a clipboard, he found the boys' names. "They're paid for the night."

"Where's mother?" Jed asked J.C.

"At a party," J.C. said.

Paul grabbed his father's hand. "We're going with you."

"We don't give refunds," the attendant said.

"No, we can stay for the party," Jed said reassuringly. The room was full of youngsters of various ages, several wore the white uniform of the hotel.

"You're staying in the hotel with Mrs. Marchion?" the attendant asked when he could.

"Yes," Jed told him. "That's right." Not seeing Julia, he asked Paul, "Is your mother here?"

"She's at her own party," Paul explained and with a yell ran across the room to help J. C. sort through the blankets piled there. Lugging their blankets the boys paraded past their father and out the door.

"Where's your mother's party?" Jed asked, following.

"At Uncle Sig's," Paul said.

"You're not supposed to call him that," J.C. said. "You're supposed to call him Uncle Proulx."

"Am not."

"Yes, sir."

Several flights downstairs J.C knelt beside a door and fished under the carpet for the key. The number on the door was 333. The room was dark. He rubbed a hand along the inside wall, locating the match safe and the striker plate. "There!" he cried, holding a lighted match in the air.

Jed raised the globe on the table lamp, and the boy fired the wick. A room chock full of Christmas jumped out of the shadows—a spruce covered with decorations, its base covered in packages, a table scattered with ribbons and gifts.

Lifting aside a heavy drape Jed looked down on the busy street. He'd never been in a building that high. A mist of ice crystals glowed a dull yellow above the street lamps. "You was gonna stay all night?" he asked, letting the drape fall back.

"Yes," the boys chorused. Yes, they were. They were jumping from the sofa onto the flowered carpet and back again.

"We get to do that a lot," Paul said.

"Not a lot," J.C. corrected him. "We only did it four times."

"Four times not counting tonight."

"Yes, counting tonight."

"Five tonight."

"No."

Back and forth they jumped, arguing.

"Let's play Run for Your Seat," Paul cried, and ran for a reclining couch, arriving there a split second before J.C.

Jed touched a match to a second lamp and carried the lamp into the bedroom. The covers were pulled tight on the beds, shoes and toys lined the wall. A small wooden box on the dresser, its lid open, caught the lamp light. Inside was a glass

compass encased in silver. A printed card beside the box read
GALT & BRO., FINE JEWELRY. On the other side of the card was
written, *My sweet cous, may you never get lost again, all my love
forever, Sig.*

Jed squeezed the box so hard the lid popped off.

It was well after midnight when the boys went to bed. Jed
sat down to wait on the sofa, and the next thing he knew it was
7:30 and there was light around the edge of the window drapes.
Warm air was pouring through a grate in the wall.

*That must be one hell of a furnace.*

He got the boys up, and they led the way downstairs to a
marble dining room as large as the lobby. The tables were spread
with white linen and decorated with little clusters of holly, and
the breakfast menu was in English and French. Jed ordered steak
and onions, and the boys ordered *blanc mange,* and *paté de foie
gras.* Uncle Proulx taught them how.

Tight as ticks and ready to tackle the Christmas tree, they ran
back upstairs.

"Do we have to wait for mama?" J.C. asked, freeing a
peppermint-stripped package from the pile.

"I think we better," Jed said. "When do you think she'll be
here?"

"I dunno, just one?"

"Sure, that's alright."

Inside was a four-bladed knife and a silver pencil. The card
read *Merry Christmas from your Uncle Proulx.*

Paul decided on a blue package, changed his mind and
pawed madly through the presents, coming up with his own
peppermint-striped package. It was a fountain pen with the word
"PRICE" inscribed on the clip.

"That's not yours," J.C. chortled.

"Yes, it is." Jed held the pen up to the light. "Price is the manufacturer, but what is it?"

"An ink pen," the boys chorused.

"Here, I'll show you." J.C. was unscrewing the cap. "Uncle Proulx has one."

"Gimme that!" Paul argued. "It's my pen."

They opened two more presents, nightshirts from their Aunt Bettina. After that, they just kept going. A toy drum, coonskin caps, toy blocks, pop-up books. Off to the side the little pile of unopened presents grew and grew. Gifts to Julia from Sigvald, to Sigvald from Julia and the boys.

"I was going to buy your presents when I got here," Jed explained to a disinterested audience.

With nothing left to open, the boys played and Jed watched out the window. Except for an occasional, heavily muffled coachman, the streets were all but empty. A thin snow fell, adding to the dismal gloom. It was a good thing he was there, Jed told himself, following the boys down to Christmas dinner, otherwise they'd be all alone.

The dining room was crowded, a silver rope hung across the entryway. A white-haired man dressed all in white required reservations to seat the party.

"Reservation for Mr. Proulx," J.C. told him.

The man couldn't find a Christmas reservation for Mr. Proulx, but he knew this lad and liked him. "Right this way."

"You look nice," J.C. said.

"I'd rather be home with my feet up," his friend whispered.

"We always have to say Mr. Proulx, because he makes our reservations," J.C. told his father. "That's the *maître d'*."

The menu included six kinds of meat, eight ornamental pyramids, twelve cakes and tarts, ten jellies and creams, six flavors of ice cream, three fruit ices, and coffee and chocolate.

The boys couldn't decide what to have. It was three o'clock before they got back upstairs again.

Of a sudden, Jed was done. He pulled the cases off the bed pillows and told the boys, "Put every present you can in these, we're going home."

"YEA!" J.C. yelled.

"Where's mama?" Paul asked.

"She'll be coming," Jed answered. *Like a house afire.*

# FORTY-TWO

NO ONE BOTHERED TO ASK about the bundles that looked suspiciously like the hotel linen. Perhaps because everyone was carrying packages about. Leaving the hotel Jed caught sight of the black porter who befriended him, and doffed his hat.

"What route?" a luggage boy asked when Jed inquired about a coach.

"B&P to New York."

Traveling bags and pillowcases loaded on the roof, the hotel coach took off down the long, wide avenue. It was snowing harder now, the street tunneling through the snow, the sleigh bells on the carriage horses jingling.

"Jingle bells, jingle bells…" sang the boys. "Come on, father, sing with us. Jingle bells…"

The train station was crowded with stranded travelers. Ordinarily the trains don't run on Christmas, the agent told Jed, but there was too much traffic backed up from earlier delays.

Jed bought one adult and two children's tickets for New York City and found a place in the station out of the draft. At 1:05 a.m., seven hours late, the New York train through Baltimore was announced. Weary and stiff, Jed rustled the traveling bags and pillowcases together and led the way through the crowded station and out on the cold platform. All evening long he'd watched for Julia. Now, moving slowly, he looked around more than once, certain he heard her call his name.

He should go back to Willard's. Getting on the train was a mistake, a bad mistake. Nevertheless, he kept walking.

The engines hooked back-to-back hissed like black swamp monsters locked in combat. Their steam in the light looked like swamp gases. At the far end of the platform a man with the word CONDUCTOR painted on his cap, attached copper tags to the handles of the traveling bags and reached for the bulging pillowcases.

"They gotta stay with us," J.C. told him.

"It's our Christmas presents," Paul explained sincerely.

The conductor was tired, it'd been another long day in a string of long days, and it wasn't over yet. He handed Jed the stubs that matched the copper tags and slung the bags on top of a loaded baggage cart. The boys waited, clutching their pillowcases. "I'd keep hold of my presents, too," the conductor allowed. "Stack 'em on your lap." He indicated the little portable step nearby.

The car looked full. A man in the back pointed, and Jed edged his way down the aisle to two seats. He put J.C. on the inside seat and took the other one—Paul on his lap, the precious horde of gifts propping up their feet. They heard the conductor shout, "Go ahead! Forward!"

The train muttered and grumbled and screeched. J.C. smiled drowsily, Paul smiled too. Jed patted J.C.'s knee. "You was good help, you both was." Clickity-click, clickity-clack, down the railroad track.

Catching himself back and forth against the seats, the conductor moved the length of the aisle collecting tickets and giving out green checks. On one side was written *Place in hat*, on the other side the names of the stations and the distances

separating them. He disappeared through the narrow door at the
end of the car and returned with a stack of pillows and blankets.

Jed paid a dime for two blankets and two pillows and checked
his timepiece. It was 1:44 a.m. The train stopped, started with a
lurch, clanged and banged and screeched and managed to keep
going. The boys were sound asleep. The conductor extinguished
the lamps above the seats, leaving the lanterns burning at the
ends of the car. In the dim light the green checks stuck in the
hatbands looked like a field of feathers.

Outside the soot-stained windows the night jerked by.
Dozing, Jed thought about Julia.

He'd been to Washington and hadn't even noticed where
the Capitol was, she'd laugh at him for that. If she ever quit
yelling. She didn't suffer embarrassment well. There was nothing
between her and Sigvald, he was certain, a harmless flirtation,
that's all. If she wanted to marry the bastard, she'd of done it
years ago.

They'd put it behind them. He wouldn't ask any questions,
and he'd apologize for not staying in Washington. And that, by
damn, was all the crawling he was doing, who was in the wrong
here anyway?

And where was she? just where in the hell was she? on
Christmas Eve for chrissake sake! and Christmas Day! Families
were supposed to be together on Christmas. Was there an
accident? did she try to get back and couldn't?

Clickity-click, clickity-clack.

Pinpoints of light came and went. People laden with packages
greeted each other in dimly lit stations in little explosions of
happiness. The two men sitting in front of Jed moved elsewhere.
Jed turned the seats to face him and eased J.C. into them.

Waking in the storm-delayed dawn, seeing men peeing out
the windows, the boys opened their own window. The car had
the usual abundance of windows, along with seats that could be

turned to face whatever direction the occupant wished. What made the car different was its newness and it unusual length.

The seats were covered with velvet and could accommodate as many as eighty people, and the walls were brightly painted with various scenes. At either end of the car were waist-high mirrors and a water tank with a dipper attached.

The snow was getting deeper. The engine plowed through to another stop, the sign said CAMBRIDGE. Jed stared at the sign thoughtfully, trying to place Cambridge. Had they already gone through Baltimore? Probably not, they weren't making very good time. Trays of bread were being loaded, their white muslin coverings flapping in the wind.

Later, the cars again on the move, a porter came by selling the bread for a penny a slice. Jed bought six slices and a little paper cup of jam. "When will we be in Philadelphia?" he asked.

"Philly ain't on this route," the porter said. "Next stop's Zanesville in about two hours."

Zanesville? They had a mechanic at the mill from Zanesville, Ohio. Jed jerked the ticket stub from his coat pocket and gave it to the porter. "We're going to Maine."

"Yep, this here's for the B&P alright," the porter said, glancing at the stub and handing it back. "But that ain't what you're on, you're on the B&O." He scratched his head under his hat, as if thinking what to do, and went on.

Well, shit!

Washed over with dismay, Jed studied the other passengers. No one seemed upset, he must of misunderstood the announcement last night in the station. He had the right tickets, the conductor should have caught the mistake. Shit!

Julia'd never believe he wasn't being mean in not returning immediately to Houlton. No matter what he said, nothing would make it better. In the slow light of the winter dawn he felt such despair and wished with all his heart he'd never gone to Washington.

The sun came out, shining on a field of wind-polished snow edged with buck fences. A well-wrapped boy leading a goat along the footpath beside the train caught Paul's attention. He waved and the boy waved back happily. Shortly afterward the train stopped at a crossroad attended only by a wagon, the team's breath frosty. There was a rush of cold air through the open door, and a man and woman and several small children got off.

Julia hurried into the lobby, her arms and those of the coachman who accompanied her, laden with packages. "My children are staying here in the care of the staff," she explained to the desk clerk. "Where will they be this afternoon?"

The clerk nodded, checked his schedule, and sent the pretty woman to the banquet room where the puppet show was going on. And waited expectantly. Sure enough, here she came, flying by headed for the stairs. The coachman who accompanied her stopped at the counter.

"Husband must of showed up," the coachman observed.

"Yep," the clerk agreed. "Now the shit's in the milk bucket."

A cold sleet rattled the front windows of the hotel. The coachman wanted to go home. Fearing Mr. Proulx's mistress would want to go back out in the storm, he dumped his armload of presents on the counter and slipped out the door.

"Hello, boys," Julia called brightly. No one answered her knock. She shoveled her packages onto the floor and tried the handle. The door wasn't locked, the note on the table read

*I took the boys home Jed*

Julia screamed and ran back downstairs.

According to the desk clerk, the children of Mrs. Jedrich Marchion checked out at 3:20 p.m. the afternoon of Wednesday, December 25, 1865, in the care of Mr. Marchion.

Julia pointed an accusing finger at the lobby clock. "What are you telling me? it's not even two o'clock yet!"

The clerk slid the book around. There it was, 3:20 p.m., Wednesday, Dec. 25, followed by entries dated December 26.

Julia stared at the clerk. "Today's the 26th? No, it can't be." She was going home today, she had the tickets upstairs. Her face whitened. "I don't care what day it is! Those children were in your care, you incompetent moron! I'll sue Willard's, I'll have you put in jail! Where's my coachman?!"

"He's gone." The clerk beckoned a porter over. "Hail a coach for the missus, please." He handed Julia the note left by Bettina's messenger, she glanced at it and threw it on the floor.

"JED, ARE YOU HERE?"

Bettina was upstairs when she heard Julia yell. She caught up with her cousin in the kitchen.

"Where's Jed?"

"He's not here, Julia."

"He was here, you sent him to the hotel!"

"I tried to warn you."

"YOU HAD NO BUSINESS SENDING HIM TO WILLARD'S!"

*Don't push me,* Bettina's face said.

Enraged, Julia hurled herself about the room. Blaming Sigvald for the decision to attend the party at the estate of General Lee in Arlington instead of staying in the city, blaming Jed for coming to Washington in the first place, blaming Bettina for betraying her.

She was still in her party dress, the red hooped skirt bouncing wildly beneath her wrap. Bettina watched silently.

"You of all people, how could you do this to me? it wasn't like I was doing anything wrong! The boys knew where I was, you knew."

"I knew where you were going, I tried to catch you."

"I didn't know Jed was coming!"

"This is the day after Christmas, Julia. He was here Christmas Eve. What did you expect him to do? live at the Willard's until you decided to come back?"

"We couldn't get back earlier, it was all the snow! AND YES," Julia screamed. "I EXPECT HIM TO LEAVE MY CHILDREN RIGHT WHERE I LEFT THEM!"

The appearance of a maid in the doorway restored some sanity to the room. Julia brushed by the servant and fled Evermay.

The bright green tree with its homemade ornaments stood forlornly in a sea of bright paper and unopened gifts. Julia broke into a fresh tide of weeping. The boys' clothing was gone from the bedroom, the beds were shorn of their pillowcases. There was only her clothing and her toiletries on the dresser.

Seeing the little wooden compass box, its lid askew, she hesitated, and shattered the box with her fist.

Despising the clerk, despising herself, sure that her face was swollen despite the application of cold towels, Julia asked for the charges. Twenty-three nights at $3.50 a night, together with the dining-room charges, came to $123.45. The cost for the children's care, let's see...

"Oh, hurry up!" she snapped. How horribly, horribly humiliating, she could hardly bear it, Jed would be *so sorry*. She had changed into a travel suit and carried only a small bag—

everything else, the unopened gifts, the red dress, abandoned in the room along with the rest of her clothes.

"Will someone be picking up your things?" the clerk asked, recalling the mountain of luggage that accompanied the woman's arrival.

"No."

The total hotel bill was $142.78. Julia counted out $150 in paper money. Unable to stand at the marble counter another second, she did not wait for her change.

At the railroad station she learned the seaboard trains were running behind schedule. It would be another twenty-four hours at least. She took a cab to Rhodes Hotel on Fifteenth Street and sent Sigvald a note. The Proulx maid gave the note to Camille Proulx, who tore it up.

# FORTY-THREE

ZANESVILLE CAME AND WENT, followed by other settlements
with unfamiliar names. The weak sun disappeared in a
wintry blast. The boys went back to sleep. Jed stared out
the window hollow-eyed.

*I gotta get off this train, I gotta go home.*

At Columbus a dignified, well-to-do man from the cut of his
clothes, thinking the seat beside Jed empty, paused upon seeing
an open sack overflowing with Christmas wrapping.

"Here," Jed said, hoisting the sack into his lap and sliding
over against the window.

J.C. looked up from his book and the fellow stuck out his
hand. "Sir Genille Cave-Browne-Cave, Twelfth baronet of
Stretton Hall at Stretton-en-le-field in the English Midlands.
And where are you chaps bound?"

"Maine," J.C. answered and turned his attention back to
his book. "Well, in that case, my good man," the Englishman
looked around as if to share the joke, his breath a flood of sweet-
smelling alcohol, "you are on…"

"…the right train," Jed said firmly, nudging the other's boot."

"The…yes, yes, yes, of course." Cave-Brown-Cave sat up very
straight, as if balancing a plate on the top of his head. "And I
too, I am on the right train too."

No one replied, and he continued as if arguing with himself.

"Actually, I do have a plan. I'm off to the wild West, I've decided to seek my fortune bringing up cows."

"You got land out there?" Jed asked.

"Actually, not quite yet." Cave-Brown-Cave covered his mouth against a belch and loosened his coat. "First I shall be going to cow school to learn to punch cows."

"I never heard of a cow school."

"I venture to say there are a great many things you've never heard of, my good man, but that doesn't affect the truth."

"No, I guess not."

"You wouldn't perhaps have a wee spot of rum?"

"Nope."

"Or anything for that matter?"

"Got a roll saved from noon." Jed unrolled the towel wrapped around a bun.

"Really, my good fellow," the passenger drew back, "I would never...oh, alright (Jed was rewrapping the bun), if you insist." And he devoured the bread in a wink, down to the last crumb. "I am deeply indebted to you."

"Forget it."

"An Englishman never forgets."

"Just try."

Which the Englishman did forthwith, dropping his chin on his chest and nodding off, occasionally jerking himself upright, mumbling something about not having been able to get a sleeping car.

Supper was sliced ham between buttered bread, balanced along with a tin cup of apple cider on the knees, Jed paying and the Englishman becoming ever so much more indebted. Late that night, staring out the window half-asleep, Jed heard the Englishman whisper, "Do you think the boys are asleep?"

"Sound asleep."

"I was just going to ask, how old is J.C.?"

"Eight."

"Well, if you don't mind my saying so, won't he soon discover that we're going the wrong direction?"

"By then we'll be going the right direction."

"Well then, old chap," the Englishman leaned close conspiratorially, "if you don't mind my asking…"

"…I do mind."

"Because I was thinking…"

"…don't."


The next morning no one came around with bread. Sure that he had seen bread loaded, Jed and the boys went looking and returned with two slices and a tin mug of coffee for the Englishman, who at first declined the feast.

"You gotta eat something, Mr. Cave-Brown-Cave," Paul said.

"Good show! Yes, yes, by all means, I shall not decline the hand of friendship." The Englishman carefully situated his handkerchief on his lap. "But first we must have an understanding, my friends call me Cave."

The day passed out its gifts. For Jed, another long and dreary ride on a train going nowhere. For Cave and his young friends, more pleasant diversions. Beginning with a pheasant shoot, the scattered flock lifting off the marshy grasses one after another as if deliberately spaced to accommodate the shootists.

Jed didn't have a gun, nor did the Englishman, to his great disappointment. But enough passengers did that the car soon filled with smoke. Next, Indians appeared. Some raced their horses alongside the train, others stood beside the rails with their hands out. A passenger lofted a chunk of bread at one and suffered a severe rebuke from a passing porter. The Indians, the porter explained, were to stay away from the rails.

The Twelfth Baronet of Stretton Hall made an amiable, if at times boring, companion. Seized with the joys of anticipation,

he overflowed with facts. The publications he carried in his
luggage—regretfully stowed away in some godforsaken place on
the train, at least he hoped so—pictured the proper classes of
cattle with regard to weight gain and overseas beef markets, in
addition to all sorts of valuable herdsman tips.

"The more open range, the more cattle that can be put out.
The more the herd multiplies, the lower the unit cost of their
maintenance. With proper management I believe I can bring
that cost down to as little as seventy cents per animal per year."

"It seems to me you ain't wrote in the weather."

"To the contrary, I am well aware of the ferocious winds.
Accordingly, there's to be plenty of broken ground for shelter.
Did I mention the hunting lodge? it's to be quite large, out
of native rock I suppose, we'll have to see. The servants will
accompany the furniture and china across. The wolfhounds and
the horses, too, they'll have to be imported. Thoroughbreds, of
course. As for the bulls, I haven't yet decided on the breed, it
will have to be hardy. Now you might have an opinion there."

Casting off his earlier reluctance, and with copious promises
to make good on the debt, the Englishman took dinner
and supper with his new friends in the kitchen car added in
Columbus. The next day, as the train pulled out of Vandalia, Jed
told Cave, "We're gonna turn around in St. Louis."

It was time, it was way past time. He'd tell Julia what
happened and that he decided the boys might as well see some
of the countryside while they were at it. She'd jump around
like a spill of cold water on a hot stove, but she'd get over it.
Probably quicker than he would. What kind of a mother would
leave her kids alone on Christmas?

"What jolly good timing!" Cave said heartily, breaking into
Jed's thoughts. "St. Louis is where I pick up my monthly draft
from the telegraph. I shall be able to repay you chaps in full
measure, and then some, for your many kindnesses."

Which Cave did, counting out eleven dollars and sweetening his gratitude with a large sack of hot-cross buns. They were standing in the busy St. Louis station, the large, double doors propped open to accommodate the crowd. It was snowing, the smells of the nearby shipping yards sharpened by the cold and wet.

Having no time to dally—the St. Joseph train was leaving in less than an hour—Cave wished his new friends godspeed and rushed outside and down the street to the closest grog shop. One double shot of whiskey and he was off to the railcars, two pint jars of cherry brandy weighing his pockets reassuringly.

Back inside the station he picked up a copy of the *Independence Occidental Messenger* and was waiting in line to pay when a large wall poster caught his eye. There in front of him, gleaming amidst the debris of older, yellowed notices.

Officers and Good Citizens
For Humanity's Sake, Help Me Locate
JEDRICH MARCHION

Reward of $2,000.00 will be paid by Zepheniah Smith for the recovery or information leading to the recovery of Mr. Jedrich Marchion; age 38, height 6 feet 4 inches, weight 180 pounds, hazel eyes, light brown hair. Wanted for arson and for kidnapping. Disappeared from his home in Houlton, Maine. Will likely seek employment in the timber business. Is traveling in the company of 2 young boys, ages 8 and 6 (older boy is lame) stolen from their mother while visiting the Capitol in Washington.

Address all information to
ZEPHENIAH SMITH, SHERIFF
Box No. 3.                          Houlton, Maine

Cave read the item twice. A crude drawing showed a lean face with a short beard at the edge of the jaw. Could it be? Very

possibly. Yes, yes indeed! What an amazing turn of events, and
what to do about it? The Englishman turned around three times
before remembering to collect his change. And then he was off
to the ticket counter.

"When does the next train leave for the east?"

"About three hours if it's on time out of...."

Cave didn't hear the rest. After a fruitless search of the lobby,
and by now delightfully committed to the adventure, he charged
full bore out to the St. Joseph-bound train, The porters were
taking up their stations, the engine was puffing loudly. Cave
waved a five-dollar bill and a luggage stub in a porter's face, and
followed the porter down the tracks to the baggage car, pausing
briefly along the way to settle his nerves with a stout nip of
cherry brandy.

Back on the street in front of the station, rescued luggage at
his feet and ticket cashed in, he secured the services of a large,
enclosed hack and scrambled up top beside the driver. He would
search diligently for one hour and return to post himself like a
bulldog outside the eastbound cars.

On the verge of return, he found them. They were watching
a puppet show in the window of a bakery, the snow falling round
them like a Christmas card.

"Why, Mr. Harris!" Cave cried jovially, clambering off the
high seat. "Here you are, my good man! I thought I'd never find
you! Get in, get in out of the weather." He took the traveling
bags from Jed's hand and slung the bags inside the hack, and
leaning close, whispered. "You are in great danger. Do as I say."

Once inside the moving carriage, Cave relaxed. "Hot-cross
buns gone already!" he teased, his friends safe and sound in their
little wooden fortress. "You boys are quite the wolves. Yes, and
don't think I exaggerate a bit."

"So who's Mr. Harris?" Jed asked softly.

"A distant cousin, Harris Drummond Stewart, Seventeenth

lord of Grandtully and Fifth baronet of Murthly, a delightful fellow. He served in the 15th King's Hussars, leading his cavalrymen in charge after change against the French, and won the Waterloo Medal for exceptional bravery. Really a most manly chap, and the name Harris has a nice, short American ring, don't you think? Here, let's draw that curtain, for all you know, you could already be in someone's sights."

"For what?"

"Arson and kidnapping, the poster's in the rail lobby."

Jed felt as if he'd been hit in the stomach with a club.

Raising his voice Cave struck a conversational tone with the boys. "We should quit the cars for the night, don't you agree? treat ourselves to a stationary bed and roof and something to eat besides endless varieties of boiled potatoes, let our heads clear of all that dismal smoke.

"Did I ever tell you," he leaned forward, "about being in the circus? Oh well now, that *is* quite a story. I was hired to ride in a steeplechase act with a girl, and here came my family looking for me, so I switched costumes with the girl and made off undetected in jolly good time."

"You were running away?" J.C. asked.

"Yes. I was quite young, only thirteen, and my parents thought I should be at Repton, a highly regarded public school and terribly dull. Oh yes, never go there! Books were my pet abomination, you see, unless they offered adventure, preferably by sea, and the more dangerous the better. You boys can understand that, I'm sure."

Jed was silent. What the hell did he expect? for Julia to sit home and twiddle her thumbs until he got over being mad? He should have known better. It's a wonder she didn't add murder to the list.

They drove to the Kansas House where Cave paid a night's lodging for the party and where Jed registered as John Harris and sons. After supper in their rooms, Cave asked Paul for the map game.

"Right here in Australia I jumped ship and got jobs clearing the land of rabbits. That was a wicked plague, thousands of the bloody hoppers swarming about like schools of fish…

"Somewhere around here," his finger wiggled back and forth, "I was employed as an apprentice on a tall-masted sailing ship…let's see, yes, right here…when we were beset by the most savage of hurricanes. The captain is screaming at the top of his lungs. 'Shorten sail!' he screams. 'Shorten sail!' And there we are, clinging like monkeys with all our might and main to the swaying yardarms and the storm inky black, making a terrible racket in the rigging, like cats fighting. But we reefed in the canvas and saved the ship."

The stories lasted until the boys went to sleep.

The Englishman was relaxing in the oversized armchair, a wonderful glow on. Jed sprawled on the couch staring at the tinned ceiling.

"It's not the end of the world, you know," Cave observed. "You have your health, the boys have theirs. You say you didn't start the fire."

"It started in the offices, someone wanting a place out of the storm it looked like."

"Well then, all you need do is explain that to the proper authorities. As for traveling about with your own sons, that could hardly be considered kidnapping."

"Trouble is, I don't think me and my wife are ever gonna get along again."

"It doesn't look like it, does it."

"If we get a divorce, the boys'll stay with her."

"Yes, that seems to be the rule in America."

"I've read a lot of men change their names when they get out of the States."

Cave, dozing off, mumbled his agreement. "Yes, you could go on being John Harris, I suppose."

The next day over breakfast they toasted the New Year and each other (the toast was Cave's idea) with a light wine that wouldn't make the boys tipsy. At the Overland Express Station Jed bought tickets on a stage bound for Jefferson City and gave Cave a twenty-dollar bill. Which, when he could, the Englishman slipped to J.C. with a wink and a nod.

The newly-christened Harris party safely on its way, the Englishman walked down the street to the train station, stopping only long enough to purchase two bottles of Scotch whiskey. A blend, unfortunately, the British being rather stingy about exporting the real article.

Now it was north to St. Joseph, then west to Omaha. In a sleeping car, thank God, his fortunes once more at high ebb. There, on the mud flats of the Big Muddy, he would bid the cars *adieu* and set off by stage into the teeth of the howling wilderness.

His final order of business in St. Louis was to remove the poster from the lobby wall, painstakingly, as if having every right to do so, and place the rolled-up paper with his things.

# FORTY-FOUR

DENVER CITY. 1866. Top dog in a nest of settlements festering at the junction of Cherry Creek and the South Platte, six hundred miles from civilization. A cocky city, given its heat-blasted cottonwoods and disemboweled waterways.

Once upon time, before the mad hatters race, the easy slippage of Cherry Creek into the South Platte must have been a lovely place—a sylvan glade dappled with deep shade and scented with cherry blossoms.

Nathan was having his hair barbered in the El Dorado Hotel, one of the few luxuries he allowed himself these days. Haircuts made him melancholy. In the old days it was a shave and a haircut and a tip for the barber. Now it was just a haircut. "When I come into my own," he would promise Count Murat, "I'll catch up." And Count Murat, scissors flying through the air, would nod as if he believed, and start another story in French to please this customer. And Daphne's feeble attempts at styling would disappear.

Yes, the actual Cherry Creek must have been lovely to see. It was too bad what passed for civilization in that desert slum didn't see it that way. All the population cared about was gold, either in the ground or in the pockets of those who mucked for it. Gold sot is what they were—the river of goods flowing in from the East and the river of gold pouring out of the mountains boiling up at their feet like the rapids at the foot of Niagara Falls.

Sadly, escape from this most despicable of wind-battered shanty towns appeared further away every day. What in the world was he thinking of three years ago! reading into a few instances of bad luck some sort of signal from a benevolent deity! He should have been more resolute, stuck to the original plan. By now they'd be back on the coast, Nancy would be with her family in Lawrenceville, and Jeremy would be…well, wherever Jeremy wanted to be.

Instead, they were like a fly with its wings pulled off. All the money carried from the coast was gone, sunk into the boarding house. The nest egg secured by selling the outfit was gone. Daphne's beloved jewels, along with their gold-filigree case— gone, all gone, along with Nancy's pony. Only Jeremy was able to keep a horse, and that's because he paid for the hay.

Nathan stared morosely at his reflection in the mirror behind the barber. Life was hard. He needed a sting—one that would get his family out of there, but even that was impossible.

He groaned inwardly, a tormented man. Old money wanted you to *be* someone, they wanted to associate with the right people, or they weren't comfortable. One had to work hard for that kind of money.

Whereas in Denver City, awash in raw gold and silver, the *nouveau riche* had no idea how to spend their money other than to parade their good fortune in the acquisition of things. A goose ripe for the plucking, with just a little corn to dribble on the ground. Just a few extra coins for keeping up appearances.

Appearances were everything, that and being seen in the right places, which meant partaking of the thin gruel of what passed for culture upstairs in the Mozart Hall.

Just a few extra coins is all it would take…but there were no extra coins.

*I should go back to the coast and peddle Phoebe's paintings,
maybe by now the market's caught on.*

Daphne wanted him to go. "Go and work your magic," she
told him. "Send for us."

To which he invariably and gallantly replied, "There is no
magic without you."

Such a mess. As long as the boarding house stayed full and he
kept his job as a clerk in Clark & Co., they could make it. But
let the slightest slip occur, and the wolf outside the door would
be in the pantry.

Oh, well, a man has to live somewhere.

The arguments with himself always came down to that. A
man has to live somewhere. But life was much easier when it
was just him and Daphne, two will-o'-the-wisps following the
rainbow.

Done, Murat dropped the handful of small coins Nathan gave
him into a little iron pot. The gesture pleased Nathan, most
customers got their change counted first.

# FORTY-FIVE

THE NEWLY MINTED HARRIS FAMILY stayed a week in Jefferson City, where Jed worked as a hod carrier. Leaving there they hop-scotched their way west, landing in Harrisonville. Here, securing work in the Overland yards, Jed signed a note with Ben Holladay promising to pay his family's fare out of the States by working for the express station at the end of the line in Pike's Peak country.

The civilization reached eight days later rose off the flat prairie like a blister. If Julia found them way out there, she'd have to work for it. And if she did, they'd hide in the mountains.

Thinking about that brought Jed the deepest heartache. The boys needed to be in school, he needed to be home in his own bed. His stubbornness had proved a leg trap that would never set him free.

A variety of broadsheets advertising rooms plastered the walls of the Overland station. Broadwell, Planter's, Fremont, Sloan, Elephant Corral. A man wearing a wooden sign hung on straps over his shoulders gave Jed a paper advertising the Missouri House at fifty cents a night. A pretty girl approached and handed Paul a flyer from the San Francisco House. In hand-drawn letters it read, ALL YOU CAN EAT + CLEAN BED $1.

"Lead on, Macduff," Jed told girl.

The narrow, stick-built house down Fifteenth Street toward the river had a slightly cockeyed roof, but stood straight enough,

propped up as it was by the Chinese laundry to one side and
the saddlery to the other. There was glass in the front door and
a small, roofed-over porch with a step and a stoop. Above the
porch, fastened to the wall with bolts, a plank sign announced
the San Francisco House.

The girl led the way into the foyer. To the left of the foyer
a wide doorway opened on a dining room. A painting of two
women hanging sheets on a line in the wind hung over the
doorway.

A blonde woman introduced herself as the landlady. She had
two rooms left, one with a single bed for a dollar, the other with
two beds for two dollars, breakfast and supper included.

"Give me the two-dollar room," Jed said. He was three
hundred and seventy-five dollars in debt to Holladay and down
to a ten-dollar bill and change. But they'd make it, they made it
this far.

"Name?"

"Harris, John Harris."

"How will momma find us?" Paul was pulling on his father's
sleeve.

"Oh, she knows," Jed answered, counting out his change,
hating himself. "Don't worry." And he followed the landlady up
a narrow flight of stairs, the boys trudging behind lugging their
dirty pillowcases.

Two miners came in looking like warmed-over death. Nancy
weighed their dust on a tiny scale and poured the house's take
into a coffee can.

Nathan came home with a loaf of stollen and was pleased to
find the house full. "Where's Jeremy?"

"Old man Burton sent a load out late," Daphne told him.

The supper table was quiet. The food plentiful, but plain.
Baked beans with molasses, roasted pork. Restless, J.C. wandered

into the kitchen. The girl who had given him the flyer was lifting cake out of a skillet. "Get out of here!" she barked, turning her face aside.

J.C. stared curiously. "That's 'dump cake.'"

"Go back to the table!"

J.C. went back to the dining room and sat down. Pretty soon he heard the girl call, "Dessert's ready."

Daphne, clearing the table, looked exasperated. Nathan put down his fork and hurried after the desserts.

*I know that fella,* Jed told himself, trying to place where. As for himself being recognized, he had no worry. His untended beard was a briar patch, his own mother wouldn't know him.

After supper he took the boys upstairs to bed and returned to sit outside on the porch. The dining room was empty, he could hear Nathan's voice and the girl's through an open window.

"Thousands of people are named Harris."

"I don't care. We could be related, he could be looking for me."

"You can't go through life being afraid, Nancy. You have to be brave, don't be a rabbit, be a..." Nathan smiled encouragingly.

"...lion," Nancy added dispiritedly.

"Yes! that's my girl! be a lion!"

Nathan stepped out on the porch to light a cigar. "Cold out tonight. They don't have much of a spring here, if it is spring, I lose track."

"That little girl got a problem with my name?" Jed asked, moving over to make room. "Tell her she shouldn't."

"No, no, of course not. It's nothing."

A figure turned in off the dark street.

"Evening, Jeremy."

"Nathan," the figure said and went inside.

"I had a stepson once named Jeremy," Jed said. "S'not a common name."

"Jeremy is not a common boy. I think he could amount to something if he had the schooling."

"Hmmmm," Jed murmured, enjoying his pipe. His father used to do this, sit out in the cold drawing on his pipe, making what Jed called his Indian sounds. "Almost lost your roof," he observed.

"Bad wind, otherwise we couldn't have afforded the building. It's anchored now to the laundry."

"Hmmmm. Where you from?"

"California for me." Nathan decided to fish a little. If the Harris family *were* looking for Nancy, the sooner it came out in the open the better. Who knew, there could be an inheritance involved. As for anyone's forcibly removing the girl, it'd be over his dead body.

"Nancy and Jeremy Harris are from Utah. Do you have relatives in Utah?"

"Nope, don't have any relatives by the name of Harris anywhere, 'cept in England," Jed said with a small laugh. And remembered George. "Who's their father?"

"I never met the chap."

"Where's their mother?"

"Dead of mountain fever, she went to sleep and never woke up. We buried her somewhere in the wilderness and kept coming."

"How'd you wind up here?"

"It's a long story. At any rate, a man's got to live somewhere, and this is where we live." Nathan sighed regretfully and got to his feet. "A cigar can only keep you so warm."

Jed sat awhile longer, remembering Ellen standing in front of her big house in Great Salt Lake, just where she wanted to be. Good Lord! now she was dead? was that who they were talking

about? no! it couldn't be. He'd have to see Jeremy in the light to
know.

Jeremy was eating alone in the dining room when the roomer
came in out of the cold. Nancy was in the kitchen, relating a
piece of gossip through the open doorway.

Jed stared at the boy and glanced toward the kitchen,
wanting to see Ellen in her daughter's face, but Nancy dodged
aside. "How's it going, Jeremiah?" he asked with a grin, taking a
chair across the table.

That night, undressing for bed in the little room marked
PRIVATE, Nathan told Daphne, "Something good's about to
happen."

"It's going to take a whole lot of something good," Daphne
muttered. She didn't do her nails anymore, didn't curl her hair,
hardly looked at herself in the mirror. What was the point? Men
didn't notice her, and worse, she didn't notice them.

"This is a sea change, my sweet." Nathan smoothed his
threadbare suit over the back of a chair. He felt the change
walking through the house to bed. It was in the way Jeremy and
the Harris fellow were visiting at the table, but it didn't start
there.

All day long there'd been coincidences.

Starting with the error uncovered on the Cheesman Drug
Store account and corrected not five minutes before Walt
Cheesman came in. Then there was the small gold coin found
while looking around for a dry place to open his lunch pail, thus
giving him money to spend at the City Bakery. Which in turn
led to his being inside the bakery when gunfire broke out on the
street.

Yo ho! Very definitely, something really quite good was on its
way!

Heartened by Jed's arrival, the much enlarged family of the San Francisco House laid their plans. Nathan and Daphne would return to the coast and wire money back while Jed kept things afloat in Denver City. As soon as finances permitted, Jed would bring everyone to California.

In the meantime a woman with credentials would be hired to take Daphne's place, and Nancy would tutor her brother in mathematics so he could make more money.

"Whose bright idea is that?" Jeremy asked.

"Mine, dimwit. Driving wagons for Hiram Burton will never make you rich. You need to be a bookkeeper, people look up to men who wear a suit and work inside."

Wonderful dreams all, to make the winter drearies go away.

Jed was promoted from feeding stock and cleaning out stalls to hauling hay, his pay went from fifty cents to sixty cents an hour. J.C. and Paul helped with the boarding-house chores and sometimes rode with their father out to the Four-mile House where the stage company kept a big hay yard.

In the evening Daphne sat in the pine rocker and read stories aloud from books borrowed from the little Pierce library in the post office—books carried west by the settlers and left with the library, pages all tattered and torn, covers worn through.

When Nancy read aloud, Daphne lay on the floor to ease her back. She wondered if not wearing a corset added to the problem. She only had the one corset, and the whalebone stays were poking through, so she put it away for special occasions, which, of course, there weren't any anymore. And even if there were, she had no hoops to poof out her skirts, no horsehair-lined petticoat —just plain old cotton petticoats too thin to hold the starch.

But what did it matter? She was never going to look like a lady again, not with her washer woman's hands. Everything the

hired woman did, she did, particularly when the house was full.
Hauled water, cooked meals, washed dishes, washed clothes,
washed sheets, made beds, scrubbed floors. All this in addition
to her own chores—keeping the books, cutting the family's hair,
ironing their clothes, mending their clothes, pulling splinters,
bandaging wounds.

She refused to learn how to cut out patterns, saying she had
no time. But she did manage, after countless disasters, to master
the art of biscuits, turning out big, fluffy masterpieces. Lodgers
expected biscuits.

Nancy helped when she could. Poor child, she didn't have
a childhood. But at least there were bright ribbons for her hair,
now that Jed was there, along with extra lamps in the dining
room.

J.C. asked Nathan if Lafitte were a real name.

"That depends," Nathan replied, making his face cautious.
"What was *your* name in the States?"

"Marchion," J.C. whispered.

"My name was Clodhopper," Nathan whispered back.

"That's a really funny name."

"'Tis not," Nathan countered petulantly. "It's horrible, that's
why I changed it, now don't tell anyone."

"Oh, I won't," J.C. promised solemnly. "And don't you tell
anyone."

Jeremy quit his job at Burton Storage and Commission
House and took off with the Indian boys that hung around the
slaughter houses. When he didn't come back in two days, Jed
made inquiry in the Indian camps out along Cherry Creek and
drew a blank.

Every night Nancy asked if he'd heard anything, and every
night Jed told her no. But the truth was, he'd stopped looking.
At nineteen, Jeremy was a man grown, he could skin his own
cats.

Daphne enrolled Nancy and the boys and herself in the free singing classes offered by the Trinity Methodist Church during the winter, but the decision proved highly impractical. Between school work and supper duties no one could spare the time, so she enrolled the boys in the free singing school run by Mr. Watson over a nearby merchant's shop.

And to ease Nancy's disappointment (although truth to tell, Daphne was the more disappointed) borrowed from the grocery jar to take Nancy to hear the Occidental Band perform Mozart's music.

# FORTY-SIX

WHEN YAM REACHED HOULTON after the spring drive, the first place he went was to the mill. The sight of new construction amidst burned debris surprised him, but not near as much as the gossip. Jed had stolen his sons from Julia and disappeared. Julia hired the Pinkerton Agency, and they almost had him in St. Louis, but he got away.

None of this made any sense to Yam.

He went immediately back to Molunkus where Mouse's people lived. Mouse had her sleep skins spread out on the ant piles and was clearing a little patch of ground for her tent. Her husband's return surprised her, his news did not surprise her. Julia Marchion went out of her way to make Yam and his wife unwelcome in Houlton. Thinking it over, Mouse decided that Julia must have been the same kind of mean to Jed.

She didn't want to go with her husband to find his brother. It was hard traveling about in the cold spring rains, always having to sleep on wet ground. It was better to stay home and sleep under a tent that stayed in one place and kept the ground dry. After the hard work of the long winter camps she wanted the companionship of her people in the summer moons.

"There's money for a train," Yam said, emptying his pockets.

Having heard wondrous stories about her husband's travels on the iron animal, Mouse had a big heart for trains. The searching would be easier on a train. She smiled.

From Portland all the way to St. Louis there was a train. The Indians sat quietly hour after hour staring out the dirty windows. The impossibility of what they were about did not occur to them. The trail was there somewhere, and beyond that was the certainty of its being there.

The first thing Yam did on reaching St. Louis was to inquire at the train station after a tall man and two small boys, one of them crippled. How long ago? the ticket agent wanted to know.

The question surprised Yam. He should have asked more questions before leaving Houlton. The agent waved him off. "There's hundreds of people come through here."

"Was he borned lame?" a boy sitting behind the counter on a pickle barrel asked.

"Yes," Yam answered.

"I remember 'cause he wanted to know how I got lamed, and I told him I fell off the shed, and he said he was borned that way, and he wanted to try out my crutch, so I let him." The boy grinned.

"Do you remember where they go?" asked Yam.

"No, 'cause he never told me."

Brooding in a cramped sleeping room near the train yards, Yam pondered what to do next. He got drunk and fell asleep wrestling with the problem. And dreamed he was north of Upper Lake, lost in the fog, the sameness of timber and bog going on and on. He couldn't tell if he were in the slough that opened on the Winisk, or further north in the deadly swamp ground of the Ogoki. In front of him in the shallow water a sea gull lifted a leg and forgot to put it down. The sun came out and the gull cast no shadow.

"Rise up, my brother," Yam ordered the bird. "Tell me what you see." The gull rose, its wings like white breakers over a beach, and disappeared. The next morning he told Mouse, "Watch for a gull."

Which she did, high and low. The streets were full of birds, but there were no gulls. She stopped in front of a shop window full of cast-iron weather vanes that vaguely resembled gulls. Yam shook his head and moved on.

Up and down the St. Louis streets the couple walked. The city didn't feel like Jed was there. Yam was sure his brother was headed for the big red timber on the other side of the desert, to follow him there would take food and horses. They had no choice but to stop searching and go to work.

That evening the two shared another pail of whiskey in their room and again went to bed drunk. But there were no dreams. Their third day in the city Yam decided to look for work in the train yards.

Waiting for her husband, Mouse sat on a bench watching the people in the cavernous station. White people always hurried along as if going to war or to a dance. The people who took their time and looked around them were not white.

Mouse was puzzling on this when, through a front window, she saw a large white woman carrying a large feather hat being helped out of a stage. The woman entered the station and stopped in front of a desk. The white feathers on the hat bobbed up and down in the pass of people.

Mouse stared at the feathers. Just then Yam came through the crowd, and Mouse pointed at the hat, now disappearing from view. Yam shook his head, but then he remembered how the gull stood on one leg as if tethered, just as the feathers were tethered.

He followed the hat out the station and down the street, uncertain what to do next. And stopped abruptly, causing Mouse to bump into him. The hat was his sign, but he'd forgotten what he told the gull to do. Now he remembered. Returning to the station he asked the man at the desk where the stage came from that just unloaded in front of the station.

"Pike's Peak country."

May 1866.

The prairie was bare as a scraped hide, but the dark line of mountains off to the west spoke of timber. Down to one dollar and twenty-one cents, Yam bought a used canvas tent at Deitsch & Bros. and went looking for work. The city was crawling with down-on-their-luck miners. What jobs they didn't hold, their wives and children did.

Making work scarcer still was the white man's contempt for Indians. It was different than in the States, where the dust-ups were done and everybody knew who won. Here in Denver City, so far from their own kind, the white people were afraid despite all their noise. Yam could see it in their faces.

That night he set up the little tent down by the Platte, but got little sleep. The banks of the Platte were a dangerous place to sleep, the fighting and gunshots went on all night long The next morning he cadged a dollar helping a teamster haul swill out the back door of the hotels to a hog feeder down along the river, while Mouse swamped out the bar in the Cherokee House.

That night they carried their tent up along Cherry Creek and chanced upon a family of Arapaho tucked down in a hollow. The Indians were roasting a dog, Mouse chipped in with her wages—a sugar sack oozing with left-over baked beans.

This went for on for several days. One night it snowed, a heavy, wet snow a foot deep. The next day the sun came out and melted most of the snow away. The next day the wind blew as if determined to lick the prairie clean of buildings. Then the Arapaho were run out of town for eating the settlers' dogs.

Without his Indian friends, Yam was forced to haul his little tent back and forth to work. "We got to get out of here," he grumbled. "Get closer to the mountains." That's where the timber was, that's where Jed was.

The teamster hauling the swill started at three a.m. and quit early afternoon, leaving Yam plenty of time to ask around for the man who called him brother. Then he ran into the bounty hunter. It happened in a saloon on Wazee Street, the hunter was showing something to a table of cardplayers and promising to spit the reward when Yam overheard the name "Marchion."

Idling close, he saw the poster spread on the table.

"Draw your wages", he told Mouse, meeting her at the Cherokee House. "We're going to the mountains." He had seven dollars saved. He wanted to save more, but seven dollars would do. That afternoon, walking up Fifteenth Street toward Cherry Creek to set up camp for the night, they found their way blocked at Larimer Street by a crowd shouting and urging on a fight.

Yam jumped on an upended barrel the better to see what was happening. Two white men, stripped to the waist, were having go of it. Enjoying himself, Yam paid little attention to the hay wagon caught at the intersection—the boys on the seat pulling on the reins, someone at the bridles.

The brawlers pummeled each other, the onlookers yelled, several nimrods shot their guns in the air. It was, as Jed would say, a hellava good fight. Thinking about Jed, Yam saw the team lunge forward and the forest of heads part briefly on a familiar figure. He couldn't see the man's face, but he didn't need to.

He eased himself down into the crowd, grabbed Mouse's braid to get her attention, and hurried as best he could through the crowd.

Jed was yelling at the boys, wanting them to jump clear. Misunderstanding, J.C. wrapped the reins around his waist and put his full weight against them. The team backed up and plunged forward again, knocking onlookers aside and dragging Jed with them.

Then Yam was on the high seat, and Mouse was pulling herself up on the other side.

"Hey, hey, hey, white man!" Yam yelled like he used to yell spinning logs on the Penobscot.

How good the sunshine looks, shining on the dark clouds of the retreating storm. The first thing Nancy said on seeing Yam was to ask if he would go looking for her brother.

Yam and Mouse rented a shack behind the Chinese laundry and took their meals in the San Francisco House. From now on they would put their money in the common pot. Mouse went back to work at the Cherokee House, Jed thought he could get Yam on with the Express.

But first Yam went hunting for Jeremy.

A Cheyenne squaw living with a blind trader spoke of the hunting ground that was there before the white men. Everything was different now. She wanted to leave, but her husband was timid.

"Where would you go to find your people?" Yam asked.

"Out along the Berrywood," she pointed toward the east.

"I always wore a red bandanna," the blind trader told him. "That way they got used to knowing it was me coming, I never had no trouble with 'em."

Yam put together some trade materials and rented a livery horse. Around his neck he wore a red bandana.

Following Cherry Creek east and south away from the white settlements he gave himself over to the lonesome prairie, the sun rolling over him, the wind pawing at him. It was good to know how to live in the world of the white man, but the world of the Indian was better.

Shortly before sundown he reached a camp of Arapaho. A boy had visited the camp asking to know where the Cheyenne lived. The boy said his father was Cheyenne. He was with some other boys, the rest of those boys went back to the settlement, but this boy went on.

The next day Yam started out again. The further east he followed the river, the scarcer grew signs of human travel. He made camp that night without a fire and the next morning picked up watchers at a distance. Now he was getting somewhere.

The camp was in the cottonwood at the mouth of a sandy wash. Here the river made a wide, flat curve. Deer hides were pegged on the ground, children ran back and forth through the water. Jeremy was resting in the shade. Bare-footed, wearing a pair of white man's trousers. His long braids were twisted with colored cord.

Yam nodded at the old woman sitting nearby. She got to her feet, making room in the shade. "You should come home," Yam told the surprised boy.

"Yes, sir. When did you get to Denver City?"

"Not long."

"I came here to ask about my father, and you'll never guess what. My aunt's here, that's her there." Jeremy indicated the woman who had moved to another piece of shade. "She remembers my mother, and I got my uncle here, and I know everything.

"My great grandfather—Indians never say 'great,' they just say 'grandfather,' all the old men are called 'grandfather'—you probably know that, being part Indian yourself—anyway, he was a Cheyenne Dog Soldier. Mother called him Okhum, but his full name was Ohkumhkakit. His daughter grew up and married a Northern Cheyenne Wolf soldier, and when her husband died in a fight with the Pawnee on Tongue River, she came back home to her family and married a Crow prisoner by the name of Big Prisoner.

"My grandmother and Big Prisoner died, and Ohkumhkakit raised their children. There were three, one was my father, Hunumpayohos. One is my Aunt Susweca, and one is Uncle Ake-lyyayapi.

"When they found my mother, she shortened their names to Ohkum and Sasha and Haskay, and you know what? the Indians still remember those names.

"My Aunt Sasha's going to take me where Grandfather Okhum died. And you wanna know what else? My little horsehair"—he fished Uergin's oversized horsehair ring out of his pocket—"is a charm. Look close, see how it's dyed red. Uergin did the medicine lodge ceremony and wore it in his hair. That's why his chest was all scarred up, they run sticks through the skin…"

Yam was nodding off when he realized Jeremy had quit talking. "You should go back to Denver City," he said.

Which Jeremy intended to do. "They're going to be so amazed."

Jeremy came home a week later with a fresh knife scar under his chin from ear to collarbone. Renegade Arapaho had visited the camp, handing out whiskey for hides. Jeremy argued against the trade, saying the hides were needed. That's when one of the visitors pulled a knife. Haskay threw a blanket over the knife, and the Arapaho went away vowing to return.

"I waited a couple of days, but they never came back, I was ready for 'em."

*Be careful,* Yam warned Jeremy silently, seeing the excitement in the boy's face. *The Indians are circling and rooting at each the way the horned ones do when cornered. Be careful, Jeremy.*

"They took my cross, it came off when the fellow knifed me."

"The wood makes its own journey," Yam replied.

Nancy thought her brother terribly foolish to have any truck whatsoever with Indians. Learning he planned to visit the mountains with Haskay, she scolded him furiously. "You've got no business going up in the mountains with the Indians."

"You don't understand, it's is a spiritual thing. My grandfather died up there to protect me, I have to go."

"That's just silly superstition. I can't think if you're dumb or just plain stupid."

"Why is thinking so hard for women, I wonder," Jeremy puzzled, shifting his feet to lessen the impact of Nancy's shoe. The horseplay reminded Jed of his own scuffles with Dinky.

"What do you think, Uncle Yam?" Nancy asked. She wanted the family J.C. and Paul had, just as they wanted an older brother and sister. That nobody had a mother made Daphne everybody's mother, although they didn't call her that.

Yam hesitated. As long as Jeremy dressed like a white man, he was safe. Living with Indians, dressed as an Indian, he wasn't. Being Indian in this part of the land was a foot-noose for trouble. "Your brother has two bloods mixing in him, he will decide what to follow."

Jeremy wanted to talk about the Indians, about how hard life was for them with the white man around. "They call the Platte the Moonshell, isn't that pretty. It comes from when they traded for pink shells along the river with tribes that came all the way from the coast. Now they can't."

"We got troubles enough without worrying about Indians," Jed told him, plainly irritated. "You worry about your own family."

"They are my family."

"They never raised you." Jed had a lot more to say in private, but didn't hold out much hope. He was young once himself, and hell bent on going somewhere, anywhere but where he was. His pa gave him a gun and a map. It was too bad they couldn't do the same for Jeremy.

# FORTY-SEVEN

NATHAN WAS WANTING to leave for the coast, it was
August, winter was coming on. He suggested Mouse's
running the boarding house, but Daphne hired a housekeeper, an Irish girl with credentials. She was the oldest of
a large brood and knew how to clean and cook, but not, as
Daphne soon discovered, how to read and write. Asked what he
thought, Jed didn't see a problem.

He didn't see it working either, none of it. They were
whistling in the dark to think they could keep the boarding
house open without Daphne. But Nathan was the only one with
a plan for getting out of the Territory, and Jed was reluctant to
shoot him down. If he had the money, he'd put everyone on the
stage, but himself and Yam and Mouse, and follow in a few days,
but he didn't have near that kind of money.

They'd probably just close the boarding house and let things
rock along through the winter. If Nathan didn't come up with
anything by next summer, they'd move to the mountains. The
bounty hunters were looking for a man with two motherless
boys, not a family of seven.

It was getting on toward the middle of September. Nathan
and Daphne were packed to leave. And, although careful to
express their regrets, could scarcely contain their enthusiasm.
Tuesday Nathan received a bonus of five dollars. He purchased

an iced chocolate cake at the Larimer Street confectionery store and a little pail of milk. That same day Daphne treated herself and Nancy to a little bottle of red polish and polished their toenails and fingernails, and discussed things Nancy needed to know when a boy asked her to walk out.

That night in bed, unable to sleep, Daphne talked about Nob Hill, wondering if there were a house on it yet. She talked about the Auction Lunch, how Nathan should eat there as often as possible and learn from the brokers what stocks to buy. About the beaches, the walrus sunning themselves on the outer rocks, the sound of the waves.

Finally she dropped off to sleep, but not before Nathan began to sense something horribly amiss. The truth of which he learned the next morning.

"I can't go."

"What's wrong?!"

"Whatever will become of Nancy? She's only fifteen. Mouse is alright with the boys, but she can't teach a girl how to be fashionable, how to wear a hat…" Daphne, in her nightshirt, preened herself in front of the mirror "…just so, on a gentle slope. And the language of the parasol…" she held an imaginary parasol over her shoulder "…that's very important, Nathan. She's such a pretty girl, and the wrong age to be alone. It would break my heart to have her end up on the dustheap."

"Don't be ridiculous! You don't give her enough credit. She can clerk in one of the banks, or in Tappan's, that's a nice store."

"Not if she doesn't finish school. If something goes wrong here at the house, and it will sooner or later, it always does, she'll quit school and never go back."

It was a sad, but true fact. Every time they hired a woman to cook and clean, she was soon gone for one reason or another.

"Daphne, I simply can not make enough money here to spit on."

"So go! do what you do so well. I'll be right here, you just make sure you come back."

"I can't believe you're doing this, Daph."

"I can't either."

Jed fired up the kitchen stove and made a fresh pot of coffee, warming the dregs of the previous evening's pot in a tin cup. Nathan was shaving at the sink.

"I remember where I saw you!"

Nathan jerked and cut his lip. "Damn!"

"It was at the mechanics fair outside Ashtabula."

*Good Lord, I hope I didn't skin you,* Nathan thought.

"At a shooting contest."

"I've never been in a shooting contest in my life."

"No, I was." Jed nodded in self-agreement. "You bet a hundred dollars against my pa's old USM 1803, and I missed. Yes, sir! I *knew* I knew you from somewhere."

Nathan kept right on shaving. "When was this?"

"Back in '46. You was wearing a fancy white suit. Whatever happened to that old gun?"

"I don't remember." But he *did* remember, kind of.

"Funny, I hadn't thought of that in years. Back then there wasn't any stages outside the States, now you're going all the way to the ocean in one."

Nathan dried his face and tested the coffee in the pot. It wasn't ready yet. "Another twenty years and there'll be a train."

"Was Daphne there?"

"Oh, probably so." Of a sudden he could see it so clearly. The lanterns hung in the trees at the edge of the road, the little row of glass bottles glinting in the shifting light, the gun smoke layering the air. Thinking *I shouldn't be leaving, this is the only family I've got,* he tried the coffee again.

He boarded the stage the most melancholy of men. The ticket cost a hundred and fifty dollars. He had a little Smith & Wesson seven-shooter in case of Indians and a little shot-bag of silver coin for breakfasts and dinners. And Daphne's ticket money to launch his fortunes in San Francisco. Informed that the luggage limit was twenty-five pounds, he smiled ruefully. His valise weighed less than nineteen.

Speaking briskly so as to hide his despondency, he instructed Daphne not to worry. Then he was off, the coach swinging and swaying, Nancy and Daphne disappearing around the corner.

By the time the stage reached Churches Station, some twelve miles distant, his customary optimism had returned, spurred on by the sheer freedom of once again being on his own, trimming his sails, running against the tide. Bowling along, crossing numerous dry rivulets and an occasional creek, the mountains on the west melting into the prairies on the east, he felt as if he were parting the Red Sea.

The stage had a canvas roof and canvas curtains on the sides and on the front, making it wonderfully cool. Explaining "it gets lonesome out here," the driver kept the front curtain up to visit with the passengers, using landmarks along the trail to illustrate his stories. Periodically he fell asleep, coach and horses continuing on like some mechanical toy.

Above Boones Station a midday rain laid the dust and sweetened the air. The departing scatter of broken clouds, patching and repatching the rolling prairie as far as the eye could reach, reminded Nathan of England, of sweet marmalade golden-tinted and sunshiny as the summer day.

Adding considerably to the pleasures of the open road was the rosy, windblown woman who boarded the stage in Laporte the next morning. Nathan made room with a friendly smile.

Fall turned into winter and Christmas came. The inhabitants of
the boarding house propped against the Chinese laundry nailed
slats crossways on a broom and stuck the broom upright in a
bucket of dirt. Pieces of mica glued to the slats made the tree
sparkle, chains of looped paper filled in the spaces.

Christmas morning the boys found a Humpty Dumpty circus
band under the tree. For Jed and Yam there were two cans of
Golden Thread tobacco, for Jeremy a pair of fancy suspenders
with braided ends. Daphne and Nancy and Mouse each got
a hair brush with white bristles and a polished walnut back.
Christmas dinner was a big grey goose, Jeremy's Christmas bonus
from Burton's.

Then it was spring. Not the lovely unfolding that spring
was meant to be, but the desert variety—one day all sweetness
and light, the next day all cold and blustery. Jed and Yam were
working for Peabody. The hours were long, but the pay was
better than the Overland, now called Wells Fargo.

Nancy filled the flower boxes with dirt and planted a little
packet of radish seeds. The boarding house stayed fairly full.
And Jeremy disappeared. Nancy called him a yo-yo on a stick .

Saturday, the 6th of June. The Planter's House ordered thirty
large kegs to be lined up beneath a row of mirrors. Filled with
dirt and used as planters, the kegs would prevent inebriated
guests from walking into the glass. Jed swung a keg into place
and was walking through the propped-open front doors for
another when he came face-to-face with Bettina.

He opened his mouth and at the same instant realized she
didn't know him. Behind her came two miniature Bettinas, and
behind them, a stout, red-faced fellow with a walrus mustache.

Everyone swathed in dusty travel linens and looking travel-worn.

An army of porters was working to unload the street hack. There didn't appear to be anyone else traveling with the family.

The mild-mannered clerk at the Planter's House spent his days off panning for gold in the abandoned Arapahoe Bar diggings. Mr. Corn was saving to bring his family out from Illinois, Daphne was helping him look for a house amongst the cabins being thrown up at the ends of the business streets.

Mr. Corn knew the gossip of the city, but this morning Daphne had her own gossip. There was a couple staying in the Planter's House come all the way from Washington, D.C.

Mr. Corn smiled, he liked Daphne, she was a real lady. He turned the register so his friend could read it—a Mr. and Mrs. Edwin Franklin and their two daughters. The Franklins were staying at Planter's until their home on Fourteenth Street was finished, he confided. Mr. Franklin was with the Union Pacific, he'd already walked up to the land office several times to look at the maps.

"Any money?" Daphne asked.

"Lots of it." Mr. Corn nodded sagely. "That's where the money is these days, in the railroads and in the mines if you're lucky."

A guest approached, and Daphne walked out on the street, enjoying her stroll in the warm sunshine even if she had no money to spend. The next morning she was back at the Planter's House.

"Have you seen the Franklins yet this morning?"

"Not yet."

They glanced at the wall clock—it was 10:40—and smiled at each other. Now it was Daphne's turn to nod sagely.

She took a chair in an out-of-the-way place. Sure enough,

here they came, standing in a knot waiting to be seated in the dining room. As soon as the food order was placed, lining herself up just so, Daphne strode purposely toward the table.

"Hello, my name is Daphne Lafitte." The card she presented smelled faintly of oil of eucalyptus (having been cut from the back of a box of eucalyptus soap). Mr. Pierce at the library had lettered it.

DAPHNE LAFITTE
LADIES CONCIERGE

"I can show you," she smiled sweetly at the girls, who stared back stonily, "where the better stores are."

Edwin Franklin frowned and tapped his plate with the edge of his fork. "I don't welcome solicitors at my table, I shouldn't think the hotel would either." He looked around as if to engage the aid of the *maître d'*.

"Oh, Edwin, don't be such a prude," Bettina scolded. "We're in the West now, people are more forward. I think the offer interesting."

"You have a carriage?" Edwin asked.

"I have no carriage," Daphne answered pertly. "What I offer is knowledge, together with a pleasurable walk."

"And your credentials?"

"Not as good as they used to be, unfortunately. But a lady must do what a lady must do. I have a small boarding house, and when I can get away, I give tours."

"For which you charge a fee."

"For which I receive a tip, if the service is satisfactory."

"Edwin, that's enough." Bettina waved her fingers at her husband as if to whisk his words away. "Allow the poor creature her dignity. Yes, by all means, you may take us on a tour…" she paused to glance at the card "…Mrs. Lafitte. Come back at two o'clock."

The tour consisted of walking up one side of Sixteenth Street toward Capitol Hill and back down the other. At which time Daphne asked Mrs. Franklin if she would like to see the San Francisco house, newly decorated in the style of an Italian courtyard.

The Franklin daughters, having encountered nothing of interest on the tour, murmured their objections.

"Oh, we really wouldn't be interested," Bettina demurred. Her daughters hurried ahead, giggling.

"I have someone who would like to meet you," Daphne said.

Bettina looked startled. "Meet me? What are you talking about?"

"His name is Jed Marchion."

Awareness flooded Bettina's face. She glanced at her daughters and back at Daphne. "Where is he?"

"Not far. There are cookies and milk set out for your daughters."

Bettina cocked her head slightly and looked into Daphne's eyes. "You pulled that off very well, I would never have guessed."

# FORTY-EIGHT

THE HOUSE SMELLED PLEASANTLY of bread rising in the oven. Daphne rang the bell on the little desk in the entryway, and Nancy, tying on an apron, walked out of the kitchen.

"These are the daughters of Mr. and Mrs. Franklin," Daphne told her. "Here for their treats."

Nancy indicated the dining room, but the girls stood their ground. "Go on now," Bettina ordered rather sharply. "Don't be rude. Take off your coats and relax and mind your manners." That the dark interior of the boarding house in no way resembled an Italian courtyard, she didn't notice.

Daphne pointed up the stairs. "The first doorway on your right."

Climbing the stairs Bettina felt like a school girl about to do something naughty. *I've been married so long I've forgotten what excitement feels like,* she told herself.

The man who answered her knock was taller than she remembered, and shabbily dressed. Without his coat he seemed too thin. There was no lamp lit, and the shade was partly drawn. Bettina felt her senses stir. Dancing with Jed Marchion back home, laughing in his arms, she'd been keenly aware of his eyes, his mouth, his hard shoulders. Not even the wild beard dispelled the memory.

"How's Julia?"

"Oh, that's nice. I wondered what you had to say. So civilized."

"How is she?"

"How do you think she is?! You stole her children! Are you married to the woman who brought me here?"

"She runs the boarding house."

"You're a horrible person, Jed, to steal children away from their own mother. Just horrible, how could you do it?!"

"I want you to write her and tell her the boys are fine."

"You write her. I'll mail it after I see the boys."

"Tell her maybe we could give it another try."

Bettina gasped. "You can't really think that!"

"It's worth another try."

"Oh, that's exactly what I'll do, I'll give her your address and let her contact you. Then her children will be where they should be, and you'll be where you should be, in jail. What are you doing in Denver City?"

"What I can 'til I can get into the timber business, that's what I know best."

"That and thievery. Surely you don't go by your real name?"

"No, and I didn't start that fire in the mill."

Bettina shrugged off the denial. "You have no idea what hell you put Julia through and are still putting her through."

"I seen my poster around."

"You don't have to worry behind that beard, it's really very nasty. What do you go by?"

Jed hesitated and Bettina chuckled wickedly. "You're right not to trust me, but it doesn't matter, now that I know where you are."

"We could start over. I never meant not to go back to Houlton, I wound up on the wrong car, and I was mad, I guess I was gonna get even. Tell her I'm sorry, she could write me in care of the boarding house."

Good God, he believed what he was saying! Bettina was astonished. "You've destroyed her life and you don't even know it?! What a fool you are! I want to see the boys."

There was no answer.

She opened the door. An aroma of meat and spices wafted up the stairs. "If you're going to run, you better run fast."

Jed's hand closed over her wrist like a vise, he pulled the door shut. "Will you take a letter to her?"

"Let go of me!" Bettina shook herself free and reached for the door again, but Jed blocked it.

"Why won't you take a letter to her?"

"Why won't you let me see the boys? they are here, aren't they? where are they?"

"With Yam."

"My god! They shouldn't be with the Indians! I know Yam's supposed to be some sort of relative, but this is madness! it's like you're making orphans of them. They can't live with their mother and they can't live with their father either? It's unbelievable, it's evil is what it is. You don't deserve them."

She fell silent, feeling the unrelieved meanness of the room and the outside street. So unlike her own well-ordered world, so far from the Clare home Julia and Jed once shared. "I am sorry for you, for both of you. But you can't hide your sons with the Indians, it's another culture, they can't adapt, it's not how they were raised."

"If I go back to Houlton, I'll never see them again."

"Julia's in Washington. She was in Houlton until Dr. Clare died, I suspect of a broken heart, then she moved back to the Capitol."

"With Sigvald?"

"Eventually. After Camille went home to New Orleans. It was quite the scandal, she was exposed as a quadroon. The marriage was nullified on the grounds of miscegenation, and…well…Sigvald married Julia. The marriage with you was annulled, it's not hard when you understand the legalities, as Sigvald does. He didn't want people thinking of his wife as a divorced woman."

Jed looked slightly dazed. "I never thought she'd do that."

"What did you think she'd do?"

"I don't know, not that."

"They couldn't marry in Washington, the first-cousin thing and all, they had to go to Canada. There won't be children, Julia's convinced there shouldn't be. Dr. Clare warned her years ago that marrying Sigvald would produce deformed children. Now, I do have to go, if you see me again, don't speak. Edwin adores Julia, if he knew you were here, he'd have you in irons."

"You're not going to the authorities?"

"I don't know what to do now, it's such a mess." Bettina pressed her hand to her chest, a manner she assumed when being dramatic, and looked around as if for a chair.

"Look," Jed pleaded, "just tell her you saw me, please. Tell her the boys are fine and that I am sorry, tell her what happened."

"You're not listening to me! I can't tell her *anything*. Once she knows you're here, she'll have you arrested. God only knows what will happen to the boys then, did you change their names too?"

"Is she happy, I mean with Sigvald?"

Such an unhappy man, he looked absolutely haunted. Bettina sat down on the edge of the bed. "I'm not used to this altitude." She sighed deeply. "Sigvald is the secretary for our ambassador to the dark-skinned countries and is gone most of the time. When he is home, there are…parties.

"The home would *not* be a good place for children. Unfortunately, oh dear, no! You realize, of course, I'm breaking a sacred oath. You do, don't you? and won't repeat this to a living soul." She took another deep breath.

And went on.

"Julia is *quite* ill and *very* lonely. When we were young and foolish, we used to drink whiskey and beer, everyone did, it was *great* fun. But the after-effects are *terrible*. Besides, beer fattens, and no fashionable lady wants to be fat. Of course, children are the final determinants."

Jed was quiet, remembering his first party in the basement of the Clare home—the wonderful array of liquors, Julia offering him what he wanted, offering herself out in the dark.

"We experimented with fruit syrups mixed with herbs and alcohol and laced with opium. *Oh dear!* just talking about it brings back the feeling!" Bettina fanned her face with her hand. "Such foolishness. Everything was right there in the Clare house, and no one the wiser, you never knew."

"No," Jed said softly.

"We gave it all up when Julia got pregnant. When I went to Washington, I refused to touch it, and I warned Julia to leave it alone. There's a great deal of partying goes on in the Capitol, ever so much more in Johnson's Washington than there ever was in Lincoln's. There are social events every afternoon and evening, and opium and alcohol are everywhere.

"Julia was in *great* demand, not having the entanglement of a husband. President Johnson's wife grew *quite* fond of her, as there is always a diplomat alone in the city requiring a suitable dinner partner.

"For awhile she was able to avoid the drugs. Until Sigvald, that naughty prankster..." Bettina wrinkled her face "...I love him dearly, after all he is our cousin, but he can be such a nuisance...added a Godfrey's Cordial to her lemonade.

*"And that was it!"* Bettina threw her arms wide. "That was all it took for the poor dear to return to the opium pleasures of her youth. Christmas Eve they all went up to Arlington and didn't come back until the day after Christmas on account of the heavy

snows. The staff at Willard's was supposedly caring for the boys. When Julia found your note, she went out of her mind. *Simply out of her mind!* She's never forgiven me for betraying her, she says I should have sent you on a wild goose chase. But I *did* try to warn her, I *did* send a note.

"You were never legally charged for the fire. Julia tried to get Shep Cary to blame you, but he wouldn't. He finally died, by the way, pneumonia, the old people's friend."

"I'm sorry to hear that."

"You must never tell Edwin any of this, or I shall deny it, and he will kill you." Bettina got to her feet, the monstrous betrayal filling her ears. "You should have stayed in Houlton, Jed."

"Yeah? Well, if 'if' was a fish, we'd all have a fry. You should of told me a long time ago, I could of helped her."

That night he visited Holladay Street. Not his first visit down the worn dirt street to the parlour houses. The two-story house with the words SPORTING MEN'S PARLOUR painted on the front windowpane was full of light and sound. Inside, seated on wooden benches along the walls, customers waited their turn to be taken upstairs. Large, brightly painted flowers decorated the walls, streamers of twisted crepe paper hung from the pressed tin ceiling. At the back of the room, sandwiched between the stairs and an upright piano, sat a woman blowing on a trumpet.

Madeline had reddened lips and splotches of rouge on her cheekbones. Seen up close, beneath the thick white powder, the pox scars made little dents. On an earlier visit, while waiting downstairs, Jed learned she was from Albany, New York. He'd never secured her favors, but he enjoyed talking to her.

Tonight was different. He paid the madam five dollars and asked for the trumpet player. Surprised, Madeline put down the instrument and flounced up the stairs, a stout woman in a bright red dress with spangles on the sleeves.

"I need to ask you some questions," Jed told her when the door was closed on the small room with its large bed and washstand and chair.

"Sure, sweetie, whatever you want, make yourself to home, get comfortable."

"Do you take drugs?"

"I figured you had something in mind besides talk." Madeline opened the washstand and set out a silver case in the shape of a miniature piano. Inside were what looked to be tiny pieces of clear quartz rock.

"What's that?"

"Opium, that's what the Chinamens smoke."

"Where do you get it?"

Madeline shrugged. "At the city hospital, I just tell 'em I'm hurting. I'll give you a little piece."

"Never mind. What if you wanted to stop?"

"Why would I wanna stop?"

"But if you did?" Jed pressed. "What would you do, would it be hard?"

"I quit all the time when I run out of money, that's when I get knives in my stomach, I always do." Madeline opened another drawer and pulled out a bottle labeled *Theriaki Painless Cure.* "This here's supposed to cure me. Ha ha, guess what, it's opium too. I can tell by the way it makes me feel." She tried again to give Jed a piece of the opium and, failing that, settled herself on the bed.

" C'mon, let's have a little fun." She grabbed Jed's hand. "C'mon, be my friend."

"I'll be back."

He did go back, stopping by during the day to see how she was doing, but he never again used the fancy women in the pretty parlour houses on Holladay Street.

# FORTY-NINE

A LETTER LEFT AT THE BOARDING HOUSe inquired as to the possibility of Mrs. Lafitte's suggesting the placement of the cupboards in the new kitchen of the Edwin Franklin mansion.

"A kitchen, for god's sake!" Daphne shrilled. "Why doesn't she ask the cooks!" Nevertheless, Daphne was pleased. She took Nancy with her to inspect the new house on Fourteenth Street, and while the Franklin daughters showed off their large bedrooms to Nancy, Daphne reviewed the plans for the kitchen. Not the placement of the cupboards, but the placement of the room's corners—some she liked, some she wanted changed.

"Really," Bettina protested. "It isn't as if I'll be entertaining guests in here."

"Old money never flaunts," Daphne warned. "The guest must always leave with a sense of something undiscovered. In this case it's the kitchen. Domestic servants gossip. That your kitchen is well-lit and functional, and the fine porcelain displayed behind glass, says you are not one to stint."

"Really, Mrs. Lafitte," Bettina scolded, only half in jest. "You forget your station."

Surprised by the charge, Daphne stared open-mouthed at her employer. "You're right!" she blurted out. "I did, and I *never* do that. You know what the problem is? I'm missing my husband."

Despite herself, Daphne broke into tears. "Very much...I...he... we're a team."

"Where is your husband?"

"In San Francisco. He buys art and sells it, and we need the money. There isn't that kind of money here." Daphne pulled a clean scrap of cloth from her sleeve and wiped her face. "Anyway, it's your house, and I'm sorry, this won't happen again."

"To the contrary." Bettina favored the poor concierge with a smile of the sort usually reserved for her family. "I expect you to speak your mind, or I shall discharge you immediately."

Rather than engage a hack, Daphne and Nancy strolled from the Franklin mansion across town to the boarding house in what Daphne called a long-overdue walk-about. "What did you think?" she asked.

"It's so big, twice as big as our house back home."

"Always remember, big houses have to be furnished and they have to be heated, and that takes money."

"Well, they have lots of money."

"Yes, and so will you someday."

"If I'm lucky."

"Anyone can get lucky. You have to be smart. That's what I want you to remember while that house is fresh in your mind. You can learn to love a rich man as well as a poor one."

"Is Uncle Nathan rich or poor?"

"Both, he's been both. And mark my words, little Miss Smarty Pants, he'll come back a richer man than he left."

Late one night, everybody in bed, Jed came home to find on the table by his waiting plate a letter addressed to *The father of the little boys, San Francisco Boarding House.* The note inside read

*Go to the Union Pacific office and talk to the man called
Meyers. He is setting up a tie camp in the mountains and is in
need of a foreman. B.*

Tied to the note was a small pair of scissors.

Meyers wanted to know who Jed talked to. Overheard it in a
saloon, Jed told him.

"No, sir, I don't think so. You got friends higher up. I just
heard the news myself this morning." The man standing before
him, hat in hand, looked poor as a church mouse, but honest,
beard neat, clothes clean. Good foremen were hard to find. Most
didn't want the job, not with the chance of hitting it big in the
mines.

"Alright, Harris, you're hired, three hundred and thirty-five
dollars a month. You been up in the mountains."

"Not yet."

"The timber north of the Vasquez is what we're looking at.
There's a wagon road up the river above Golden City into the
interior. And the Gregory road out of Gate City.* Everything's
got a toll on it, just let the gatekeepers know who you work for.

"We own every odd section, I'll get you a map. Lease what
you have to, it won't be cheap, the mines are driving the market
way up. We'll have a yard in Golden City."

"What about the mill?"

"Coming from Atchison."

"How many men?"

"Whatever you can hire, we'll set up an account with the
Carter banking house in the city."

"What about wages?"

"Three a day, bed and board, pay at the end of the week so
they'll stick around. Any complaints, remind 'em the mines only
pay two dollars and fifty cents."

---

* For place names in this paragraph, see "The History" on page 515.

"I got a brother comes with me."

"Too bad you don't have thirty."

Jed turned in his notice along with Yam and the two took off on livery horses for the mountains, using Meyer's map from the land office showing sections and roads.

Gate City was little more a ghost town. The wagon road though the middle of town led up a ravine. At a place too narrow to turn a wagon around a gatekeeper collected toll.

"I don't have anything shows you pass free."

"You will," Jed told him, and paid fifteen cents a horse.

The Gregory road wasn't much of a road to pay toll on, snaking back and forth across the creekbed countless times and scattered with dead livestock. The timber in the drainage was spotty—some good stands on the northern slopes, nothing to speak of on the southern. Toward the top of the drainage a roadhouse advertised as 8 MILE HOUSE boasted a dance hall and a piano.

Above the roadhouse the grade steepened, then flattened off across a pass through the mountain range. Beyond to the southwest a wild batter of black mountains ended in a broken, far-away edge of snow. The heavy blanket of timber reminded Jed of a verse in a schoolhouse dance.

> Never marry a man from the piney woods,
> he's got the itchy foot.
> His pockets are filled with sawdust,
> and his boots are filled with soot.

A deep north-south gulch lay dead ahead. The map showed a wagon road swinging off the river and through Guy's gulch to the Gregory road. If this was the gulch, the junction was below in the bottom.

"I hope to god that river road never washes out," Jed said, eying the windlass at the edge of the slope.

In the bottom was a roadhouse much like the earlier one— large, white, two-story, signed GUY HOUSE. The carcass of a steer hung from the barn roof, chickens scratched at the dirt. The proprietor, a balding, mustached man by the name of Wiggins, dished up information along with the meal. The gulch was named for John Guy, a homesteader. Folks called the steep climb to the east the Big Hill.

"Folks coming down from the mines are always asking me is the river road passable. I tell them, hell, it's two miles away, go look for yourself. They don't like this Big Hill.

"River road's built by Mr. Loveland. I'm supposed to collect the toll on this end, but I quit that. Too much of a hassle. Folks go down there, don't like what they see, and come back wanting their money back."

Making their way toward the diggings Jed and Yam poked around for several days. The higher trees were full of mills. Jed asked questions about supplies and animals and techniques, and saw several things he'd never seen before. Including a forty-foot bandsaw, too new to have a patent, hauled from Indiana, and a portable sawmill engine from Ohio oddly mounted horizontal on a horizontal boiler.

People everywhere talked about the railroad's coming and the good times it was bringing. But to the men from Maine, life in the terrible up and downs looked like nothing so much as hard times. And no place looked harder than the diggings themselves. The timber here ended where the mine dumps started. Clinging in the cracks of the mountains, mill operators and town builders scoured the nearby slopes bare as a shaved hog.

There were good stands of virgin timber in the higher reaches to either side of Guy's gulch. The gulch's steep walls made the timber hard to get at, but an easy skid out. A tie camp in the bottom would provide a straight, relatively short haul to the river.

Jed stuck an dead stick upright between two rocks. "What d'you think, Yam?"

Yam studied the small patch of level ground and the steep walls to either side. No place in the gulch looked any worse or any better. He grinned and gestured his acceptance, it was as good a place as any to count coup.

According to Wiggins, the timber up the gulch from the roadhouse was owned by a Cousin Jack named Tom Robinson. Robinson lived in Black Hawk, and finding him proved easier than dealing with him.

Robinson owned four sections in the Guy Gulch country, he had his own map, hand-drawn and colored in like a patchwork quilt. People talked about needing timber, but talk was cheap, he wanted twelve hundred dollars for a year's lease, up front.

"Some of it's burned," Jed said.

Robinson shook off the argument. "You want the lease or not?"

"We'll take it."

Headed back for the prairie they followed Mr. Loveland's wagon road. The narrow floor of the gulch was all but level, the steep walls were awash in brush. A tiny stream wandered back and forth through a litter of ruined beaver dams. Long before the riders reached the river they could hear it roar. At the water's edge they stared up in awe at grey, gloomy cliffs over a thousand feet high.

"You ever been a place this deep in the earth?" Jed asked.

Yam shook his head. It felt like sacred ground, a deep cave open to the sky where men came to be alone.

Except for an occasional flood plain marked by thick clumps of willows, and water spruce and cottonwood with trunks as big around as wagon wheels, the toll road down the Vasquez was little more than a gravel path shored up with stonework between the water and the granite walls.

Broad, deceptively quiet pools followed fields of immense boulders all but lost in a froth of white water. Islands surfaced in the race—deep grass waving in the breeze, sandy beaches sparkling. Birds swooped and dived, the ramparts of the beaver were spotted at the entrances to the larger drainages, along with an occasional Indian fishing.

A brief, but furious storm darkened the narrow ribbon of sky overhead. Rain pelted the riders, thunder cracked, lightning licked the canyon rim and bounced rocks down the cliff faces. Like the man said, the Vasquez was a better grade—but it was sure god-awful spooky as hell.

Down in the Union Pacific office on Market Street Jed described good stands of timber with some fire scarring, mostly along the ridge lines.

"The miners set fires to find the rock outcroppings," Meyers explained, "and burn themselves up, or the poor bastard behind them. I warrant you'll find bodies before all's said and done. Salvage what you can of the charred timber for yard posts."

## F I F T Y

J ED DECIDED TO MOVE the family to Golden City. Daphne
objected, so did Nancy. But the truth was, the boarding
house was falling down around their ears. The roof needed to
be replaced, there were patches on patches, and still it
leaked. A corner of the kitchen floor was slowly giving way
under the weight of the stove. Determined to put a good face on
the move, Daphne told Nancy that the nicer homes were closer
to the mines.

This didn't turn out to be the case. But whatever Golden
City lacked in finesse, it more than made up for in derring-do.
Stuck like a cocklebur between the mountains and the mesas,
Golden City was busier than a cranberry merchant the day
before Thanksgiving. False-fronted buildings were rising like
mushrooms, some so poorly constructed that they appeared to be
on their last leg, with the paint still fresh.

A most pretentious settlement, what with its title of
Territorial Capitol and rusty red river, faster and deeper than
the prairie rivers. Full of uppity people walking around twirling
their gold watch fobs, bragging that their mines, once properly
developed, would stand toe to toe with any of those upriver in
the Little Kingdom of Gilpin, and looking down their noses at
that poor wannabe called Denver City.

North of the Vasquez on Platte Street a two-story house
of unhewn stone displayed a FOR RENT sign in the window.

The lady who answered the door said she was moving up to Nevadaville, that's where the big money was. She wanted thirty dollars a month deposited in her account with Carter's banking house. It wasn't worth thirty dollars, the chinking between the stones was crumbling, but beggars can't be choosers. Shortly after that, Daphne wrote Nathan.

> We are well at present and are moved closer to the mountans to Golden City which is the capital. Nancy is not happy but I tell her she will make friends here. we got $75 for the house in Denver City and rented a big house here and put out 3 rooms for let. There is a nice room for me and Nancy and a room under the stair for the boys excep Jeremy is gone most of the time with the lazie indians. I will keep decorating for Mrs. Franklin so will take the coach to that city 1 day a week Jed and Yam are gone off to the pinaries Take care of yourself. Write us at the Golden City post office. Love and kisses Daphne

Yam spent the first week in the city looking for stock, while Jed put together a crew. With both men sleeping in the boarding house, Yam and his wife took the room under the stairs, and Jed and the boys and Jeremy slept in the unheated porch behind the house—much to Daphne's irritation. She had not anticipated the Indians living with them.

Yam was no problem, he wouldn't be there that much anyway, but what to do with Mouse? As soon as the men took off for the mountains, she declared her intention to move J.C. and Paul under the stairs and partition off the porch for Jeremy and Mouse. But the boys liked their porch, they called it their fort. So Mouse stayed under the stairs.

Daphne's irritation deepened. She gave orders, Mouse argued back in Indian. Daphne accused the squaw of having a low and shriveled nature, Mouse acted as if she didn't understand. In desperation Daphne hired an emigrant woman to clean. But the day she took off to Denver City, the emigrant woman got

in an argument with Mouse and quit. Daphne hired another
emigrant woman. By then she had enrolled Nancy and the boys
in Golden City's public school, a one-story brick school house
across the river on Third Street.

That the school was free made the enrollment possible. In
Denver City the tuition was ten dollars a month per child. In
their new surroundings, at least until they got on their feet,
there was no money for schooling.

On one of Jed's trips down to Golden City, Jeremy hit him up
to work in the timber. "I want you here," Jed told him. "You're
the one holding everything together."

Hearing the conversation, Daphne felt a real apprehension. It
wasn't Jeremy holding everything together.

Cold weather came on. Daphne and Mouse draped a canvas
across the room under the stairs and moved J.C. and Paul into
one side. Mouse stayed on the other side. Jeremy was gone most
of the time, working as a market hunter for the hotels. He could
have the cold porch to himself when he was around.

The renters wanted more meat on the table, Daphne asked
for credit at the slaughter house on Ford Street and was turned
down.

A spider bite swelled her face and neck, and she told Mouse
to wash the sheets. "They have to be washed every week."

Jed was in town that day to pick up tools, and Mouse rode
around with him instead.

That night the house was full—seven men in the bedrooms.
Jed pulled the sheets out of the dirty-clothes pile and put them
back on the beds. Mouse and Nancy fried up beef liver and
onions and served it with dried peas boiled into mush. There
was no dessert, so Jed promised double helpings the next night.
The kitchen was a mess. He sent the boys to bed, and with
Mouse and Nancy's help, scrubbed everything up and got wood

and water in for the next day. It was midnight. He shared the boys' blankets and got up at three a.m. and put the water on.

At breakfast the boarders complained they'd been promised eggs, there were no eggs in the house. Two said they wouldn't be back, another complained his bed stunk.

Hard times. Hard times.

Mouse said she'd take over in the kitchen as long as Daphne stayed in bed. So Jed paid a neighbor woman three dollars to wash the sheets and make up the beds, and went down to the billiard hall to see if anyone wanted work in the tie camp. Next he stopped at Sarell's hardware for tools, and after that at the slaughter house for a leg of mutton.

"Go back to the mountains," Mouse told him when he returned with the mutton. "Nothing bad will happen."

Daphne sent Bettina a note saying her services were no longer available, and Bettina replied with a note offering to recommend Mrs. Lafitte for employment elsewhere should the occasion arise. A large fruitcake accompanied that note.

Daphne spent most of the daylight hours sitting in the sun behind the windows. Eventually she got to where she could chew meat, but had little strength otherwise. Much less the stomach for arguing with Mouse, who hired a swamper away from Sauter's Saloon and put the woman to work down at the creek washing the sheets. The sand had to be shook out before making up the beds, but the house stayed full.

Mouse's idea of editable food also left something to be desired. Stews, always popular with the miners, rapidly evolved into a mix of unfamiliar roots and herbs which Mouse secured from mysterious sources, along with strips of meat. At Daphne's insistence, potatoes continued to be used in the mix. Also at Daphne's insistence, the meat, which she suspected as having come from dogs, was cut into even smaller pieces to disguise it.

When one of the miners called it rattlesnake meat, she

stopped eating stew meat altogether. Even so, when she bought a mess of turnip greens and mushrooms from a peddler, and Mouse threw the mushrooms out, she didn't complain. Given the strange mixes of roots and herbs the Indian cooked up every day, the mushrooms must really be bad.

Eventually Mouse took pity on her nemesis and cut a plug of Kentucky burley tobacco with kinnikinnick and red-willow bark and skunk leaves and rolled the mixture in cabbage leaves. Dried in the oven the cabbage leaves resembled fat, brown cigars.

Feeling silly, Daphne agreed to smoke one. After that, she smoked one every night before going to bed. They really weren't that bad.

Eventually she got back to making biscuits, and life in the boarding house returned to normal. But for all anyone's hard work, the boarding house never made a cracker more than what it cost to put food on the table. The wages the men drew paid for everything else.

Daphne joined the Baptist Church and took Nancy and the boys to services and prayed fervently to be healed, of what she wasn't sure. In time her prayers lost their intensity and she relaxed. She didn't struggle with the sermons, thinking them none too practical, but she did enjoy the singing, joining in with great gusto.

"I always thought I could have done very well as a singer," she told Nancy. "If only I had applied myself."

One Sunday morning they found themselves seated next to Miss Bell Dixon, the school teacher. After the service Miss Dixon asked Nancy, "Would you audition to sing in the opening ceremony of the Metropolitan Hall?"

Nancy was astonished. "No, I can't do that, I'm sorry, I can't sing that good."

"I think you can, you won't be alone. There's supposed to be a group, but no one seems to have the courage to try."

Actually, some thirty people had the courage to audition in the new frame building above the Davis real estate office. Nancy and nine others were chosen. Daphne was thrilled to pieces! A few days after the festivities, an effusive tub-shaped Italian with Doughterty and Hunter, a theatrical company out of Denver City, paid a call on Daphne.

"We'd like Miss Harris to audition for future presentations in the Metropolitan Hall."

"Yes!" Daphne cried.

"Perhaps I should confirm this with Miss Harris?"

"Never mind that, just let us know when."

Learning of the offer, Nancy was less sanguine. "It makes me nervous to sing with everybody looking at me."

"Oh," Daphne moaned. "Nancy, dear, all your life people are going to be looking at you whether you're singing or not. You might as well show them you have a brain."

"What's singing got to do with a brain? You just open your mouth...ahahahahahahah." Her voice went up and down the scale.

"Singing is not braying like a donkey, it's an *art*, you're going to learn an *art* and be paid for it, you'll have money of your own to spend."

Nancy auditioned wearing a pink Dotted Swiss dress borrowed from the world-famous Mademoiselle Heydee, who performed often in Golden City, and was hired.

Her first part was a short solo as the handmaiden in "Betsy Baker." Daphne bought a brown switch from the hair dressing saloon and a lace collar from Ferris Millinery Shop. Mouse dyed a dozen feed sacks in a dishpan full of hot water and a concoction of cream-of-tarter and tin spirits. The end result was a scarlet red cape. Nancy was the prettiest girl on the stage, everyone said so.

Jed and Yam didn't get to see the performance, so the next time they were in the city Nancy put on her costume and repeated the solo. She appeared in several sketches after that, for which she was paid a dollar each, and even went so far as to sign up for lessons in classical elocution at St. John's College on the south side of Golden City.

The son of the woman who owned the house stopped by. His mother needed more income, she wanted sixty dollars a month for rent.

"She'll never get it," Daphne told him. "Not from us or anyone else, look at the walls, they're crumbling."

"I dunno." He didn't look interested.

"I'll write her a note."

"I'll be collecting the rent from now on." Something about the way he said it....

"Why don't I just keep depositing the usual thirty dollars and give you twenty dollars to fix the walls."

"Alright."

Nancy was watching the exchange. "How did you know he was lying?"

"Those are the things you learn when you travel a great deal, and that's what your voice will enable you to do, travel a great deal."

They didn't have the extra dollars. Nancy stopped attending the elocution lessons and unpacked her mother's silver ewer. It was a beautiful piece, P. B. Cheney, the owner of the Chicago Saloon, paid sixty dollars to display the ewer behind his long bar. Daphne used the money to buy bright yellow bedspreads and corn-patterned dishes from Armor, Harris. And laid ironed scarves on all the dressers, and raised the bed-and-board price to three dollars a night, and put a FAMILY LODGING sign in the window.

Families came with their own set of problems. A noon meal had to be provided, along with chamber sets in the rooms— women guests, along with their children, preferring not to use the outhouse at night. Mouse mumbled and grumbled and alternated between refusing to empty the pots and refusing to cook noon meals. Too busy to argue, and feeling much better, Daphne simply gathered up the slack.

Jeremy came home and went to work for Barnes flouring mills. Restless as a tumbleweed caught against a wall, he quit and enrolled in public school, quit and went to work in Dollison's market, and disappeared.

"I don't even worry about him anymore," Nancy said, and almost believed it.

The landlady's son, after a few desultory swipes at cleaning the crumbling clay off the outside walls, gave up. The next time he came to collect his twenty dollars, Daphne pointed at a sack of fire-clay purchased from the brick yard north of the city. "I'll get the supplies and give you the receipts."

"Alright," the boy said, and was never seen again. Daphne and Mouse mixed the fire-clay and plastured over the cracks, but it didn't go far.

The tie camp in the bottom of the gulch.

A party from Michigan worked a week on a corral and sheds before going up to Nevadaville to work in the mines. Miners looking to pick up money for the long trek back across the desert to the States hollowed out the hillside for a storehouse and the main building—a long rock barracks with a pole roof overlaid with sod. An inside wall divided the barracks long-ways. The half facing the road was left open for the stove and living area. The half hunched into the mountain was portioned off into five bedrooms.

Jed was digging the outhouse hole when Meyers showed up with the saw. "This place is hell for stout," he observed. "Downright cozy, got your teams lined up?"

"Horses, no oxen."

"You can't buy 'em, not what you want. Quick as they get to the edge of the mountains they're being fattened for beef."

A week later Jeremy led four red Duran steers into the corral. He bought them from the Indians.

"You know, don't you, they're stolen?" Jed asked him.

"I dunno that, and neither do you." Jeremy looked like the cat that swallowed the cream.

Jed opened his purse. "What have you got on 'em?"

"Fifty apiece," Jeremy grinned, "and my neck, they ain't paid for yet."

Jed counted out an extra hundred dollars. The company could easily afford that kind of money for these kind of oxen. "Be careful, Jeremy, it ain't all fun and games out there."

# FIFTY-ONE

AUTUMN 1867.

A farmer living below Golden City decided to go hunting. Not that he'd run out of work—a farmer never runs out of work, just out of anything better to do. He kissed his wife and told her he'd be back in a day or so and rode happily off on the plow horse.

As a rule he hunted the big mesa behind his farm, only occasionally did he get up into the mountains. The prairie that morning from the top of the mountains looked like an old, worn carpet streaked here and there with yellow. The mesa behind his farm looked like a big brown tabletop with a few yellow speckles. The Indians camped there lot. In fact, he thought he could see some smoke there now, near the lake. Did they still think the white traffic would go away, he wondered.

The farmer liked to be up high looking out. He guessed it was the nature of men and animals to want to see out as far as they could. He didn't get any game that day, and the next morning decided to mosey back home.

Keeping to the high parks north of the Vasquez, following a game trail, he reached the rim of a wide, heavily grassed bench thinly scattered with aspen and old-growth pine. The bench sloped gently downhill for several miles to the edge of the canyon of the Vasquez. Below him, too far to pick out, the travois trail made its way west toward the back range.

He tied the horse, and perched on a stoney overlook, hefted a rock as far as he could. A rabbit jumped out. He sat awhile longer, enjoying the view, when he heard a rifle crack off to the west. Now that might shake something out.

And it did. A doe bounced by below, stopped to look over her shoulder, and bounced out of sight. Too far for a shot. Then the farmer saw the man on foot running full out.

The farmer's first thought was that the man was running to where he could get a better shot at the doe. But then he saw the runner, like the doe, pause and look back before taking off again. Three riders showed up in the distance, moving toward the bench from the west at a stiff trot.

The runner had turned and was working his way uphill, keeping low, headed for the stoney points. He didn't appear to be carrying a rifle.

Now the men were off their horses and taking aim. It was too far away for the farmer to mix in, even so he took the safety off his old single-shot.

Rifle fire sounded, the runner dodged and dodged again. And went down. Hurriedly mounting their horses, the rifleman rode toward their quarry.

That's when the farmer saw another man on foot. He was standing out in the open not far from where the runner went down. Crossing the watercourses, the riders bobbed in and out of sight. When they got to where they could see the second man, he took off downhill and out across the bench toward the canyon.

The farmer never in his life saw a man run like that. Fast as a coyote he was, and nimble, clearing fallen timber like an elk.

*That's an Indian out there*, the farmer told himself.

The horsemen had a hard time following, and for awhile the farmer lost sight of everybody. Then he spotted the riders at the edge of the canyon. They looked to be tying their horses in the brush.

He closed the chamber on the single-shot and headed for the downed man, picking his way across the rough ground and keeping an eye on the horses on the distant rim. When he saw the horses spook as if jumped by a bear and head for the prairie, he relaxed. That took care of having to worry about his back for awhile.

The runner lay scrunched against the rocks, unconscious. A young fellow, half-breed. He'd been hit in the neck. The farmer straightened the boy around to where his head was uphill and the ugly wound open to the sky. There was a lot of blood, but it was beginning to cake up. The farmer rolled his undershirt into a bandage of a sort and put his old brown coat over the still form.

"You sit tight," he ordered. "Don't move, I gotta get my horse." It took awhile. He watered the horse at a little seep lower in the basin and picketed it there in the trees. When he returned with blankets, the boy lay still as death, but didn't appear to be bleeding.

The farmer built a fire in the low shelter of the rocks and rustled enough wood to last through the night and ate a couple of boiled eggs. "Let me know if you get hungry," he said. "I saved a couple."

The sky darkened and one or two dim stars came out. The wolves talked amongst themselves, the coyotes getting in their two cents worth. Down toward the canyon a mountain lion screamed. A tiny whirlwind sprang up, flaring the flames and scattering a brief rain of embers.

It was getting cold. The farmer eased down against the boy, pulling the blankets over them both, and dozed. He was at Vicksburg, in the dugouts behind the Union lines, and men were

yelling and falling all around him. That's when he woke up and
saw the Indian.

Holy Jesus Christ!!

Standing at the edge of the fire, head thrown back, howling
at the top of his lungs, an old man with a knife in one hand and
what looked to be fresh scalps in the other. The screams went on
and on. And stopped. The Indian came close, intent on the boy.
Careful not to look into the man's eyes, the farmer doubled up
his fist.

Straightening, the Indian let out one last cry and walked
away into the darkness. Leaving a hole in the night noises. The
farmer lay still, listening. After what seemed like a long time, a
coyote yipped.

"You didn't hear that racket?" the farmer asked softly. "It
sure as hell scared the shit out of me." He freshened the fire and
remained awake the rest of the night, breaking camp early the
next morning.

This farmer, being a provident fellow, had a travois.
Otherwise he would have no choice but to go for help. As it
was, he rolled the boy onto the travois. The bandage rubbed off
and the wound broke open, and the farmer packed the hole with
ashes from the campfire and replaced the bandage. The storm
coming in turned the sky linty and paled the sun. The back
range was clear, the canyon of the Vasquez was a wide river of
fog.

His cargo covered with blankets and lashed down, the farmer
led the plow horse downhill around the rocks as best he could
and across the basin to the good trail. All this took a long time.
At the top of the mountains overlooking Golden City, the
farmer ate the last two eggs. "Too late for you kid, you shoulda
woke up."

Low clouds were rolling in from the north, hiding the prairie.

Taking it slow, occasionally explaining where they were, the farmer led the horse down the travois trail to the pastures above Golden City and slogged wearily around the northern edge of his mesa. It was the long way home, but it wouldn't be a good idea to haul a wounded Indian through the city, not with someone scalped up top.

"I sure hope to hell you ain't dead," he told the silent form on the travois. "I'd hate to be taking all this trouble for nothing."

By the time the farmer reached his farm, it was dusk. A thin, heavy snow had turned the road white, and the farmer's feet were numb with cold.

## FIFTY-TWO

H E'D ALWAYS BEEN ABLE to gin out a living, but running that tie camp was the hardest work Jed ever tackled. The mountains were a terrible place to team. There wasn't a path or a road that wasn't full of rocks and ruts. The twitch paths were steep and narrow and crooked, the main roads were no more than funnels, with few turnouts. Flooding turned the poorly grassed roads into ditches, leading to new road cuts, leading to more ditches. Ditches and cuts made a braid of the Gregory road.

There was no scratching new roads in the granite walls of the Vasquez. Wash-outs there demanded rebuilding with rock and gravel, and hauls up Big Hill in the meantime. Even so, the hard surface and easy grade more than made up for the occasional wash-out and the little nuisances like rattlesnakes, thick as fleas and big around as a man's arm, dropping onto the moving loads from the overhead rocks. And the rocks up higher sloughing off the walls. Seeing those doanies scattered across the road sure woke a man up.

Right now, with eight men including the cook, he was in good shape, but that wouldn't last. Chasing the rainbow the crews disappeared overnight. Some men came back, most didn't.

Keeping the teams sound was a big problem. They lamed up and skinned up regularly, and that's when he was lucky. Get unlucky and he had camp meat, tough as a boot.

Oddly enough, the burned-over patches on the lease ground proved no problem at all. Most of the timber was still standing, making it an easy pass through—a silent graveyard sentineled with an occasional macabre scattering of metal and bones.

On this day Jed was after draft animals. Oxen, as usual, if he could get them. He needed six yoke to ship out twice a week with a day's turn-around at the yards, and right now he had two horse teams in the mix. Oxen were no good at dragging timber downhill in that country. They got hit by runaway logs and tangled in the heavy chains, whereas horses were able to scramble aside. And horses could back up if need be, whereas oxen had to be unyoked. But for pulling loaded cargo wagons on the straight-away oxen couldn't be beat.

With Yam in charge, he walked down to the Guy House. And because he wanted to see if Miller at the freighters' stop at Four-mile gulch still had hay, followed the Gregory road over the top of Big Hill. It was enjoyable, this walking along stretching his legs, kind of like fishing. What would winter be like in the mountains, he wondered. He needed to bury a pipe from the spring to the barn and the road tank. The open ditch was no good.

At the Eight-mile house he bought two dill pickles, savoring the treat as long as possible. Down at four-mile a big stack of hay was selling for twenty dollars a wagon load. Not a bad price, not that bad looking. Jed bought what was left of the stack.

Miller was full of news. "There won't be a train up Guy Gulch, Loveland's blasting a road right through the bottom of the canyon all the way to Black Hawk. Freighters are crying like babies."

"I'll be damned," Jed said. "He must have deep pockets. He's gonna be one sick pup when he loses a train in that creek."

"He ain't gonna let that happen, it's gonna be a law. And

guess what else, the United States paid seven million dollars for a chunk of ice called Alaska, you know why?"

"Nope."

"So we can have ice in the summer, I'd of thought you could of figured that one out on your own."

"Anything else I need to know?"

"Not that's free, you're gotta pay for the rest of it."

Down at the edge of the prairie the old Gate City was all but deserted. Several women standing in the doorway of an abandoned hotel called out to the man walking by.

"I'm living on pennies myself," Jed told them cheerily.

"Your credit's good," one answered.

He hesitated, then walked on. Jeez, he was getting old, he never used to worry about the clap.

At the boarding house in Golden City someone had nailed the SAN FRANCISCO HOUSE sign above the front entrance.

"You guys making any money?" Jed called, entering the back door. A woman he'd never seen before planted herself in front of him. "Use the front door."

Jed grinned and backed up. Things were pretty bad when a man couldn't get respect in his own house. His easy actions belied his fear. Every time he came down to the valley, until he heard a familiar voice, it was like this. What if the boys weren't there? what if they were gone?

Entering the front door, he heard a bell jingle. And here came J.C. and Paul, tearing inside like fire engines.

"Did you hear my bell?" J.C. asked, giving his father a hug. "I made that all myself."

The world righted itself, life went on.

No one had seen hide nor hair of Jeremy for several weeks. It was easier finding oxen. Jed got lucky and found two the next morning at the Eagle Corral. There were no draft horses in, so he rented a horse and went looking.

The recent snow was all but gone. The cottonwoods were mostly bare, except for the occasional holdout lit up like a torch. Out on the prairie in Arvada City the sale-barn stock was pretty well picked over. The new gold strike above Black Hawk had tightened the market on horses and mules. There was no way in hell a man could team dirt with oxen up in those rabbit warrens.

Headed back to Golden City, Jed checked out the pastures around Arapahoe Bar. A white Percheron mule, a big thousand-pounder like what was used on the canals in the States, trotted up.

Hoping he might be onto something, Jed turned up the nearby trace—the Percheron keeping pace across a pole fence. In a thicket of old cottonwoods on the lower slope of the northerly mesa was a log cabin and the usual outbuilding. A dog chewing on a deer leg lifted its head watchfully.

A stocky, ruddy-faced man with one arm answered the door. It was hard to say who was the more surprised.

"Chinkos! is that you with no arm?"

"Well, I'll be damned!! Jed Marchion! Come in, come in! Well, I'll be goddamned!" The man in the faded military-issue shirt and pants was heavier than Jed remembered, the red hair looked more roan, but the eyes were as bright blue as ever.

Jed swung a chair around and made himself comfortable. "What happened to your arm?"

"Lost it at Petersburg, almost made it to Richmond. Got a pension out of it, retired a lieutenant. You go in?"

"Tried once. Got messed up in a boiler explosion two days ahead of when I was leaving, never tried again."

Charlie rattled the stove grates, shaking down the coals, and added more wood. "What are you doing out here in this neck of the woods?"

"Running a tie camp up Guy Gulch. Right now I'm looking for something to put together for teams."

"That mule out there ain't mine. Belongs to Churches, he won't sell. D'you try Wall? he generally has horses."

"Talked to him, he values his horses."

"Yeah," Charlie said with a grin. "Values his peas too. Next spring I'll have my own crop in."

The house smelled terrible, like trap bait. The flour-sack curtains on the kitchen windows were pulled back on iron pots of wildflowers gone to seed. A soiled, red-checked oilcloth covered the table.

A woman came out of a back room carrying a wash pan. She smiled at Jed and filled the pan at the sink pump.

"My wife, Sarah," Charlie said. "Got a sick boy in back, pretty bad shot up, come damned near going under."

The sight of the woman triggered an old memory. Years ago up on the Laramie, when Jed was grousing about Charlie's having run off with his sweetheart, a Canadian free trapper by the name of Perrault called the sergeant a squaw man. This woman looked to be part-Cherokee, what the trappers called high-born Cherokee.

"I'm sorry to hear that."

"Not mine, I don't have any. I was up in the mountains and saw the whole thing, but I was too far away to argue it. Three men on horseback and this kid on foot. He dodged up through the rocks and almost made it before they pumped a couple in him. Got one in the neck and another in the leg. He'll be alright, Sarah's good at fixing people up."

"I get lots of advice from him." Sarah tipped her head toward her husband. "He was a sergeant too long."

Dinner was white beans and dried meat which, to Jed's great relief, did not taste like the room smelled. After dinner Charlie emptied the coffee cups of their grounds and set a jug on the table.

"You want any, Sarah?" he called. There was no answer.

"Probably gone to sleep, she's got a cot in there by the bed. You find any gold yet?"

"Not yet, don't really have time to look."

"It's out there." Charlie shook a handful of small nuggets out of a tin can. "Whatever happened to that pretty woman, the one you followed all the way down to QueQue?"

"I married her, what'd you expect?"

"Well, that's what I expected."

"And she left me and went out to Utah Territory and married a Mormon preacher man, the same one she run away from."

"There's no figuring women, specially good-looking women. And she was good-looking."

"Yep. Then I married a doctor's daughter, she was good-looking too. Got a good job with a big cooker, and the damn mill burned down. Long story short, my wife's back east and I'm here."

"You ain't too good at this marrying business."

"Piss poor, as a matter of fact."

"Squaws are your best bet, they're just glad to have a solid roof over their head."

"Nope, I'm done with it. D'you know Ellen had a baby by the Indians."

"No!"

"Oh, Christ yes. A nice kid, course he won't hit a lick at a snake. Ellen's dead, did I say?"

"What happened?"

"Not sure, she was on her way back to the States."

"Where's her husband?"

"Dead. And that Uergin, remember him?"

"Can't say as I do."

"He's dead, too."

"I'll tell you a story about Indians."

"Was we talking about Indians?"

"I was up there on the mountain with this boy overnight, and here come some juiced-up redskin screaming and dancing around and carrying on. Goddamn! I didn't know what was happening. And, get this, he's carrying fresh scalps."

"I never seen a scalp fresh, I don't think. What'd you do?"

"Nothing! just possumed. Pretty soon away he goes. I never shut my eyes the rest of the night."

Jed laughed. This was nice, this tying one on, it'd been awhile.

"What was odd was them scalps."

"How so?"

"The fellows that was doing the shooting, remember them?"

"What was they shooting?"

"Wait! wait, just a goddamned minute here, I got to back up here. There was three men after this kid, see. Shooting at him. They was on horses and he was on foot. They come charging across the mountain after him, but they got sidetracked. They'd of got him, he was down, but they jumped another fellow who took off running, and they went after that fellow instead. Thought he was the one they hit, I guess. Never seen any of 'em again.

"Then ole crazy pants shows up after dark with fresh scalps, you follow?" Charlie asked owl-eyed.

Actually, Jed didn't, he nodded nevertheless.

"That's why I didn't take the kid into Golden City to the doc."

Jed closed his eyes and blew air through his teeth, and got to his feet. The boys would be out of school by now, they wanted him to see their hide-out. He pulled on his coat. "I got to go, and before I go, I got to know, why does this house stink so bad?"

"Injun medicine. You want me to spot horses for you? mules'd be better."

"Yeah, do that, whatever you find."

Jed bridled the livery horse and tightened the cinch, wishing he could stay drunk all night. It never worked that way, not even when he was young and practiced hard at it.

Riding along, the sun warm on his old felt hat, pulled low over his eyes, he thought about how the sweet, long days of fall lulled a man into forgetting what the sun was doing. He thought about Julia. Did she miss him at all? was she ever sorry?

*She hates you, you stole her kids. Well, they're my kids too.*

Across the valley that was Golden City the rumpled rim of mountains black against the sun looked like a giant's wall. No wonder people wouldn't go into the mountains until they knew where the gold was. According to Jeremy, not even the Indians liked going up there. Nancy was always telling boarders about her mother's being taken there against her will. How brave her mother was, how everything came out all right in the end.

*Oh, yeah, fell right into place.* He'd be happy if he never heard that dumb story again.

A little ways further and he reined in the livery horse.


The room looked like it might be a storeroom, everything—clothing, barrels, tools—hollowed out away from the bed Jeremy lay on beside a narrow cot. He'd been there a week.

"Is he gonna be alright?" Jed asked.

"Sarah says his fever broke," Charlie explained.

"I'm going after his sister," Jed said, absently rubbing Jeremy's head, aware of his own head. And off he went again. Reaching Golden City, he washed his face in the creek, and drank deeply of the cold water.

An hour later he was back at Charlie's farm, everyone with him in a rented buggy. Dusk was in the house. Carrying a tin lantern, Sarah led the way into the back room. Nancy cried, Daphne cooed.

# FIFTY-THREE

HALLOWEEN CAME AND BROUGHT ghosts and goblins and winter. Dressed as coal miners, charcoal smeared across their faces, J.C. and Paul trudged through the snow to collect all sorts of sweet-smelling loot. The hour grew late, porch lanterns were extinguished, and the entreaties of ghosts and goblins faded away. But winter stayed.

The world turned black and white and grey, and the wind blew something fierce, and Mouse collected buckets of fresh cow pies from the streets and replaced the chinking where the wind came in the worst. And black coal smoke from the foundries plumed the skies and papered over the snow with soot. And folks said things like "storm's not done 'til the snow's off the trees," and "that west wind now, that's a snow eater." But it seemed like the wind that blew the storms out and brushed the trees off was the same wind that blew them in.

Jeremy piled wood scraps from the lumberyards inside the back porch, leaving a narrow passageway through to the kitchen door, and Daphne bought a cart-load of coal from Buckman's coal yard to bank the cookstove and the dining-room stove through the cold nights. That the upstairs rooms had chimneys, but no stoves, she thought just as well, coal being so dear, and plugged the chimneys with rags.

But the coal, being hard coal, burned too hot to bank the

stoves. So they were allowed to go out, which meant waking up in a house with the buckets on the drain board iced over.

Daphne warmed river stones in the oven for the family's beds, and bought rubber boots for Nancy and the boys and took her old leather boots to the cobbler.

And rented ice skates from the shoemaker and took everyone ice skating on the river and taught them what she could and trudged home cold and wet and bruised all over. The next day she did it again and managed to crack her elbow. After that she gave Nancy the skate money and stayed home. And stayed home, too, when Nancy and the boys went sledding on the nearby table mountain—the hike up to the top being so long they usually only made one trip.

Up in the mountains the wind bared the ridges and plugged up the deep canyons with snow, making Guy Gulch the best stretch of the road. Not too cold, not much wind. The canyon of the Vasquez, on the other hand, was a mean sonofabitch, full of wicked updrafts that drifted the snow as high as a loaded wagon.

At least winter made using the Big Hill unnecessary.

The biggest disappointment was the twitching paths. The timber on the furthest reaches of the cut had been left in lots to be drug out after snow cushioned the ground. But the cushioning snow that made the drag to the twitching paths so easy, under the prairie sun did not linger on the paths themselves, leaving behind steep ribbons of mud and ice that wore out the runners on the bobsled.

Indian sightings stopped altogether, but there was no trouble with the natives anyway, unlike out on the prairie. And camp meat was plentiful. All that was needed was to stay high on the south slopes and move easy.

Keeping a crew got harder. Back East there wasn't much winter work to be had, out West the mines took up the slack.

The mines were more dangerous, but the even temperature in the tunnels made them preferable to the bad roads and rough weather topside.

But worse than anything else was the loneliness. Lord was it lonely.

Spring 1868. Slow but sure the days lengthened, cold and disagreeable as a harlot's heart, coaxing the new grass out of hiding with vinegary gifts.

Embedded in its great canyon the Vasquez melted and refroze, jamming the ice up against the bridges. The wagon road that through the dark winter months swung out over the ice was pulled back. Great frozen waterfalls, all winter in the making, oozed across the floor of the canyon, turning it into a skating rink.

Little rock slides off the rims of the mesas overlooking Golden City tumbled helter-skelter down the slopes, while in the city itself the icebergs floated by, causing a curious booming.

In far off San Francisco the sun was not shining, at least not on Monsieur Nathaniel Lafitte. Utterly unable to craft even the most miserly of windfalls, Nathan slogged through the days and nights as he would a foggy bottom. The paintings he'd shipped from Great Salt Lake City brought but a pittance, not even enough to keep himself suitably dressed, and this in a profession where appearances were everything!

Worse, he'd received only one shipment of two paintings from the artist's representative, a Mrs. Stenhouse, who enclosed a note explaining that Sister Straw's paintings were on display in the lobby of the Salt Lake Theatre, together with an address for the artist's share of the sales. Ha!

Adding insult to injury, shortly after receiving this shipment, he received a note saying there would be no more paintings for the foreseeable future. The artist was pregnant and suffering from morning sickness.

Poor Nathan, forced to content himself with newspapers wheedled piecemeal from merchants uncrating boxes and betrayed by his good-luck signs. Take, for instance, the time he won a free lunch in the bakery after his business card was drawn from the bowl. Later that very day he was walking down the street when plop! at his feet fell what looked to be a new suit. Gathering up the suit he entered the bank below the window and inquiring, learned that the widow of the newly deceased banker wished to dispose of the clothing.

Sure his luck was turning, he grew careless, sauntering along the boardwalk, thinking how the rain-cleansed air smelled of mint, when he drew too close to the edge and the suit draped over his arm received a fine sheen of street mud from a passing buggy.

That night his boarding house suffered a chimney fire, charring his belongings and necessitating a draw on his wages to replenish his wardrobe and toiletries.

How very, very difficult life had become. He never ate in public, dining instead on day-old bread and canned goods in his room—a mere cubicle with a drafty window and noisy neighbors. In these close quarters the amazing mix of nationalities that made the city a perfect roundhouse of the world, instead of proving stimulating, proved utterly annoying. Why, for God's sake, couldn't they learn to speak English!

Leaving Colorado, he'd felt sorry for Daphne, he now felt much sorrier for himself. At least Daphne had family there, here he had no one, not a soul. His weekly letter always began *Ne sois pas découragé*, followed by glowing descriptions of the city cleverly interspersed with oblique references to promising projects "best not committed to paper."

Lies, all lies!

His first month in San Francisco he sent twenty-five dollars home. (How absolutely dreadful, having to think of that abominable desert as home!) Now, two years later, he was still sending only twenty-five dollars whenever he could, and scrimping on groceries to do that.

> *I used to be a rich man, full of airs,*
> *Little boys scrambled for the nickels I threw.*
> *I used to be a rich man, welcome anywheres,*
> *Daphne darling, where are you.*

He was walking down Washington Street one dreary Saturday morning, entertaining himself with doggerel to offset the feeling of pushing against the ocean, so great was his gloom, when he noticed the LUCKY LADY SALOON signage overhead. He really should let someone know of Mr. Uergin's fate. Berating himself for his negligence, he turned into the entrance.

The aubergine carpeted anteroom was lit with long, tapered candles in slender glass chimneys placed in front of faceted mirrors—the flutter of light lending the room a kind of ethereal shimmer. Various *objets d'art* occupied a scatter of recessed alcoves. Beyond in the large gaming room several people were drinking quietly at the bar. The silver-beaded drapes on the stage were pulled back, and a Chinaman with a long queue was mopping the floor.

*A most respectable establishment. The ambience hasn't changed a bit.*

A man approached.

"I should like to speak with the manager."

"What are you selling?"

"I buy and sell art. Mr. Uergin previously purchased some

paintings from me, and I thought someone might like news of him." Another time Nathan might have offered his card, but he had no cards left, and no funds with which to purchase more.

"Wait here," the fellow said, and disappeared down a hall.

A few minutes later a rather large man with a receding grey hairline and military bearing approached. "Mr. Uergin is out of the city today. May I help you?" A pleasant, clipped voice, British to the bootstraps. Ah, yes, this explained the well-appointed bar seen on the way in, as British as a rainy day.

"Mr. Uergin..." Nathan hesitated, hating to jab anyone with such a truth, "...died at Fort Laramie out on the Oregon Trail five years ago."

"I'm afraid that's impossible." The Brit's expression, the tone of his voice, changed not a whit.

"It was an accident, an emigrant dropped a weapon on the ground and it discharged. Death was instant."

"And your name?"

"Nathaniel Lafitte."

"Do you have identification?"

"Do I need it?"

"Yes, I'm afraid you do."

Ordinarily Nathan would have taken umbrage, but he had a soft spot for anything that bespoke England, and so produced a payroll stub from the brokerage house of Flood and O'Brien showing him to be the recipient of twelve dollars and fifty cents in one week's wages.

"What was your business with Mr. Uergin?"

"I sold him some paintings."

"And you can identify those paintings?"

"Of course. I believe they're in his office, or were the last I knew."

Without further adieu the Brit led the way to Uergin's office and unlocked the door. Seeing Phoebe's raucous paintings, Nathan felt as if he were being greeted by old friends.

*Good Lord! Uergin, what were you thinking of to trade all this for the desert?!!*

"If you will but look on the back, you'll see the name *Phoebe Taggart* and the words *only for the money.*"

The Brit lifted the painting of the children off the wall hook and stared at the back. "I'm afraid your nasty game is all for naught," he said evenly, returning the painting to its hook. "We correspond regularly with Mr. Uergin. Rest assured, he is quite well."

Nathan smiled with genuine warmth. "Let's hope so. At any rate, I have done my duty and shall not trouble you further."

"I do have a letter from him."

"If it is truly from Mr. Uergin, the last place it could have been posted is Fort Laramie five years ago."

"I anticipated someone's coming along sooner or later, if not Mr. Uergin himself, but still, it is a bit of a shock to learn of his death."

"Yes, I suppose it would be. Yes."

"How did you happen to be with him?"

So Nathan told the story, and enjoying his audience, drew out the details, circumventing the grim ending with numerous misadventures. (He was a very good raconteur, if he did say so himself.)

Mr. Leith wondered if Mr. Lafitte might like a drink to ward off the chill.

Harold Leith was the Brit's name. He had worked for the establishment since before Mr. Uergin won the building, along with the business, in a poker game. Of his employers, Harold vastly preferred Mr. Uergin, who was smart enough to realize what he'd won and turn it into a fine gentlemen's club.

Nathan nodded his agreement, enjoying the incomparable

bouquet of the Moselle. Oh, but he did very definitely feel a kinship with this man, the damp London fog outside, the warm, dark wood inside.

"When there was no word from Mr. Uergin in a reasonable time, I launched an investigation, which has since been expanded to include his heirs, all of it discreetly of course. There are people who, learning he is missing, will claim kinship."

"Yes, most assuredly, they will come out of the woodwork, won't they. That's the way it is with inheritances."

"Yes, isn't it."

"Still, people must suspect the worst."

"His friends think he is exploring the tropical rain forest in Madagascar, he spoke often of wishing to visit the region, such travels take years."

"Humm. I didn't really know very much about the chap. Did he have family?"

"A daughter whose whereabouts is unknown."

A comfortable silence enveloped the room. Mr. Leith refilled the glasses. "I thought it rather odd he liked these paintings so much. Americans, given their joyless Puritan backgrounds, have very little appreciation of bright colors."

"It's an odd story, really. Putting two and two together, I think he fell in love with the wife of a Mormon, and that the artist herself was another wife of the same Mormon. At any rate, Mr. Uergin seemed to have great affection for the women, and they for him."

"He was a fine man, I would say beloved. Certainly he made enemies, but the right kind."

They reminisced for awhile about England before Nathan reluctantly allowed himself to remember that a gentleman never overstays his welcome. Getting to his feet, he extended his hand.

"It has been a pleasure, sir. I commend you on your efforts to

do the right thing, Mr. Uergin would be quite pleased." Wishing
to part on a lighter note, Nathan recalled the hill road on the
Sweetwater. "He taught me to drive mules, if you can imagine
such a preposterous thing."

"Did he! And how did you get on?"

"It was a bloody disaster, extremely dangerous. Actually there
were two horses and four mules, they didn't like each other and
they jolly well hated me. The feeling was mutual, I assure you.
Well, I'm off. I promise not to let the cat out. It's the least I can
do, being the bearer of bad news and all."

Mr. Leith was unlocking a small iron safe in the wall recess
behind the desk. "As I told you, there was a letter." He lay a
paper on the table, smoothing it out as he did. "It did come
from Fort Laramie. There is also an earlier will. I should like to
continue to manage the business."

"I certainly hope for your sake that this is the case," Nathan
said warmly. Oh, yes, he loved the Brits! so proper, so bloody
civilized. He must visit England again soon, life was too short.

"The letter is dated July 23, 1863, and gives the building and
its contents to a Nathan Lafitte and to a Daphne Lafitte. And
Mr. Uergin's other holdings to his daughter, Nancy Harris, and
Jeremy Harris, her brother." Mr. Leith turned the paper so that
Nathan might read it. At the top was written *In the event of my
death.*

"This is not Mr. Uergin's handwriting, but it is his signature."
Mr. Leith pointed to the bottom of the paper.

Stunned, Nathan stared at the wrinkled paper. The names
had been misspelled, but the text, what did it say...?! He must
be mistaken. Did it say what he thought it said?!

The Brit was going on about the need to verify Mr. Uergin's
death. "Sadly, that appears to be just a formality. I did write Fort
Laramie several years back, but received no reply. Was the grave
marked?"

"Yes, a board with the name and the date, the wheelwright burned it on the wood."

"That would give me more to go on, wouldn't it. Then there's your identity, which would also need to be verified."

"Yes. Yes, quite." Nathan resumed his seat abruptly. "Forgive me, this *is* a bit of a shock, almost more than I can comprehend." He opened his mouth and closed it. Finally he said, "Nancy is Uergin's daughter?"

"It would appear so."

"She has no idea, absolutely no idea whatsoever. Well, that's remarkable, isn't it? And Daphne and I...*this* building? is he talking about *this* building?"

"Yes."

"Well, yes...that's superb...absolutely superb, isn't it? Yes. Well...what shall I do?" Nathan's face registered a sudden panic. "You wouldn't by chance be sporting with me?"

"Not at all. To the contrary, as I stated, I should like to work for you. I must warn you that an earlier will left everything to a Mrs. Ellen Harris of Great Salt Lake City, so there may be trouble from that quarter during probate."

"Mrs. Ellen Harris is dead, she died in the wilderness."

"Before Mr. Uergin?"

"Before...? yes...oh yes, quite. He buried her, we all did. Nancy is her daughter."

"Perhaps you would care to see the rooms."

"The rooms?"

"Mr. Uergin kept rooms here, and, of course, there's my room and..."

"...why yes, I suppose so. Excuse me, I'm just a little unstrung is all. Excuse me. First I have to make arrangements for Mrs. Lafitte and the Harris children to come here. I don't suppose it would be possible to arrange a loan."

"Yes, by all means."

Gathering his wits about him, Nathan drummed the marble desk top with his fingers. "You could have destroyed that paper."

"I suppose so. But that would have left everything up in the air, wouldn't it have. Better the man Mr. Uergin picked, than a magsman eager to pluck the establishment clean. Would you care to hear about the holdings?"

"The holdings?" Good Lord, he was behaving like a dunce! "Yes, by all means."

"The Harris children inherit rather extensively. If they are not of an age to look after their interests, we should perhaps consider an executor."

"Yes, we'll work something out."

"A large brownstone in San Francisco, the controlling shares in a winery at Sonoma, a summer home overlooking San Pablo Bay, the Wells Fargo shares, seventy in all, and one-half interest in both the John Parrot building and the Miners Exchange Building."

Nathan gasped. It was unbelievable, absolutely unbelievable! "Mr. Leith, you are both a gentleman and a scholar, a *sterling* scholar! I insist you give yourself a raise, immediately."

"Yes, sir." Mr. Leith smiled faintly. "And then, of course, there are the funds accumulating in Mr. Uergin's personal account. With interest, those funds currently total $192,000."

Nathan stopped breathing, and realizing he was in danger of fainting dead away, roused himself.

"For how much should I make the loan?"

"The loan? Oh, yes, the loan!" Nathan wanted to leap up and embrace the man, instead he answered primly, or at least he tried to sound prim, "One thousand dollars should do quite nicely."

The Brit removed a metal tray from the safe and counted out ten one-hundred dollar bills. Pocketing the money, Nathan expected some sort of paperwork to sign, but Mr. Leith merely

extended his hand in a firm, sealing-the-bargain handshake (was
how Nathan later described it to Daphne.)

"A healthy raise, do you understand, Mr. Leith?" Nathan
said and strode purposefully back the way he'd come—through
the large gambling room with its smaller gaming rooms situated
to either side like the leaves on a four-leaf clover—out the dim
anteroom into the cool fog and across the wet paving bricks to
the Well-Fargo office down the street.

Mr. Uergin, I salute you, sir, and I thank you. From the
bottom of my miserable, undeserving heart I thank you. I am
deeply, deeply grateful, so very deeply grateful.

Within the hour a letter was on its way, together with a
check for six hundred dollars.

> *Dear Daphne, Return to San Francisco immediately. It is*
> *absolutely imperative you bring Nancy and Jeremy. Do not*
> *delay, but be careful. Considerable opportunity has opened up*
> *here. Confirm departure date by return mail. You MUST bring*
> *the children and come as soon as possible. Love Nathan*

# FIFTY-FOUR

*Dearest Nathan,*
*Jeremy is not home right now we will leave as soon as he*
*comes back. We have new curtains in the dinning room and*
*Nancy likes singing better. We have bought some chickens and*
*a pig to kill the rattle snaks but the pig ran off. There is not very*
*much news around here.*
*Love from your Daphne*

LEAVING THE POST OFFICE, strolling through town in the dry,
hard sunshine, Daphne wondered what Nathan was
cooking up. She glanced at her reflection in the store
windows and looked quickly away. Such a dowdy figure. She
glanced at her hands, they weren't pretty anymore, nothing
about her was pretty. She used to have such lovely silk-plaited
hosiery, but she didn't even wear hose anymore, not in the
summer. Nathan would be sad to see her.

She thought about beaches and water as far as the eye could
see. It was too bad J.C. and Paul couldn't come with them,
beaches were made for little boys. Maybe no one would be
seeing beaches for awhile, she had no idea where Jeremy was. He
came and went, to and fro, like bat wings on a saloon. Everyone
thought, after the second brush with death, that he'd stay away
from the Indians, but he didn't have enough sense to do that.
Maybe she could hire one of his friends to go looking for him.
Who were his friends anyway, besides Indians?

Life was so complicated. Nancy wouldn't want to leave, she loved Golden City, she loved singing, even if she did complain about what she was given to sing. And Paul and J.C., who'd take care of them? It wouldn't do to have them running the streets, wandering like flies in and out the saloons and billiard halls. If ever they were to amount to anything, they had to stay on the right foot.

*Oh, Nathan, you'll just have to get along without me until I can finish raising these children.*

Jeremy was at the boarding house when Daphne got home. He'd exchanged his leather clothing for Jed's old shirt and trousers and cut off his long hair. He wanted Daphne to barber it.

"We'll go right now," he said, reading Nathan's letter.

Nancy came home and objected loudly. "We're always moving somewhere! I'm tired of moving, I don't want to start again with another boarding house, this one's just fine."

"Then stay," Jeremy told her. "I'm going to California."

"Ride up to the tie camp and tell Jed," Daphne said. "Tell him we'll send for him as soon as we can."

Jeremy shook his head. "I can't do that."

"Why not?" Nancy asked.

"I don't have time."

"What happened? what'd you do?"

"Nothing."

"Nothing? You're in a terrible hurry for nothing. You're on the run, aren't you. That's why you chopped off your hair, I know you."

"You don't know beans from Arbuckle coffee."

"What if I wait 'til after the Fourth of July program?" Nancy asked Daphne. She'd been anticipating the program at the German House for months. She was seventeen years old and in her last year of schooling. Leaving now meant missing all the festivities that whirled around saying good-bye. Plus, she was in love, nobody knew it, it was nobody's business. He was very shy. He always came to hear her sing, and she always sang to him. He was the son of the lumber-yard owner and could mimic people's voices.

"We all have to go together," Daphne said. "I know Nathan, he's not getting us out there to run a boarding house. He's made some very good investments, and they're paying off."

She was not absolutely sure about this. After all, when Nathan left, he promised to send money for the common pot, which he did, but very little. So if all the sudden he got his hands on a lot money, why didn't he just send it? And what was all this business about leaving immediately? It was really very peculiar.

Nancy went upstairs and sat on her bed. The iron spring creaked, it was terribly uncomfortable, but the noises it made reminded her of the porch swing at home. And that reminded her of other noises, children playing in the road, the tolling church bell. She would never get back there. She was like the trail-worn cattle curled on the ground under their yokes, waiting for the signal to get up and pull further and further away from home. Eventually she bent down and dragged her travel bag from beneath the bed.

Daphne engaged a buggy and drove immediately to Charlie's farm. Mouse could take care of the boys, but she wouldn't make them go to school, and they had to go to school, they were only nine and eleven. Then too, the long walk back and forth from the farm to Golden City would keep them out of mischief.

Charlie agreed. He'd bring a wagon in for their things.

Next, Daphne left a note backed "Jed Harris at ty camp" at the Wells Fargo station for the Mountain City driver.

*Nathan wants us in Californa right away and sent the money
for tickets. Jeremy is home and is in a hury to go I think there
is more to it but at any rate we should go right away I will put
Mrs. Bartunic in charge of the house she lives next door untel
you get down and leave the boys with Charles and Sarra. We
will send for you as soon as possible.*
　　　*Daphne*

Seven months later.

Jed was sitting on a stump outside the front door smoking
his pipe in the half-light of late afternoon, the sun having long
dropped from sight behind the high ridge of mountain. He had a
letter in his coat pocket from Nancy telling of yet another delay
with inheriting Uergin's estate. He liked hearing from her, all
the goings on in San Francisco, but he wasn't counting on any
old promises. He had things pretty well nailed down as it was. It
wasn't much of a life, but it was his life.

The stage up from Golden City stopped at the water tank.

"Lo, Billy," Jed said, walking over to hold the team called the
Mountain Maids. "You got a hard pull ahead of you, wind's been
blowing all day, probably closed the road up higher."

"I ain't going nowhere," Billy Opdyke answered, climbing off
the box. "The only reason I'm here is Guy's is full up, got a big
hunting party in there."

"You hauling any women?"

"I got two ladies with me, respectable ladies."

"Shit, Billy! you can't stay here. I got Madam Wright's girls
down from Central City in there."

"Well, clean her up, sonny."

"Jesus! you must be kidding! Just keep going, you can make it
up to the Michigan House."

"If I could, we wouldn't be standing out here talking about it, now would we. Quit your bitchin', we all got our troubles."

A man buried in a fur coat was working himself out of the stage. "What are we doing stopping in front of a bloody hen coop?!" He walked toward Jed. "Why, I believe I know you! Mr. Marchion?…well, I do know you! What bloody good luck!"

Jed froze in his tracks. The Englishman was pumping his hand furiously.

"It's Harris," Jed said, keeping his head down.

"Harris? Oh, Harris! Yes! right you are, old chap. I forgot. Sir Genille Cave-Browne-Cave at your service."

"What are you doing here?" Jed asked. "I thought you was off raising cattle."

"I might ask you the same question."

"It's a long story."

"Everything with you is a long story." Cave looked around expectantly. "Well, alright then. Already this place looks better."

"Hold your horses," Billy growled. "Keep the women in the stage till Harris here says."

"Oh? Why is that?" Cave walked over to the window and peered above the frost. "Woo my! Well, well then, what jolly good fun."

A second man crawled out of the stage. Standing at the window, swathed in fur, the men resembled two large bears.

Billy unhooked his team and led the horses around to the barn. Jed went inside and ordered his crew to move the party to the other end of the building away from the cookstove. The Eureka Street girls, in various stages of undress and well into their cups, giggled as they collected their belongings.

Next, Jed stretched a rope from one wall to another and hung a wagon canvas over it, allowing his crew about a third of the building. "You boys hold it down to a low roar back there," he ordered. "No profanity."

"There ain't much room back here," one of the men complained.

"Plenty of room outside," Jed answered and hollered out the door at Cave, "Go get 'em."

"A wonderful show!" the Englishman exclaimed, hurrying over to the coach. "The very last thing I expected in this godforsaken desolation."

Jed propped open the front door with a chunk of wood and went to work on the cookstove. He had it tamped down for the night, now he opened the damper and and stirred the smoldering wood. Billy came in with a frozen deer haunch found hanging in the barn and slung it on the table, and began working his way out from under his coats.

Hearing the cabin door close, Jed looked to see how many there'd be to feed. Three men counting Billy, two women. An older woman bundled into a black fur coat, and a younger woman with long, honey-colored hair. Cheeks reddened by the cold. Wearing a long, white ermine cape.

Forgetting himself, Jed stared open-mouthed.

"Now what was that about the Michigan House?" Billy asked under his breath.

Cave was helping the girl with her cape. Her dark velvet dress showed white lace at the neck and sleeves, and she was saying something to the Englishman about keeping his promise to introduce her to the West.

"Mr. Harris, my sister Blanche and my cousin Spencer Ogilvy and his wife. Alas, they have come to fetch me home. Sir Mylles, my father, seems to be spending money faster even than I. We are waiting for the warmer weather to cross, in the meantime I'm showing them the countryside."

"What sort of an establishment is this?" Blanche asked, dark-eyed in the shadowy lantern light.

"It's a tie camp, ma'am." Dazzled, Jed glanced away. A corset fallen against the table leg trailed a pink ribbon across the floor. He edged the corset out of sight with his boot and organized the chairs.

"Where's Yam?" Billy asked.

"Up top." Jed lifted the dishpan off its hook, put the pan on the stove and emptied the water bucket into it. The rest of the buckets were empty.

Billy grabbed a bucket, opened the door to a wild gust of snow, pronounced it not a fit night out for man nor beast, and slammed the door shut. Everybody laughed, and he opened it again and went outside.

Dirty dishes were everywhere on the table and on the counter. Jed went to work on the mess feeling like a bug on a pin. Smothered laughter seeped through the make-shift wall.

With the water buckets full, Billy attacked the frozen deer haunch, sawing away furiously. His passengers had drawn the scatter of chairs into a circle and were huddled around a map considering the next day's journey.

"Will we get to Central City tomorrow?" Cave asked.

"If you don't mind shoveling part of the way," Billy said with a wink at Jed. Two hours later fried potatoes and onions and venison appeared on the trestle table.

Everybody busy eating, Jed considered the bedroom situation. The impromptu canvas wall left him with three bedrooms on the stove side of the room, including the room he and Yam shared. Fortunately, in building his long cabin, he'd partitioned off the sleeping rooms. Back home in Maine in the Big Woods everything would have been left open, but it was nice to have walls to hang things on.

He scooped two rooms clean of what was on the beds and the floor and dumped everything in his room. Next order of business, the filthy bedding. The stack of wagon sheeting that yielded the room's partition now lent itself to bed sheets. After experimenting, he lay a piece of wagon sheeting over a lumpy mattress and folded it back. The grimy blankets went on top and were covered with a second fold in the sheeting. In the dim light the results didn't look all that bad.

His last order of business was to clear the outhouse path of loose snow and shovel around the door so it closed all the way.

All's well that ends well. The next morning, after another meal of venison and potatoes embellished with a tin can of oysters, the Gilpin stage was on its way again with no one the worse for wear, except the hungry crew huddled under blankets at the far end of the building.

"I owe you, Billy," Jed said when the driver gathered up the reins.

"You ain't getting paid for the meals," Billy said with a grin. "You ain't on the itin'ry."

"Screw the meals."

Billy snapped his hat down and cracked the whip, and the stage was off in a cloud of snow under a brilliant blue sky.

But that wasn't the end of it. No sirree, not by a long shot.

Unbelievable as it may seem, for a man stuck in the loneliest gulch on the loneliest road in the territory to have such good luck twice in a row in the dead of winter, it happened nonetheless.

Jed was chopping ice out of the water tank at the edge of the road when the stage approached on its regular run to Denver City. And stopped.

"Got someone here wants a word with you," Billy said. The way he looked, Jed knew who was inside that coach.

He walked back to the door and Blanche drew aside the curtain. The sun shining on her face revealed her eyes to be hazel flecked with gold. *Enchantants*. That's what his father called them. Bewitching eyes.

The cousin and the cousin's wife stared out curiously from a sea of robes. Cave was in the far corner dead to the world, mouth open, snoring.

Blanche seemed little discomforted by her brother's actions. "He was hoping to have a word with you, he planned to ask about your sons."

"Yeah, they're fine," Jed said, his face stiff with cold. "They live down in the valley." His nose dripped, he wiped it with his sleeve.

"We'll be in Denver City over Christmas. Perhaps you'll find time to visit, we're staying at the Broadwell House."

"Gotta go," Billy yelled and snapped the whip, leaving Jed staring down the road long after the coach was out of sight.

It snowed and snowed some more. On December 20 Jed laid the crew off for a week, and he and Yam caught the Wells Fargo coach for the prairie. Jake Hawk was at the ribbons, he had a full load, but no one up top. The news was mostly of the mines, the accidents, the pay dirt. The railroad was less than three hundred miles east of Denver City, a telegraph line was going up between Denver City and Cheyenne. Grant was the new President.

In the canyon of the Vasquez the road drifted back and forth out over the ice, dodging river boulders and stubborn banks of wind-polished snow. "Like that new snow," Jake observed. "When you can't see the ice, passengers don't holler about falling in."

Down in Golden City the brothers had rented a little house on Fayette Street and let the boarding house go. For Mouse, with no white people to look after, life was much better. Occasionally she was able to rent the porch out to Indians passing through. Colorow and his friends paid in pelts, which

Mouse traded with Dr. Kelly for various and sundry articles at his Golden City drug store.

Seeing Jed and Yam at the Fayette Street house, the next-door neighbor took Jed aside. The Indians were stealing his chickens, he had a double-barreled shotgun waiting by the window. Sooner or later....

"If they take a liking to you, they might tell you where the gold is," Jed said softly.

The neighbor's eyes grew big. "They know where the gold is?"

"They keep it in big caves up in the mountains. Every time they come around the camp? we give 'em a big feast."

Later he warned Yam, "The Utes ain't welcome in the city, you tell Mouse to keep her friends lined up, no stealing from the neighbors."

Downriver at the farm Charlie and the boys were peeling a deer head for head cheese. Sarah was off to St. Joe to the bedside of her dying mother.

"If I'd of knowed you were batching it," Jed groused, "I'd of stayed in Golden City and eaten with Yam, Mouse's got a big kettle of noodles and chicken." His whining bought him no sympathy. The boys wanted him to make cookies. Paul tied a dish towel around his father's waist and J.C. set out the fixings.

"You don't look like the safest crew to be working with," Jed said.

Paul was missing his eyebrows and some of his hair from having doused the stove kindling with too much coal oil. J.C. had a smashed thumb wrapped in a rag.

"The boys say they got an aunt lives with the Indians," Charlie said, dropping withered turnips in a pot of hot water.

"Yeah, my sister. She lives somewhere down in New Mexico, I guess with Indians, I don't know."

"Indians ain't so bad," Charlie said. "I wish my Indian was here, I don't like cooking."

"Her mind's off, she got tangled up with the Mormons and they did a number on her. She was in that train they hit in Utah. She jumped ship before they got it, but then something happened, I'm not sure what. All I know for sure is that the Indians got her, and the Mormons got her kids."

"They stole her kids?"

"Tried to. I found them, and the army found her. My brother went and got her, but she was pregnant. So my sister-in-law takes her back there along with her Indian kid. Jesus!" Jed shook his head. "You'd have to know my sister-in-law, she is certifiably nuts."

"You say the army found your sister?"

"Yeah, somewhere out in the desert."

"And she went back?"

"Yep."

"I'll be damned, how 'bout that, and blind as a bat."

"Yeah, she was, she ain't now. Did I say that?"

"No, I said that, I was the one found her. The Mormons was after her, it was over on the Colorado River. She was with a Paiute called Dancer. She'd be dead if it wasn't for that Indian, he was her eyes."

His audience stared at him.

"That Paiute said she'd be back, he believed it, I never thought she would. Hell, what are the chances of that? You say she did get her sight back?"

"Yeah, but not her mind."

"She's got more of a mind than you think. Well, I'll be damned." And Charlie told his amazing story about the runner's stopping at Fort Defiance, and Dancer and his big yellow dog, and Dinky's being able to say her name and where she came from.

"I remembered that name, I was gonna ask her if she knew you, but it never worked out. Then I forgot about it."

The turnips burned dry and got thrown out. But no one much liked boiled turnips anyway. And anyway, the cookies got made, that's what counted.

Jed wanted the boys and Charlie to go to Denver City the next day and stay in the Overland House.

"I ain't spending good money to stay down there!"

"You can see how pretty everything is after dark, all lit up for Christmas. It'll be like a little vacation."

"A vacation? in Denver City?"

"I met a lady in the tie camp."

"Ho, ho, ho! A lady in the tie camp. Them ain't the kind of women you meet in tie camps."

"Billy brought her up, she was one of his passengers. She's staying at the Broadwell. I thought maybe I'd just stroll by and say hello, and I can't leave the boys home, it's Christmas."

"Stroll by! You ain't gonna get a poke?"

"She's a lady, I told you."

Charlie grinned and went to rub his hands together. It was funny how he kept forgetting. "Why don't we just all stroll by, have a look-see?"

"'Cause I don't want you cramping my style."

Denver City, two days before Christmas.

The streets were full of mud and snow and ice all churned together under a brilliant blue sky. Holiday pretties and evergreen trees hung with ribbons decorated the store windows. The displays of sweetmeats and toys weren't anywhere as fancy as those in the Capitol, J.C. allowed, but only to Paul, not wanting to spoil his father's fun. His father, who was blowing on tin horns, tapping drums, rolling a little wooden engine along a track fashioned from nails.

"Isn't this fun?" Jed asked over and over. "Look at this."

"Mother would like that," Paul said, eyeing a glass bowl on a glassware shelf.

"Yes, she would," Jed agreed cheerily.

"When is she coming?" J.C. asked, but his father, stepping aside for the crowd, stepped away from the question, and J.C. didn't ask again. The answer was always the same anyway. She'd be along later. When? Just later.

Dusk came on. Candles were lit in the store windows. Propped in the window of the Cheesman Drug Store was a large painting of a jolly, red-suited Santa Claus sitting in a sleigh pulled by reindeer. Little platforms holding little candles were fastened to the painting. Each reindeer had a candle above its nose, as did the sleigh lanterns and the tip of Santa's hat. The flickering candles made the sleigh appear to be flying down Blake Street. That was the best decoration of all.

After supper at the Elephant Corral, Charlie took the boys back to the boarding house and Jed walked up Sixteenth Street to the Broadwell. The mud was hardening in the streets and there was a cold wind blowing.

The Cave-Browne-Caves were hosting a private supper in an upstairs room when Jed arrived. The streaks on his dark suit showed it to have recently been wiped down with a wet rag.

"Were you expected?" the clerk asked, looking down his nose at the patched boots on the tomato-red carpets.

"No, but it's important."

"It always is with these Englishmen," the clerk muttered, scribbling a note for his assistant.

"I see we have a visitor," Blanche said, discreetly placing the note beside her brother's plate. "I'll take care of it, Cave, you finish your story." It was a story about gold mining in the South Indian state of Mysore. She knew it by heart, complete with variations. She pecked her brother on the cheek, nodded

at their guests, all well into their cups, and walked down the
hallway to the stair. Before reaching the head of the stairs, she
brushed her hair with her fingers and straightened her collar.

"Why, Mr. Harris." She wore a red plaid hoopskirt with thick
black fringe at the bottom and a similarly fringed plaid jacket
with a white cameo at her throat. Except for a few loose curls,
her honey-colored hair was upswept. "What a nice surprise, how
are you?"

Bowled over, that's what he was, just plain bowled over.
Seeing his face, Blanche looked down modestly. "Shall we sit by
the street, so we can view the lights?"

They sat at a small round table covered with green felt cloth
and looked wordlessly out on the traffic on Larimer Street—Jed
terribly discomforted, Blanche enjoying his struggle.

At length he asked, "So…what'd you think of the
mountains?"

"They were extremely disappointing. I had no idea how
utterly gold mining ruins the appearance of the countryside."

"The more dirt you see up top, the more gold's been dug out."

"Poor bald, scarred mountains, all pitted up like a smallpox
epidemic, the mills puffing away. And those rickety little
buildings on stilts jammed into the crevices. There were unusual
things, but no one feature I'd call attractive, except perhaps the
Presbyterian Church. That was rather charming, stuck up as it
was above the mess in the bottom and painted white. I believe
churches, if wooden, should be painted white, don't you?"

"Oh definitely, that's how they are."

"I had a nosebleed every morning I was there." Blanche made
a face. "From the elevation."

A waiter approached. Blanche ordered a glass of Fendant
de Sion. Jed ordered a whiskey. He'd forgot how to talk to real
ladies, just forgot. Nevertheless it was pleasant sitting there in

the Broadwell being part, if only for a little while, of the world he'd left behind.

"In Central City we stayed at the St. Nicholas." Blanche sighed deeply. "It was recommended as the cleanest in the city, unfortunately, the bar was set rather too low."

Another silence.

The waiter brought the drinks. Jed reached for his purse, but the waiter was walking away.

"We have an account here," Blanche explained. "So, Mr. Harris, may I call you Jed? what do you do on that road to the Little Kingdom of Gilpin?"

"Run a tie camp."

"I remember something's being said about that, but I'm not sure what a tie camp is."

"Railroad ties for under the rails."

"So you're the one responsible for cutting down those huge trees. Couldn't you go further up the mountainside and leave the trees in the bottom? They're really quite ancient, you know. They remind me of England, of the roads made dark by old trees."

Jed laughed self-consciously. "We cut high and low, depending on what we get into. If we cut those big water spruce in the bottom, sun'll get in there and melt the snow, make the road easier going."

He downed the whiskey and waved off the watchful waiter. His English princess was toying with him, having nothing better to do on a cold winter's night far away from home. And so what? He didn't have anything better to do either. She hated the mountains. Hell, he hated the mountains. He was tired of throwing himself against them. Tired of worrying that Bettina would spill the beans, tired of missing Julia every goddamned day.

Blanche was talking about investing in American railroads.

"We've been hearing a good deal lately about railroads in the West. Where do your ties go?"

"Down to Golden City."

"And then where?"

"Nowhere, they're being stockpiled."

"Hmmm." Blanche nodded as if having suspected as much. "We were introduced to a Nathaniel Hill at supper, I believe he just opened a smelter in Black Hawk. He said that a Mr. Loveland, who lives in Golden City, spent fifty thousand dollars to open a road cut into the mountains and has now secured a charter to build a railroad. Perhaps you could introduce us when I return."

"Sure."

A group of children entered the front door caroling and passed by the table. Watching them, Blanche's face was absolutely radiant. "You don't think I'm serious do you," she said when she could.

"It's Christmas," Jed replied warmly. "You can believe anything you want to."

"In that case, I want you to tell Mr. Loveland that you have a friend with ten thousand dollars to invest in his railroad." She laughed at the disbelief in Jed's face. "Actually I have very little money of my own, daughters are supposed to *marry* money, not worry about *making* it. But since I'm the only daughter, and now Cave is the only son—we lost our older brother Geoffrey—he is very generous with me."

"Are you really coming back? I didn't think you liked it here."

"I like Americans, you don't show the underbelly, you aren't so inbred and so delicate." She leaned forward as if sharing a confidence. "Your father was French."

"Yes. My mother was Dutch."

Blanche nodded. "But the French will out. Lean and

hawkish, a fighter *and* a lover." She smiled provocatively, her head slightly tipped. "And your sons, where are they tonight?"

"At a party down the street."

"Why don't you bring them here tomorrow for supper?" Without waiting for an answer, Blanche got to her feet. "Shall we say seven?"

"Seven's good," Jed agreed, hastily abandoning his chair, almost knocking the table over.

Blanche glanced out the window with the sparest of glances and gestured ever so slightly with her fan.

"Do you think she saw us?" Paul asked excitedly.

"I think she did!" exclaimed J.C.

"No, she didn't!" Charlie argued, actually having no idea one way or the other. "We better get while the gettin's good." And they hotfooted it back to the Overland House, arriving just in the nick of time to shed their coats, their faces still reddened by cold, when Jed showed up.

"How was the strolling?" Charlie asked.

"S'good," Jed said. "Got invited out to supper tomorrow night, along with the boys."

"You didn't wrangle me one?"

"Hell, I never wrangled this one, it just come at me right out of the blue."

"We're gonna go eat wit…" Paul stopped when J.C. clamped a hand over his mouth.

Jed never noticed.

"Kind of in a fog, ain't he?" Charlie observed, and the boys snickered.

The next day Charlie caught a ride back across the prairie to the old settlement on Arapahoe Bar and walked home from there, and Jed and the boys went shopping. It was Christmas Eve. Up and down the boardwalks, in and out the open doorways, the festive crowds ebbed and flowed, hunting and gathering. That night at the Broadwell House the boys looked dandy in their new calico shirtwaists and striped cottonade trousers. Jed had splurged for a red silk tie, and smiled at everybody he met.

Christmas Eve was the hardest night of the year. He was at the window in the Willard's Hotel watching the street. J.C. and Paul were waiting for their mother to unwrap packages. Just when they all seemed to be easing past the worst of the heartache, back came Christmas Eve.

Surrounded by a swirl of lustrous green taffeta, Blanche was waiting for them in the lobby, a book in her lap. "You look familiar," she told J.C. "Have we met somewhere before?"

"Ah..." J.C. glanced at his father "...I don't think so."

Blanche winked at the boy and said to Paul, "You look familiar also."

Paul hung his head wordlessly. "He's real shy," Jed explained.

Blanche took Jed's arm. "Cave made reservations in the dining room." Her perfume smelled like Christmas, and Jed realized it was a perfume Julia wore.

Cave was exuberant. His dear friends with him on the loveliest night of the year? what more could a man ask. And he had something for them. Yes, for each and every one of them. Something they could not repay. Oh my no! it was a gift.

"Do you still believe in Santa Claus?" he asked Paul, whose careful consideration of the question set the table to laughing. "By jove! you're covering all your bets, and well you should, that's a smart lad. Don't open this tonight, put it under the tree and open it tomorrow with what Santa brings."

Blanche gave the boys the book she was reading when they arrived—a collection of early-day mining stories by Mr. Bret Harte, a new author of immense promise. During the course of the meal, having seen to it that she was seated next to J.C., she remarked quietly, "I notice your shoe is built up like mine."

J.C. ducked his head to look under the table linen, and Blanche lifted the hem of her skirt. The boy stared in astonishment at the black, specially-made boot with its thick sole and heel. Uncertain what to say, he looked over at his father, who grimaced, wondering what his son had dropped.

"She's like me," J.C. said, a grin splitting his face in two.

After supper, Cave and his cousin off to check out the bar in the hotel across the street, Blanche suggested the boys might enjoy the puppet show taking place in a corner of the Broadwell lobby.

"I thought we might listen to the music," she told Jed, taking his arm to stroll toward the sound of violins. That's when Jed realized she had a slight limp.

"Do you dance?"

"No," Jed said. "It don't interest me."

"Me either."

Jed did a double-take. What woman didn't like to dance? They had reached a small ballroom. Several couples were dancing, others sat at tables along the edge of the room.

Jed thought about his son, the many times he'd had to remind the boy that he could do anything anyone else could. Anything.

"Yes, you can dance," he said firmly. "It's easy, c'mon, I'll show you."

And there he was, lurching across the floor like a hobbled horse, doggedly encouraging the woman in his arms with, "One, two, three. One, two, three…that's it, listen to the music, that's how you know it's a waltz, see. You count. One, two, three…." Hearing Julia's no-nonsense voice in his head, closing his eyes and holding Julia in his arms.

# FIFTY-FIVE

I T WAS NOT A LONG COURTSHIP as courtships go, so much as a long-distance one. Blanche accompanied Cave to England, and in the spring of 1869 returned with her brother to America. They traveled west together as far as Denver City, where Cave left her to explore the unorganized territory below the headwaters of the Missouri River.

"I shall return for the wedding," he teased, "if there is to be a wedding."

"Never fear," Blanche replied with a laugh. "I have only, how do you cow people say? to rope him in."

She sent a note up to the tie camp arranging to meet Jed in Golden City at the Astor House. And he came, all lean and brown and smelling of resin, sandy hair caught in a leather string, wild beard washed down with water. Blanche wanted to throw her arms around him, instead they merely exchanged pleasantries. Jed inquired about England, she inquired about the boys. He didn't have a lot of time, but Blanche thought there should be time for the latest eating craze—potato chips and root beer—in Dr. Kelly's drug store on Washington Avenue.

Had Jed spoken with Mr. Loveland about her investment?

"I ain't the one to introduce you," Jed said, having had several run-ins with Bill Loveland over the condition of his wagon road, which in places more resembled a cow trail. "He's not the easiest man to get along with. You just hook it on over to his store, he won't turn away a pretty lady with money to spend."

"When will you be back?"

"Next Saturday."

By the next Saturday, good as her word, Blanche had invested ten thousand dollars in Bill Loveland's railroad. She and Jed rented a buggy and drove out to Charlie's farm to pick up the boys, then back to the mouth of the Vasquez canyon where they learned that four hundred feet of rail had already been laid. Afterward they took a drive up graveyard hill to enjoy the view, ate fried chicken in the Overland Hotel, and walked down the street to the drug store for ice cream. Blanche hugged the boys and made over them, and they lapped it up like puppies in front of a bowl of warm milk.

Jed was taking them hunting the next day, Blanche was meeting friends in Denver City. She lingered at the front door of the Astor House. When would Jed be back?

"Probably Friday to pick up chain." He smiled boyishly. "But I ain't got time for any more monkey business."

"Friday it is, and no monkey business, I promise."

*Why am I romancing a total stranger?* Blanche asked herself, watching her tall woodman walk away. *I know nothing about his habits and very little about his background. I'm buying a pig in a poke.* Still, she so wished she were walking with him.

That Monday Jed received a packet from the Union Pacific office. Inside was an envelope marked personal, and inside that a note from Bettina.

> Julia had a baby girl, both are healthy. B.
> p.s. I have done as you asked.

He burned the note in the stove and went to splitting wood with a vengeance. Toward dark he walked down the gulch to Guy's and visited with a blind fiddler working his way up to the

diggings. "Play me some music," Jed said, dropping his coins
in the wooden box. The fiddler played, and Jed sat back in the
corner, eyes closed, chair tipped against the wall.

Friday he was in a hurry. The sun was shining, but it'd rained
every afternoon for the past week, and he was afraid of a run-off
in the canyon. Blanche wanted him to see her house, purchased,
she explained, to be nearer her investment. Surely he had time
for that, it was just around the corner up along the river.

The house, a two-story, gabled brick, was brand new. There
were no curtains yet on the windows. A man on a long ladder
was painting one of the gables.

"What are you doing?" Jed asked. "You're just throwing your
money away, you won't even be here."

"Perhaps your brother's wife would look after it for me."

"Mouse? Well…sure, she could do that good as any, I guess,
but what's your long-range plan? Are you gonna run a boarding
house? 'cause that's your best money with a big house like this.
But why bother?"

"It will be a bit of a new experience, being a landlady and all.
I thought just rooms for now. I'm assuming men hired to build
the railroad will need places to sleep."

"Sure, you're right, they will."

"You're surprised I'd think of that?"

Jed didn't know what he thought. They were walking down
First Street back to the Astor House. The jays were making a
racket in the cottonwoods, the path was dappled in shade.

"I'll keep a room for myself, that will save the hostel fees
when I'm in the city."

"It's none of my business, but why here of all places? The
prairie's just a big desert, and the mountains are rough to get
around in. No water that amounts to anything, lots of wind."

"And the bluest skies I've ever seen. Actually, I rather like it here, the sudden rise of mountains, having my back to them. You're here."

"I got business here."

"So do I. You don't find me attractive?"

"Look." Jed stopped in front of her. Good lord, she was beautiful! the sun in her hair, the prettiest eyes, He ought to kiss her, that's what he wanted to do. Instead he scolded her. "This is like a big game to you, and that's alright, that's what you know, that other life. But I can't just...you can't depend on me to help you, I don't have time."

"Oh, I would never depend on you to *help* me. I was thinking more of a partnership."

Jed looked down at his boots to hide his grin. And then he kissed her, and the world spun him round and round, and he promised himself he'd never do that again even as he whispered softly "I do appreciate you" against her neck.

"Couldn't you love me instead?"

Jed shook his head and walked on, a man in control of his own destiny.

"Give me a month," Blanche teased, "to convince you I'm a good businesswoman. When you come down out of your lonely old mountains to see your sons, stop by and say hello."

"You're going to hang around here for a month?!"

They'd turned away from the river and were approaching the boarding house. A dog fight broke out in the middle of the road, a buggy team veered aside. Jed took Blanche's arm, holding her back from crossing.

"So you don't like games, Mr. Harris?"

"I don't have time for them."

"You would surely guess that brothers have no secrets from their sisters, that I know your real name."

Jed's face hardened.

"Perhaps I should tell you what Mr. Caruthers, who is with

the Pinkerton Agency, told me. Their file on Julia Marchion, who is now Mrs. Sigvald Proulx, yes? has recently been closed by Mrs. Proulx herself, and she is no longer a client."

Jed studied Blanche's face so intently that she blushed and looked away.

Blanche Dianna Cave-Brown-Cave became Mrs. Jedrich Thomas Marchion November 10, 1869, in a ceremony performed in the Presbyterian Church in Golden City. Jed was forty-one years old. Shaved bare as a schoolboy, he looked like a stranger to everyone but his sons. Blanche, twenty-seven, was a princess in a white mound of silk and lace.

Cave escorted his sister down the aisle, Yam was Jed's best man. When the minister asked, "Who gives this woman in marriage," J.C. and Paul replied in one voice, "We do." Charlie and Sarah tanned a spotted bull hide for the occasion. Billy Opdyke presented Blanche with a sterling silver snuff case to calm her nerves. And Col. Parker B. Cheney, who made it a point to appear at the city's weddings and funerals to underscore the respectability of his Chicago Saloon, handed out cigars.

The couple honeymooned high in the mountains, staying in the Hotel de Paris in Georgetown. That night the moon was full, clumps of silver clouds sailed overhead trailing little veils of snow. A festival was being held on Argentine Street, lanterns swayed gently in the pines, musicians played and people danced. And Jed waltzed with his wife.

"And who is it you are thinking of tonight, my lord?" Blanche asked gaily, leaning back in his arms.

Jed laughed, swinging her off her feet. "I'm thinking of the beautiful woman I met in the woods who wouldn't take no for an answer. And counting my lucky stars."

# A  HEMMING  UP

In the spring of 1872 a white woman burned black as a cinder
and wearing hides, walked to the Moenkopi trading house with
three Paiute women and several children.

She said she came from the other side of the river and wanted
to go home to the States.

A blistery old Morman by the name of Lake, guessing this
woman to be the same woman the church was offering a reward
for back in the '50s, put her up in his home. Very early the next
morning Brother Lake propped a board against the bedroom
door and rode off up Tanner wash to the ferry to ask Brother Lee
if the church ever found the woman it was looking for.

Fearing her husband meant to take another wife, good Sister
Lake filled a small sugar sack with cured meat and a bladder with
water and tied the items to either end of a short rope. Next she
caught up the jackass recently purchased in Oraibi and hung the
rope across the animal's withers.

And waking the white woman, warned her to leave
immediately. "Let the jackass go where it will, when you reach
Oraibi, tell them that the Americans will pay a reward for you.
But whatever you do, don't stay with the white people. The
Indians live there, stay with them."

The Paiute refused to accompany their friend to Oraibi. It

wasn't necessary to go any further. The only reason they came this far south was because Icamani wanted to cross the river to find her people.

Late the next morning, some forty miles across the scorched earth to the east, the white woman reached Oraibi. On hearing that the Americans would pay a reward for her return, the Mormon settlers at Oraibi dispatched a Navajo runner to Fort Verde. Before the American soldiers arrived, Brother Lake arrived with John Lee. But the Navajo, with whom the white woman had taken refuge, refused to turn her over to the moronie.

Soldiers from the First Cavalry rode in a week later. At Fort Verde the woman was put on a coach for Albuquerque. She visited little with the other passengers, spending most of her time staring silently out the window.

From the post at Albuquerque she wrote,

> Dear mother, I am well and coming home. I have been well in my mind for some time. It was a terrible awakening. I was bathing in a thicket, and there were birds everywhere, and all the sudden I knew it was an oriole I was hearing and that I smelled juniper and I was in the West. It was an awful jolt and left me quite ill for several days. I felt as if I had been cut loose from the earth and was looking down on everything from a great height, my sweet children, my old home along the Hudson, the great canyon I lived beside. Forgive my ramblings, it's hard to explain.
>
> Before I could determine how best to leave, a Mexican found wandering through the mountain died in our camp. Soon others died and it was determined to move the camp, but before that happened my dear devoted Dancer was gone. Little Stephen died several days later. I was filled with a great despondency and thought I might die as the others, but instead I remained well by some miracle.
>
> There were only a few of us left to make the journey off the mountain. We were led by a boy who had walked the trail

*only once before with his father. He is a brave little lad, I never
will forget him. I write hoping you have heard from Mun and
knowing you have not. He is still here, lost forever in this poor
tortured land. Words can not convey how my heart aches for
him. I pray this finds you all well. I will be home soon. Much
love from your daughter Dinky*

Back in New York Dinky stayed a brief time with Katherine
and Walker before moving upriver to the old Marchion
farm with her children and a widowed aunt. There she
was interviewed by officials from West Point and later by a
delegation from the LDS Church.

The army placed Mrs. Miller's story in the file cabinet labeled
*Mountain Meadows Massacre.*

The LDS delegation sent their report to John Bernhisel,
Utah's delegate to Washington. A skeptical Bernhisel sent two
staff members to interview friends and members of Mrs. Miller's
family. Based on these findings, he concluded that Editha Miller
had been out of her mind for a number of years. As for his own
investigation into the matter, there was no evidence whatsoever
of Mrs. Miller's having ever been a member of the unfortunate
party massacred at Mountain Meadows.

The LDS report, together with Bernhisel's conclusions, was
quietly sealed away with the rest of the Fancher papers in the
Church Buttress in Little Cottonwood Canyon.

The more Dinky read about the passage of the Fancher party
through Utah Territory, the more she felt compelled to set
the story straight. She wrote out everything she remembered
in detail, including what others of the party had told her, and
contacted Appleton publishers in New York. Mr. Thomas
Stenhouse, a Mormon apostate who had recently published his
mammoth *The Rocky Mountain Saints* with Appleton, replied
and subsequently visited the farm.

Tom took great interest in Dinky's story and made copious

notes. A wickedly good-humored Scotsman, he outlined the events leading to the isolation and destruction of the wagon train in tragicomical fashion, and warned strongly against publishing the manuscript.

"Brigham's power is such that all he need do is give the word, and every man who participated in the massacre will be delivered to the front door of the Salt Lake jail. That he refuses to do so makes him doubly dangerous to those who know the truth. Although you weren't in the meadows, you are the only person living who knows what happened prior to the massacre itself. For your safety, the story can not be told until the church accepts full responsibility."

※

Uergin's estate survived numerous challenges to be settled in 1871 in favor of the inheritors named in his will. Waiting for this auspicious day, Nathan kept his family together with yet another boarding house.

※

Bill Loveland's rails reached Black Hawk in 1872. Shortly afterward, Jed was made superintendent of the railroad yards on Wall Street in Golden City.

That same year Blanche took her stepsons to England. J.C. was fifteen and Paul thirteen. On the way over they stopped off in Washington where the boys stayed a week with Julia—the first of what would become yearly visits. That his sons took great pleasure in recounting their adventures in the Capitol, and mentioned nothing untoward about their mother's actions, enabled Jed to believe what he wanted to believe—that Julia had put aside her use of opium.

In 1873 both boys enrolled in the Territorial School of Mines. The Professor in Charge gave them flyers to distribute amongst the people coming into the region. Even so, enrollment remained low, it wasn't until nine years later that the first Engineer of Mines degrees were awarded.

※

Nancy never for a minute believed she was Uergin's daughter, but that he had simply wanted to make inheriting easier.

She traveled to Europe to study voice and language, and returned to San Francisco to audition for *Adrienne Lecouvreu*. She was hired as first understudy after singing the *Marseillaise*, and went on to appear in a variety of leading roles that included *Frou Frou*, *Hermai*, and *Le Sphinx*. The *San Francisco Chronicle* labeled her "the Canary of the Gold Coast" and noted that "...the impulses of passion inform her singing, she spends her voice abundantly, even recklessly, as she is carried along by the dramatic situations, and she never spares herself in the climaxes."

That Nancy was a close friend of the wealthy Crocker family and a frequent guest at their Hotel del Monte in Monterey was a source of great pride to the Lafittes.

She never married.

※

Nathan made Harold Leith principal partner in the Lucky Lady Gaming Establishment (he'd changed the name, "saloon" being so low-class) and for the next decade traveled the world. In 1883 Daphne was badly injured by a runaway team while crossing California Street. Facing a long convalescence, she wanted to live where she could hear the ocean. Nathan purchased a modest bungalow on the coast not far from Nancy and took up the invigorating game of baseball.

※

Sarah Reeves died of pleurisy in her forty-third year, and Charlie took up with a widow who lived in a stone house atop the mesa behind his farm. They raised cows and chickens and pigs, along with a big flock of turkeys to thin out the locusts.

Yam and Mouse moved back to the North Woods. But Yam missed the nighttime sky and Mouse couldn't find her people, scattered to the four winds by the European tide. Within the year the pair returned and squatted in the little swale to the south of Charlie's stone house.

Their stick-and-stone house consisted of one large room with a little iron stove in the center. Yam hunted wild rabbits and collected wild honey, which he peddled in Golden City. He also domesticated coyotes, selling the hides for three to five dollars apiece for women's furs.

The visits of Arapaho and Cheyenne to the mesa top caused no worries in the city below, and the stories they told enriched many an evening in the households of their friends.

Katherine never returned to the desert. When she dreamed, she dreamed of red mesas and smoke-colored mountains and Henry Chee riding beside her quoting poetry, lying beside her whispering in her ear. Every year at Christmastime she sent a package to Taos, New Mexico, addressed to Henry Chee Dodge in care of Mr. Kit Carson. The homage continued until she read of the death of Kit Carson at Fort Lyon, Colorado, in 1868.

In 1886, when she was fifty-eight years old, she circled New York Harbor in a boatload of suffragettes protesting that, of the more than six hundred dignitaries invited to witness the unveiling of the beautiful lady from France, only two were women. It was, Katherine declared, her finest hour.

✖

Phoebe never left the Valley. Her paintings traveled far and wide and in the 20th century gained sufficient following to merit inclusion in a show in the Smithsonian entitled "Modern Art Before Modern Art." The Taggart section was divided into three periods—*The Taggarts, The Abysmals, The Straws.* The San Francisco Lyceum sent all six of its paintings, including the scene of the women in white dresses hanging clothes in the wind.

✖

By the time Jeremy located his Cheyenne relatives, the long death of the Plains Indian that began with treaties signed prior to the 1840s and ended at Wounded Knee in 1890, was well into its third decade. On May 19, 1868, at the mouth of the Musselshell River, Captain Robert Nugent, 13th Infantry, engaged a band of Cheyenne and Sioux and killed ten of the Indians. Jeremy and his brother Haskay rode with the band, and Haskay was killed.

Determined to live the rest of his life on the white side of the law, Jeremy stayed in California, eventually marrying a Spanish woman, a calm, quiet descendent of the Arguello family, a good listener. She died of leakage of the heart while pregnant with their first child. Jeremy gave what he had left of Uergin's estate to Nancy and returned to the sacred places of his grandfathers.

## ✢◗ THE HISTORY ◖✢

T. B. H. Stenhouse, a well-educated Scotsman and journalist, pressured to live his faith by taking extra wives, reluctantly married twice more. The first of these extra wives was Parley Pratt's daughter, Belinda. As a member of a small group of dissenters called the Godbeites (after founder W. S. Godbe), Thomas grew increasingly disenchanted with Brigham's absolute authority over matters both secular and ecclesiastical and eventually left the church. He and his first wife, Fanny, moved to the States, where both published their experiences with the Mormons. Their publications are listed in the Bibliography.

※

Brigham's sermons and letters are part of the historical record. The private conversations of the churchman are told here as fiction, with the exception of Brigham's meetings with John Lee. Those meetings were recorded by Wilford Woodruff, as was the churchman's dashing the contents of Lee's hat to the floor, to later be picked up by his wives.

※

The Gunnison massacre, like that of the Mountain Meadows, was widely considered to be the work of "white Indians," Mormons painted as Indians. In both cases the accusations of Mormon involvement came from within the church community itself, despite vigorous denials by Church Authority.

※

Elizabeth Cumming's observation on the so-called happy women of Zion is an actual quote recorded by Fanny Stenhouse.

Sir Genille Cave-Browne-Cave, a remittance man and heir apparent to one of England's oldest titles, arrived in America in the 1890s bent on adventure and excitement. He did not, that I know of, have a sister. For an entertaining account of this charming Englishman's true adventures, read Lee Olson's highly acclaimed book, *Marmalade and Whiskey, British Remittance Men in the West,* Fulcrum Publishing, 1993.

Henry Chee Dodge was not born until 1860. Other than that, the background of the scout and interpreter is as described.

The comet seen over the Southwest was Donati's Comet, one of the brightest comets on record, visible even at noon in broad daylight. First recorded in June 1858 the comet reached its maximum brilliancy that October.

Vasquez Creek in Colorado is now called Clear Creek. Early pioneers changed the name to reflect the clear waters of the creek, which rises in the southwest mountains of Clear Creek County and flows east into the South Platte River. Mining in the mountains turned the river the colors of the mine dumps.

Gate City, no longer in existence, was a mining supply town at the entrance to Golden Gate Canyon northwest of present-day Golden, Colorado.

Gate City was extracted from the name Golden's Gate City. A second, more common name, was Golden Gate City. Tom Golden laid out the city on the road to the mining districts in the mountains and built a toll gate inside the mouth of the nearby canyon.

The term "gate" refers not to the toll gate but to the two tall rock pillars at the canyon entrance. The pillars were destroyed by road construction in the 1900s. The city itself was much shorter lived as a result of competition from nearby Golden City, which usurped Tom's name.

※

John Richard's bridge below Devil's Gate on the Platte was over a thousand feet long and fifteen feet wide. The piers were huge tree trunks filled with stones.

Crossing fees were five dollars per wagon, four dollars per every hundred head of stock. Tolls were taken in cash and goods, leaving the bridge tender's house well-stocked with furniture and tools. When water levels were low (tempting travelers to cross on their own), bridge fees were lowered.

Soldiers sent to guard the bridge from Indian raids during the winter months called the site Camp Payne.

※

Jim Bridger is the first white man known to have seen the Great Salt Lake and is the best known of the Rocky Mountain frontiersmen next to Kit Carson.

Bridger and Louis Vasquez built Fort Bridger on the Green River in 1843. It was Louis Vasquez who, with his own fort on the South Platte River, lent his name to Vasquez Creek, now known as Clear Creek.

Bridger's Fort carried on a lively business with local Indians and passing emigrants. In 1855, when Bridger was away, Vasquez sold the fort to the Mormons, who in 1857 burned the buildings

to prevent American soldiers escorting Brigham's replacement,
Alfred Cumming, from taking shelter there.

In 1858 the American Army built a permanent fort on the
site and named it in honor of Bridger. The fort remained an
active military post until 1890.

⁕

In 1873 Isabella Bird wrote, "Golden City by daylight showed
its meanness and belied its name. It is ungraded, with here and
there a piece of wooden sidewalk, supported on posts, up to
which you ascend by planks. Brick, pine, and log houses are
huddled together, every other house is a saloon...." *A Lady's Life
in the Rocky Mountains*, by Isabella Bird.

Joseph Bowden, who lived in Golden City in the 1870's,
wrote of the city:

> It was a little village but a wild one, no law or order in
> those days. It was nothing to go out and see a dead man
> picked up on the street and no one thought any thing of it.
> I remember one beautiful Sunday afternoon in particular,
> a man was found lying dead and a bunch of us small boys,
> only 9 or 10 yrs. old, went to see him. A little later in the
> day, another man was found dead (both had been shot) and
> we went and had a look at him.
>
> They had been taken to a building on the flats, at that
> time the camping ground for the freighters, mule teams,
> oxen and horse teams. When they all came in from
> different parts of the country, it was a busy time round there
> as they came in droves....
>
> Ford Street was a tough joint in those days. There were
> all kinds of old stables, log shacks, blacksmith shops, livery
> barns as well as a couple of saloons and brand houses as
> well....
>
> The style they had in the saloons in those days was—
> they had one long table down the center of the room and
> a long bench on each side. You sat down and called for

your pint, quart, or gallon and glasses according to the size of your crowd. Everybody was welcome, kids and all, so everybody drank that wanted to and nothing said....

[The Indians] were a fine looking tribe of red men. They used to pitch their tents or tepees in a camp north of the town. As soon as they established themselves, the squaws got busy on their buffalo robes. They used to stretch them on the ground and peg them down. When they had them cured and pliable to suit them, they drew all kinds of fancy Indian figures on them with different colored native paints, then sold them at five dollars a robe when finished.

They would come to your door begging and if you gave them anything they would come and stand around the door in dozens and look in your windows. [One] morning when we got up the town was full of Indians. That was the way they always arrived. Not one to be seen at night but the town would be full of them in the morning.

Excerpted from: *The Story of My Life*, unpublished autobiography of Joseph Thomas Bowden, 1862-?, in the private collection of Andrew R. Patten, Jr., a great nephew.

※

The treaty medal, the blue-stone necklace, the wooden cross are somewhere in the West in museums.

## ✦═ THE CAST OF FICTIONAL CHARACTERS ═✦

The story told in *Over the Mountains of the Moon* and *Down the Valley of the Shadow* continues. The year is 1857.

◈ **Blanche Cave-Brown-Cave.** An English noblewoman visiting the Pike's Peak mining district with her brother. Walks with a slight limp as the result of a riding accident. Romanced by the raw American wilderness, Blanche is immediately drawn to the tall woodman in his lonely dell.

◈ **Dancer.** Paiute runner who witnesses the Fancher train massacre. Returning to his home on the Kaibab Plateau, Dancer sees a white woman fleeing the Mormons and leads her to safety.

### Harris Family:

◈ **Appella Harris.** The one outside wife George trusts. It is in Appella's home, away from the prying eyes of his neighbors, that the bishop meets with friends to discuss the troubled times.

◈ **Constance Harris.** (Referenced) George's first wife. Abhorred polygamy and refused to acknowledge her husband's additional wives.

◈ **Ellen Harris.** The last wife the bishop took and the only wife who shares his bed. Safe in George's shadow, Ellen convinces herself that the violence in the church will not touch her family.

◈ **George Harris.** Wealthy Mormon bishop, seven wives, six houses. LDS Tax Collector and Chief Tithe Collector. Fearful of the growing violence within the church, the bishop welcomes the approach of the American Army.

◈ **Jeremy Harris.** Ellen's son by a Cheyenne warrior and the adopted son of Bishop Harris. Fiercely anxious to prove himself in the Lord's army, Jeremy has complete faith in Brigham Young.

◈ **Nancy Jane Harris.** Daughter of George and Ellen Harris. A spoiled, happy little girl with black curly hair and dark green eyes.

§ **Phoebe (Taggart) Harris.** The only wife allowed to live in the Harris mansion with George and Ellen. Paints bright, blurry landscapes which she is forbidden to sign with her married name.

§ **Emil and Verity James.** Emigrated to the West with George Harris in 1846. Live in southern Utah outside Cedar City on a hog farm.

§ **Nathaniel and Daphne Lafitte.** A handsome pair of thieves, well-traveled, resourceful. Having stumbled across Phoebe's paintings in San Francisco, they make plans to visit the artist as soon as the Utah War is over.

§ **Alfredo Luna.** Mexican horse dealer and Charlie's friend.

## *Marchion Family:*

§ **Christina Marchion.** Widow of Jean Paul Marchion. Mother of Walker, Jed, and Dinky. Christina has no idea that Jed considers Yam his half-brother.

§ **Dinky (Marchion) Miller.** The wife of Mun Miller and mother of twins Anne and Emily and a younger son Lymund. Traveling through Utah to meet Mun in California, Dinky suffers a terrible betrayal followed by an accident that blinds her and clouds her mind.

§ **J.C. Marchion.** Short for Jedrich Cyrus. Jed's oldest son. Born with a shortened Achilles tendon, J.C. wears a built-up shoe and walks with a limp.

§ **Jed Marchion.** Dinky's brother. Married Ellen after her Indian sojourn to give Ellen and Jeremy a home, but the marriage didn't last. Happily remarried, Jed operates a sawmill in Houlton, Maine.

§ **Julia (Clare) Marchion.** Jed Marchion's wife and the mother of his sons. A French-English beauty used to her father's prominence in the Houlton community, Julia is anxious that her husband achieve the same level of recognition.

§ **Katherine Marchion.** Walker's wife and the mother of his two daughters. Katherine's deep affection for Dinky will be rewarded in a most unexpected way.

⚘ **Paul Marchion.** Jed Marchion's younger son.

⚘ **Walker Marchion.** Jed and Dinky's brother. A successful farmer and much-respected member of the Hudson Valley community. Melancholy and self-absorbed, Walker hates Jed with a mindless passion.

⚘ **Yam Marchion.** The son of Jean Paul Marchion and a Seneca squaw. Yam does not believe he has a white father, nevertheless, he partners up with Jed, who calls him a brother.

⚘ **Stephen Abraham Miller.** Dinky's son by Dancer.

⚘ **Mouse.** A Malicite squaw and Yam's common-law wife.

⚘ **Sigvald Proulx.** Julia Marchion's first cousin. An exceedingly handsome Nordic fellow with important friends in Washington. That Sigvald enjoys Julia's company perhaps more than he should is readily apparent.

⚘ **Bettina Putnam.** Julia's cousin and closest confidant.

⚘ **Charlie Reeves.** A hearty, well-met sergeant in the U.S. Army of the West. Fate has made Sergeant Reeves a linchpin in the affairs of the Marchion and Harris families.

⚘ **Sarah Reeves.** The wife of Charlie Reeves. Lives in St. Joe, Missouri.

⚘ **Sasha.** Cheyenne squaw. Sister of Whonow, a Cheyenne warrior killed by Mexican traders on the Arkansas in 1847. Whonow is Jeremy's father. It was Sasha, her younger brother Haskay and her grandfather Okhum who found Ellen lost on the prairie and took her into the mountains. Sasha calls Ellen her sister-by-choice.

⚘ **Jack Straw.** Illiterate Mormon emigrant from Wales.

⚘ **Conrad Uergin.** A good-looking, devil-may-care fellow whom women find dangerous in a delicious sort of way. An old friend of George's wives, Uergin buys Phoebe's artwork from the Lafittes.

# BIBLIOGRAPHY
## A SAMPLING

The history shapes the story. A few of the books and periodicals drawn upon are listed below.

Adjutant General's Office, 1979, Chronological list of actions, &c., with Indians from January 15, 1837 to January, 1891: Old Army Press.

Agnew, S. G., 1974, Garrisons of the Regular U.S. Army, Arizona 1851-1899: Virginia, Council on Abandoned Military Posts.

Arrington, L. J., 1970, Great Basin Kingdom, economic history of the Latter-Day Saints, 1830-1900: Lincoln, University of Nebraska Press.

Backus, A. J., 1995, Mountain Meadows witness: Spokane, Arthur H. Clark Co.

Bagley, Will, 2002, Blood of the prophets, Brigham Young and the massacre at mountain meadows: Norman, University of Oklahoma Press.

Broad, Richard, Jr., 1922, When Golden was the capital: typed manuscript, Colorado Room, Colorado School of Mines Library, Golden, Colorado School of Mines.

Brooks, Juanita, 1950, The Mountain Meadows massacre: Norman, University of Oklahoma Press, 1970 edition.

Brown, Georgina, 1976, The shining mountains: Gunnison, Colorado, B&B Printers, privately published.

Burton, R. F., 1862, The city of the Saints: New York, Harper & Brothers Publishers.

Crampton, C. G., 1986, Ghosts of Glen Canyon: Salt Lake City, Tower Productions.

Crampton, C. G., editor., 1975, Sharlot Hall on the Arizona Strip: Northland Press.

Department of the Army, 1956, American military history 1607-1953: ROTC Manual 145-20, U.S. Government Printing Office.

Dorsett, L. W., 1977, The Queen City, A history of Denver, in Western Urban History Series: Boulder, Pruett Publishing Co.

Erb, L. B.; Brown, A. B.; and Hughes, G. B., 1989, Overland Trail, 1862-1869: Greeley, Journal Pub.

Flanagan, Mike, 1995, The old West day by day: New York, Facts on File, Inc.

Frazer, R. W., 1983, Forts and supplies, the role of the army in the economy of the Southwest, 1846-1861, Albuquerque, University of New Mexico Press.

Frink, Maurice, 1968, Fort Defiance & the Navajos: Boulder, Pruett Press.

Garraty, John A., 1966, The American nation, a history of the United States: New York, American Heritage Publishing Co.

Hafen, LeRoy, and Young, F. M., 1938, Fort Laramie and the pageant of the West, 1834-1890, Glendale, California, Arthur H. Clark Co.

Hauck, C. W., 1972, Narrow gauge to Central and Silver Plume: Colorado Rail Annual No. 10, Golden, Colorado, Colorado Railroad Museum.

Holt, R. R., 1949, Beneath these red cliffs: Albuquerque, University of New Mexico Press.

Hungerford, Edward, 1949, Wells Fargo, advancing the American frontier: New York, Bonanza Books.

Jackson, W. T., 1952, Wagon roads west: University of California Press.

Jones, W. C., and Forrest, Kenton, 1993, Denver: A pictorial history: Golden, Colorado Railroad Museum.

Manley, J. A., 1989, Arapahoe City to Fairmount: Boulder, Colorado, Johnson Publishing.

Mattes, Merrill, 1969, The great Platte River road: Nebraska State Historical Society, Publications v. 25.

Moffat, Frances, 1977, Dancing on the brink of the world: New York, G. P. Putnam's Sons.

Nibley, Preston, 1936, Brigham Young, the man and his work: Independence, Missouri, Zion's Printing & Publishing Co.

Olson, Lee, 1993, Marmalade and whiskey, British remittance men in the west: Golden, Colorado, Fulcrum Publishing.

Peterson, C. S., 1973, Take up your mission, Mormon colonizing along the Little Colorado River, 1870-1900, Tucson, University of Arizona Press.

Peterson, N. M., 1984, People of the Moonshell: Frederick, Colorado, Renaissance House.

Propst, Nell Brown, 1979, The South Platte trail: Boulder, Colorado, Pruett Publishing.

Putnam, C. M., 1958, The story of Houlton: Portland, Maine, House of Falmouth.

Railway Passenger Travel, 1962, from Scribner's, September 1888: Scotia, New York, Americana Review.

Simmons, Marc, 1982, Albuquerque: Albuquerque, University of New Mexico Press.

Smart, Donna, editor, 1997, Mormon midwife, the 1846-1888 diaries of Patty Bartlett Sessions: Logan, Utah, Utah State University Press.

Stenhouse, T. B. H., 1873, The Rocky Mountain Saints: New York, D. Appleton and Co.

Stenhouse, Mrs. T. B. H., 1875, Tell it all, the story of a life's experience in Mormonism: Chicago, Illinois, Louis Lloyd and Co.

Ubbelohde, Carl; Benson, Maxine; and Smith, Duane, 1976, A Colorado history: Boulder, Colorado, Pruett Publishing Co.

Wagner, Henry, 1953, The plains and the Rockies, 1800-1865: Columbus, Ohio, Long's Publishing Co.

Wagenbach, Lorraine, and Jo Ann Thistlewood, 1987, Golden, the 19th cenury: Littleton, Colorado, Harbinger House Publishing Co.

Wilson, D. R., 1980, Fort Kearny on the Platte: Crossroads Communications, Dundee, Illinois.

Wise, William, 1976, Massacre at Mountain Meadows: New York, Thomas Y. Crowell Publishing Co.

# C Lazy Three
## PRESS

## HISTORICAL FICTION

## Over the Mountains of the Moon: An American Novel

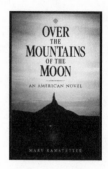

By Mary Ramstetter
Softbound, 5½×8½", 496 pages, map and bibliography
ISBN 0-9643283-0-5

&#10752; *Winner, American Regional History Publishing Award, Western States, 1999.*

&#10752; *Bronze Award, Non-Fiction Essay, Colorado Independent Publishers Association.*

&#10752; *Recommended Reading, Southwest Education Classes, Adams State College, Alamosa, Colorado.*

&#10752; *First Place Overall Design Winner—Best Design of a Novel, Colorado Independent Publishers Association, 1997*

Vol. I—The West of the American emigrant in the late 1840s. A would-be trapper traps himself in a shadowy love affair. The first wife of a Mormon polygamist clings to shards of past happiness. A Fort Laramie bourgeois philosophizes about the Oregon Trail. Intrigue and betrayal, unexpected partings and surprising reunions pop up like dust devils. Plus dramatic river crossings, Indian captures, and dozens of well-drawn winners and losers from New York to New Mexico intermixed with true historic places and events—an irresistible, page-turning, history-rich experience from start to finish.

# C Lazy Three
## P R E S S

## HISTORICAL FICTION

---

## Down the Valley of the Shadow:
## An American Novel

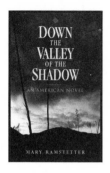

By Mary Ramstetter
Softbound, 5½ × 8½", 488 pages, map and bibliography
ISBN 0-9643283-1-3

✪ *Best Fiction, Best Design, Colorado Independent Publishers Association, 2002.*

✪ *Finalist, ForeWord Magazine's Book of the Year Awards, BookExpo, Los Angeles, 2003.*

✪ *Western Writers of America, Roundup Magazine Review, June 2002. "This may be the single best fictional account of the Mountain Meadows Massacre."*

Vol. II—The saga begun in *Over the Mountains of the Moon* continues as the friendship between the Marchion and Harris families deepens. In Maine, an Indian puts a face on an old love affair. In San Francisco, a flimflam artist peddling emigrant paintings finds a gold mine in a saloon keeper. While in the heart of the West, the Utah Reformation maims itself with the violent betrayal known as the Mountain Meadows Massacre. The steady drumbeat of events makes for a fascinating, history-haunted story.

## Ride, Boldly Ride: An American Novel

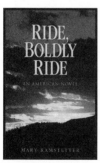

By Mary Ramstetter
Softbound, 5½ × 8½", 544 pages, map and bibliography
ISBN 0-9643283-4-8

Vol. III—The wide-ranging conclusion to the Marchion and Harris saga in mid-1800s America. No longer mere desert and Indians, the West floods with a rising tide of those seeking escape, wealth, love. In Great Salt Lake City, George Harris, seeing the future, calls for Brigham Young's resignation. In San Francisco, Nathan works a sting that goes bad, washing him penniless into the booming gold camps of the Rocky Mountains. And in New York, Katherine Marchion receives a strange letter leading her into a delicious love affair in the desert Southwest. A narrative history rich in the day-to-day events of life in the lands beyond the States.

# C Lazy Three
### PRESS

## HISTORY

---

## John Gregory Country:
## Place Names and History of Ralston Buttes
## Quadrangle, Jefferson County, Colorado

Charles and Mary Ramstetter, Editors
ISBN 0-9643283-2-1
Softbound, 8½ × 11", 280 pages, nearly 200 photographs, USGS topographic
quad and location maps, bibliography and index

⊙ *Winner, 1999 American Regional History Publishing Award, Western States:
   New Mexico, Arizona, Texas, Utah, Colorado, Nevada, Wyoming, Montana,
   Idaho.*

⊙ *Bronze Award, Non-Fiction Essay, Colorado Independent Publishers
   Association, 2000.*

⊙ *Best Regional History, Ladies of the Columbine, 1999.*

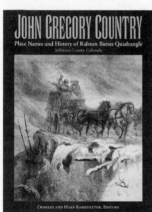

An amazing collection of every scrap of
history known to exist surrounding the first
road through the mountains to the fabulous
gold strikes in Blackhawk and Central City,
Colorado. Richly illustrated with photographs old and new, the book doesn't con-
fine itself to the origin of place names, but
ranges across the countryside to show how
the dreamers who followed in Gregory's
footsteps suffered and coped.

# C Lazy Three
## P R E S S

*All books are available from your local bookstore or
directly from the publisher.
Distributed by Baker & Taylor, Ingram, and Books West*

To order directly from the press, send a check or money order to:

C Lazy Three Press
5957 Crawford Gulch
Golden, CO 80403
Telephone 303-277-0134

☐ Send ___ copies of *Over the Mountains of the Moon* at $14 each.

☐ Send ___ copies of *Down the Valley of the Shadow* at $14 each.

☐ Send ___ copies of *Ride, Boldly Ride* at $16 each.

☐ Send ___ complete trilogy sets of *Over the Mountains of the Moon, Down the Valley of the Shadow,* and *Ride, Boldly Ride* at the reduced price of $38 per set.

☐ Send ___ copies of *John Gregory Country* at $24 each.

Please add $4.00 postage for the first book and 75¢ for each additional book (each trilogy set counts as one book).

PLEASE ALLOW UP TO 3 TO 4 WEEKS FOR DELIVERY

*If you represent a non-profit organization or a business interested in purchasing copies of this book for educational or resale purposes, please write or call the publisher for detailed discount information.*